THE PARISIANS

Edward Bulwer-Lytton

Vol. II.

Graham reclines at her feet, his face upturned to hers.—Page 302.

THE PARISIANS

Edward Bulwer-Lytton

Vol. II.

WILDSIDE PRESS

PREFATORY NOTE.

(BY THE AUTHOR'S SON.)

The Parisians and *Kenelm Chillingly* were begun about
the same time, and had their common origin in the same
central idea. That idea first found fantastic expression in
The Coming Race; and the three books, taken together, constitute a special group distinctly apart from all the other
works of their author.

The satire of his earlier novels is a protest against false
social respectabilities; the humour of his later ones is a
protest against the disrespect of social realities. By the
first he sought to promote social sincerity, and the free play
of personal character; by the last, to encourage mutual
charity and sympathy amongst all classes on whose inter-
relation depends the character of society itself. But in
these three books, his latest fictions, the moral purpose is
more definite and exclusive. Each of them is an expostu-
lation against what seemed to him the perilous popularity
of certain social and political theories, or a warning against
the influence of certain intellectual tendencies upon individual character and national life. This purpose, however, though common to the three fictions, is worked out
in each of them by a different method. *The Coming Race*
is a work of pure fancy, and the satire of it is vague and
sportive. The outlines of a definite purpose are more distinctly drawn in *Chillingly*—a romance which has the

source of its effect in a highly-wrought imagination. The humour and pathos of *Chillingly* are of a kind incompatible with the design of *The Parisians*, which is a work of dramatised observation. *Chillingly* is a Romance; *The Parisians* is a Novel. The subject of *Chillingly* is psychological; that of *The Parisians* is social. The author's object in *Chillingly* being to illustrate the effects of "modern ideas" upon an individual character, he has confined his narrative to the biography of that one character. Hence the simplicity of plot and small number of *dramatis personæ;* whereby the work gains in height and depth what it loses in breadth of surface. *The Parisians,* on the contrary, is designed to illustrate the effect of "modern ideas" upon a whole community. This novel is therefore panoramic in the profusion and variety of figures presented by it to the reader's imagination. No exclusive prominence is vouchsafed to any of these figures. All of them are drawn and coloured with an equal care, but by means of the bold broad touches necessary for their effective presentation on a canvas so large and so crowded. Such figures are, indeed, but the component features of one great Form, and their actions only so many modes of one collective impersonal character—that of the Parisian Society of Imperial and Democratic France;—a character everywhere present and busy throughout the story, of which it is the real hero or heroine. This society was doubtless selected for characteristic illustration as being the most advanced in the progress of "modern ideas." Thus, for a complete perception of its writer's fundamental purpose, *The Parisians* should be read in connection with *Chillingly,* and these two books in connection with *The Coming Race.* It will then be perceived that, through the medium of alternate fancy, sentiment, and observation assisted by humour and passion, these three books (in all other respects so different from each other) complete the presentation of the same purpose under different aspects; and thereby constitute a group of fictions which claims a separate place of its own in any thoughtful classification of their author's works.

One last word to those who will miss from these pages the connecting and completing touches of the master's hand. It may be hoped that such a disadvantage, though irreparable, is somewhat mitigated by the essential character of the work itself. The æsthetic merit of this kind of novel is in the vivacity of a general effect produced by large swift strokes of character; and in such strokes, if they be by a great artist, force and freedom of style must still be apparent, even when they are left rough and unfinished. Nor can any lack of final verbal correction much diminish the intellectual value which many of the more thoughtful passages of the present work derive from a long, keen, and practical study of political phenomena, guided by personal experience of public life, and enlightened by a large, instinctive knowledge of the human heart.

Such a belief is, at least, encouraged by the private communications spontaneously made, to him who expresses it, by persons of political experience and social position in France; who have acknowledged the general accuracy of the author's descriptions, and noticed the suggestive sagacity and penetration of his occasional comments on the circumstances and sentiments he describes.

L.

THE PARISIANS.

BOOK IX.

CHAPTER I.

On waking some morning, have you ever felt, reader, as if a change for the brighter in the world, without and within you, had suddenly come to pass—some new glory has been given to the sunshine, some fresh balm to the air—you feel younger, and happier, and lighter, in the very beat of your heart—you almost fancy you hear the chime of some spiritual music far off, as if in the deeps of heaven? You are not at first conscious how, or wherefore, this change has been brought about. Is it the effect of a dream in the gone sleep, that has made this morning so different from mornings that have dawned before? And while vaguely asking yourself that question, you become aware that the cause is no mere illusion, that it has its substance in words spoken by living lips, in things that belong to the work-day world.

It was thus that Isaura woke the morning after the conversation with Alain de Rochebriant, and as certain words, then spoken, echoed back on her ear, she knew why she was so happy, why the world was so changed.

In those words she heard the voice of Graham Vane— no! she had not deceived herself—she was loved! she was loved! What mattered that long cold interval of absence? She had not forgotten—she could not believe that absence had brought forgetfulness. There are moments when we insist on judging another's heart by our own. All would be explained some day—all would come right.

How lovely was the face that reflected itself in the glass as she stood before it, smoothing back her long hair, murmuring sweet snatches of Italian love-song, and blushing with sweeter love-thoughts as she sang! All that had passed in that year so critical to her outer life—the authorship, the fame, the public career, the popular praise—vanished from her mind as a vapour that rolls from the face of a lake to which the sunlight restores the smile of a brightened heaven.

She was more the girl now than she had ever been since the day on which she sat reading Tasso on the craggy shore of Sorrento.

Singing still as she passed from her chamber, and entering the sitting-room, which fronted the east, and seemed bathed in the sunbeams of deepening May, she took her bird from its cage, and stopped her song to cover it with kisses, which perhaps yearned for vent somewhere.

Later in the day she went out to visit Valérie. Recalling the altered manner of her young friend, her sweet nature became troubled. She divined that Valérie had conceived some jealous pain which she longed to heal; she could not bear the thought of leaving any one that day unhappy. Ignorant before of the girl's feelings towards Alain, she now partly guessed them—one woman who loves in secret is clairvoyante as to such secrets in another.

Valérie received her visitor with a coldness she did not attempt to disguise. Not seeming to notice this, Isaura commenced the conversation with frank mention of Rochebriant. "I have to thank you so much, dear Valérie, for a pleasure you could not anticipate—that of talking about an absent friend, and hearing the praise he deserved from one so capable of appreciating excellence as M. de Rochebriant appears to be."

"You were talking to M. de Rochebriant of an absent

friend—ah! you seemed indeed very much interested in the conversation——"

"Do not wonder at that, Valérie; and do not grudge me the happiest moments I have known for months."

"In talking with M. de Rochebriant! No doubt, Mademoiselle Cicogna, you found him very charming."

To her surprise and indignation, Valérie here felt the arm of Isaura tenderly entwining her waist, and her face drawn towards Isaura's sisterly kiss.

"Listen to me, naughty child—listen and believe. M. de Rochebriant can never be charming to me—never touch a chord in my heart or my fancy except as friend to another, or—kiss me in your turn, Valérie—as suitor to yourself."

Valérie here drew back her pretty childlike head, gazed keenly a moment into Isaura's eyes, felt convinced by the limpid candour of their unmistakable honesty, and flinging herself on her friend's bosom, kissed her passionately, and burst into tears.

The complete reconciliation between the two girls was thus peacefully effected; and then Isaura had to listen, at no small length, to the confidences poured into her ears by Valérie, who was fortunately too engrossed by her own hopes and doubts to exact confidences in return. Valérie's was one of those impulsive eager natures that longs for a confidante. Not so Isaura's. Only when Valérie had unburthened her heart, and been soothed and caressed into happy trust in the future, did she recall Isaura's explanatory words, and said, archly: "And your absent friend? Tell me about him. Is he as handsome as Alain?"

"Nay," said Isaura, rising to take up the mantle and hat she had laid aside on entering, "they say that the colour of a flower is in our vision, not in the leaves." Then with a grave melancholy in the look she fixed upon Valérie, she added: "Rather than distrust of me should occasion you pain, I have pained myself, in making clear to you the reason why I felt interest in M. de Rochebriant's conversation. In turn, I ask of you a favour—do not on this point question me farther. There are some things in our past which influence the present, but to which we dare not assign a future—on which we cannot talk to another. What soothsayer can tell us if the dream of a yesterday will be renewed on the night of a morrow? All is said—we trust one another, dearest."

CHAPTER II.

THAT evening the Morleys looked in at Isaura's on their way to a crowded assembly at the house of one of those rich Americans, who were then outvying the English residents at Paris in the good graces of Parisian society. I think the Americans get on better with the French than the English do—I mean the higher class of Americans. They spend more money; their men speak French better; the women are better dressed, and, as a general rule, have read more largely, and converse more frankly. Mrs. Morley's affection for Isaura had increased during the last few months. As so notable an advocate of the ascendency of her sex, she felt a sort of grateful pride in the accomplishments and growing renown of so youthful a member of the oppressed sisterhood. But, apart from that sentiment, she had conceived a tender mother-like interest for the girl who stood in the world so utterly devoid of family ties, so destitute of that household guardianship and protection which, with all her assertion of the strength and dignity of woman, and all her opinions as to woman's right of absolute emancipation from the conventions fabricated by the selfishness of man, Mrs. Morley was too sensible not to value for the individual, though she deemed it not needed for the mass. Her great desire was that Isaura should marry well, and soon. American women usually marry so young that it seemed to Mrs. Morley an anomaly in social life, that one so gifted in mind and person as Isaura should already have passed the age in which the belles of the great Republic are enthroned as wives and consecrated as mothers.

We have seen that in the past year she had selected from our unworthy but necessary sex, Graham Vane as a suitable spouse to her young friend. She had divined the state of his heart—she had more than suspicions of the state of Isaura's. She was exceedingly perplexed and exceedingly chafed at the Englishman's strange disregard to his happiness and her own projects. She had counted, all this past winter, on his return to Paris; and she became convinced that some misunderstanding, possibly some lover's quarrel, was the cause of his protracted absence, and a cause that, if ascertained, could be removed. A good opportunity now presented itself—Colonel Morley was going to London the next day. He had business there which would detain him at least a week. He would see Graham; and as she considered her husband the shrewdest and wisest person in the world—I mean of the male sex—she had no doubt of his being able to turn Graham's mind thoroughly inside out, and ascertain his exact feelings and intentions. If the Englishman, thus assayed, were found of base metal, then, at least, Mrs. Morley would be free to cast him altogether aside, and coin for the uses of the matrimonial market some nobler effigy in purer gold.

"My dear child," said Mrs. Morley, in a low voice, nestling herself close to Isaura, while the Colonel, duly instructed, drew off the Venosta, "have you heard anything lately of our pleasant friend Mr. Vane?"

You can guess with what artful design Mrs. Morley put that question point-blank, fixing keen eyes on Isaura while she put it. She saw the heightened colour, the quivering lip of the girl thus abruptly appealed to, and she said inly: "I was right—she loves him!"

"I heard of Mr. Vane last night—accidentally."

"Is he coming to Paris soon?"

"Not that I know of. How charmingly that wreath becomes you! it suits the earrings so well, too."

"Frank chose it; he has good taste for a man. I trust him with my commissions to Hunt and Roskell's but I limit him as to price, he is so extravagant—men are, when they make presents. They seem to think we value things according to their cost. They would gorge us with jewels, and let us starve for want of a smile. Not that Frank is so bad as the rest of them. But à *propos* of Mr. Vane— Frank will be sure to see him, and scold him well for deserting us all. I should not be surprised if he brought the deserter back with him, for I send a little note by Frank, inviting him to pay us a visit. We have spare rooms in our apartments."

Isaura's heart heaved beneath her robe, but she replied in a tone of astonishing indifference: "I believe this is the height of the London season, and Mr. Vane would probably be too engaged to profit even by an invitation so tempting."

"*Nous verrons.* How pleased he will be to hear of your triumphs! He admired you so much before you were famous: what will be his admiration now! men are so vain— they care for us so much more when people praise us. But till we have put the creatures in their proper place, we must take them for what they are."

Here the Venosta, with whom the poor Colonel had exhausted all the arts at his command for chaining her attention, could be no longer withheld from approaching Mrs. Morley, and venting her admiration of that lady's wreath, earrings, robes, flounces. This dazzling apparition had on her the effect which a candle has on a moth—she fluttered round it, and longed to absorb herself in its blaze. But the wreath especially fascinated her—a wreath which no prudent lady with colourings less pure, and features less exquisitely delicate than the pretty champion of the rights of women, could have fancied on her own brows without a shudder. But the Venosta in such matters was not prudent. "It can't be dear," she cried piteously, extending her arms towards Isaura. "I must have one exactly like. Who made it? *Cara signora,* give me the address."

"Ask the Colonel, dear Madame; he chose and bought it," and Mrs. Morley glanced significantly at her well-tutored Frank.

"Madame," said the Colonel, speaking in English, which he usually did with the Venosta—who valued herself on knowing that language and was flattered to be addressed in it—while he amused himself by introducing into its forms the dainty Americanisms with which he puzzled the Britisher—he might well puzzle the Florentine,—"Madame, I am too anxious for the appearance of my wife to submit to the test of a rival schemer like yourself in the same apparel. With all the homage due to a sex of which I am enthused dreadful, I decline to designate the florist from whom I purchased Mrs. Morley's head-fixings."

"Wicked man!" cried the Venosta, shaking her finger at him coquettishly. "You are jealous! Fie! a man should never be jealous of a woman's rivalry with women;" and then, with a cynicism that might have become a greybeard, she added, "but of his own sex every man should be jealous—though of his dearest friend. Isn't it so, *Colonello?*"

The Colonel looked puzzled, bowed, and made no reply.

"That only shows," said Mrs. Morley, rising, "what villains the Colonel has the misfortune to call friends and fellow-men."

"I fear it is time to go," said Frank, glancing at the clock.

In theory the most rebellious, in practice the most obedient, of wives, Mrs. Morley here kissed Isaura, resettled her crinoline, and shaking hands with the Venosta, retreated to the door.

"I shall have the wreath yet," cried the Venosta, impishly. "*La speranza è femmina*" (Hope is female).

"Alas!" said Isaura, half mournfully, half smiling,—"alas! do you not remember what the poet replied when asked what disease was most mortal?—'the hectic fever caught from the chill of hope.'"

CHAPTER III.

GRAHAM VANE was musing very gloomily in his solitary apartment one morning, when his servant announced Colonel Morley.

He received his visitor with more than the cordiality with which every English politician receives an American citizen. Graham liked the Colonel too well for what he was in himself to need any national title to his esteem. After some preliminary questions and answers as to the health of Mrs. Morley, the length of the Colonel's stay in London, what day he could dine with Graham at Richmond or Gravesend, the Colonel took up the ball. "We have been reckoning to see you at Paris, sir, for the last six months."

"I am very much flattered to hear that you have thought of me at all; but I am not aware of having warranted the expectation you so kindly express."

"I guess you must have said something to my wife which led her to do more than expect—to reckon on your return. And, by the way, sir, I am charged to deliver to you this note from her, and to back the request it contains that you will avail yourself of the offer. Without summarising the points I do so."

Graham glanced over the note addressed to him:

"DEAR MR. VANE,—Do you forget how beautiful the environs of Paris are in May and June? how charming it was last year at the lake of Enghien? how gay were our little dinners out of doors in the garden arbours, with the Savarins and the fair Italian, and her incomparably amusing chaperon? Frank has my orders to bring you back to renew these happy days, while the birds are in their first song, and the leaves are in their youngest green. I have prepared your rooms *chez nous*—a chamber that looks out on the Champs Elysées, and a quiet *cabinet de travail* at the back, in which you can read, write, or sulk undisturbed. Come, and we will again visit Enghien and Montmorency. Don't talk of engagements. If man proposes, woman disposes. Hesitate not—obey. Your sincere little friend, . LIZZY."

"My dear Morley," said Graham, with emotion, "I cannot find words to thank your wife sufficiently for an invitation so graciously conveyed. Alas! I cannot accept it."

"Why?" asked the Colonel, drily.

"I have too much to do in London."

"Is that the true reason, or am I to suspicion that there is anything, sir, which makes you dislike a visit to Paris?"

The Americans enjoy the reputation of being the frankest putters of questions whom liberty of speech has yet educated into *la recherche de la vérité*, and certainly Colonel Morley in this instance did not impair the national reputation.

Graham Vane's brow slightly contracted, and he bit his lip as if stung by a sudden pang; but after a moment's pause, he answered with a good-humoured smile:

"No man who has taste enough to admire the most beautiful city, and appreciate the charms of the most brilliant society in the world, can dislike Paris."

"My dear sir, I did not ask you if you disliked Paris, but if there were anything that made you dislike coming back to it on a visit."

"What a notion! and what a cross-examiner you would have made if you had been called to the bar! Surely, my dear friend, you can understand that when a man has in one place business which he cannot neglect, he may decline going to another place, whatever pleasure it would give him to do so. By the way, there is a great ball at one of the Ministers' to-night; you should go there, and I will point out to you all those English notabilities in whom Americans

naturally take interest. I will call for you at eleven o'clock.
Lord ——, who is a connection of mine, would be charmed
to know you."

Morley hesitated; but when Graham said, "How your
wife will scold you if you lose such an opportunity of telling her whether the Duchess of M—— is as beautiful as
report says, and whether Gladstone or Disraeli seems to
your phrenological science to have the finer head!" the
Colonel gave in, and it was settled that Graham should call
for him at the Langham Hotel.

That matter arranged, Graham probably hoped that his
inquisitive visitor would take leave for the present, but the
Colonel evinced no such intention. On the contrary, settling himself more at ease in his arm-chair, he said, "If I
remember aright, you do not object to the odour of tobacco?"

Graham rose and presented to his visitor a cigar-box
which he took from the mantelpiece.

The Colonel shook his head, and withdrew from his
breast pocket a leather case, from which he extracted a
gigantic regalia; this he lighted from a gold match-box in
the shape of a locket attached to his watch-chain, and took
two or three preliminary puffs, with his head thrown back
and his eyes meditatively intent upon the ceiling.

We know already that strange whim of the Colonel's
(than whom, if he so pleased, no man could speak purer
English as spoken by the Britisher) to assert the dignity
of the American citizen by copious use of expressions and
phrases familiar to the lips of the governing class of the
great Republic—delicacies of speech which he would have
carefully shunned in the polite circles of the Fifth Avenue
in New York. Now the Colonel was much too experienced
a man of the world not to be aware that the commission
with which his Lizzy had charged him was an exceedingly
delicate one; and it occurred to his mother wit that the
best way to acquit himself of it, so as to avoid the risk of
giving or of receiving serious affront, would be to push that
whim of his into more than wonted exaggeration. Thus he

could more decidedly and briefly come to the point; and should he, in doing so, appear too meddlesome, rather provoke a laugh than a frown—retiring from the ground with the honours due to a humorist. Accordingly, in his deepest nasal intonation, and withdrawing his eyes from the ceiling, he began:

"You have not asked, sir, after the signorina, or as we popularly call her, Mademoiselle Cicogna?"

"Have I not? I hope she is quite well, and her lively companion, Signora Venosta."

"They are not sick, sir; or at least they were not so last night when my wife and I had the pleasure to see them. Of course you have read Mademoiselle Cicogna's book—a bright performance, sir, age considered."

"Certainly, I have read the book; it is full of unquestionable genius. Is Mademoiselle writing another? But of course she is."

"I am not aware of the fact, sir. It may be predicated; such a mind cannot remain inactive; and I know from M. Savarin and that rising young man Gustave Rameau, that the publishers bid high for her brains considerable. Two translations have already appeared in our country. Her fame, sir, will be world-wide. She may be another George Sand, or at least another Eulalie Grantmesnil."

Graham's cheek became as white as the paper I write on. He inclined his head as in assent, but without a word. The Colonel continued:

"We ought to be very proud of her acquaintance, sir. I think you detected her gifts while they were yet unconjectured. My wife says so. You must be gratified to remember that, sir—clear grit, sir, and no mistake."

"I certainly more than once have said to Mrs. Morley, that I esteemed Mademoiselle's powers so highly that I hoped she would never become a stage-singer and actress. But this M. Rameau? You say he is a rising man. It struck me when at Paris that he was one of those charlatans with a great deal of conceit and very little information, who are always found in scores on the ultra-Liberal side of politics;—possibly I was mistaken."

"He is the responsible editor of *Le Sens Commun*, in which talented periodical Mademoiselle Cicogna's book was first raised."

"Of course, I know that; a journal which, so far as I have looked into its political or social articles, certainly written by a cleverer and an older man than M. Rameau, is for unsettling all things and settling nothing. We have writers of that kind among ourselves—I have no sympathy with them. To me it seems that when a man says, 'Off with your head,' he ought to let us know what other head he would put on our shoulders, and by what process the change of heads shall be effected. Honestly speaking, if you and your charming wife are intimate friends and admirers of Mademoiselle Cicogna, I think you could not do her a greater service than that of detaching her from all connection with men like M. Rameau, and journals like *La Sens Commun*."

The Colonel here withdrew his cigar from his lips, lowered his head to a level with Graham's, and relaxing into an arch significant smile, said: "Start to Paris, and dissuade her yourself. Start—go ahead—don't be shy—don't seesaw on the beam of speculation. You will have more influence with that young female than we can boast."

Never was England in greater danger of quarrel with America than at that moment; but Graham curbed his first wrathful impulse, and replied coldly:

"It seems to me, Colonel, that you, though very unconsciously, derogate from the respect due to Mademoiselle Cicogna. That the counsel of a married couple like yourself and Mrs. Morley should be freely given to and duly heeded by a girl deprived of her natural advisers in parents, is a reasonable and honourable supposition; but to imply that the most influential adviser of a young lady so situated is a young single man, in no way related to her, appears to me a dereliction of that regard to the dignity of

her sex which is the chivalrous characteristic of your countrymen—and to Mademoiselle Cicogna herself, a surmise
which she would be justified in resenting as an impertinence."

"I deny both allegations," replied the Colonel serenely.
"I maintain that a single man whips all connubial creation
when it comes to gallantising a single young woman; and
that no young lady would be justified in resenting as impertinence my friendly suggestion to the single man so de-
serving of her consideration as I estimate you to be, to
solicit the right to advise her for life. And that's a caution."

Here the Colonel resumed his regalia, and again gazed
intent on the ceiling.

"Advise her for life! You mean, I presume, as a candidate for her hand."

"You don't Turkey now. Well, I guess, you are not
wide of the mark there, sir."

"You do me infinite honour, but I do not presume so
far."

"So, so—not as yet. Before a man who is not without
gumption runs himself for Congress, he likes to calculate
how the votes will run. Well, sir, suppose we are in cau-
cus, and let us discuss the chances of the election with
closed doors."

Graham could not help smiling at the persistent officious-
ness of his visitor, but his smile was a very sad one.

"Pray change the subject, my dear Colonel Morley—it
is not a pleasant one to me; and as regards Mademoiselle
Cicogna, can you think it would not shock her to suppose
that her name was dragged into the discussions you would
provoke, even with closed doors?"

"Sir," replied the Colonel, imperturbably, "since the
doors are closed, there is no one, unless it be a spirit-lis-
tener under the table, who can wire to Mademoiselle Cicogna the substance of debate. And, for my part, I do not believe in spiritual manifestations. Fact is, that I have the

most amicable sentiments towards both parties, and if there is a misunderstanding which is opposed to the union of the States, I wish to remove it while yet in time.   Now, let us suppose that you decline to be a candidate; there are plenty of others who will run; and as an elector must choose one representative or other, so a gal must choose one husband or other.   And then you only repent when it is too late. It is a great thing to be first in the field.   Let us approximate to the point; the chances seem good—will you run?— Yes or no?"

"I repeat, Colonel Morley, that I entertain no such presumption."

The Colonel here, rising, extended his hand, which Graham shook with constrained cordiality, and then leisurely walked to the door; there he paused, as if struck by a new thought, and said gravely, in his natural tone of voice, "You have nothing to say, sir, against the young lady's character and honour?"

"I!—heavens, no! Colonel Morley, such a question insults me."

The Colonel resumed his deepest nasal bass: "It is only, then, because you don't fancy her now so much as you did last year—fact, you are soured on her and fly off the handle. Such things do happen.   The same thing has happened to myself, sir.   In my days of celibacy, there was a gal at Saratoga whom I gallantised, and whom, while I was at Saratoga, I thought Heaven had made to be Mrs. Morley: I was on the very point of telling her so, when I was suddenly called off to Philadelphia; and at Philadelphia, sir, I found that Heaven had made another Mrs. Morley.   I state this fact, sir, though I seldom talk of my own affairs, even when willing to tender my advice in the affairs of another, in order to prove that I do not intend to censure you if Heaven has served you in the same manner.   Sir, a man may go blind for one gal when he is not yet dry behind the ears, and then, when his eyes are skinned, go in for one better.   All things mortal meet with a change, as my sis-

ter's little boy said when, at the age of eight, he quitted
the Methodys and turned Shaker. Threep and argue as we
may, you and I are both mortals—more's the pity. Good
morning, sir (glancing at the clock, which proclaimed the
hour of 3 P.M.),—I err—good evening."

By the post that day the Colonel transmitted a condensed
and laconic report of his conversation with Graham Vane.
I can state its substance in yet fewer words. He wrote
word that Graham positively declined the invitation to
Paris; that he had then, agreeably to Lizzy's instruction,
ventilated the Englishman, in the most delicate terms, as
to his intentions with regard to Isaura, and that no intentions at all existed. The sooner all thoughts of him were
relinquished, as a new suitor on the ground, the better it
would be for the young lady's happiness in the only state
in which happiness should be, if not found, at least sought,
whether by maid or man.

Mrs. Morley was extremely put out by this untoward
result of the diplomacy she had intrusted to the Colonel;
and when, the next day, came a very courteous letter from
Graham, thanking her gratefully for the kindness of her
invitation, and expressing his regret briefly, though cordially, at his inability to profit by it, without the most distant allusion to the subject which the Colonel had brought
on the *tapis*, or even requesting his compliments to the
Signoras Venosta and Cicogna, she was more than put out,
more than resentful,—she was deeply grieved. Being,
however, one of those gallant heroes of womankind who
do not give in at the first defeat, she began to doubt whether
Frank had not rather overstrained the delicacy which he
said he had put into his "soundings." He ought to have
been more explicit. Meanwhile she resolved to call on
Isaura, and, without mentioning Graham's refusal of her
invitation, endeavour to ascertain whether the attachment
which she felt persuaded the girl secretly cherished for this
recalcitrant Englishman were something more than the first
romantic fancy—whether it were sufficiently deep to justify

farther effort on Mrs. Morley's part to bring it to a prosperous issue.

She found Isaura at home and alone; and, to do her justice, she exhibited wonderful tact in the fulfilment of the task she had set herself. Forming her judgment by manner and look—not words—she returned home, convinced that she ought to seize the opportunity afforded to her by Graham's letter. It was one to which she might very naturally reply, and in that reply she might convey the object at her heart more felicitously than the Colonel had done. "The cleverest man is," she said to herself, "stupid compared to an ordinary woman in the real business of life, which does not consist of fighting and money-making."

Now there was one point she had ascertained by words in her visit to. Isaura—a point on which all might depend. She had asked Isaura when and where she had seen Graham last; and when Isaura had given her that information, and she learned it was on the eventful day on which Isaura gave her consent to the publication of her MS. if approved by Savarin, in the journal to be set up by the handsome-faced young author, she leapt to the conclusion that Graham had been seized with no unnatural jealousy, and was still under the illusive glamoury of that green-eyed fiend. She was confirmed in this notion, not altogether an unsound one, when asking with apparent carelessness, "And in that last interview, did you see any change in Mr. Vane's manner, especially when he took leave?"

Isaura turned away pale, and involuntarily clasping her hands—as women do when they would suppress pain—replied, in a low murmur, "His manner was changed."

Accordingly, Mrs. Morley sat down and wrote the following letter:

"DEAR MR. VANE,—I am very angry indeed with you for refusing my invitation—I had so counted on you, and I don't believe a word of your excuse. Engagements! To balls and dinners, I suppose, as if you were not much too clever to care about such silly attempts to enjoy solitude in crowds. And as to what you men call business, you have no right to have any business at all. You are not in commerce; you are not in Parliament; you told me yourself that you had no great landed estates to give you trouble; you are rich, without any necessity to take pains to remain rich, or to become richer; you have no business in the world except to please yourself: and when you will not come to Paris to see one of your truest friends—which I certainly am—it simply means, that no matter how such a visit would please me, it does not please yourself. I call that abominably rude and ungrateful.

"But I am not writing merely to scold you. I have something else on my mind, and it must come out. Certainly, when you were at Paris last year you did admire, above all other young ladies, Isaura Cicogna. And I honoured you for doing so. I know no other young lady to be called her equal. Well, if you admired her then, what would you do now if you met her? Then she was but a girl—very brilliant, very charming, it is true—but undeveloped, untested. Now she is a woman, a princess among women, but retaining all that is most lovable in a girl; so courted, yet so simple—so gifted, yet so innocent. Her head is not a bit turned by all the flattery that surrounds her. Come and judge for yourself. I still hold the door of the rooms destined to you open for repentance.

"My dear Mr. Vane, do not think me a silly match-making little woman, when I write to you thus, à cœur ouvert.

"I like you so much that I would fain secure to you the rarest prize which life is ever likely to offer to your ambition. Where can you hope to find another Isaura? Among the stateliest daughters of your English dukes, where *is* there one whom a proud man would be more proud to show to the world, saying, 'She is mine!' where one more distinguished—I will not say by mere beauty, there she might be eclipsed—but by sweetness and dignity combined—in aspect, manner, every movement, every smile?

"And you, who are yourself so clever, so well read—you who would be so lonely with a wife who was not your companion, with whom you could not converse on equal terms of intellect,—my dear friend, where could you find a companion in whom you would not miss the poet-soul of Isaura? Of course I should not dare to obtrude all these questionings on your innermost reflection, if I had not some idea, right or wrong, that since the days when at Enghien and Montmorency, seeing you and Isaura side by side, I whispered to Frank, 'So should those two be through life,' some cloud has passed between your eyes and the future on which they gazed. Cannot that cloud be dispelled? Were you so unjust to yourself as to be jealous of a rival, perhaps of a Gustave Rameau? I write to you frankly—answer me frankly; and if you answer, 'Mrs. Morley, I don't know what you mean; I admired Mademoiselle Cicogna as I might admire any other pretty, accomplished girl, but it is really nothing to me whether she marries Gustave Rameau or any one else,'—why, then, burn this letter—forget that it has been written; and may you never know the pang of remorseful sigh, if, in the days to come, you see her—whose name in that case I should profane did I repeat it—the comrade of another man's mind, the half of another man's heart, the pride and delight of another man's blissful home."

CHAPTER IV.

THERE is somewhere in Lord Lytton's writings—writings so numerous that I may be pardoned if I cannot remember where—a critical definition of the difference between dramatic and narrative art of story, instanced by that marvellous passage in the loftiest of Sir Walter Scott's works, in which all the anguish of Ravenswood on the night before he has to meet Lucy's brother in mortal combat is conveyed without the spoken words required in tragedy. It is only to be conjectured by the tramp of his heavy boots to and fro all the night long in his solitary chamber, heard below by the faithful Caleb. The drama could not have allowed that treatment; the drama must have put into words, as "soliloquy," agonies which the non-dramatic narrator knows that no soliloquy can describe. Humbly do I imitate, then, the great master of narrative in declining to put into words the conflict between love and reason that tortured the heart of Graham Vane when, dropping noiselessly the letter I have just transcribed, he covered his face with his hands and remained—I know not how long—in the same position, his head bowed, not a sound escaping from his lips.

He did not stir from his rooms that day; and had there been a Caleb's faithful ear to listen, his tread, too, might have been heard all that sleepless night passing to and fro, but pausing oft, along his solitary floors.

Possibly love would have borne down all opposing reasonings, doubts, and prejudices, but for incidents that occurred the following evening. On that evening Graham dined *en famille* with his cousins the Altons. After dinner, the Duke produced the design for a cenotaph inscribed to the memory of his aunt, Lady Janet King, which he proposed to place in the family chapel at Alton.

"I know," said the Duke, kindly, "you would wish the old house from which she sprang to preserve some such record of her who loved you as her son; and even putting you out of the question, it gratifies me to attest the claim of our family to a daughter who continues to be famous for her goodness, and made the goodness so lovable that envy forgave it for being famous. It was a pang to me when poor Richard King decided on placing her tomb among strangers; but in conceding his rights as to her resting-place, I retain mine to her name, *Nostris liberis virtutis exemplar.*"

Graham wrung his cousin's hand—he could not speak, choked by suppressed tears.

The Duchess, who loved and honoured Lady Janet almost as much as did her husband, fairly sobbed aloud. She had, indeed, reason for grateful memories of the deceased: there had been some obstacles to her marriage with the man who had won her heart, arising from political differences and family feuds between their parents, which the gentle mediation of Lady Janet had smoothed away. And never did union founded on mutual and ardent love more belie the assertions of the great Bichat (esteemed by Dr. Buckle the finest intellect which practical philosophy has exhibited since Aristotle), that "Love is a sort of fever which does not last beyond two years," than that between those eccentric specimens of a class denounced as frivolous and heartless by philosophers, English and French, who have certainly never heard of Bichat.

When the emotion the Duke had exhibited was calmed down, his wife pushed towards Graham a sheet of paper, inscribed with the epitaph composed by his hand. "Is it not beautiful," she said, falteringly—"not a word too much or too little?"

Graham read the inscription slowly, and with very dimmed eyes. It deserved the praise bestowed on it; for the Duke, though a shy and awkward speaker, was an incisive and graceful writer.

Yet, in his innermost self, Graham shivered when he read that epitaph, it expressed so emphatically the reverential nature of the love which Lady Janet had inspired—the genial influences which the holiness of a character so active in doing good had diffused around it. It brought vividly before Graham that image of perfect spotless womanhood. And a voice within him asked, "Would that cenotaph be placed amid the monuments of an illustrious lineage if the secret known to thee could transpire? What though the lost one were really as unsullied by sin as the world deems, would the name now treasured as an heirloom not be a memory of gall and a sound of shame?"

He remained so silent after putting down the inscription,

that the Duke said modestly: "My dear Graham, I see that you do not like what I have written. Your pen is much more practised than mine. If I did not ask you to compose the epitaph, it was because I thought it would please you more in coming, as a spontaneous tribute due to her, from the representative of her family. But will you correct my sketch, or give me another according to your own ideas?"

"I see not a word to alter," said Graham; "forgive me if my silence wronged my emotion; the truest eloquence is that which holds us too mute for applause."

"I knew you would like it. Leopold is always so disposed to underrate himself," said the duchess, whose hand was resting fondly on her husband's shoulder. "Epitaphs are so difficult to write—especially epitaphs on women of whom in life the least said the better. Janet was the only woman I ever knew whom one could praise in safety."

"Well expressed," said the Duke, smiling: "and I wish you would make that safety clear to some lady friends of yours, to whom it might serve as a lesson. Proof against every breath of scandal herself, Janet King never uttered and never encouraged one ill-natured word against another. But I am afraid, my dear fellow, that I must leave you to a *tête-à-tête* with Eleanor. You know that I must be at the House this evening—I only paired till half-past nine."

"I will walk down to the House with you, if you are going on foot."

"No," said the Duchess; "you must resign yourself to me for at least half an hour. I was looking over your aunt's letters to-day, and I found one which I wish to show you; it is all about yourself, and written within the last few months of her life." Here she put her arm into Graham's, and led him into her own private drawing-room, which, though others might call it a boudoir, she dignified by the name of her study. The Duke remained for some minutes thoughtfully leaning his arm on the mantelpiece. It was no unimportant debate in the Lords that night, and on a subject in which he took great interest, and the details of

which he had thoroughly mastered.   He had been requested
to speak, if only a few words, for his high character and his
reputation for good sense gave weight to the mere utterance
of his opinion.   But though no one had more moral courage in action, the Duke had a terror at the very thought of
addressing an audience, which made him despise himself.

"Ah!" he muttered, "if Graham Vane were but in Parliament, I could trust him to say exactly what I would
rather be swallowed up by an earthquake than stand up
and say for myself.   But now he has got money he seems
to think of nothing but saving it."

CHAPTER V.

THE letter from Lady Janet, which the Duchess took
from the desk and placed in Graham's hand, was in strange
coincidence with the subject that for the last twenty-four
hours had absorbed his thoughts and tortured his heart.
Speaking of him in terms of affectionate eulogy, the writer
proceeded to confide her earnest wish that he should not
longer delay that change in life which, concentrating so
much that is vague in the desires and aspirations of man,
leaves his heart and his mind, made serene by the content-
ment of home, free for the steadfast consolidation of their
warmth and their light upon the ennobling duties that unite
the individual to his race.

"There is no one," wrote Lady Janet, "whose character
and career a felicitous choice in marriage can have greater
influence over than this dear adopted son of mine. ˙ I do
not fear that in any case he will be liable to the errors of
his brilliant father.   His early reverse of fortune here
seems to me one of those blessings which Heaven conceals
in the form of affliction.   For in youth, the genial freshness of his gay animal spirits, a native generosity mingled
with desire of display and thirst for applause, made me

somewhat alarmed for his future. But, though he still
retains these attributes of character, they are no longer
predominant; they are modified and chastened. He has
learned prudence. But what I now fear most for him is
that which he does not show in the world, which neither
Leopold nor you seem to detect,—it is an exceeding sensi-
tiveness of pride. I know not how else to describe it. It
is so interwoven with the highest qualities, that I sometimes dread injury to them could it be torn away from the
faultier ones which it supports.

"It is interwoven with that lofty independence of spirit
which has made him refuse openings the most alluring to
his ambition; it communicates a touching grandeur to his
self-denying thrift; it makes him so tenacious of his word
once given, so cautious before he gives it. Public life to
him is essential; without it he would be incomplete; and
yet I sigh to think that whatever success he may achieve
in it will be attended with proportionate pain. Calumny
goes side by side with fame, and courting fame as a man,
he is as thin-skinned to calumny as a woman.

"The wife for Graham should have qualities, not taken
individually, uncommon in English wives, but in combination somewhat rare.

"She must have mind enough to appreciate his—not to
clash with it. She must be fitted with sympathies to be
his dearest companion, his confidante in the hopes and fears
which the slightest want of sympathy would make him keep
ever afterwards pent within his breast. In herself worthy
of distinction, she must merge all distinction in his. You
have met in the world men who, marrying professed beau·
ties, or professed literary geniuses, are spoken of as the
husband of the beautiful Mrs. A——, or of the clever Mrs.
B——: can you fancy Graham Vane in the reflected light
of one of those husbands? I trembled last year when I
thought he was attracted by a face which the artists raved
about, and again by a tongue which dropped *bons mots* that
went the round of the club. I was relieved, when, sound-

ing him, he said, laughingly, 'No, dear aunt, I should be one sore from head to foot if I married a wife that was talked about for anything but goodness.'

"No,—Graham Vane will have pains sharp enough if he live to be talked about himself. But that tenderest half of himself, the bearer of the name he would make, and for the dignity of which he alone would be responsible,—if that were the town talk, he would curse the hour he gave any one the right to take on herself his man's burden of calumny and fame. I know not which I should pity the most, Graham Vane or his wife.

"Do you understand me, dearest Eleanor? No doubt you do so far, that you comprehend that the women whom men most admire are not the women we, as women ourselves, would wish our sons or brothers to marry. But perhaps you do not comprehend my cause of fear, which is this—for in such matters men do not see as we women do— Graham abhors, in the girls of our time, frivolity and insipidity. Very rightly, you will say. True, but then he is too likely to be allured by contrasts. I have seen him attracted by the very girls we recoil from more than we do from those we allow to be frivolous and insipid. I accused him of admiration for a certain young lady whom you call 'odious,' and whom the slang that has come into vogue calls 'fast;' and I was not satisfied with his answer, 'Certainly I admire her; she is not a doll—she has ideas.' I would rather of the two see Graham married to what men call a doll, than to a girl with ideas which are distasteful to women."

Lady Janet then went on to question the Duchess about a Miss Asterisk, with whom this tale will have nothing to do, but who, from the little which Lady Janet had seen of her, might possess all the requisites that fastidious correspondent would exact for the wife of her adopted son.

This Miss Asterisk had been introduced into the London world by the Duchess. The Duchess had replied to Lady Janet, that if earth could be ransacked, a more suitable wife for Graham Vane than Miss Asterisk could not be found; she was well born—an heiress; the estates she inherited were in the county of —— (viz., the county in which the ancestors of D'Altons and Vanes had for centuries established their whereabout). Miss Asterisk was pretty enough to please any man's eye, but not with the beauty of which artists rave; well informed enough to be companion to a well-informed man, but certainly not witty enough to supply *bons mots* to the clubs. Miss Asterisk was one of those women of whom a husband might be proud, yet with whom a husband would feel safe from being talked about.

And in submitting the letter we have read to Graham's eye, the Duchess had the cause of Miss Asterisk pointedly in view. Miss Asterisk had confided to her friend, that, of all men she had seen, Mr. Graham Vane was the one she would feel the least inclined to refuse.

So when Graham Vane returned the letter to the Duchess, simply saying, "How well my dear aunt divined what is weakest in me!" the Duchess replied quickly, "Miss Asterisk dines here to-morrow; pray come; you would like her if you knew more of her."

"To-morrow I am engaged—an American friend of mine dines with me; but 'tis no matter, for I shall never feel more for Miss Asterisk than I feel for Mont Blanc."

CHAPTER VI.

ON leaving his cousin's house Graham walked on, he scarce knew or cared whither, the image of the beloved dead so forcibly recalled the solemnity of the mission with which he had been intrusted, and which hitherto he had failed to fulfil. What if the only mode by which he could, without causing questions and suspicions that might result in dragging to day the terrible nature of the trust he held, enrich the daughter of Richard King, repair all wrong hitherto done to her, and guard the sanctity of Lady

Janet's home,—should be in that union which Richard
King had commended to him while his heart was yet free?

In such a case, would not gratitude to the dead, duty to
the living, make that union imperative at whatever sacrifice
of happiness to himself? The two years to which Richard
King had limited the suspense of research were not yet expired. Then, too, that letter of Lady Janet's,—so tenderly anxious for his future, so clear-sighted as to the elements
of his own character in its strength or its infirmities—combined with graver causes to withhold his heart from its
yearning impulse, and—no, not steel it against Isaura, but
forbid it to realise, in the fair creature and creator of romance, his ideal of the woman to whom an earnest, sagacious, aspiring man commits all the destinies involved in
the serene dignity of his hearth. He could not but own
that this gifted author—this eager seeker after fame—this
brilliant and bold competitor with men on their own stormy
battle-ground—was the very person from whom Lady Janet
would have warned away his choice. She (Isaura) merge
her own distinctions in a husband's;—she leave exclusively
to him the burden of fame and calumny!—she shun "to be
talked about!" she who could feel her life to be a success
or a failure, according to the extent and the loudness of the
talk which it courted!

While these thoughts racked his mind, a kindly hand was
laid on his arm, and a cheery voice accosted him. "Well
met, my dear Vane! I see we are bound to the same place;
there will be a good gathering to-night."

"What do you mean, Bevil? I am going nowhere, except to my own quiet rooms."

"Pooh! Come in here at least for a few minutes,"—and
Bevil drew him up to the door-step of a house close by,
where, on certain evenings, a well-known club drew together men who seldom meet so familiarly elsewhere—men
of all callings; a club especially favoured by wits, authors,
and the *flâneurs* of polite society.

Graham shook his head, about to refuse, when Bevil

added, "I have just come from Paris, and can give you the
last news, literary, political, and social. By the way, I
saw Savarin the other night at the Cicogna's—he introduced me there." Graham winced; he was spelled by the
music of a name, and followed his acquaintance into the
crowded room, and, after returning many greetings and
nods, withdrew into a remote corner, and motioned Bevil
to a seat beside him.

"So you met Savarin? Where, did you say?"

"At the house of the new lady-author—I hate the word
authoress—Mademoiselle Cicogna! Of course you have
read her book?"

"Yes."

"Full of fine things, is it not?—though somewhat high-
flown and sentimental: however, nothing succeeds like success. No book has been more talked about at Paris: the
only thing more talked about is the lady-author herself."

"Indeed, and how?"

"She doesn't look twenty, a mere girl—of that kind of
beauty which so arrests the eye that you pass by other faces
to gaze on it, and the dullest stranger would ask, 'Who,
and what is she?' A girl, I say, like that—who lives as
independently as if she were a middle-aged widow, receives
every week (she has her Thursdays), with no other chaperon than an old *ci-devant* Italian singing woman, dressed
like a guy—must set Parisian tongues into play even if she
had not written the crack book of the season."

"Mademoiselle Cicogna receives on Thursdays, —no harm
in that; and if she have no other chaperon than the Italian
lady you mention, it is because Mademoiselle Cicogna is an
orphan, and having a fortune, such as it is, of her own, I
do not see why she should not live as independently as
many an unmarried woman in London placed under similar
circumstances. I suppose she receives chiefly persons in
the literary or artistic world, and if they are all as respectable as the Savarins, I do not think ill-nature itself could
find fault with her social circle."

"Ah! you know the Cicogna, I presume. I am sure I did not wish to say anything that could offend her best friends, only I do think it is a pity she is not married, poor girl!"

"Mademoiselle Cicogna, accomplished, beautiful, of good birth (the Cicognas rank among the oldest of Lombard families), is not likely to want offers."

"Offers of marriage,—h'm—well, I dare say, from authors and artists. You know Paris better even than I do, but I don't suppose authors and artists there make the most desirable husbands; and I scarcely know a marriage in France between a man-author and lady-author which does not end in the deadliest of all animosities—that of wounded *amour propre*. Perhaps the man admires his own genius too much to do proper homage to his wife's."

"But the choice of Mademoiselle Cicogna need not be restricted to the pale of authorship—doubtless she has many admirers beyond that quarrelsome borderland."

"Certainly—countless adorers. Enguerrand de Vandemar—you know that diamond of dandies?"

"Perfectly—is he an admirer?"

"*Cela va sans dire*—he told me that though she was not the handsomest woman in Paris, all other women looked less handsome since he had seen her. But, of course, French lady-killers like Enguerrand, when it comes to marriage, leave it to their parents to choose their wives and arrange the terms of the contract. Talking of lady-killers, I beheld amid the throng at Mademoiselle Cicogna's the *ci-devant* Lovelace whom I remember some twenty-three years ago as the darling of wives and the terror of husbands—Victor de Mauléon."

"Victor de Mauléon at Mademoiselle Cicogna's!—what, is that man restored to society?"

"Ah! you are thinking of the ugly old story about the jewels—oh, yes, he has got over that; all his grand relations, the Vandemars, Beauvilliers, Rochebriant, and others, took him by the hand when he reappeared at Paris last year;

and though I believe he is still avoided by many, he is courted by still more—and avoided, I fancy, rather from political than social causes. The Imperialist set, of course, execrate and prescribe him. You know he is the writer of those biting articles signed *Pierre Firmin* in the *Sens Commun;* and I am told he is the proprietor of that very clever journal, which has become a power."

"So, so—that is the journal in which Mademoiselle Cicogna's *roman* first appeared. So, so—Victor de Mauléon one of her associates, her counsellor and friend—ah!"

"No, I didn't say that; on the contrary, he was presented to her the first time the evening I was at the house. I saw that young silk-haired coxcomb, Gustave Rameau, introduce him to her. You don't perhaps know Rameau, editor of the *Sens Commun*—writes poems and criticisms. They say he is a Red Republican, but De Mauléon keeps truculent French politics subdued if not suppressed in his cynical journal. Somebody told me that the Cicogna is very much in love with Rameau; certainly he has a handsome face of his own, and that is the reason why she was so rude to the Russian Prince X——."

"How rude! Did the Prince propose to her?"

"Propose! you forget—he is married. Don't you know the Princess? Still there are other kinds of proposals than those of marriage which a rich Russian prince may venture to make to a pretty novelist brought up for the stage."

"Bevil!" cried Graham, grasping the man's arm fiercely, "how dare you?"

"My dear boy," said Bevil, very much astonished, "I really did not know that your interest in the young lady was so great. If I have wounded you in relating a mere *on dit* picked up at the Jockey Club, I beg you a thousand pardons. I dare say there was not a word of truth in it."

"Not a word of truth, you may be sure, if the *on dit* was injurious to Mademoiselle Cicogna. It is true, I *have* a strong interest in her; any man—any gentleman—would

have such interest in a girl so brilliant and seemingly so
friendless.   It shames one of human nature to think that
the reward which the world makes to those who elevate its
platitudes, brighten its dulness, delight its leisure, is—
Slander!   I have had the honour to make the acquaintance
of this lady before she became a 'celebrity,' and I have
never met in my paths through life a purer heart or a nobler
nature.   What is the wretched *on dit* you condescend to
circulate?   Permit me to add:

    " 'He who repeats a slander shares the crime.' "

"Upon my honour, my dear Vane," said Bevil seriously
(he did not want for spirit), "I hardly know you this evening.   It is not because duelling is out of fashion that a man
should allow himself to speak in a tone that gives offence
to another who intended none; and if duelling is out of
fashion in England, it is still possible in France.   *Entre
nous*, I would rather cross the Channel with you than submit to language that conveys unmerited insult."

Graham's cheek, before ashen pale, flushed into dark
red.   "I understand you," he said quietly, "and will be at
Boulogne to-morrow."

"Graham Vane," replied Bevil, with much dignity, "you
and I have known each other a great many years, and
neither of us has cause to question the courage of the other;
but I am much older than yourself—permit me to take the
melancholy advantage of seniority.   A duel between us in
consequence of careless words said about a lady in no way
connected with either, would be a cruel injury to her; a
duel on grounds so slight would little injure me—a man
about town, who would not sit an hour in the House of
Commons if you paid him a thousand pounds a minute.
But you, Graham Vane—you whose destiny it is to canvass
electors and make laws—would it not be an injury to you
to be questioned at the hustings why you broke the law, and
why you sought another man's life?   Come, come! shake
hands and consider all that seconds, if we chose them,

would exact, is said, every affront on either side retracted, every apology on either side made."

"Bevil, you disarm and conquer me. I spoke like a hot-headed fool; forget it—forgive. But—but—I can listen calmly now—what is that *on dit?*"

"One that thoroughly bears out your own very manly upholding of the poor young orphan, whose name I shall never again mention without such respect as would satisfy her most sensitive champion. It was said that the Prince X—— boasted that before a week was out Mademoiselle Cicogna should appear in his carriage at the Bois de Boulogne, and wear at the opera diamonds he had sent to her; that this boast was enforced by a wager, and the terms of the wager compelled the Prince to confess the means he had taken to succeed, and produce the evidence that he had lost or won. According to this *on dit*, the Prince had written to Mademoiselle Cicogna, and the letter had been accompanied by a *parure* that cost him half a million of francs; that the diamonds had been sent back with a few words of such scorn as a queen might address to an upstart lackey. But, my dear Vane, it is a mournful position for the girl to receive such offers; and you must agree with me in wishing she were safely married, even to Monsieur Rameau, coxcomb though he be. Let us hope that they will be an exception to French authors, male and female, in general, and live like turtle-doves."

CHAPTER VII.

A FEW days after the date of the last chapter, Colonel Morley returned to Paris. He had dined with Graham at Greenwich, had met him afterwards in society, and paid him a farewell visit on the day before the Colonel's depart-ure; but the name of Isaura Cicogna had not again been uttered by either. Morley was surprised that his wife did not question him minutely as to the mode in which he had executed her delicate commission, and the manner as well as words with which Graham had replied to his "ventilations." But his Lizzy cut him short when he began his recital:

"I don't want to hear anything more about the man. He has thrown away a prize richer than his ambition will ever gain, even if it gained him a throne."

"That it can't gain him in the old country. The people are loyal to the present dynasty, whatever you may be told to the contrary."

"Don't be so horribly literal, Frank; that subject is done with. How was the Duchess of M—— dressed?"

But when the Colonel had retired to what the French call the *cabinet de travail*—and which he more accurately termed his "smoke den"—and there indulged in the cigar which, despite his American citizenship, was forbidden in the drawing-room of the tyrant who ruled his life, Mrs. Morley took from her desk a letter received three days before, and brooded over it intently, studying every word. When she had thus reperused it, her tears fell upon the page. "Poor Isaura!" she muttered—"poor Isaura! I know she loves him—and how deeply a nature like hers can love! But I must break it to her. If I did not, she would remain nursing a vain dream, and refuse every chance of real happiness for the sake of nursing it." Then she mechanically folded up the letter—I need not say it was from Graham Vane—restored it to the desk, and remained musing till the Colonel looked in at the door and said peremptorily, "Very late—come to bed."

The next day Madame Savarin called on Isaura.

"*Chère enfant,*" said she, "I have bad news for you. Poor Gustave is very ill—an attack of the lungs and fever; you know how delicate he is."

"I am sincerely grieved," said Isaura, in earnest tender tones; "it must be a very sudden attack: he was here last Thursday."

"The malady only declared itself yesterday morning, but

surely you must have observed how ill he has been looking for several days past? It pained me to see him."

"I did not notice any change in him," said Isaura, somewhat conscience-stricken. Wrapt in her own happy thoughts, she would not have noticed change in faces yet more familiar to her than that of her young admirer.

"Isaura," said Madame Savarin, "I suspect there are moral causes for our friend's failing health. Why should I disguise my meaning? You know well how madly he is in love with you, and have you denied him hope?"

"I like M. Rameau as a friend; I admire him—at times I pity him."

"Pity is akin to love."

"I doubt the truth of that saying, at all events as you apply it now. I could not love M. Rameau; I never gave him cause to think I could."

"I wish for both your sakes that you could make me a different answer; for his sake, because, knowing his faults and failings, I am persuaded that they would vanish in a companionship so pure, so elevating as yours: you could make him not only so much happier but so much better a man. Hush! let me go on, let me come to yourself,—I say for your sake I wish it. Your pursuits, your ambition, are akin to his; you should not marry one who could not sympathise with you in these. If you did, he might either restrict the exercise of your genius or be chafed at its dis-play. The only authoress I ever knew whose married lot was serenely happy to the last, was the greatest of English poetesses married to a great English poet. You cannot, you ought not, to devote yourself to the splendid career to which your genius irresistibly impels you, without that counsel, that support, that protection, which a husband alone can give. My dear child, as the wife myself of a man of letters, and familiarised to all the gossip, all the scandal, to which they who give their names to the public are exposed, I declare that if I had a daughter who inherited Savarin's talents, and was ambitious of attaining to his

renown, I would rather shut her up in a convent than let
her publish a book that was in every one's hands until she
had sheltered her name under that of a husband; and if I
say this of my child, with a father so wise in the world's
ways, and so popularly respected as my *bon homme*, what
must I feel to be essential to your safety, poor stranger in
our land! poor solitary orphan! with no other advice or
guardian than the singing mistress whom you touchingly
call '*Madre!*' I see how I distress and pain you—I cannot
help it. Listen! The other evening Savarin came back
from his favourite *café* in a state of excitement that made
me think he came to announce a revolution. It was about
you; he stormed, he wept—actually wept—my philosophical
laughing Savarin. He had just heard of that atrocious wager
made by a Russian barbarian. Every one praised you for
the contempt with which you had treated the savage's insolence. But that *you* should have been submitted to such
an insult without one male friend who had the right to resent and chastise it,—you cannot think how Savarin was
chafed and galled. You know how he admires, but you
cannot guess how he reveres you; and since then he says
to me every day: 'That girl must not remain single. Better
marry any man who has a heart to defend a wife's honour
and the nerve to fire a pistol: every Frenchman has those
qualifications!' "

Here Isaura could no longer restrain her emotions; she
burst into sobs so vehement, so convulsive, that Madame
Savarin became alarmed; but when she attempted to embrace and soothe her, Isaura recoiled with a visible shudder,
and gasping out, "Cruel, cruel!" turned to the door, and
rushed to her own room.

A few minutes afterwards a maid entered the *salon* with
a message to Madame Savarin that Mademoiselle was so
unwell that she must beg Madame to excuse her return to
the *salon*.

Later in the day Mrs. Morley called, but Isaura would
not see her.

Meanwhile poor Rameau was stretched on his sick-bed, and in sharp struggle between life and death. It is difficult to disentangle, one by one, all the threads in a nature so complex as Rameau's; but if we may hazard a conjecture, the grief of disappointed love was not the immediate cause of his illness, and yet it had much to do with it. The goad of Isaura's refusal had driven him into seeking distraction in excesses which a stronger frame could not have courted with impunity. The man was thoroughly Parisian in many things, but especially in impatience of any trouble. Did love trouble him—love could be drowned in absinthe; and too much absinthe may be a more immediate cause of congested lungs than the love which the absinthe had lulled to sleep.

His bedside was not watched by hirelings. When first taken thus ill—too ill to attend to his editorial duties—information was conveyed to the publisher of the *Sens Commun*, and in consequence of that information, Victor de Mauléon came to see the sick man. By his bed he found Savarin, who had called, as it were by chance, and seen the doctor, who had said, "It is grave. He must be well nursed."

Savarin whispered to De Mauléon, "Shall we call in a professional nurse, or a *sœur de charité?*"

De Mauléon replied, also in a whisper, "Somebody told me that the man had a mother."

It was true—Savarin had forgotten it. Rameau never mentioned his parents—he was not proud of them.

They belonged to a lower class of the *bourgeoisie*, retired shopkeepers, and a Red Republican is sworn to hate of the *bourgeoisie*, high or low; while a beautiful young author pushing his way into the Chaussée d'Antin does not proclaim to the world that his parents had sold hosiery in the Rue St. Denis.

Nevertheless Savarin knew that Rameau had such parents still living, and took the hint. Two hours afterwards Rameau was leaning his burning forehead on his mother's breast.

The next morning the doctor said to the mother, "You are worth ten of me. If you can stay here we shall pull him through."

"Stay here!—my own boy!" cried indignantly the poor mother.

CHAPTER VIII.

THE day which had inflicted on Isaura so keen an anguish was marked by a great trial in the life of Alain de Rochebriant.

In the morning he received the notice " of *un commandement tendant à saisie immobilière,*" on the part of his creditor, M. Louvier; in plain English, an announcement that his property at Rochebriant would be put up to public sale on a certain day, in case all debts due to the mortgagee were not paid before. An hour afterwards came a note from Duplessis stating that " he had returned from Bretagne on the previous evening, and would be very happy to see the Marquis de Rochebriant before two o'clock, if not inconvenient to call."

Alain put the "*commandement*" into his pocket, and repaired to the Hotel Duplessis.

The financier received him with very cordial civility. Then he began: "I am happy to say I left your excellent aunt in very good health. She honoured the letter of introduction to her which I owe to your politeness with the most amiable hospitalities; she insisted on my removing from the *auberge* at which I first put up and becoming a guest under your venerable roof-tree—a most agreeable lady, and a most interesting *château.*"

"I fear your accommodation was in striking contrast to your comforts at Paris; my *château* is only interesting to an antiquarian enamoured of ruins."

"Pardon me, 'ruins' is an exaggerated expression. I do not say that the *château* does not want some repairs, but

they would not be costly; the outer walls are strong enough
to defy time for centuries to come, and a few internal deco-
rations and some modern additions of furniture would make
the old *manoir* a home fit for a prince. I have been over the
whole estate, too, with the worthy M. Hébert,—a superb
property."

"Which M. Louvier appears to appreciate," said Alain,
with a somewhat melancholy smile, extending to Duplessis
the menacing notice.

Duplessis glanced at it, and said drily: "M. Louvier
knows what he is about. But I think we had better put
an immediate stop to formalities which must be painful to
a creditor so benevolent. I do not presume to offer to pay
the interest due on the security you can give for the repay-
ment. If you refused that offer from so old a friend as
Lemercier, of course you could not accept it from me. I
make another proposal, to which you can scarcely object.
I do not like to give my scheming rival on the Bourse the
triumph of so profoundly planned a speculation. Aid me
to defeat him. Let me take the mortgage on myself, and
become sole mortgagee—hush!—on this condition, that
there should be an entire union of interests between us
two; that I should be at liberty to make the improvements
I desire, and when the improvements be made, there should
be a fair arrangement as to the proportion of profits due to
me as mortgagee and improver, to you as original owner.
Attend, my dear Marquis,—I am speaking as a mere man
of business. I see my way to adding more than a third—
I might even say a half—to the present revenues of Rochebriant. The woods have been sadly neglected, drainage
alone would add greatly to their produce. Your orchards
might be rendered magnificent supplies to Paris with better
cultivation. Lastly, I would devote to building purposes
or to market gardens all the lands round the two towns
of —— and ——. I think I can lay my hands on suitable
speculators for these last experiments. In a word, though
the market value of Rochebriant, as it now stands, would

not be equivalent to the debt on it, in five or six years it
could be made worth—well, I will not say how much—but
we shall be both well satisfied with the result. Meanwhile, if you allow me to find purchasers for your timber,
and if you will not suffer the Chevalier de Finisterre to
regulate your expenses, you need have no fear that the interest due to me will not be regularly paid, even though I
shall be compelled, for the first year or two at least, to ask
a higher rate of interest than Louvier exacted—say a quarter per cent. more; and in suggesting that, you will comprehend that this is now a matter of business between us,
and not of friendship."

Alain turned his head aside to conceal his emotion, and
then, with the quick affectionate impulse of the genuine
French nature, threw himself on the financier's breast and
kissed him on both cheeks.

"You save me! you save the home and the tombs of my
ancestors! Thank you I cannot; but I believe in God—I
pray—I will pray for you as for a father; and if ever," he
hurried on in broken words, "I am mean enough to squan-
der on idle luxuries one franc that I should save for the
debt due to you, chide me as a father would chide a grace-
less son."

Moved as Alain was, Duplessis was moved yet more
deeply. "What father would not be proud of such a son?
Ah, if I had such a one!" he said softly. Then, quickly
recovering his wonted composure, he added, with the sar-
donic smile which often chilled his friends and alarmed his
foes, "Monsieur Louvier is about to pass that which I ventured to promise him, a '*mauvais quart d'heure.*' Lend me
that *commandement tendant à saisie.* I must be off to my
avoué with instructions. If you have no better engagement, pray dine with me to-day and accompany Valérie and
myself to the opera."

I need not say that Alain accepted the invitation. How
happy Valérie was that evening!

CHAPTER IX.

THE next day Duplessis was surprised by a visit from M. Louvier—that magnate of *millionaires* had never before set foot in the house of his younger and less famous rival.

The burly man entered the room with a face much flushed, and with more than his usual mixture of jovial *brusquerie* and opulent swagger.

"Startled to see me, I dare say," began Louvier, as soon as the door was closed. "I have this morning received a communication from your agent containing a cheque for the interest due to me from M. Rochebriant, and a formal notice of your intention to pay off the principal on behalf of that popinjay prodigal. Though we two have not hitherto been the best friends in the world, I thought it fair to a man in your station to come to you direct and say, '*Cher confrère*, what swindler has bubbled you? You don't know the real condition of this Breton property, or you would never so throw away your millions. The property is not worth the mortgage I have on it by 30,000 louis.'"

"Then, M. Louvier, you will be 30,000 louis the richer if I take the mortgage off your hands."

"I can afford the loss—no offence—better than you can; and I may have fancies which I don't mind paying for, but which cannot influence another. See, I have brought with me the exact schedule of all details respecting this property. You need not question their accuracy; they have been arranged by the Marquis's own agents, M. Gandrin and M. Hébert. They contain, you will perceive, every possible item of revenue, down to an apple-tree. Now, look at that, and tell me if you are justified in lending such a sum on such a property."

"Thank you very much for an interest in my affairs that I scarcely ventured to expect M. Louvier to entertain; but

I see that I have a duplicate of this paper, furnished to me very honestly by M. Hébert himself. Besides, I, too, have fancies which I don't mind paying for, and among them may be a fancy for the lands of Rochebriant."

"Look you, Duplessis, when a man like me asks a favour, you may be sure that he has the power to repay it. Let me have my whim here, and ask anything you like from me in return!"

"*Désolé* not to oblige you, but this has become not only a whim of mine, but a matter of honour; and honour you know, my dear M. Louvier, is the first principle of sound finance. I have myself, after careful inspection of the Rochebriant property, volunteered to its owner to advance the money to pay off your *hypothèque;* and what would be said on the Bourse if Lucien Duplessis failed in an obligation?"

"I think I can guess what will one day be said of Lucien Duplessis if he make an irrevocable enemy of Paul Louvier. *Corbleu! mon cher*, a man of thrice your capital, who watched every speculation of yours with a hostile eye, might some *beau jour* make even you a bankrupt!"

"Forewarned, forearmed!" replied Duplessis, imperturbably, "*Fas est ab hoste doceri*,—I mean, 'It is right to be taught by an enemy;' and I never remember the day when you were otherwise, and yet I am not a bankrupt, though I receive you in a house which, thanks to you, is so modest in point of size!"

"Bah! that was a mistake of mine,—and, ha! ha! you had your revenge there—that forest!"

"Well, as a peace offering, I will give you up the forest, and content my ambition as a landed proprietor with this bad speculation of Rochebriant!"

"Confound the forest, I don't care for it now! I can sell my place for more than it has cost me to one of your imperial favourites. Build a palace in your forest. Let me have Rochebriant, and name your terms."

"A thousand pardons! but I have already had the honour to inform you, that I have contracted an obligation which does not allow me to listen to terms."

As a serpent, that, after all crawlings and windings, rears itself on end, Louvier rose, crest erect:

"So then it is finished. I came here disposed to offer peace—you refuse, and declare war."

"Not at all, I do not declare war; I accept it if forced on me."

"Is that your last word, M. Duplessis?"

"Monsieur Louvier, it is."

"*Bon jour!*"

And Louvier strode to the door; here he paused: "Take a day to consider."

"Not a moment."

"Your servant, Monsieur,—your very humble servant."

Louvier vanished.

Duplessis leaned his large thoughtful forehead on his thin nervous hand. "This loan will pinch me," he muttered. "I must be very wary now with such a foe. Well, why should I care to be rich? Valérie's *dot*, Valérie's happiness, are secured."

CHAPTER X.

MADAME SAVARIN wrote a very kind and very apologetic letter to Isaura, but no answer was returned to it. Madame Savarin did not venture to communicate to her husband the substance of a conversation which had ended so painfully. He had, in theory, a delicacy of tact, which, if he did not always exhibit it in practice, made him a very severe critic of its deficiency in others. Therefore, unconscious of the offence given, he made a point of calling at Isaura's apartments, and leaving word with her servant that "he was sure she would be pleased to hear M. Rameau was somewhat better, though still in danger."

II.—4

It was not till the third day after her interview with Madame Savarin that Isaura left her own room,—she did so to receive Mrs. Morley.

The fair American was shocked to see the change in Isaura's countenance. She was very pale, and with that indescribable appearance of exhaustion which betrays continued want of sleep; her soft eyes were dim, the play of her lips was gone, her light step weary and languid.

"My poor darling!" cried Mrs. Morley, embracing her, "you have indeed been ill! What is the matter?—who attends you?"

"I need no physician, it was but a passing cold—the air of Paris is very trying. Never mind me, dear—what is the last news?"

Therewith Mrs. Morley ran glibly through the principal topics of the hour: the breach threatened between M. Ollivier and his former liberal partisans; the tone unexpectedly taken by M. de Girardin; the speculations as to the result of the trial of the alleged conspirators against the Emperor's life, which was fixed to take place towards the end of that month of June,—all matters of no slight importance to the interests of an empire. Sunk deep into the recesses of her *fauteuil*, Isaura seemed to listen quietly, till, when a pause came, she said in cold clear tones:

"And Mr. Graham Vane—he has refused your invitation?"

"I am sorry to say he has—he is so engaged in London."

"I knew he had refused," said Isaura, with a low bitter laugh.

"How? who told you?"

"My own good sense told me. One may have good sense, though one is a poor scribbler."

"Don't talk in that way; it is beneath you to angle for compliments."

"Compliments, ah! And so Mr. Vane has refused to come to Paris; never mind, he will come next year. I shall not be in Paris then. Did Colonel Morley see Mr. Vane?"

"Oh, yes; two or three times."

"He is well?"

"Quite well, I believe—at least Frank did not say to the contrary; but, from what I hear, he is not the person I took him for. Many people told Frank that he is much changed since he came into his fortune—is grown very stingy, quite miserly indeed; declines even a seat in Parliament because of the expense. It is astonishing how money does spoil a man."

"He had come into his fortune when he was here. Money had not spoiled him then."

Isaura paused, pressing her hands tightly together; then she suddenly rose to her feet, the colour on her cheek mantling and receding rapidly, and fixing on her startled visitor eyes no longer dim, but with something half fierce, half imploring in the passion of their gaze, said: "Your husband spoke of me to Mr. Vane: I know he did. What did Mr. Vane answer? Do not evade my question. The truth! the truth! I only ask the truth!"

"Give me your hand; sit here beside me, dearest child."

"Child!—no, I am a woman!—weak as a woman, but strong as a woman too!—The truth!"

Mrs. Morley had come prepared to carry out the resolution she had formed and "break" to Isaura "the truth," that which the girl now demanded. But then she had meant to break the truth in her own gentle, gradual way. Thus suddenly called upon, her courage failed her. She burst into tears. Isaura gazed at her dry-eyed.

"Your tears answer me. Mr. Vane has heard that I have been insulted. A man like him does not stoop to love for a woman who has known an insult. I do not blame him; I honour him the more—he is right."

"No—no—no!—you insulted! Who dared to insult you? (Mrs. Morley had never heard the story about the Russian Prince.) Mr. Vane spoke to Frank, and writes of you to me as of one whom it is impossible not to admire, to respect; but—I cannot say it—you will have the

truth,—there, read and judge for yourself." And Mrs.
Morley drew forth and thrust into Isaura's hands the letter
she had concealed from her husband. The letter was not
very long; it began with expressions of warm gratitude to
Mrs. Morley, not for her invitation only, but for the interest she had conceived in his happiness. It went on thus:

"I join with my whole heart in all that you say, with
such eloquent justice, of the mental and personal gifts so
bounteously lavished by nature on the young lady whom
you name.

"No one can feel more sensible than I of the charm of
so exquisite a loveliness; no one can more sincerely join
in the belief that the praise which greets the commencement of her career is but the whisper of the praise that
will cheer its progress with louder and louder plaudits.

"He only would be worthy of her hand, who, if not equal
to herself in genius, would feel raised into partnership with
it by sympathy with its objects and joy in its triumphs.
For myself, the same pain with which I should have learned
she had adopted the profession which she originally contemplated, saddened and stung me when, choosing a career
that confers a renown yet more lasting than the stage, she
no less left behind her the peaceful immunities of private
life. Were I even free to consult only my own heart in
the choice of the one sole partner of my destinies (which I
cannot at present honestly say that I am, though I had expected to be so ere this, when I last saw you at Paris);
could I even hope—which I have no right to do—that I
could chain to myself any private portion of thoughts
which now flow into the large channels by which poets
enrich the blood of the world,—still (I say it in self-reproach, it may be the fault of my English rearing, it may
rather be the fault of an egotism peculiar to myself)—still I
doubt if I could render happy any woman whose world could
not be narrowed to the Home that she adorned and blessed.

"And yet not even the jealous tyranny of man's love could
dare to say to natures like hers of whom we speak, 'Limit

to the household glory of one the light which genius has placed in its firmament for the use and enjoyment of all.' "

"I thank you so much," said Isaura, calmly; "suspense makes a woman so weak—certainty so strong." Mechanically she smoothed and refolded the letter—mechanically, with slow, lingering hands—then she extended it to her friend, smiling.

"Nay, will you not keep it yourself?" said Mrs. Morley. "The more you examine the narrow-minded prejudices, the English arrogant *man's* jealous dread of superiority—nay, of equality—in the woman he can only value as he does his house or his horse, because she is his exclusive property, the more you will be rejoiced to find yourself free for a more worthy choice. Keep the letter; read it till you feel for the writer forgiveness and disdain."

Isaura took back the letter, and leaned her cheek on her hand, looking dreamily into space. It was some moments before she replied, and her words then had no reference to Mrs. Morley's consolatory exhortation.

"He was so pleased when he learned that I renounced the career on which I had set my ambition. I thought he would have been so pleased when I sought in another career to raise myself nearer to his level—I see now how sadly I was mistaken. All that perplexed me before in him is explained. I did not guess how foolishly I had deceived myself till three days ago,—then I did guess it; and it was that guess which tortured me so terribly that I could not keep my heart to myself when I saw you to-day; in spite of all womanly pride it would force its way—to the truth. Hush! I must tell you what was said to me by another friend of mine—a good friend, a wise and kind one. Yet I was so angry when she said it that I thought I could never see her more."

"My sweet darling! who was this friend, and what did she say to you?"

"The friend was Madame Savarin."

"No woman loves you more except myself—and she said?"

"That she would have suffered no daughter of hers to commit her name to the talk of the world as I have done—be exposed to the risk of insult as I have been—until she had the shelter and protection denied to me. And I have thus overleaped the bound that a prudent mother would prescribe to her child, have become one whose hand men do not seek, unless they themselves take the same roads to notoriety. Do you not think she was right?"

"Not as you so morbidly put it, silly girl,—certainly not right. But I do wish that you had the shelter and protection which Madame Savarin meant to express; I do wish that you were happily married to one very different from Mr. Vane—one who would be more proud of your genius than of your beauty—one who would say, 'My name, safer far in its enduring nobility than those that depend on titles and lands—which are held on the tenure of the popular breath—must be honoured by posterity, for She has deigned to make it hers. No democratic revolution can disennoble *me*.'"

"Ay, ay, you believe that men will be found to think with complacency that they owe to a wife a name they could not achieve for themselves. Possibly there are such men. Where?—among those that are already united by sympathies in the same callings, the same labours, the same hopes and fears with the women who have left behind them the privacies of home. Madame de Grantmesnil was wrong. Artists should wed with artists. True—true!"

Here she passed her hand over her forehead—it was a pretty way of hers when seeking to concentrate thought—and was silent a moment or so.

"Did you ever feel," she then asked dreamily, "that there are moments in life when a dark curtain seems to fall over one's past that a day before was so clear, so blended with the present? One cannot any longer look behind; the gaze is attracted onward, and a track of fire flashes upon the future,—the future which yesterday was invisible. There is a line by some English poet—Mr. Vane once quoted it, not to me, but to M. Savarin, and in illustration of his argument, that the most complicated recesses of thought are best reached by the simplest forms of expression. I said to myself, 'I will study that truth if ever I take to literature as I have taken to song;' and—yes—it was that evening that the ambition fatal to woman fixed on me its relentless fangs—at Enghien—we were on the lake—the sun was setting."

"But you do not tell me the line that so impressed you," said Mrs. Morley, with a woman's kindly tact.

"The line—which line? Oh, I remember; the line was this:

"'I see as from a tower the end of all. "

And now—kiss me, dearest—never a word again to me about this conversation: never a word about Mr. Vane—the dark curtain has fallen on the past."

CHAPTER XI.

MEN and women are much more like each other in certain large elements of character than is generally supposed, but it is that very resemblance which makes their differences the more incomprehensible to each other; just as in politics, theology, or that most disputatious of all things disputable, metaphysics, the nearer the reasoners approach each other in points that to an uncritical bystander seem the most important, the more sure they are to start off in opposite directions upon reaching the speck of a pin-prick.

Now there are certain grand meeting-places between man and woman—the grandest of all is on the ground of love, and yet here also is the great field of quarrel. And here the teller of a tale such as mine ought, if he is sufficiently wise to be humble, to know that it is almost profanation if, as man, he presumes to enter the penetralia of a woman's innermost heart, and repeat, as a man would repeat, all the vibrations of sound which the heart of a woman sends forth undistinguishable even to her own ear.

I know Isaura as intimately as if I had rocked her in her cradle, played with her in her childhood, educated and trained her in her youth; and yet I can no more tell you faithfully what passed in her mind during the forty-eight hours that intervened between her conversation with that American lady and her reappearance in some commonplace drawing-room, than I can tell you what the Man in the Moon might feel if the sun that his world reflected were blotted out of creation.

I can only say that when she reappeared in that commonplace drawing-room world, there was a change in her face not very perceptible to the ordinary observer. If anything, to his eye she was handsomer—the eye was brighter—the complexion (always lustrous, though somewhat pale, the limpid paleness that suits so well with dark hair) was yet more lustrous,—it was flushed into delicate rose hues—hues that still better suit with dark hair. What, then, was the change, and change not for the better? The lips, once so pensively sweet, had grown hard; on the brow that had seemed to laugh when the lips did, there was no longer sympathy between brow and lip; there was scarcely seen a fine threadlike line that in a few years would be a furrow on the space between the eyes; the voice was not so tenderly soft; the step was haughtier. What all such change denoted it is for a woman to decide—I can only guess. In the mean while, Mademoiselle Cicogna had sent her servant daily to inquire after M. Rameau. That, I think, she would have done under any circumstances. Meanwhile, too, she had called on Madame Savarin—made it up with her—sealed the reconciliation by a cold kiss. That, too, under any circumstances, I think she would have done—under some circumstances the kiss might have been less cold.

There was one thing unwonted in her habits. I mention it, though it is only a woman who can say if it means anything worth noticing.

For six days she had left a letter from Madame de Grantmesnil unanswered. With Madame de Grantmesnil was connected the whole of her innermost life—from the day when the lonely desolate child had seen, beyond the dusty thoroughfares of life, gleams of the faery land in poetry and art—onward through her restless, dreamy, aspiring youth—onward—onward—till now, through all that constitutes the glorious reality that we call romance.

Never before had she left for two days unanswered letters which were to her as Sibylline leaves to some unquiet neophyte yearning for solutions to enigmas suggested whether by the world without or by the soul within. For six days Madame de Grantmesnil's letter remained unanswered, unread, neglected, thrust out of sight; just as when some imperious necessity compels us to grapple with a world that is, we cast aside the romance which, in our holiday hours, had beguiled us to a world with which we have interests and sympathies no more.

CHAPTER XII.

Gustave recovered, but slowly. The physician pronounced him out of all immediate danger, but said frankly to him, and somewhat more guardedly to his parents, "There is ample cause to beware." "Look you, my young friend," he added to Rameau, "mere brain-work seldom kills a man once accustomed to it like you; but heart-work, and stomach-work, and nerve-work, added to brain-work, may soon consign to the coffin a frame ten times more robust than yours. Write as much as you will—that is your vocation; but it is not your vocation to drink absinthe— to preside at orgies in the *Maison Dorée*. Regulate yourself, and not after the fashion of the fabulous Don Juan. Marry—live soberly and quietly—and you may survive the grandchildren of *viveurs*. Go on as you have done, and before the year is out you are in *Père la Chaise*."

Rameau listened languidly, but with a profound conviction that the physician thoroughly understood his case.

Lying helpless on his bed, he had no desire for orgies at the *Maison Dorée*, with parched lips thirsty for innocent *tisane* of lime-blossoms, the thought of absinthe was as odious to him as the liquid fire of Phlegethon. If ever sinner became suddenly convinced that there was a good deal to be said in favour of a moral life, that sinner at the moment I speak of was Gustave Rameau. Certainly a moral life—'*Domus et placens uxor*,' were essential to the poet who, aspiring to immortal glory, was condemned to the ailments of a very perishable frame.

"Ah," he murmured plaintively to himself, "that girl Isaura can have no true sympathy with genius! It is no ordinary man that she will kill in me!"

And so murmuring he fell asleep. When he woke and found his head pillowed on his mother's breast, it was much as a sensitive, delicate man may wake after having drunk too much the night before. Repentant, mournful, maudlin, he began to weep, and in the course of his weeping he confided to his mother the secret of his heart.

Isaura had refused him—that refusal had made him desperate.

"Ah! with Isaura how changed would be his habits! how pure! how healthful!" His mother listened fondly, and did her best to comfort him and cheer his drooping spirits.

She told him of Isaura's messages of inquiry duly twice a day. Rameau, who knew more about women in general, and Isaura in particular, than his mother conjectured, shook his head mournfully. "She could not do less," he said. "Has no one offered to do more?"—he thought of Julie when he asked that—Madame Rameau hesitated.

These poor Parisians! it is the *mode* to preach against them; and before my book closes, I shall have to preach— no, not to preach, but to imply—plenty of faults to consider and amend. Meanwhile I try my best to take them, as the philosophy of life tells us to take other people, for what they are.

I do not think the domestic relations of the Parisian *bourgeoisie* are as bad as they are said to be in French novels. Madame Rameau is not an uncommon type of her class. She had been when she first married singularly handsome. It was from her that Gustave inherited his beauty; and her husband was a very ordinary type of the French shopkeeper—very plain, by no means intellectual, but gay, good-humoured, devotedly attached to his wife, and with implicit trust in her conjugal virtue. Never was trust better placed. There was not a happier nor a more faithful couple in the *quartier* in which they resided. Madame Rameau hesitated when her boy, thinking of Julie, asked if no one had done more than send to inquire after him as Isaura had done.

After that hesitating pause she said, "Yes—a young lady calling herself Mademoiselle Julie Caumartin wished to instal herself here as your nurse. When I said, 'But I am his mother—he needs no other nurses,'" she would have retreated, and looked ashamed—poor thing! I don't blame her if she loved my son. But, my son, I say this, —if you love her, don't talk to me about that Mademoiselle Cicogna; and if you love Mademoiselle Cicogna, why, then your father will take care that the poor girl who loved you not knowing that you loved another is not left to the temptation of penury."

Rameau's pale lips withered into a phantom-like sneer! Julie! the resplendent Julie!—true, only a ballet-dancer, but whose equipage in the Bois had once been the envy of duchesses—Julie! who had sacrificed fortune for his sake —who, freed from him, could have *millionaires* again at her feet!—Julie! to be saved from penury, as a shopkeeper would save an erring nursemaid—Julie! the irrepressible Julie! who had written to him, the day before his illness, in a pen dipped, not in ink, but in blood from a vein she had opened in her arm:

"Traitor!—I have not seen thee for three days. Dost thou dare to love another? If so, I care not how thou attempt to conceal it—woe to her! *Ingrat!* woe to thee! Love is not love, unless, when betrayed by Love, it appeals to death. Answer me quick—quick.   JULIE."

Poor Gustave thought of that letter and groaned. Certainly his mother was right—he ought to get rid of Julie; but he did not clearly see how Julie was to be got rid of. He replied to Madame Rameau peevishly, "Don't trouble your head about Mademoiselle Caumartin; she is in no want of money. Of course, if I could hope for Isaura—but, alas! I dare not hope. Give me my *tisane.*"

When the doctor called next day, he looked grave, and, drawing Madame Rameau into the next room, he said, "We are not getting on so well as I had hoped; the fever is gone, but there is much to apprehend from the debility left behind. His spirits are sadly depressed." Then added the doctor, pleasantly, and with that wonderful insight into our complex humanity in which physicians excel poets, and in which Parisian physicians are not excelled by any physicians in the world: "Can't you think of any bit of good news—that 'M. Thiers raves about your son's last poem'— that 'it is a question among the Academicians between him and Jules Janin'—or that 'the beautiful Duchesse de —— has been placed in a lunatic asylum because she has gone mad for love of a certain young Red Republican whose name begins with R.'—can't you think of any bit of similar good news? If you can, it will be a tonic to the relaxed state of your dear boy's *amour propre,* compared to which all the drugs in the Pharmacopœia are moonshine and water; and meanwhile be sure to remove him to your

own house, and out of the reach of his giddy young friends,
as soon as you possibly can."

When that great authority thus left his patient's case in
the hands of the mother, she said, "The boy shall be
saved."

CHAPTER XIII.

ISAURA was seated beside the Venosta,—to whom, of
late, she seemed to cling with greater fondness than ever,
—working at some piece of embroidery—a labour from
which she had been estranged for years; but now she had
taken writing, reading, music, into passionate disgust.
Isaura was thus seated, silently intent upon her work, and
the Venosta in full talk, when the servant announced Madame Rameau.

The name startled both; the Venosta had never heard
that the poet had a mother living, and immediately jumped
to the conclusion that Madame Rameau must be a wife he
had hitherto kept unrevealed. And when a woman, still
very handsome, with a countenance grave and sad, entered the *salon*, the Venosta murmured, "The husband's
perfidy reveals itself on a wife's face," and took out her
handkerchief in preparation for sympathising tears.

"Mademoiselle," said the visitor, halting, with eyes fixed
on Isaura. "Pardon my intrusion—my son has the honour
to be known to you. Every one who knows him must share
in my sorrow—so young—so promising, and in such danger—my poor boy!" Madame Rameau stopped abruptly.
Her tears forced their way—she turned aside to conceal
them.

In her twofold condition of being—womanhood and genius—Isaura was too largely endowed with that quickness
of sympathy which distinguishes woman from man, and
genius from talent, not to be wondrously susceptible to
pity.

Already she had wound her arm round the grieving mother—already drawn her to the seat from which she herself had risen—and bending over her had said some words—true, conventional enough in themselves,—but cooed forth in a voice the softest I ever expect to hear, save in dreams, on this side of the grave.

Madame Rameau swept her hand over her eyes, glanced round the room, and noticing the Venosta in dressing-robe and slippers, staring with those Italian eyes, in seeming so quietly innocent, in reality so searchingly shrewd, she whispered pleadingly, "May I speak to you a few minutes alone?" This was not a request that Isaura could refuse, though she was embarrassed and troubled by the surmise of Madame Rameau's object in asking it; accordingly she led her visitor into the adjoining room, and making an apologetic sign to the Venosta, closed the door.

* * *

CHAPTER XIV.

WHEN they were alone, Madame Rameau took Isaura's hand in both her own, and, gazing wistfully into her face, said, "No wonder you are so loved—yours is the beauty that sinks into the hearts and rests there. I prize my boy more, now that I have seen you. But, oh, Mademoiselle! pardon me—do not withdraw your hand—pardon the mother who comes from the sick-bed of her only son and asks if you will assist to save him! A word from you is life or death to him!"

"Nay, nay, do not speak thus, Madame; your son knows how much I value, how sincerely I return, his friendship; but—but," she paused a moment, and continued sadly and with tearful eyes—"I have no heart to give to him—to any one."

"I do not—I would not if I dared—ask what it would be violence to yourself to promise. I do not ask you to

bid me return to my son and say, 'Hope and recover,' but
let me take some healing message from your lips. If I
understand your words rightly, I at least may say that you
do not give to another the hopes you deny to him?"

"So far you understand me rightly, Madame. It has
been said, that romance-writers give away so much of their
hearts to heroes or heroines of their own creation, that they
leave nothing worth the giving to human beings like themselves. Perhaps it is so; yet, Madame," added Isaura,
with a smile of exquisite sweetness in its melancholy, "I
have heart enough left to feel for you."

Madame Rameau was touched. "Ah, Mademoiselle, I
do not believe in the saying you have quoted. But I must
not abuse your goodness by pressing further upon you subjects from which you shrink. Only one word more: you
know that my husband and I are but quiet tradesfolks, not
in the society, nor aspiring to it, to which my son's talents
have raised himself; yet dare I ask that you will not close
here the acquaintance that I have obtruded on you?—dare
I ask, that I may, now and then, call on you—that now
and then I may see you at my own home? Believe that I
would not here ask anything which your own mother would
disapprove if she overlooked disparities of station. Humble
as our home is, slander never passed its threshold."

"Ah, Madame, I and the Signora Venosta, whom in our
Italian tongue I call mother, can but feel honoured and
grateful whenever it pleases you to receive visits from us."

"It would be a base return for such gracious compliance
with my request if I concealed from you the reason why I
pray Heaven to bless you for that answer. The physician
says that it may be long before my son is sufficiently convalescent to dispense with a mother's care, and resume his
former life and occupation in the great world. It is everything for us if we can coax him into coming under our own
roof-tree. This is difficult to do. It is natural for a young
man launched into the world to like his own *chez lui*.
Then what will happen to Gustave? He, lonely and heart-

stricken, will ask friends, young as himself, but far stronger,
to come and cheer him; or he will seek to distract his
thoughts by the overwork of his brain; in either case he is
doomed.   But I have stronger motives yet to fix him a
while at our hearth.   This is just the moment, once lost
never to be regained, when soothing companionship, gentle
reproachless advice, can fix him lastingly in the habits and
modes of life which will banish all fears of his future from
the hearts of his parents.   You at least honour him with
friendship, with kindly interest—you at least would desire
to wean him from all that a friend may disapprove or lament—a creature whom Providence meant to be good, and
perhaps great.   If I say to him, 'It will be long before you
can go out and see your friends, but at my house your
friends shall come and see you—among them Signora Venosta and Mademoiselle Cicogna will now and then drop
in'—my victory is gained, and my son is saved."

"Madame," said Isaura, half sobbing, "what a blessing
to have a mother like you!   Love so noble ennobles those
who hear its voice.   Tell your son how ardently I wish
him to be well, and to fulfil more than the promise of his
genius; tell him also this—how I envy him his mother."

CHAPTER XV.

It needs no length of words to inform thee, my intelligent reader, be thou man or woman—but more especially
woman—of the consequences following each other, as wave
follows wave in a tide, that resulted from the interview
with which my last chapter closed.   Gustave is removed
to his parents' house; he remains for weeks confined within
doors, or, on sunny days, takes an hour or so in his own
carriage, drawn by the horse bought from Rochebriant, into
by-roads remote from the fashionable world; Isaura visits
his mother, liking, respecting, influenced by her more and

more; in those visits she sits beside the sofa on which
Rameau reclines. Gradually, gently—more and more by
his mother's lips—is impressed on her the belief that it is
in her power to save a human life, and to animate its career towards those goals which are never based wholly upon
earth in the earnest eyes of genius, or perhaps in the yet
more upward vision of pure-souled believing woman.

And Gustave himself, as he passes through the slow
stages of convalescence, seems so gratefully to ascribe to
her every step in his progress—seems so gently softened in
character—seems so refined from the old affectations, so
ennobled above the old cynicism—and, above all, so needing her presence, so sunless without it, that—well, need I
finish the sentence?—the reader will complete what I leave
unsaid.

Enough, that one day Isaura returned home from a visit
at Madame Rameau's with the knowledge that her hand
was pledged—her future life disposed of; and that, escaping from the Venosta, whom she so fondly, and in her hunger for a mother's love, called *Madre*, the girl shut herself
up in her own room with locked doors.

Ah, poor child! ah, sweet-voiced Isaura! whose delicate
image I feel myself too rude and too hard to transfer to
this page in the purity of its outlines, and the blended soft-
nesses of its hues—thou who, when saying things serious
in the words men use, saidst them with a seriousness so
charming, and with looks so feminine—thou, of whom no
man I ever knew was quite worthy—ah, poor, simple, miserable girl, as I see thee now in the solitude of that white-
curtained virginal room; hast thou, then, merged at last
thy peculiar star into the cluster of all these commonplace
girls whose lips have said "Ay," when their hearts said
"No"?—thou, O brilliant Isaura! thou, O motherless
child!

She had sunk into her chair—her own favourite chair,—
the covering of it had been embroidered by Madame de
Grantmesnil, and bestowed on her as a birthday present

II.—5

last year—the year in which she had first learned what it
is to love—the year in which she had first learned what it
is to strive for fame. And somehow uniting, as many young
people do, love and fame in dreams of the future, that
silken seat had been to her as the Tripod of Delphi was to
the Pythian: she had taken to it, as it were intuitively, in
all those hours, whether of joy or sorrow, when youth seeks
to prophesy, and does but dream.

There she sat now, in a sort of stupor—a sort of dreary
bewilderment—the illusion of the Pythian gone—desire of
dream and of prophecy alike extinct—pressing her hands
together, and muttering to herself, "What has happened?
—what have I done?"

Three hours later you would not have recognised the
same face that you see now. For then the bravery, the
honour, the loyalty of the girl's nature had asserted their
command. Her promise had been given to one man—it
could not be recalled. Thought itself of any other man
must be banished. On her hearth lay ashes and tinder—
the last remains of every treasured note from Graham
Vane; of the hoarded newspaper extracts that contained
his name; of the dry treatise he had published, and which
had made the lovely romance-writer first desire "to know
something about politics." Ay, if the treatise had been
upon fox-hunting, she would have desired "to know something about" that! Above all, yet distinguishable from the
rest—as the sparks still upon stem and leaf here and there
faintly glowed and twinkled—the withered flowers which
recorded that happy hour in the arbour, and the walks of
the forsaken garden—the hour in which she had so blissfully pledged herself to renounce that career in art wherein
fame would have been secured, but which would not have
united Fame with Love—in dreams evermore over now.

BOOK X.

CHAPTER I.

GRAHAM VANE had heard nothing for months from M. Renard, when one morning he received the letter I translate:

"MONSIEUR,—I am happy to inform you that I have at last obtained one piece of information which may lead to a more important discovery. When we parted after our fruitless research in Vienna, we had both concurred in the persuasion that, for some reason known only to the two ladies themselves, Madame Marigny and Madame Duval had exchanged names—that it was Madame Marigny who had deceased in the name of Madame Duval, and Madame Duval who had survived in that of Marigny.

"It was clear to me that the *beau Monsieur* who had visited the false Duval must have been cognisant of this exchange of name, and that, if his name and whereabouts could be ascertained, he, in all probability, would know what had become of the lady who is the object of our research; and after the lapse of so many years he would probably have very slight motive to preserve the concealment of facts which might, no doubt, have been convenient at the time. The lover of the *soi-disant* Mademoiselle Duval was by such accounts as we could gain a man of some rank—very possibly a married man; and the *liaison*, in short, was one of those which, while they last, necessitate precautions and secrecy.

"Therefore, dismissing all attempts at further trace of

the missing lady, I resolved to return to Vienna as soon as the business that recalled me to Paris was concluded, and devote myself exclusively to the search after the amorous and mysterious Monsieur.

"I did not state this determination to you, because, possibly, I might be in error—or, if not in error, at least too sanguine in my expectations—and it is best to avoid disappointing an honourable client.

"One thing was clear, that, at the time of the *soi-disant* Duval's decease, the *beau Monsieur* was at Vienna.

"It appeared also tolerably clear that when the lady friend of the deceased quitted Munich so privately, it was to Vienna she repaired, and from Vienna comes the letter demanding the certificates of Madame Duval's death. Pardon me, if I remind you of all these circumstances no doubt fresh in your recollection. I repeat them in order to justify the conclusions to which they led me.

"I could not, however, get permission to absent myself from Paris for the time I might require till the end of last April. I had meanwhile sought all private means of ascertaining what Frenchmen of rank and station were in that capital in the autumn of 1849. Among the list of the very few such Messieurs I fixed upon one as the most likely to be the mysterious Achille—Achille was, indeed, his *nom de baptême.*

"A man of intrigue—*à bonnes fortunes*—of lavish expenditure withal; very tenacious of his dignity, and avoiding any petty scandals by which it might be lowered; just the man who, in some passing affair of gallantry with a lady of doubtful repute, would never have signed his titular designation to a letter, and would have kept himself as much incognito as he could. But this man was dead—had been dead some years. He had not died at Vienna—never visited that capital for some years before his death. He was then, and had long been, the *ami de la maison* of one of those *grandes dames* of whose intimacy *grands seigneurs* are not ashamed. They parade there the *bonnes fortunes*

they conceal elsewhere. Monsieur and the *grande dame*
were at Baden when the former died. Now, Monsieur, a
Don Juan of that stamp is pretty sure always to have a
confidential Leporello. If I could find Leporello alive I
might learn the secrets not to be extracted from a Don
Juan defunct. I ascertained, in truth, both at Vienna, to
which I first repaired in order to verify the *renseignements*
I had obtained at Paris, and at Baden, to which I then
bent my way, that this brilliant noble had a favourite valet
who had lived with him from his youth—an Italian, who had
contrived in the course of his service to lay by savings
enough to set up a hotel somewhere in Italy, supposed to
be Pisa. To Pisa I repaired, but the man had left some
years; his hotel had not prospered—he had left in debt.
No one could say what had become of him. At last, after
a long and tedious research, I found him installed as man-
ager of a small hotel at Genoa—a pleasant fellow enough;
and after friendly intercourse with him (of course I lodged
at his hotel), I easily led him to talk of his earlier life and
adventures, and especially of his former master, of whose
splendid career in the army of '*La Belle Déese*' he was not
a little proud. It was not very easy to get him to the particular subject in question. In fact, the affair with the
poor false Duval had been so brief and undistinguished an
episode in his master's life, that it was not without a
strain of memory that he reached it.

"By little and little, however, in the course of two or
three evenings, and by the aid of many flasks of Orviette
or bottles of Lacrima (wines, Monsieur, that I do not commend to any one who desires to keep his stomach sound
and his secrets safe), I gathered these particulars.

"Our Don Juan, since the loss of a wife in the first year
of marriage, had rarely visited Paris where he had a domi-
cile—his ancestral hotel there he had sold.

"But happening to visit that capital of Europe a few
months before we come to our dates at Aix-la-Chapelle, he
made acquaintance with Madame Marigny, a natural daugh-

ter of high-placed parents, by whom, of course, she had
never been acknowledged, but who had contrived that she
should receive a good education at a convent; and on leaving it also contrived that an old soldier of fortune—which
means an officer without fortune—who had served in Al-
giers with some distinction, should offer her his hand, and
add the modest *dot* they assigned her to his yet more modest income. They contrived also that she should understand the offer must be accepted. Thus Mademoiselle
'*Quelque Chose*' became Madame Marigny, and she, on her
part, contrived that a year or so later she should be left a
widow. After a marriage, of course the parents washed
their hands of her—they had done their duty. At the
time Don Juan made this lady's acquaintance nothing
could be said against her character; but the milliners and
butchers had begun to imply that they would rather have
her money than trust to her character. Don Juan fell in
love with her, satisfied the immediate claims of milliner
and butcher, and when they quitted Paris it was agreed
that they should meet later at Aix-la-Chapelle. But when
he resorted to that sultry and, to my mind, unalluring
spa, he was surprised by a line from her saying that she
had changed her name of Marigny for that of Duval.

" 'I recollect,' said Leporello, 'that two days afterwards
my master said to me, "Caution and secrecy. Don't mention my name at the house to which I may send you with
any note for Madame Duval. I don't announce my name
when I call. *La petite* Marigny has exchanged her name
for that of Louise Duval; and I find that there is a Louise
Duval here, her friend, who is niece to a relation of my
own, and a terrible relation to quarrel with—a dead shot
and unrivalled swordsman — Victor de Mauléon." My
master was brave enough, but he enjoyed life, and he did
not think *la petite* Marigny worth being killed for.'

"Leporello remembered very little of what followed.
All he did remember is that Don Juan, when at Vienna,
said to him one morning, looking less gay than usual, 'It

is finished with *la petite* Marigny—she is no more.' Then
he ordered his bath, wrote a note, and said with tears in
his eyes, 'Take this to Mademoiselle Celeste; not to be
compared to *la petite* Marigny; but *la petite* Celeste is
still alive.' Ah, Monsieur! if only any man in France
could be as proud of his ruler as that Italian was of
my countrymen! Alas! we Frenchmen are all made to
command—or at least we think ourselves so—and we
are insulted by one who says to us, 'Serve and obey.'
Nowadays, in France, we find all Don Juans and no
Leporellos.

"After strenuous exertions upon my part to recall to Leporello's mind the important question whether he had ever
seen the true Duval, passing under the name of Marigny—
whether she had not presented herself to his master at Vienna or elsewhere—he rubbed his forehead, and drew from
it these reminiscences.

"'On the day that his Excellency,'—Leporello generally
so styled his master—'Excellency,' as you are aware, is the
title an Italian would give to Satan if taking his wages,—
'told me that *la petite* Marigny was no more, he had received previously a lady veiled and mantled, whom I did
not recognise as any one I had seen before, but I noticed
her way of carrying herself—haughtily—her head thrown
back; and I thought to myself, that lady is one of his
grandes dames. She did call again two or three times,
never announcing her name; then she did not reappear.
She might be Madame Duval—I can't say.'

"'But did you never hear his Excellency speak of the
real Duval after that time?'

"'No—*non mi ricordo*—I don't remember.'

"'Nor of some living Madame Marigny, though the real
one was dead?'

"'Stop, I do recollect; not that he ever named such a
person to me, but that I have posted letters for him to a
Madame Marigny—oh, yes! even years after the said *petite*
Marigny was dead; and once I did venture to say, "Pardon

me, Eccellenza, but may I ask if that poor lady is really
dead, since I have to prepay this letter to her?"

" '"Oh," said he, "Madame Marigny! Of course the one
you know is dead, but there are others of the same name;
this lady is of my family. Indeed, her house, though noble
in itself, recognises the representative of mine as its head,
and I am too *bon prince* not to acknowledge and serve any
one who branches out of my own tree.' "

" A day after this last conversation on the subject, Leporello said to me: 'My friend, you certainly have some interest in ascertaining what became of the lady who took
the name of Marigny (I state this frankly, Monsieur, to
show how difficult even for one so prudent as I am to beat
about a bush long but what you let people know the sort of
bird you are in search of).

" 'Well,' said I, 'she does interest me. I knew something of that Victor de Mauléon, whom his Excellency did
not wish to quarrel with; and it would be a kindly act to
her relation if one could learn what became of Louise
Duval.'

" 'I can put you on the way of learning all that his Excellency was likely to have known of her through correspondence. I have often heard him quote, with praise, a
saying so clever that it might have been Italian, "Never
write, never burn;" that is, never commit yourself by a
letter—keep all letters that could put others in your power.
All the letters he received were carefully kept and labelled.
I sent them to his son in four large trunks. His son, no
doubt, has them still.'

" Now, however, I have exhausted my budget. I arrived at Paris last night. I strongly advise you to come
hither at once, if you sitll desire to prosecute your search.

" You, Monsieur, can do what I could not venture to do;
you can ask the son of Don Juan if, amid the correspondence of his father, which he may have preserved, there be
any signed Marigny or Duval—any, in short, which can
throw light on this very obscure complication of circum-

stances. A *grand seigneur* would naturally be more complaisant to a man of your station than he would be to an agent of police. Don Juan's son, inheriting his father's title, is Monsieur le Marquis de Rochebriant; and permit me to add, that at this moment, as the journals doubtless inform you, all Paris resounds with the rumour of the coming war; and Monsieur de Rochebriant—who is, as I have ascertained, now in Paris—it may be difficult to find anywhere on earth a month or two hence.—I have the honour, with profound consideration, &c., &c.,   I. RENARD."

The day after the receipt of this letter Graham Vane was in Paris.

CHAPTER II.

AMONG things indescribable is that which is called "Agitation" in Paris—"Agitation without riot or violence—showing itself by no disorderly act, no turbulent outburst. Perhaps the *cafés* are more crowded; passengers in the streets stop each other more often, and converse in small knots and groups; yet, on the whole, there is little externally to show how loudly the heart of Paris is beating. A traveller may be passing through quiet landscapes, unconscious that a great battle is going on some miles off, but if he will stop and put his ear to the ground he will recognise, by a certain indescribable vibration, the voice of the cannon.

But at Paris an acute observer need not stop and put his ear to the ground; he feels within himself a vibration—a mysterious inward sympathy which communicates to the individual a conscious thrill—when the passions of the multitude are stirred, no matter how silently.

Tortoni's *café* was thronged when Duplessis and Frederic Lemercier entered it: it was in vain to order breakfast; no table was vacant either within the rooms or under the awnings without.

But they could not retreat so quickly as they had entered. On catching sight of the financier several men rose and gathered round him, eagerly questioning:

"What do you think, Duplessis? Will any insult to France put a drop of warm blood into the frigid veins of that miserable Ollivier?"

"It is not yet clear that France has been insulted, Messieurs," replied Duplessis, phlegmatically.

"Bah! Not insulted! The very nomination of a Hohenzollern to the crown of Spain was an insult —what would you have more?"

"I tell you what it is, Duplessis," said the Vicomte de Brézé, whose habitual light good temper seemed exchanged for insolent swagger—"I tell you what it is, your friend the Emperor has no more courage than a chicken. He is grown old, and infirm, and lazy; he knows that he can't even mount on horseback. But if, before this day week, he has not declared war on the Prussians, he will be lucky if he can get off as quietly as poor Louis Philippe did under shelter of his umbrella, and ticketed 'Schmidt.' Or could you not, M. Duplessis, send him back to London in a bill of exchange?"

"For a man of your literary repute, M. le Vicomte," said Duplessis, "you indulge in a strange confusion of metaphors. But, pardon me, I came here to breakfast, and I cannot remain to quarrel. Come, Lemercier, let us take our chance of a cutlet at the *Trois Frères.*"

"Fox, Fox," cried Lemercier, whistling to a poodle that had followed him into the *café,* and, frightened by the sudden movement and loud voices of the *habitués,* had taken refuge under the table.

"Your dog is *poltron,*" said De Brézé; "call him Nap."

At this stroke of humour there was a general laugh, in the midst of which Duplessis escaped, and Frederic, having discovered and caught his dog, followed with that animal tenderly clasped in his arms. "I would not lose Fox for a great deal," said Lemercier with *effusion;* "a pledge

of love and fidelity from an English lady the most distinguished: the lady left me—the dog remains."

Duplessis smiled grimly: "What a thoroughbred Parisian you are, my dear Frederic! I believe if the tramp of
the last angel were sounding, the Parisians would be divided into two sets: one would be singing the Marseillaise,
and parading the red flag; the other would be shrugging
their shoulders and saying, 'Bah! as if *le Bon Dieu* would
have the bad taste to injure Paris—the Seat of the
Graces, the School of the Arts, the Fountain of Reason,
the Eye of the World;' and so be found by the destroying
angel caressing poodles and making *bons mots* about *les
femmes.*"

"And quite right, too," said Lemercier, complacently;
"what other people in the world could retain lightness of
heart under circumstances so unpleasant? But why do you
take things so solemnly? Of course there will be war—
idle now to talk of explanations and excuses. When a
Frenchman says, 'I am insulted,' he is not going to be told
that he is not insulted. He means fighting, and not apologising. But what if there be war? Our brave soldiers
beat the Prussians—take the Rhine—return to Paris covered with laurels; a new *Boulevard de Berlin* eclipses the
Boulevard Sebastopol. By the way, Duplessis, a Boulevard de Berlin will be a good speculation—better than the
Rue de Louvier. Ah! is not that my English friend, Grarm
Varn?" here, quitting the arm of Duplessis, Lemercier
stopped a gentleman who was about to pass him unnotic-
ing. "*Bon jour, mon ami!* how long have you been at
Paris?"

"I only arrived last evening," answered Graham, "and
my stay will be so short that it is a piece of good luck, my
dear Lemercier, to meet with you, and exchange a cordial
shake of the hand."

"We are just going to breakfast at the *Trois Frères*—
Duplessis and I—pray join us."

"With great pleasure—ah, M. Duplessis, I shall be glad

to hear from you that the Emperor will be firm enough to
check the advances of that martial fever which, to judge
by the persons I meet, seems to threaten delirium."

Duplessis looked very keenly at Graham's face, as he
replied slowly: "The English, at least, ought to know
that when the Emperor by his last reforms resigned his
personal authority for constitutional monarchy, it ceased
to be a question whether he could or could not be firm in
matters that belonged to the Cabinet and the Chambers. I
presume that if Monsieur Gladstone advised Queen Victoria
to declare war upon the Emperor of Russia, backed by a
vast majority in Parliament, you would think me very ignorant of constitutional monarchy and Parliamentary government if I said, "I hope Queen Victoria will resist that
martial fever.'"

"You rebuke me very fairly, M. Duplessis, if you can
show me that the two cases are analogous; but we do not
understand in England that, despite his last reforms, the
Emperor has so abnegated his individual ascendency, that
his will, clearly and resolutely expressed, would not pre-
vail in his Council and silence opposition in the Chambers.
Is it so? I ask for information."

The three men were walking on towards the Palais Royal
side by side while this conversation proceeded.

"That all depends," replied Duplessis, "upon what may
be the increase of popular excitement at Paris. If it slack-
ens, the Emperor, no doubt, could turn to wise account that
favourable pause in the fever. But if it continues to swell,
and Paris cries, 'War,' in a voice as loud as it cried to
Louis Philippe 'Revolution,' do you think that the Emperor could impose on his ministers the wisdom of peace?
His ministers would be too terrified by the clamour to
undertake the responsibility of opposing it—they would
resign. Where is the Emperor to find another Cabinet?
a peace Cabinet? What and who are the orators for peace?
—what a handful!—who? Gambetta, Jules Favre, avowed
Republicans,—would they even accept the post of ministers

to Louis Napoléon? If they did, would not their first step
be the abolition of the Empire? Napoléon is therefore so
far a constitutional monarch in the same sense as Queen
Victoria, that the popular will in the country (and in
France in such matters Paris is the country) controls the
Chambers, controls the Cabinet; and against the Cabinet
the Emperor could not contend. I say nothing of the army
—a power in France unknown to you in England, which
would certainly fraternise with no peace party. If war is
proclaimed,—let England blame it if she will—she can't
lament it more than I should: but let England blame the
nation; let her blame, if she please, the form of the government, which rests upon popular suffrage; but do not let
her blame our sovereign more than the French would blame
her own, if compelled by the conditions on which she holds
her crown to sign a declaration of war, which vast majorities in a Parliament just elected, and a Council of Ministers
whom she could not practically replace, enforced upon her
will."

"Your observations, M. Duplessis, impress me strongly,
and add to the deep anxieties with which, in common with
all my countrymen, I regard the menacing aspect of the
present hour. Let us hope the best. Our Government, I
know, is exerting itself to the utmost verge of its power,
to remove every just ground of offence that the unfortunate nomination of a German Prince to the Spanish throne
could not fail to have given to French statesmen."

"I am glad you concede that such a nomination was a
just ground of offence," said Lemercier, rather bitterly;
"for I have met Englishmen who asserted that France had
no right to resent any choice of a sovereign that Spain
might make."

"Englishmen in general are not very reflective politicians
in foreign affairs," said Graham; "but those who are must
see that France could not, without alarm the most justifi-
able, contemplate a cordon of hostile states being drawn
around her on all sides,—Germany, in itself so formidable

since the field of Sadowa, on the east; a German prince in
the southwest; the not improbable alliance between Prussia and the Italian kingdom, already so alienated from the
France to which it owed so much. If England would be
uneasy were a great maritime power possessed of Antwerp,
how much more uneasy might France justly be if Prussia
could add the armies of Spain to those of Germany, and
launch them both upon France. But that cause of alarm
is over—the Hohenzollern is withdrawn. Let us hope for
the best."

The three men had now seated themselves at a table in
the *Trois Frères*, and Lemercier volunteered the task of
inspecting the *menu* and ordering the repast, still keeping
guard on Fox.

"Observe that man," said Duplessis, pointing towards a
gentleman who had just entered; "the other day he was
the popular hero—now, in the excitement of threatened
war, he is permitted to order his *bifteck* uncongratulated,
uncaressed; such is fame at Paris! here to-day and gone
to-morrow."

"How did the man become famous?"

"He is a painter, and refused a decoration—the only
French painter who ever did."

"And why refuse?"

"Because he is more stared at as the man who refused
than he would have been as the man who accepted. If
ever the Red Republicans have their day, those among
them most certain of human condemnation will be the
coxcombs who have gone mad for the desire of human
applause."

"You are a profound philosopher, M. Duplessis."

"I hope not—I have an especial contempt for philosophers. Pardon me a moment—I see a man to whom I
would say a word or two."

Duplessis crossed over to another table to speak to a
middle-aged man of somewhat remarkable countenance,
with the red ribbon in his buttonhole, in whom Graham

recognised an ex-minister of the Emperor, differing from most of those at that day in his Cabinet, in the reputation of being loyal to his master and courageous against a mob.

Left thus alone with Lemercier, Graham said:

"Pray tell me where I can find your friend the Marquis de Rochebriant. I called at his apartment this morning, and I was told that he had gone on some visit into the country, taking his valet, and the *concierge* could not give me his address. I thought myself so lucky on meeting with you, who are sure to know."

"No, I do not; it is some days since I saw Alain. But Duplessis will be sure to know." Here the financier rejoined them.

"*Mon cher*, Grarm Varn wants to know for what Sabine shades Rochebriant has deserted the '*fumum opes strepitumque*' of the capital."

"Ah! the Marquis is a friend of yours, Monsieur?"

"I can scarcely boast that honour, but he is an acquaintance whom I should be very glad to see again."

"At this moment he is at the Duchesse de Tarascon's country-house near Fontainebleau; I had a hurried line from him two days ago stating that he was going there on her urgent invitation. But he may return to-morrow; at all events he dines with me on the 8th, and I shall be charmed if you will do me the honour to meet him at my house."

"It is an invitation too agreeable to refuse, and I thank you very much for it."

Nothing worth recording passed further in conversation between Graham and the two Frenchmen. He left them smoking their cigars in the garden, and walked homeward by the Rue de Rivoli. As he was passing beside the Magasin du Louvre he stopped, and made way for a lady crossing quickly out of the shop towards her carriage at the door. Glancing at him with a slight inclination of her head in acknowledgment of his courtesy, the lady recognised his features,—

"Ah, Mr. Vane!" she cried, almost joyfully—"you are then at Paris, though you have not come to see me."

"I only arrived last night, dear Mrs. Morley," said Graham, rather embarrassed, "and only on some matters of business which unexpectedly summoned me. My stay will probably be very short."

"In that case let me rob you of a few minutes—no, not rob you even of them; I can take you wherever you want to go, and as my carriage moves more quickly than you do on foot, I shall save you the minutes instead of robbing you of them."

"You are most kind, but I was only going to my hotel, which is close by."

"Then you have no excuse for not taking a short drive with me in the Champs Elysées—come."

Thus bidden, Graham could not civilly disobey. He handed the fair American into her carriage, and seated himself by her side.

----------◆----------

CHAPTER III.

"MR. VANE, I feel as if I had many apologies to make for the interest in your life which my letter to you so indiscreetly betrayed."

"Oh, Mrs. Morley! you cannot guess how deeply that interest touched me."

"I should not have presumed so far," continued Mrs. Morley, unheeding the interruption, "if I had not been altogether in error as to the nature of your sentiments in a certain quarter. In this you must blame my American rearing. With us there are many flirtations between boys and girls which come to nothing; but when in my country a man like you meets with a woman like Mademoiselle Cicogna, there cannot be flirtation. His attentions, his looks, his manner, reveal to the eyes of those who care enough for him to watch, one of two things—either he coldly admires and esteems, or he loves with his whole heart and soul a woman worthy to inspire such a love. Well, I did watch, and I was absurdly mistaken. I imagined that I saw love, and rejoiced for the sake of both of you to think so. I know that in all countries, our own as well as yours, love is so morbidly sensitive and jealous that it is always apt to invent imaginary foes to itself. Esteem and admiration never do that. I thought that some misunderstanding, easily removed by the intervention of a third person, mght have impeded the impulse of two hearts towards each other—and so I wrote. I had assumed that you loved—I am humbled to the last degree—you only admired and esteemed."

"Your irony is very keen, Mrs. Morley, and to you it may seem very just."

"Don't call me Mrs. Morley in that haughty tone of voice,—can't you talk to me as you would talk to a friend? You only esteemed and admired—there is an end of it."

"No, there is not an end of it," cried Graham, giving way to an impetuosity of passion, which rarely, indeed, before another, escaped his self-control; "the end of it to me is a life out of which is ever stricken such love as I could feel for woman. To me true love can only come once. It came with my first look on that fatal face—it has never left me in thought by day, in dreams by night. The end of it to me is farewell to all such happiness as the one love of a life can promise—but——"

"But what?" asked Mrs. Morley, softly, and very much moved by the passionate earnestness of Graham's voice and words.

"But," he continued with a forced smile, "we Englishmen are trained to the resistance of absolute authority; we cannot submit all the elements that make up our being to the sway of a single despot. Love is the painter of existence, it should not be its sculptor."

"I do not understand the metaphor."

"Love colours our life, it should not chisel its form."

ii.—6

"My dear Mr. Vane, that is very cleverly said, but the human heart is too large and too restless to be quietly packed up in an aphorism. Do you mean to tell me that if you found you had destroyed Isaura Cicogna's happiness as well as resigned your own, that thought would not somewhat deform the very shape you would give to your life? Is it colour alone that your life would lose?"

"Ah, Mrs. Morley, do not lower your friend into an ordinary girl in whom idleness exaggerates the strength of any fancy over which it dreamily broods. Isaura Cicogna has her occupations—her genius—her fame—her career. Honestly speaking, I think that in these she will find a happiness that no quiet hearth could bestow. I will say no more. I feel persuaded that were we two united I could not make her happy. With the irresistible impulse that urges the genius of the writer towards its vent in public sympathy and applause, she would chafe if I said, 'Be contented to be wholly mine.' And if I said it not, and felt I had no right to say it, and allowed the full scope to her natural ambition, what then? She would chafe yet more to find that I had no fellowship in her aims and ends—that where I should feel pride, I felt humiliation. It would be so; I cannot help it, 'tis my nature."

"So be it then. When, next year perhaps, you visit Paris, you will be safe from my officious interference— Isaura will be the wife of another."

Graham pressed his hand to his heart with the sudden movement of one who feels there an agonising spasm—his cheek, his very lips were bloodless.

"I told you," he said bitterly, "that your fears of my influence over the happiness of one so gifted, and so strong in such gifts, were groundless; you allow that I should be very soon forgotten?"

"I allow no such thing—I wish I could. But do you know so little of a woman's heart (and in matters of heart, I never yet heard that genius had a talisman against emotion),—do you know so little of a woman's heart as not to know that the very moment in which she may accept a marriage the least fitted to render her happy, is that in which she has lost all hope of happiness in another?"

"Is it indeed so?" murmured Graham—"ay, I can conceive it."

"And have you so little comprehension of the necessities which that fame, that career to which you allow she is impelled by the instincts of genius, impose on this girl, young, beautiful, fatherless, motherless? No matter how pure her life, can she guard it from the slander of envious tongues? Will not all her truest friends—would not you, if you were her brother—press upon her by all the arguments that have most weight with the woman who asserts independence in her modes of life, and yet is wise enough to know that the world can only judge of virtue by its shadow—reputation, not to dispense with the protection which a husband can alone secure? And that is why I warn you, if it be yet time, that in resigning your own happiness you may destroy Isaura's. She will wed another, but she will not be happy. What a chimera or dread your egotism as man conjures up! Oh! forsooth, the qualities that charm and delight a world are to unfit a woman to be helpmate to a man. Fie on you!—fie!"

Whatever answer Graham might have made to these impassioned reproaches was here checked.

Two men on horseback stopped the carriage. One was Enguerrand de Vandemar, the other was the Algerine Colonel whom we met at the supper given at the *Maison Dorée* by Frederic Lemercier.

"*Pardon*, Madame Morley," said Enguerrand; "but there are symptoms of a mob-epidemic a little further up: the fever began at Belleville, and is threatening the health of the Champs Elysées. Don't be alarmed—it may be nothing, though it may be much. In Paris, one can never calculate an hour beforehand the exact progress of a politico-epidemic fever. At present I say, 'Bah! a pack of ragged boys, *gamins de Paris;*' but my friend the Colonel,

twisting his *moustache en souriant amèrèment*, says, 'It is
the indignation of Paris at the apathy of the Government
under insult to the honour of, France;' and Heaven only
knows how rapidly French *gamins* grow into giants when
Colonels talk about the indignation of Paris and the honour
of France!"

"But what has happened?" asked Mrs. Morley, turning
to the Colonel.

"Madame," replied the warrior, "it is rumoured that the
King of Prussia has turned his back upon the ambassador
of France; and that the *pékin* who is for peace at any price
—M. Ollivier—will say to-morrow in the Chamber, that
France submits to a slap in the face."

"Please, Monsieur de Vandemar, to tell my coachman
to drive home," said Mrs. Morley.

The carriage turned and went homeward. The Colonel
lifted his hat, and rode back to see what the *gamins* were
about. Enguerrand, who had no interest in the *gamins*,
and who looked on the Colonel as a bore, rode by the side
of the carriage.

"Is there anything serious in this?" asked Mrs.
Morley.

"At this moment, nothing. What it may be this hour
to-morrow I cannot say. Ah! Monsieur Vane, *bon jour*—I
did not recognise you at first. Once, in a visit at the
château of one of your distinguished countrymen, I saw
two game-cocks turned out facing each other: they needed
no pretext for quarrelling—neither do France and Prussia—
no matter which game-cock gave the first offence, the
two game-cocks must have it out. All that Ollivier can do,
if he be wise, is to see that the French cock has his steel
spurs as long as the Prussians. But this I do say, that if
Ollivier attempts to put the French cock back into its bag,
the Empire is gone in forty-eight hours. That to me is a
trifle—I care nothing for the Empire; but that which is
not a trifle is anarchy and chaos. Better war and the Empire than peace and Jules Favre. But let us seize the pres-

ent hour, Mr. Vane; whatever happens to-morrow, shall we
dine together to-day? Name your *restaurant*."

"I am so grieved," answered Graham, rousing himself—
"I am here only on business, and engaged all the evening."

"What a wonderful thing is this life of ours!" said Enguerrand. "The destiny of France at this moment hangs
on a thread—I, a Frenchman, say to an English friend,
'Let us dine—a cutlet to-day and a fig for to-morrow;' and
my English friend, distinguished native of a country with
which we have the closest alliance, tells me that in this
crisis of France he has business to attend to! My father is
quite right; he accepts the Voltairean philosophy, and
cries, *Vivent les indifférents!*"

"My dear M. de Vandemar," said Graham, "in every
country you will find the same thing. All individuals
massed together constitute public life. Each individual has
a life of his own, the claims and the habits and the needs
of which do not suppress his sympathies with public life,
but imperiously overrule them. Mrs. Morley, permit me
to pull the check-string—I get out here."

"I like that man," said Enguerrand, as he continued to
ride by the fair American, "in language and *esprit* he is so
French."

"I use to like him better than you can," answered Mrs.
Morley, "but in prejudice and stupidity he is so English.
As it seems you are disengaged, come and partake, *pot au
feu,* with Frank and me."

"Charmed to do so," answered the cleverest and best bred
of all Parisian *beaux garçons*, "but forgive me if I quit you
soon. This poor France! *Entre nous,* I am very uneasy
about the Parisian fever. I must run away after dinner to
clubs and *cafés* to learn the last bulletins."

"We have nothing like that French Legitimist in the
States," said the fair American to herself, "unless we
should ever be so silly as to make Legitimists of the ruined
gentlemen of the South."

Meanwhile Graham Vane went slowly back to his apartment. No false excuse had he made to Enguerrand; this evening was devoted to M. Renard, who told him little he had not known before; but his private life overruled his public, and all that night he, professed politician, thought sleeplessly, not over the crisis to France, which might alter the conditions of Europe, but the talk on his private life of that intermeddling American woman.

CHAPTER IV.

THE next day, Wednesday, July 6th, commenced one of those eras in the world's history in which private life would vainly boast that it overrules Life Public. How many private lives does such a terrible time influence, absorb, darken with sorrow, crush into graves?

It was the day when the Duc de Gramont uttered the fatal speech which determined the die between peace and war. No one not at Paris on that day can conceive the popular enthusiasm with which that speech was hailed—the greater because the warlike tone of it was not anticipated; because there had been a rumour amidst circles the best informed that a speech of pacific moderation was to be the result of the Imperial Council. Rapturous indeed were the applauses with which the sentences that breathed haughty defiance were hailed by the Assembly. The ladies in the tribune rose with one accord, waving their handkerchiefs. Tall, stalwart, dark, with Roman features and lofty presence, the Minister of France seemed to say with Catiline in the fine tragedy: "Lo! where I stand, I am war!"

Paris had been hungering for some hero of the hour—the Duc de Gramont became at once raised to that eminence.

All the journals, save the very few which were friendly to peace, because hostile to the Emperor, resounded with praise, not only of the speech, but of the speaker. It is with a melancholy sense of amusement that one recalls now

to mind those organs of public opinion—with what romantic
fondness they dwelt on the personal graces of the man who
had at last given voice to the chivalry of France: "The
charming gravity of his countenance—the mysterious expression of his eye!"

As the crowd poured from the Chambers, Victor de Mauléon and Savarin, who had been among the listeners, encountered.

"No chance for my friends the Orleanists now," said
Savarin. "You who mock at all parties are, I suppose,
at heart for the Republican—small chance, too, for that."

"I do not agree with you. Violent impulses have quick
reactions."

"But what reaction could shake the Emperor after he
returns a conqueror, bringing in his pocket the left bank of
the Rhine?"

"None—when he does that. Will he do it? Does he
himself think he will do it? I doubt——"

"Doubt the French army against the Prussian?"

"Against the German people united—yes, very much."

"But war will disunite the German people. Bavaria
will surely assist us—Hanover will rise against the spoli-
ator—Austria at our first successes must shake off her present enforced neutrality?"

"You have not been in Germany, and I have. What
yesterday was a Prussian army, to-morrow will be a German population; far exceeding our own in numbers, in
hardihood of body, in cultivated intellect, in military discipline. But talk of something else. How is my ex-edi-
tor—poor Gustave Rameau?"

"Still very weak, but on the mend. You may have him
back in his office soon."

"Impossible! even in his sick-bed his vanity was more
vigorous than ever. He issued a war-song, which has
gone the round of the war journals signed by his own name.
He must have known very well that the name of such a
Tyrtæus cannot reappear as the editor of *Les Sens Com-*

mun; that in launching his little firebrand he burned all vessels that could waft him back to the port he had quitted. But I dare say he has done well for his own interests; I doubt if *Les Sens Commun* can much longer hold its ground in the midst of the prevalent lunacy."

"What! it has lost subscribers?—gone off in sale already, since it declared for peace?"

"Of course it has; and after the article which, if I live over to-night, will appear to-morrow, I should wonder if it sell enough to cover the cost of the print and paper."

"Martyr to principle! I revere, but I do not envy thee."

"Martyrdom is not my ambition. If Louis Napoléon be defeated, what then? Perhaps *he* may be the martyr; and the Favres and Gambettas may roast their own eggs on the gridiron they heat for his majesty."

Here an English gentleman, who was the very able correspondent to a very eminent journal, and in that capacity had made acquaintance with De Mauléon, joined the two Frenchmen; Savarin, however, after an exchange of salutations, went his way.

"May I ask a frank answer to a somewhat rude question, M. le Vicomte?" said the Englishman. "Suppose that the Imperial Government had to-day given in their adhesion to the peace party, how long would it have been before their orators in the Chamber and their organs in the press would have said that France was governed by *poltrons?*"

"Probably for most of the twenty-four hours. But there are a few who are honest in their convictions; of that few I am one."

"And would have supported the Emperor and his Government?"

"No, Monsieur—I do not say that."

"Then the Emperor would have turned many friends into enemies, and no enemies into friends."

"Monsieur—you in England know that a party in opposition is not propitiated when the party in power steals its measures. Ha!—pardon me, who is that gentleman, evidently your countryman, whom I see yonder talking to the Secretary of your Embassy?"

"He.—Mr. Vane—Graham Vane. Do you not know him? He has been much in Paris, attached to our Embassy formerly; a clever man—much is expected from him."

"Ah! I think I have seen him before, but am not quite sure. Did you say Vane? I once knew a Monsieur Vane, a distinguished parliamentary orator."

"That gentleman is his son—would you like to be introduced to him?"

"Not to-day—I am in some hurry." Here Victor lifted his hat in parting salutation, and as he walked away cast at Graham another glance keen and scrutinising. "I have seen that man before," he muttered, "where?—when?—can it be only a family likeness to the father? No, the features are different; the profile is—ha!—Mr. Lamb, Mr. Lamb— but why call himself by that name?—why disguised?—what can he have to do with poor Louise? Bah—these are not questions I can think of now. This war—this war—can it yet be prevented? How it will prostrate all the plans my ambition so carefully schemed! Oh!—at least if I were but in the *Chambre.* Perhaps I yet may be before the war is ended—the Clavignys have great interest in their department."

CHAPTER V.

GRAHAM had left a note with Rochebriant's *concierge* requesting an interview on the Marquis's return to Paris, and on the evening after the day just commemorated he received a line, saying that Alain had come back, and would be at home at nine o'clock. Graham found himself in the Breton's apartment punctually at the hour indicated.

Alain was in high spirits: he burst at once into enthusiastic exclamations on the virtual announcement of war.

"Congratulate me, *mon cher !"* he cried—"the news was

a joyous surprise to me. Only so recently as yesterday morning I was under the gloomy apprehension that the Imperial Cabinet would continue to back Ollivier's craven declaration 'that France had not been affronted!' The Duchesse de Tarascon, at whose *campagne* I was a guest, is (as you doubtless know) very much in the confidence of the Tuileries. On the first signs of war, I wrote to her, saying that whatever the objections of my pride to enter the army as a private in time of peace, such objections ceased on the moment when all distinctions of France must vanish in the eyes of sons eager to defend her banners. The Duchesse in reply begged me to come to her *campagne* and talk over the matter. I went; she then said that if war should break out it was the intention to organise the *Mobiles* and officer them with men of birth and education, irrespective of previous military service, and in that case I might count on my epaulets. But only two nights ago she received a letter—I know not of course from whom—evidently from some high authority—that induced her to think the moderation of the Council would avert the war, and leave the swords of the *Mobiles* in their sheaths. I suspect the decision of yesterday must have been a very sudden one. *Ce cher Gramont!* See what it is to have a well-born man in a sovereign's councils."

"If war must come, I at least wish all renown to yourself. But——"

"Oh! spare me your '*buts*'; the English are always too full of them where her own interests do not appeal to her. She had no 'buts' for war in India or a march into Abyssinia."

Alain spoke petulantly; at that moment the French were very much irritated by the monitory tone of the English journals. Graham prudently avoided the chance of rousing the wrath of a young hero yearning for his epaulets.

"I am English enough," said he, with good-humoured courtesy, "to care for English interests; and England has no interest abroad dearer to her than the welfare and dignity of France. And now let me tell you why I presumed on an acquaintance less intimate than I could desire, to solicit this interview on a matter which concerns myself, and in which you could perhaps render me a considerable service."

"If I can, count it rendered; move to this sofa—join me in a cigar, and let us talk at ease *comme de vieux amis,* whose fathers or brothers might have fought side by side in the Crimea." Graham removed to the sofa beside Rochebriant, and after one or two whiffs laid aside the cigar and began:

"Among the correspondence which Monsieur your father has left, are there any letters of no distant date signed Marigny—Madame Marigny? Pardon me, I should state my motive in putting this question. I am intrusted with a charge, the fulfilment of which may prove to the benefit of this lady or her child; such fulfilment is a task imposed upon my honour. But all the researches to discover this lady which I have instituted stop at a certain date, with this information,—viz., that she corresponded occasionally with the late Marquis de Rochebriant; that he habitually preserved the letters of his correspondents; and that these letters were severally transmitted to you at his decease."

Alain's face had taken a very grave expression while Graham spoke, and he now replied with a mixture of haughtiness and embarrassment:

"The boxes containing the letters my father received and preserved were sent to me as you say—the larger portion of them were from ladies—sorted and labelled, so that in glancing at any letter in each packet I could judge of the general tenor of these in the same packet without the necessity of reading them. All packets of that kind, Monsieur Vane, I burned. I do not remember any letters signed 'Marigny.'"

"I perfectly understand, my dear Marquis, that you would destroy all letters which your father himself would have destroyed if his last illness had been sufficiently prolonged. But I do not think the letters I mean would have come under that classification; probably they were short, and on matters of business relating to some third person— some person, for instance, of the name of Louise, or of Duval!"

"Stop! let me think. I have a vague remembrance of one or two letters which rather perplexed me, they were labelled, 'Louise D——. Mem.: to make further inquiries as to the fate of her uncle.' "

"Marquis, these are the letters I seek. Thank heaven, you have not destroyed them?"

"No; there was no reason why I should destroy, though I really cannot state precisely any reason why I kept them. I have a very vague recollection of their existence."

"I entreat you to allow me at least a glance at the hand-writing, and compare it with that of a letter I have about me; and if the several handwritings correspond, I would ask you to let me have the address, which, according to your father's memorandum, will be found in the letters you have preserved."

"To compliance with such a request I not only cannot demur, but perhaps it may free me from some responsibility which I might have thought the letters devolved upon my executorship. I am sure they did not concern the honour of any woman of any family, for in that case I *must* have burned them."

"Ah, Marquis, shake hands there! In such concord be-tween man and man, there is more *entente cordiale* between England and France than there was at Sebastopol. Now let me compare the handwritings."

"The box that contained the letters is not here—I left it at Rochebriant; I will telegraph to my aunt to send it; the day after to-morrow it will no doubt arrive. Breakfast with me that day—say at one o'clock, and after breakfast the Box!"

"How can I thank you?"

"Thank me! but you said your honour was concerned in

your request—requests affecting honour between men *comme
il faut* is a ceremony of course, like a bow between them.
One bows, the other returns the bow—no thanks on either
side. Now that we have done with that matter, let me say
that I thought your wish for our interview originated in a
very different cause."

"What could that be?"

"Nay, do you not recollect that last talk between us,
when with such loyalty you spoke to me about Mademoiselle Cicogna, and supposing that there might be rivalship
between us, retracted all that you might have before said to
warn me against fostering the sentiment with which she had
inspired me; even at the first slight glance of a face which
cannot be lightly forgotten by those who have once seen it."

"I recollect perfectly every word of that talk, Marquis,"
answered Graham, calmly, but with his hand concealed
within his vest and pressed tightly to his heart. The
warning of Mrs. Morley flashed upon him. "Was this the
man to seize the prize he had put aside—this man, younger
than himself—handsomer than himself—higher in rank?"

"I recollect that talk, Marquis! Well, what then?"

"In my self-conceit I supposed that you might have heard
how much I admired Mademoiselle Cicogna—how, having
not long since met her at the house of Duplessis (who by
the way writes me word that I shall meet you *chez lui* to-
morrow), I have since sought her society wherever there
was a chance to find it. You may have heard, at our
club, or elsewhere, how I adore her genius—how, I say,
that nothing so *Breton*—that is, so pure and so lofty—has
appeared and won readers since the days of Châteaubriand—
and you, knowing that *les absens ont toujours tort,* come to
me and ask Monsieur de Rochebriant, Are we rivals? I
expected a challenge—you relieve my mind—you abandon
the field to me?"

At the first I warned the reader how improved from his
old *mauvaise honte* a year or so of Paris life would make
our *beau Marquis.* How a year or two of London life with

its horsey slang and its fast girls of the period would have vulgarised an English Rochebriant! Graham gnawed his lips and replied quietly, "I do not challenge! Am I to congratulate you?"

"No, that brilliant victory is not for me. I thought that was made clear in the conversation I have referred to. But if you have done me the honour to be jealous I am exceedingly flattered. Speaking, seriously, if I admired Mademoiselle Cicogna when you and I last met, the admiration is increased by the respect with which I regard a character so simply noble. How many women older than she would have been spoiled by the adulation that has followed her literary success!—how few women so young, placed in a position so critical, having the courage to lead a life so independent, would have maintained the dignity of their character free from a single indiscretion! I speak not from my own knowledge, but from the report of all, who would be pleased enough to censure if they could find a cause. Good society is the paradise of *mauvaises langues*."

Graham caught Alain's hand and pressed it, but made no answer.

The young Marquis continued:

"You will pardon me for speaking thus freely in the way that I would wish any friend to speak of the *demoiselle* who might become my wife. I owe you much, not only for the loyalty with which you address me in reference to this young lady, but for words affecting my own position in France, which sank deep into my mind—saved me from deeming myself a *proscrit* in my own land—filled me with a manly ambition, not stifled amidst the thick of many effeminate follies—and, in fact, led me to the career which is about to open before me, and in which my ancestors have left me no undistinguished examples. Let us speak, then, *à cœur ouvert*, as one friend to another. Has there been any misunderstanding between you and Mademoiselle Cicogna which has delayed your return to Paris? If so, is it over now?"

"There has been no such misunderstanding."

"Do you doubt whether the sentiments you expressed in regard to her when we met last year, are returned?"

"I have no right to conjecture her sentiments. You mistake altogether."

"I do not believe that I am dunce enough to mistake your feelings towards Mademoiselle—they may be read in your face at this moment. Of course I do not presume to hazard a conjecture as to those of Mademoiselle towards yourself. But when I met her not long since at the house of Duplessis, with whose daughter she is intimate, I chanced to speak to her of you; and if I may judge, by looks and manner, I chose no displeasing theme. You turn away—I offend you?"

"Offend!—no, indeed; but on this subject I am not prepared to converse. I came to Paris on matters of business much complicated and which ought to absorb my attention. I cannot longer trespass on your evening. The day after to-morrow, then, I will be with you at one o'clock."

"Yes, I hope then to have the letters you wish to consult; and, meanwhile, we meet to-morrow at the Hotel Duplessis."

CHAPTER VI.

GRAHAM had scarcely quitted Alain, and the young Marquis was about to saunter forth to his club, when Duplessis was announced.

These two men had naturally seen much of each other since Duplessis had returned from Bretagne and delivered Alain from the gripe of Louvier. Scarcely a day had passed but what Alain had been summoned to enter into the financier's plans for the aggrandisement of the Rochebriant estates, and delicately made to feel that he had become a partner in speculations, which, thanks to the capital and the

abilities Duplessis brought to bear, seemed likely to result
in the ultimate freedom of his property from all burdens,
and the restoration of his inheritance to a splendour correspondent with the dignity of his rank.

On the plea that his mornings were chiefly devoted to
professional business, Duplessis arranged that these consultations should take place in the evenings. From those
consultations Valérie was not banished; Duplessis took her
into the council as a matter of course. "Valérie," said the
financier to Alain, "though so young, has a very clear head
for business, and she is so interested in all that interests
myself, that even where I do not take her opinion, I at
least feel my own made livelier and brighter by her sympathy."

So the girl was in the habit of taking her work or her
book into the *cabinet de travail*, and never obtruding a suggestion unasked, still, when appealed to, speaking with a
modest good sense which justified her father's confidence
and praise; and *à propos* of her book, she had taken Châteaubriand into peculiar favour. Alain had respectfully
presented to her beautifully bound copies of *Atala* and *Le
Génie du Christianisme;* it is astonishing, indeed, how he
had already contrived to regulate her tastes in literature.
The charms of those quiet family evenings had stolen into
the young Breton's heart.

He yearned for none of the gayer reunions in which he
had before sought for a pleasure that his nature had not
found; for, amidst the amusements of Paris, Alain remained
intensely Breton—viz., formed eminently for the simple joys
of domestic life, associating the sacred hearthstone with the
antique religion of his fathers; gathering round it all the
images of pure and noble affections which the romance of
a poetic temperament had evoked from the solitude which
had surrounded a melancholy boyhood—an uncontaminated
youth.

Duplessis entered abruptly, and with a countenance
much disturbed from its wonted saturnine composure.

"Marquis, what is this I have just heard from the Duchesse de Tarascon? Can it be? You ask military service in this ill-omened war?—you?"

"My dear and best friend," said Alain, very much startled, "I should have thought that you, of all men in the world, would have most approved of my request—you, so devoted an Imperialist—you, indignant that the representative of one of these families, which the First Napoléon so eagerly and so vainly courted, should ask for the grade of sous-lieutenant in the armies of Napoléon the Third—you, who of all men know how ruined are the fortunes of a Rochebriant—you, feel surprised that he clings to the noblest heritage his ancestors have left to him—their sword! I do not understand you."

"Marquis," said Duplessis, seating himself, and regarding Alain with a look in which were blended the sort of admiration and the sort of contempt with which a practical man of the world, who, having himself gone through certain credulous follies, has learned to despise the follies, but retains a reminiscence of sympathy with the fools they bewitch,—"Marquis, pardon me; you talk finely, but you do not talk common sense. I should be extremely pleased if your Legitimist scruples had allowed you to solicit, or rather to accept, a civil appointment not unsuited to your rank, under the ablest sovereign, as a civilian, to whom France can look for rational liberty combined with established order. Such openings to a suitable career you have rejected; but who on earth could expect you, never trained to military service, to draw a sword hitherto sacred to the Bourbons, on behalf of a cause which the madness, I do not say of France but of Paris, has enforced on a sovereign against whom you would fight to-morrow if you had a chance of placing the descendant of Henry IV. on his throne."

"I am not about to fight for any sovereign, but for my country against the foreigner."

"An excellent answer if the foreigner had invaded your

II.—7

country; but it seems that your country is going to invade
the foreigner—a very different thing. *Chut!* all this discussion is most painful to me. I feel for the Emperor a
personal loyalty, and for the hazards he is about to encounter a prophetic dread, as an ancestor of yours might
have felt for Francis I. could he have foreseen Pavia. Let
us talk of ourselves and the effect the war should have upon
our individual action. You are aware, of course, that,
though M. Louvier has had notice of our intention to pay
off his mortgage, that intention cannot be carried into effect
for six months; if the money be not then forthcoming his
hold on Rochebriant remains unshaken—the sum is large."

"Alas! yes."

"The war must greatly disturb the money-market, affect
many speculative adventures and operations when at the
very moment credit may be most needed. It is absolutely
necessary that I should be daily at my post on the Bourse,
and hourly watch the ebb and flow of events. Under these
circumstances I had counted, permit me to count still, on
your presence in Bretagne. We have already begun nego-
tiations on a somewhat extensive scale, whether as regards
the improvement of forests and orchards, or the plans for
building allotments, as soon as the lands are free for disposal—for all these the eye of a master is required. I entreat you, then, to take up your residence at Rochebriant."

"My dear friend, this is but a kindly and delicate mode
of relieving me from the dangers of war. I have, as you
must be conscious, no practical knowledge of business.
Hébert can be implicitly trusted, and will carry out your
views with a zeal equal to mine, and with infinitely more
ability."

"Marquis, pray neither to Hercules nor to Hébert; if you
wish to get your own cart out of the ruts, put your own
shoulder to the wheel."

Alain coloured high, unaccustomed to be so bluntly addressed, but he replied with a kind of dignified meekness:

"I shall ever remain grateful for what you have done,

and wish to do for me. But, assuming that you suppose rightly, the estates of Rochebriant would, in your hands, become a profitable investment, and more than redeem the mortgage, and the sum you have paid Louvier on my account, let it pass to yours irrespectively of me. I shall console myself in the knowledge that the old place will be restored, and those who honoured its old owners prosper in hands so strong, guided by a heart so generous."

Duplessis was deeply affected by these simple words; they seized him on the tenderest side of his character—for his heart was generous, and no one, except his lost wife and his loving child, had ever before discovered it to be so. Has it ever happened to you, reader, to be appreciated on the one point of the good or the great that is in you—on which secretly you value yourself most—but for which nobody, not admitted into your heart of hearts, has given you credit? If that has happened to you, judge what Duplessis felt when the fittest representative of that divine chivalry which, if sometimes deficient in head, owes all that exalts it to riches of heart, spoke thus to the professional moneymaker, whose qualities of head were so acknowledged that a compliment to them would be a hollow impertinence, and whose qualities of heart had never yet received a compliment!

Duplessis started from his seat and embraced Alain, murmuring, "Listen to me, I love you—I never had a son—be mine—Rochebriant shall be my daughter's *dot*."

Alain returned the embrace, and then recoiling, said:

"Father, your first desire must be honour for your son. You have guessed my secret—I have learned to love Valérie. Seeing her out in the world, she seemed like other girls, fair and commonplace—seeing her—at your house, I have said to myself, 'There is the one girl fairer than all others in my eyes, and the one individual to whom all other girls are commonplace.' "

"Is that true?—is it?"

"True! does a *gentilhomme* ever lie? And out of that

love for her has grown this immovable desire to be something worthy of her—something that may lift me from the vulgar platform of men who owe all to ancestors, nothing to themselves. Do you suppose for one moment that I, saved from ruin and penury by Valérie's father, could be base enough to say to her, 'In return be Madame la Marquise de Rochebriant'? Do you suppose that I, whom you would love and respect as son, could come to you and say: 'I am oppressed by your favours—I am crippled with debts—give me your millions and we are quits.' No, Duplessis! You, so well descended yourself—so superior as man amongst men that you would have won name and position had you been born the son of a shoeblack,—you would eternally despise the noble who, in days when all that we Bretons deem holy in *noblesse* are subjected to ridicule and contempt, should so vilely forget the only motto which the scutcheons of all *gentilhommes* have in common, '*Noblesse oblige.*' War, with all its perils and all its grandeur,—war lifts on high the banners of France,—war, in which every ancestor of mine whom I care to recall aggrandised the name that descends to me. Let me then do as those before me have done; let me prove that I am worth something in myself, and then you and I are equals; and I can say with no humbled crest, 'Your benefits are accepted:' the man who has fought not ignobly for France may aspire to the hand of her daughter. Give me Valérie; as to her *dot*,— be it so, Rochebriant,—it will pass to her children."

"Alain! Alain! my friend! my son!—but if you fall."

"Valérie will give you a nobler son."

Duplessis moved away, sighing heavily; but he said no more in deprecation of Alain's martial resolves.

A Frenchman, however practical, however worldly, however philosophical he may be, who does not sympathise with the follies of honour—who does not concede indulgence to the hot blood of youth when he says, "My country is insulted and her banner is unfurled," may certainly be a man of excellent common sense; but if such men had been in the majority, Gaul would never have been France—Gaul would have been a province of Germany.

And as Duplessis walked homeward—he the calmest and most far-seeing of all authorities on the Bourse—the man who, excepting only De Mauléon, most decidedly deemed the cause of the war a blunder, and most forebodingly antic-ipated its issues, caught the prevalent enthusiasm. Every-where he was stopped by cordial hands, everywhere met by congratulating smiles. "How right you have been, Duples-sis, when you have laughed at those who have said, 'The Emperor is ill, decrepit, done up.'"

" *Vive l'Empereur!* at least we shall be face to face with those insolent Prussians!"

Before he arrived at his home, passing along the Boule-vards, greeted by all the groups enjoying the cool night air before the *cafés*, Duplessis had caught the war epidemic.

Entering his hotel, he went at once to Valérie's chamber. "Sleep well to-night, child; Alain has told me that he adores thee, and if he will go to the war, it is that he may lay his laurels at thy feet. Bless thee, my child, thou couldst not have made a nobler choice."

Whether, after these words, Valérie slept well or not 'tis not for me to say; but if she did sleep, I venture to guess that her dreams were rose-coloured.

CHAPTER VII.

ALL the earlier part of that next day, Graham Vane remained in-doors—a lovely day at Paris that 8th of July, and with that summer day all hearts at Paris were in uni-son. Discontent was charmed into enthusiasm—Belleville and Montmartre forgot the visions of Communism and So-cialism and other "isms" not to be realised except in some undiscovered Atlantis!

The Emperor was the idol of the day—the names of

Jules Favre and Gambetta were by-words of scorn. Even Armand Monnier, still out of work, beginning to feel the pinch of want, and fierce for any revolution that might turn topsy-turvy the conditions of labour,—even Armand Monnier was found among groups that were laying *immortelles* at the foot of the column in the Place Vendôme, and heard to say to a fellow malcontent, with eyes uplifted to the statue of the First Napoleon, "Do you not feel at this moment that no Frenchman can be long angry with the Little Corporal? He denied *La Liberté*, but he gave *La Gloire*."

Heeding not the stir of the world without, Graham was compelling into one resolve the doubts and scruples which had so long warred against the heart which they ravaged, but could not wholly subdue.

The conversations with Mrs. Morley and Rochebriant had placed in a light in which he had not before regarded it, the image of Isaura.

He had reasoned from the starting-point of his love for her, and had sought to convince himself that against that love it was his duty to strive.

But now a new question was addressed to his conscience as well as to his heart. What though he had never formally declared to her his affection—never, in open words, wooed her as his own—never even hinted to her the hopes of a union which at one time he had fondly entertained,—still was it true that his love had been too transparent not to be detected by her, and not to have led her on to return it?

Certainly he had, as we know, divined that he was not indifferent to her: at Enghien, a year ago, that he had gained her esteem, and perhaps interested her fancy.

We know also how he had tried to persuade himself that the artistic temperament, especially when developed in women, is too elastic to suffer the things of real life to have lasting influence over happiness or sorrow,—that in the pursuits in which her thought and imagination found employ, in the excitement they sustained, and the fame to which they conduced, Isaura would be readily consoled for a momentary pang of disappointed affection. And that a man so alien as himself, both by nature and by habit, from the artistic world, was the very last person who could maintain deep and permanent impression on her actual life or her ideal dreams. But what if, as he gathered from the words of the fair American—what if, in all these assumptions, she was wholly mistaken? What if, in previously revealing his own heart, he had decoyed hers—what if, by a desertion she had no right to anticipate, he had blighted her future? What if this brilliant child of genius could love as warmly, as deeply, as enduringly as any simple village girl to whom there is no poetry except love? If this were so—what became the first claim on his honour, his conscience, his duty?

The force which but a few days ago his reasonings had given to the arguments that forbade him to think of Isaura, became weaker and weaker, as now in an altered mood of reflection he resummoned and reweighed them.

All those prejudices—which had seemed to him such rational common-sense truths, when translated from his own mind into the words of Lady Janet's letter,—was not Mrs. Morley right in denouncing *them* as the crotchets of an insolent egotism? Was it not rather to the favour than to the disparagement of Isaura, regarded even in the man's narrow-minded view of woman's dignity, that this orphan girl could, with character so unscathed, pass through the trying ordeal of the public babble, the public gaze—command alike the esteem of a woman so pure as Mrs. Morley, the reverence of a man so chivalrously sensitive to honour as Alain de Rochebriant?

Musing thus, Graham's countenance at last brightened—a glorious joy entered into and possessed him. He felt as a man who had burst asunder the swathes and trammels which had kept him galled and miserable with the sense of captivity, and from which some wizard spell that took strength from his own superstition had forbidden to struggle.

He was free!—and that freedom was rapture!—yes, his resolve was taken.

The day was now far advanced. He should have just time before the dinner with Duplessis to drive to A——, where he still supposed Isaura resided.   How, as his *fiacre* rolled along the well-remembered road—how completely he lived in that world of romance of which he denied himself to be a denizen.

Arrived at the little villa, he found it occupied only by workmen—it was under repair.   No one could tell him to what residence the ladies who occupied it the last year had removed.

"I shall learn from Mrs. Morley," thought Graham, and at her house he called in going back, but Mrs. Morley was not at home; he had only just time, after regaining his apartment, to change his dress for the dinner to which he was invited.   As it was, he arrived late, and while apologising to his host for his want of punctuality, his tongue faltered.   At the farther end of the room he saw a face, paler and thinner than when he had seen it last—a face across which a something of grief had gone.

The servant announced that dinner was served.

"Mr. Vane," said Duplessis, "will you take into dinner Mademoiselle Cicogna?"

BOOK XI.

CHAPTER I.

AMONG the frets and checks to the course that "never did run smooth," there is one which is sufficiently frequent, for many a reader will remember the irritation it caused him. You have counted on a meeting with the beloved one unwitnessed by others, an interchange of confessions and vows which others may not hear. You have arranged almost the words in which your innermost heart is to be expressed; pictured to yourself the very looks by which those words will have their sweetest reply. The scene you have thus imagined appears to you vivid and distinct, as if foreshown in a magic glass. And suddenly, after long absence, the meeting takes place in the midst of a common companionship: nothing that you wished to say can be said. The scene you pictured is painted out by the irony of Chance; and groups and backgrounds of which you had never dreamed start forth from the disappointing canvas. Happy if that be all! But sometimes, by a strange, subtle intuition, you feel that the person herself is changed; and sympathetic with that change, a terrible chill comes over your own heart.

Before Graham had taken his seat at the table beside Isaura, he felt that she was changed to him. He felt it by her very touch as their hands met at the first greeting,—by the tone of her voice in the few words that passed between them,—by the absence of all glow in the smile which had once lit up her face, as a burst of sunshine lights up a day in spring, and gives a richer gladness of colour to

all its blooms.   Once seated side by side they remained for
some moments silent.   Indeed, it would have been rather
difficult for anything less than the wonderful intelligence
of lovers between whom no wall can prevent the stolen interchange of tokens, to have ventured private talk of their
own amid the excited converse which seemed all eyes, all
tongues, all ears, admitting no one present to abstract himself from the common emotion.   Englishmen do not recognise the old classic law which limited the number of guests,
where banquets are meant to be pleasant, to that of the
Nine Muses.   They invite guests so numerous, and so shy
of launching talk across the table, that you may talk to the
person next to you not less secure from listeners than you
would be in talking with the stranger whom you met at a
well in the Sahara.   It is not so, except on state occasions,
at Paris.   Difficult there to retire into solitude with your
next neighbour.   The guests collected by Duplessis completed with himself the number of the Sacred Nine—the
host, Valérie, Rochebriant, Graham, Isaura, Signora Venosta, La Duchesse de Tarascon, the wealthy and high-born
Imperialist, Prince ——, and last and least, one who shall
be nameless.

I have read somewhere, perhaps in one of the books which
American superstition dedicates to the mysteries of Spirit-
ualism, how a gifted seer, technically styled medium, sees
at the opera a box which to other eyes appears untenanted
and empty, but to him is full of ghosts, well dressed in
costume de règle, gazing on the boards and listening to the
music.   Like such ghosts are certain beings whom I call
Lookers-on.   Though still living, they have no share in the
life they survey, they come as from another world to hear
and to see what is passing in ours.   In ours they lived
once, but that troubled sort of life they have survived.
Still we amuse them as stage-players and puppets amuse
ourselves.   One of these Lookers-on completed the party
at the house of Duplessis.

How lively, how animated the talk was at the finan-

cier's pleasant table that day, the 8th of July! The excitement of the coming war made itself loud in every
Gallic voice, and kindled in every Gallic eye. Appeals at
every second minute were made, sometimes courteous,
sometimes sarcastic, to the Englishman—promising son of
an eminent statesman, and native of a country in which
France is alway coveting an ally, and always suspecting
an enemy. Certainly Graham could not have found a
less propitious moment for asking Isaura if she really
were changed. And certainly the honour of Great Brit-
ain was never less ably represented (that is saying a great
deal) than it was on this occasion by the young man
reared to diplomacy and aspiring to Parliamentary distinction. He answered all questions with a constrained voice
and an insipid smile,—all questions pointedly addressed to
him as to what demonstrations of admiring sympathy with
the gallantry of France might be expected from the English
Government and people; what his acquaintance with the
German races led him to suppose would be the effect on the
Southern States of the first defeat of the Prussians; whether
the man called Moltke was not a mere strategist on paper,
a crotchety pedant; whether, if Belgium became so enamoured of the glories of France as to solicit fusion with her
people, England would have a right to offer any objection,—
&c., &c. I do not think that during that festival Graham
once thought one-millionth so much about the fates of Prussia and France as he did think, " Why is that girl so changed
to me? Merciful heaven! is she lost to my life?"

By training, by habit, even by passion, the man was a
genuine politician, cosmopolitan as well as patriotic, accustomed to consider what effect every vibration in that bal-
ance of European power, which no deep thinker can despise,
must have on the destinies of civilised humanity, and on
those of the nation to which he belongs. But are there not
moments in life when the human heart suddenly narrows
the circumference to which its emotions are extended? As
the ebb of a tide, it retreats from the shores it had covered

on its flow, drawing on with contracted waves the treasure-trove it has selected to hoard amid its deeps.

CHAPTER II.

ON quitting the dining-room, the Duchesse de Tarascon said to her host, on whose arm she was leaning, " Of course you and I must go with the stream. But is not all the fine talk that has passed to-day at your table, and in which we too have joined, a sort of hypocrisy? I may say this to you; I would say it to no other."

"And I say to you, Madame la Duchesse, that which I would say to no other. Thinking over it as I sit alone, I find myself making a 'terrible hazard;' but when I go abroad and become infected by the general enthusiasm, I pluck up gaiety of spirit, and whisper to myself, 'True, but it may be an enormous gain.' To get the left bank of the Rhine is a trifle; but to check in our next neighbour a growth which a few years hence would overtop us,—that is no trifle. And, be the gain worth the hazard or not, could the Emperor, could any Government likely to hold its own for a week, have declined to take the chance of the die?"

The Duchesse mused a moment, and meanwhile the two seated themselves on a divan in the corner of the *salon*. Then she said very slowly:

"No Government that held its tenure on popular suffrage could have done so. But if the Emperor had retained the personal authority which once allowed the intellect of one man to control and direct the passions of many, I think the war would have been averted. I have reason to know that the Emperor gave his emphatic support to the least belli-cose members of the Council, and that Gramont's speech did not contain the passage that precipitates hostilities when the Council in which it was framed broke up. These fatal words were forced upon him by the temper in which the

Ministers found the Chamber, and the reports of the popular excitement which could not be resisted without imminent danger of revolution. It is Paris that has forced the war on the Emperor. But enough of this subject. What must be, must, and, as you say, the gain may be greater than the hazard. I come to something else you whispered to me before we went in to dinner,—a sort of complaint which wounds me sensibly. You say I had assisted to a choice of danger and possibly of death a very distant connection of mine, who might have been a very near connection of yours. You mean Alain de Rochebriant?"

"Yes; I accept him as a suitor for the hand of my only daughter."

"I am so glad, not for your sake so much as for his. No one can know him well without appreciating in him the finest qualities of the finest order of the French noble; but having known your pretty Valérie so long, my congratulations are for the man who can win her. Meanwhile, hear my explanation: when I promised Alain any interest I can command for the grade of officer in a regiment of Mobiles, I knew not that he had formed, or was likely to form, ties or duties to keep him at home. I withdraw my promise."

"No, Duchesse, fulfil it. I should be disloyal indeed if I robbed a sovereign under whose tranquil and prosperous reign I have acquired, with no dishonour, the fortune which Order proffers to Commerce, of one gallant defender in the hour of need. And, speaking frankly, if Alain were really my son, I think I am Frenchman enough to remember that France is my mother."

"Say no more, my friend—say no more," cried the Duchesse, with the warm blood of the heart rushing through all the delicate coatings of pearl-powder. "If every Frenchman felt as you do; if in this Paris of ours all hostilities of class may merge in the one thought of the common country; if in French hearts there yet thrills the same sentiment as that which, in the terrible days when all other ties were rent asunder, revered France as mother,

and rallied her sons to her aid against the confederacy of
Europe,—why, then, we need not grow pale with dismay
at the sight of a Prussian needle-gun.   Hist! look yonder:
is not that a tableau of Youth in Arcady?   Worlds rage
around, and Love, unconcerned, whispers to Love!"   The
Duchesse here pointed to a corner of the adjoining room
in which Alain and Valérie sat apart, he whispering into
her ear: her cheek downcast, and, even seen at that distance, brightened by the delicate tenderness of its blushes.

CHAPTER III.

But in that small assembly there were two who did not
attract the notice of Duplessis or of the lady of the Imperial Court.   While the Prince —— and the placid Looker-on
were engaged at a contest of *écarté*, with the lively Venosta,
for the gallery, interposing criticisms and admonitions,
Isaura was listlessly turning over a collection of photo-
graphs, strewed on a table that stood near to an open window in the remoter angle of the room, communicating with
a long and wide balcony filled partially with flowers and
overlooking the Champs Elysées, softly lit up by the innu-
merable summer stars.   Suddenly a whisper, the command
of which she could not resist, thrilled through her ear, and
sent the blood rushing back to her heart.

"Do you remember that evening at Enghien? how I said
that our imagination could not carry us beyond the question whether we two should be gazing together that night
twelve months on that star which each of us had singled
out from the hosts of heaven?   That was the 8th of July.
It is the 8th of July once more.   Come and seek for our
chosen star—come.   I have something to say, which say I
must.   Come."

Mechanically, as it were,—mechanically, as they tell us
the Somnambulist obeys the Mesmeriser,—Isaura obeyed

that summons. In a kind of dreamy submission she followed his steps, and found herself on the balcony, flowers
around her and stars above, by the side of the man who
had been to her that being ever surrounded by flowers and
lighted by stars,—the ideal of Romance to the heart of
virgin Woman.

"Isaura," said the Englishman, softly. At the sound of
her own name for the first time heard from those lips, every
nerve in her frame quivered. "Isaura, I have tried to live
without you. I cannot. You are all in all to me: without
you it seems to me as if earth had no flowers, and even
heaven had withdrawn its stars. Are there differences between us, differences of taste, of sentiments, of habits, of
thought? Only let me hope that you can love me a tenth
part so much as I love you, and such differences cease to
be discord. Love harmonises all sounds, blends all colours
into its own divine oneness of heart and soul. Look up!
is not the star which this time last year invited our gaze
above, is it not still there? Does it not still invite our
gaze? Isaura, speak!"

"Hush, hush, hush,"—the girl could say no more, but
she recoiled from his side.

The recoil did not wound him: there was no hate in it.
He advanced, he caught her hand, and continued, in one
of those voices which become so musical in summer nights
under starry skies:

"Isaura, there is one name which I can never utter without a reverence due to the religion which binds earth to
heaven—a name which to man should be the symbol of life
cheered and beautified, exalted, hallowed. That name is
'wife.' Will you take that name from me?"

And still Isaura made no reply. She stood mute, and
cold, and rigid as a statue of marble. At length, as if
consciousness had been arrested and was struggling back,
she sighed heavily, and passed her hands slowly over her
forehead.

"Mockery, mockery," she said then, with a smile half

bitter, half plaintive, on her colourless lips. "Did you
wait to ask me that question till you knew what my answer must be? I have pledged the name of wife to another."

"No, no; you say that to rebuke, to punish me! Unsay
it! unsay it!"

Isaura beheld the anguish of his face with bewildered
eyes. "How can my words pain you?" she said, drearily.
"Did you not write that I had unfitted myself to be wife
to you?"

"I?"

"That I had left behind me the peaceful immunities
of private life? I felt you were so right! Yes! I am
affianced to one who thinks that in spite of that misfortune——"

"Stop, I command you—stop! You saw my letter to
Mrs. Morley. I have not had one moment free from torture and remorse since I wrote it. But whatever in that
letter you might justly resent——"

"I did not resent——"

Graham heard not the interruption, but hurried on.
"You would forgive could you read my heart. No matter. Every sentiment in that letter, except those which
conveyed admiration, I retract. Be mine, and instead of
presuming to check in you the irresistible impulse of genius
to the first place in the head or the heart of the world, I
teach myself to encourage, to share, to exult in it. Do you
know what a difference there is between the absent one and
the present one—between the distant image against whom
our doubts, our fears, our suspicions, raise up hosts of imaginary giants, barriers of visionary walls, and the beloved
face before the sight of which the hosts are fled, the walls
are vanished? Isaura, we meet again. You know now
from my own lips that I love you. I think your lips will
not deny that you love me. You say that you are affianced
to another. Tell the man frankly, honestly, that you mis-
took your heart. It is not yours to give. Save yourself,

save him, from a union in which there can be no happiness."

"It is too late," said Isaura, with hollow tones, but with no trace of vacillating weakness on her brow and lips. "Did I say now to that other one, 'I break the faith that I pledged to you,' I should kill him, body and soul. Slight thing though I be, to him I am all in all; to you, Mr. Vane, to you a memory—the memory of one whom a year, perhaps a month, hence, you will rejoice to think you have escaped."

She passed from him—passed away from the flowers and the starlight; and when Graham,—recovering from the stun of her crushing words, and with the haughty mien and step of the man who goes forth from the ruin of his hopes, leaning for support upon his pride,—when Graham re-entered the room, all the guests had departed save only Alain, who was still exchanging whispered words with Valérie.

CHAPTER IV.

THE next day, at the hour appointed, Graham entered Alain's apartment. "I am glad to tell you," said the Marquis, gaily, "that the box has arrived, and we will very soon examine its contents. Breakfast claims precedence." During the meal Alain was in gay spirits, and did not at first notice the gloomy countenance and abstracted mood of his guest. At length, surprised at the dull response to his lively sallies on the part of a man generally so pleasant in the frankness of his speech, and the cordial ring of his sympathetic laugh, it occurred to him that the change in Graham must be ascribed to something that had gone wrong in the meeting with Isaura the evening before; and remembering the curtness with which Graham had implied disinclination to converse about the fair Italian, he felt perplexed how to reconcile the impulse of his good nature with the discretion imposed on his good-breeding. At all events, a compliment to the lady whom Graham had so admired could do no harm.

"How well Mademoiselle Cicogna looked last night!"

"Did she?   It seemed to me that, in health at least, she did not look very well. Have you heard what day M. Thiers will speak on the war?"

"Thiers? No. Who cares about Thiers? Thank heaven his day is past! I don't know any unmarried woman in Paris, not even Valérie—I mean Mademoiselle Duplessis— who has so exquisite a taste in dress as Mademoiselle Ci-cogna.   Generally speaking, the taste of a female author is atrocious."

"Really—I did not observe her dress. I am no critic on subjects so dainty as the dress of ladies, or the tastes of female authors."

"Pardon me," said the *beau* Marquis, gravely.   "As to dress, I think that so essential a thing in the mind of wo-man, that no man who cares about women ought to disdain critical study of it.   In woman, refinement of character is never found in vulgarity of dress.   I have only observed that truth since I came up from Bretagne."

"I presume, my dear Marquis, that you may have read in Bretagne books which very few not being professed scholars have ever read at Paris; and possibly you may re-member that Horace ascribes the most exquisite refinement in dress, denoted by the untranslatable words, '*simplex mun-ditiis,*' to a lady who was not less distinguished by the ease and rapidity with which she could change her affection. Of course that allusion does not apply to Mademoiselle Ci-cogna, but there are many other exquisitely dressed ladies at Paris of whom an ill-fated admirer

" 'fidem
Mutatosque deos flebit.'

Now, with your permission, we will adjourn to the box of letters."

The box being produced and unlocked, Alain looked with conscientious care at its contents before he passed over to Graham's inspection a few epistles, in which the Englishman immediately detected the same handwriting as that of the letter from Louise which Richard King had bequeathed to him.

They were arranged and numbered chronologically.

LETTER I.

DEAR M. LE MARQUIS,—How can I thank you sufficiently for obtaining and remitting to me those certificates? You are too aware of the unhappy episode in my life not to know how inestimable is the service you render me. I am saved all further molestation from the man who had indeed no right over my freedom, but whose persecution might compel me to the scandal and disgrace of an appeal to the law for protection, and the avowal of the illegal marriage into which I was duped. I would rather be torn limb from limb by wild horses, like the Queen in the history books, than dishonour myself and the ancestry which I may at least claim on the mother's side, by proclaiming that I had lived with that low Englishman as his wife, when I was only—O heavens, I cannot conclude the sentence!

"No, Mons. le Marquis, I am in no want of the pecuniary aid you so generously wish to press on me. Though I know not where to address my poor dear uncle,—though I doubt, even if I did, whether I could venture to confide to him the secret known only to yourself as to the name I now bear—and if he hear of me at all he must believe me dead,—yet I have enough left of the money he last remitted to me for present support; and when that fails, I think, what with my knowledge of English and such other slender accomplishments as I possess, I could maintain myself as a teacher or governess in some German family. At all events, I will write to you again soon, and I entreat you to let me know all you can learn about my uncle. I feel

so grateful to you for your just disbelief of the horrible
calumny which must be so intolerably galling to a man so
proud, and, whatever his errors, so incapable of a base-
ness.

"Direct to me *Poste restante,* Augsburg.
    "Yours with all consideration,
                        "————— —————.''

LETTER II.

(Seven months after the date of Letter I.)

"AUGSBURG.

"DEAR M. LE MARQUIS,—I thank you for your kind
little note informing me of the pains you have taken, as
yet with no result, to ascertain what has become of my unfortunate uncle. My life since I last wrote has been a very
quiet one. I have been teaching among a few families
here; and among my pupils are two little girls of very high
birth. They have taken so great a fancy to me that their
mother has just asked me to come and reside at their house
as governess. What wonderfully kind hearts those Germans have,—so simple, so truthful! They raise no troublesome questions,—accept my own story implicitly." Here
follow a few commonplace sentences about the German
character, and a postscript. "I go into my new home
next week. When you hear more of my uncle, direct to
me at the Countess von Rudesheim, Schloss N—— M——,
near Berlin."

"Rudesheim!" Could this be the relation, possibly the
wife, of the Count von Rudesheim with whom Graham had
formed acquaintance last year?

LETTER III.

(Between three and four years after the date of the last.)

"YOU startle me indeed, dear M. le Marquis. My uncle
said to have been recognised in Algeria under another name,

a soldier in the Algerian army? My dear, proud, luxurious uncle! Ah, I cannot believe it, any more than you do: but I long eagerly for such further news as you can learn of him. For myself, I shall perhaps surprise you when I say I am about to be married. Nothing can exceed the amiable kindness I have received from the Rudesheims since I have been in their house. For the last year especially I have been treated on equal terms as one of the family. Among the habitual visitors at the house is a gentleman of noble birth, but not of rank too high, nor of fortune too great, to make a marriage with the French widowed governess a *mésalliance*. I am sure that he loves me sincerely; and he is the only man I ever met whose love I have cared to win. We are to be married in the course of the year. Of course he is ignorant of my painful history, and will never learn it. And after all, Louise D—— is dead. In the home to which I am about to remove, there is no probability that the wretched Englishman can ever cross my path. My secret is as safe with you as in the grave that holds her whom in the name of Louise D—— you once loved. Henceforth I shall trouble you no more with my letters; but if you hear anything decisively authentic of my uncle's fate, write me a line at any time, directed as before to Madame M——, enclosed to the Countess von Rudesheim.

"And accept, for all the kindness you have ever shown me, as to one whom you did not disdain to call a kinswoman, the assurance of my undying gratitude. In the alliance she now makes, your kinswoman does not discredit the name through which she is connected with the yet loftier line of Rochebriant."

To this letter the late Marquis had appended in pencil. "Of course Rochebriant never denies the claim of a kinswoman, even though a drawing-master's daughter. Beautiful creature, Louise, but a termagant. I could not love Venus if she were a termagant. L.'s head turned by the unlucky discovery that her mother was noble. In one form or other, every woman has the same disease—vanity. Name of her intended not mentioned—easily found out."

The next letter was dated May 7, 1859, on black-edged paper, and contained but these lines: "I was much comforted by your kind visit yesterday, dear Marquis. My affliction has been heavy: but for the last two years my poor husband's conduct has rendered my life unhappy, and I am recovering the shock of his sudden death. It is true that I and the children are left very ill provided for; but I cannot accept your generous offer of aid. Have no fear as to my future fate. Adieu, my dear Marquis! This will reach you just before you start for Naples. *Bon voyage.*" There was no address on this note—no postmark on the envelope—evidently sent by hand.

The last note, dated 1861, March 20, was briefer than its predecessor. "I have taken your advice, dear Marquis; and, overcoming all scruples, I have accepted his kind offer, on the condition that I am never to be taken to England. I had no option in this marriage. I can now own to you that my poverty had become urgent.—Yours, with inalienable gratitude,   ——."

This last note, too, was without postmark, and was evidently sent by hand.

"There are no other letters, then, from this writer?" asked Graham; "and no further clue as to her existence?"

"None that I have discovered; and I see now why I preserved these letters. There is nothing in their contents not creditable to my poor father. They show how capable he was of good-natured disinterested kindness towards even a distant relation of whom he could certainly not have been proud, judging not only by his own pencilled note, or by the writer's condition as a governess, but by her loose sentiments as to the marriage tie. I have not the slightest idea who she could be. I never at least heard of one connected, however distantly, with my family, whom I could identify with the writer of these letters."

"I may hold them a short time in my possession?"

"Pardon me a preliminary question. If I may venture to form a conjecture, the object of your search must be connected with your countryman, whom the lady politely calls the 'wretched Englishman;' but I own I should not like to lend, through these letters, a pretence to any steps that may lead to a scandal in which my father's name or that of any member of my family could be mixed up."

"Marquis, it is to prevent the possibility of all scandal that I ask you to trust these letters to my discretion."

"*Foi de gentilhomme?*"

"*Foi de gentilhomme!*"

"Take them. When and where shall we meet again?"

"Soon, I trust; but I must leave Paris this evening. I am bound to Berlin in quest of this Countess von Rudesheim: and I fear that in a very few days intercourse between France and the German frontier will be closed upon travellers."

After a few more words not worth recording, the two young men shook hands and parted.

CHAPTER V.

IT was with an interest languid and listless indeed, compared with that which he would have felt a day before, that Graham mused over the remarkable advances towards the discovery of Louise Duval which were made in the letters he had perused. She had married, then, first a foreigner, whom she spoke of as noble, and whose name and residence could be easily found through the Countess von Rudesheim. The marriage did not seem to have been a happy one. Left a widow in reduced circumstances, she had married again, evidently without affection. She was living so late as 1861, and she had children living in 1859: was the child referred to by Richard King one of them?

The tone and style of the letters served to throw some light on the character of the writer: they evinced pride, stubborn self-will, and unamiable hardness of nature; but her rejection of all pecuniary aid from a man like the late Marquis de Rochebriant betokened a certain dignity of sentiment. She was evidently, whatever her strange ideas about her first marriage with Richard King, no vulgar woman of gallantry; and there must have been some sort of charm about her to have excited a friendly interest in a kinsman so remote, and a man of pleasure so selfish, as her high-born correspondent.

But what now, so far as concerned his own happiness, was the hope, the probable certainty, of a speedy fulfilment of the trust bequeathed to him? Whether the result, in the death of the mother, and more especially of the child, left him rich, or, if the last survived, reduced his fortune to a modest independence, Isaura was equally lost to him, and fortune became valueless. But his first emotions on recovering from the shock of hearing from Isaura's lips that she was irrevocably affianced to another, were not those of self-reproach. They were those of intense bitterness against her who, if really so much attached to him as he had been led to hope, could within so brief a time reconcile her heart to marriage with another. This bitterness was no doubt unjust; but I believe it to be natural to men of a nature so proud and of affections so intense as Graham's, under similar defeats of hope. Resentment is the first impulse in a man loving with the whole ardour of his soul, rejected, no matter why or wherefore, by the woman by whom he had cause to believe he himself was beloved; and though Graham's standard of honour was certainly the reverse of low, yet man does not view honour in the same light as woman does, when involved in analogous difficulties of position. Graham conscientiously thought that if

Isaura so loved him as to render distasteful an engagement
to another which could only very recently have been contracted, it would be more honourable frankly so to tell the
accepted suitor than to leave him in ignorance that her
heart was estranged.   But these engagements are very solemn things with girls like Isaura, and hers was no ordinary
obligation of woman-honour.   Had the accepted one been
superior in rank—fortune—all that flatters the ambition of
woman in the choice of marriage; had he been resolute,
and strong, and self-dependent amid the trials and perils
of life—then possibly the woman's honour might find excuse in escaping the penalties of its pledge.   But the poor,
ailing, infirm, morbid boy-poet, who looked to her as his
saving angel in body, in mind, and soul—to say to him,
"Give me back my freedom," would be to abandon him to
death and to sin.   But Graham could not of course divine
why what he as a man thought right was to Isaura as
woman impossible: and he returned to his old prejudiced
notion that there is no real depth and ardour of affection for
human lovers in the poetess whose mind and heart are devoted to the creation of imaginary heroes.   Absorbed in
reverie, he took his way slowly and with downcast looks
towards the British embassy, at which it was well to ascertain whether the impending war yet necessitated special
passports for Germany.

"*Bon jour, cher ami,*" said a pleasant voice; "and how
long have you been at Paris?"

"Oh, my dear M. Savarin! charmed to see you looking
so well!   Madame well too, I trust?   My kindest regards
to her.   I have been in Paris but a day or two, and I leave
this evening."

"So soon?   The war frightens you away, I suppose.
Which way are you going now?"

"To the British embassy."

"Well, I will go with you so far—it is in my own direction.   I have to call at the charming Italian's with my congratulations—on news I only heard this morning."

"You mean Mademoiselle Cicogna—and the news that demands congratulations—her approaching marriage!"

"*Mon Dieu!* when could you have heard of that?"

"Last night at the house of M. Duplessis."

"*Parbleu!* I shall scold her well for confiding to her new friend Valérie the secret she kept from her old friends, my wife and myself."

"By the way," said Graham, with a tone of admirably-feigned indifference, "who is the happy man? That part of the secret I did not hear."

"Can't you guess?"

"No."

"Gustave Rameau."

"Ah!" Graham almost shrieked, so sharp and shrill was his cry. "Ah! I ought indeed to have guessed that!"

"Madame Savarin, I fancy, helped to make up the marriage. I hope it may turn out well; certainly it will be his salvation. May it be for her happiness!"

"No doubt of that! Two poets—born for each other, I dare say. Adieu, my dear Savarin! Here we are at the embassy."

CHAPTER VI.

THAT evening Graham found himself in the *coupé* of the express train to Strasbourg. He had sent to engage the whole *coupé* to himself, but that was impossible. One place was bespoken as far as C——, after which Graham might prosecute his journey alone on paying for the three places.

When he took his seat another man was in the further corner whom he scarcely noticed. The train shot rapidly on for some leagues. Profound silence in the *coupé*, save at moments those heavy impatient sighs that came from the very depths of the heart, and of which he who sighs is unconscious, burst from the Englishman's lips, and drew on him the observant side-glance of his fellow-traveller.

At length the fellow-traveller said in very good English,

though with French accent, "Would you object, sir, to my lighting my little carriage-lantern? I am in the habit of reading in the night train, and the wretched lamp they give us does not permit that. But if you wish to sleep, and my lantern would prevent you doing so, consider my request unasked."

"You are most courteous, sir. Pray light your lantern—that will not interfere with my sleep."

As Graham thus answered, far away from the place and the moment as his thoughts were, it yet faintly struck him that he had heard that voice before.

The man produced a small lantern, which he attached to the window-sill, and drew forth from a small leathern bag sundry newspapers and pamphlets. Graham flung himself back, and in a minute or so again came his sigh. "Allow me to offer you those evening journals—you may not have had time to read them before starting," said the fellow-traveller, leaning forward, and extending the newspapers with one hand, while with the other he lifted his lantern. Graham turned, and the faces of the two men were close to each other—Graham with his travelling-cap drawn over his brows, the other with head uncovered.

"Monsieur Lebeau!"

"*Bon soir*, Mr. Lamb!"

Again silence for a moment or so. Monsieur Lebeau then broke it:

"I think, Mr. Lamb, that in better society than that of the Faubourg Montmartre you are known under another name."

Graham had no heart then for the stage-play of a part, and answered, with quiet haughtiness, "Possibly—and what name?"

"Graham Vane. And, sir," continued Lebeau, with a haughtiness equally quiet, but somewhat more menacing, "since we two gentlemen find ourselves thus close, do I ask too much if I inquire why you condescend to seek my acquaintance in disguise?"

"Monsieur le Vicomte de Mauléon, when you talk of disguise, is it too much to inquire why my acquaintance was accepted by Monsieur Lebeau?"

"Ha! Then you confess that it was Victor de Mauléon whom you sought when you first visited the *Café Jean Jacques?*"

"Frankly I confess it."

Monsieur Lebeau drew himself back, and seemed to reflect.

"I see! Solely for the purpose of learning whether Victor de Mauléon could give you any information about Louise Duval. Is it so?"

"Monsieur le Vicomte, you say truly."

Again M. Lebeau paused as if in reflection; and Graham, in that state of mind when a man who may most despise and detest the practice of duelling, may yet feel a thrill of delight if some homicide would be good enough to put him out of his misery, flung aside his cap, lifted his broad frank forehead, and stamped his foot impatiently as if to provoke a quarrel.

M. Lebeau lowered his spectacles, and, with those calm, keen, searching eyes of his, gazed at the Englishman.

"It strikes me," he said, with a smile, the fascination of which not even those faded whiskers could disguise—"it strikes me that there are two ways in which gentlemen such as you and I are can converse: firstly, with reservation and guard against each other; secondly, with perfect openness. Perhaps of the two I have more need of reservation and wary guard against any stranger than you have. Allow me to propose the alternative—perfect openness. What say you?" and he extended his hand.

"Perfect openness," answered Graham, softened into sudden liking for this once terrible swordsman, and shaking, as an Englishman shakes, the hand held out to him in peace by the man from whom he had anticipated quarrel.

"Permit me now, before you address any questions to me, to put one to you. How did you learn that Victor de Mauléon was identical with Jean Lebeau?"

"I heard that from an agent of the police."

"Ah!"

"Whom I consulted as to the means of ascertaining whether Louise Duval was alive,—if so, where she could be found."

"I thank you very much for your information. I had no notion that the police of Paris had divined the original *alias* of poor Monsieur Lebeau, though something occurred at Lyons which made me suspect it. Strange that the Government, knowing through the police that Victor de Mauléon, a writer they had no reason to favour, had been in so humble a position, should never, even in their official journals, have thought it prudent to say so! But, now I think of it, what if they had? They could prove nothing against Jean Lebeau. They could but say, 'Jean Lebeau is suspected to be too warm a lover of liberty, too earnest a friend of the people, and Jean Lebeau is the editor of *La Sens Commun.*' Why, that assertion would have made Victor de Mauléon the hero of the Reds, the last thing a prudent Government could desire. I thank you cordially for your frank reply. Now, what question would you put to me?"

"In one word, all you can tell me about Louise Duval."

"You shall have it. I had heard vaguely in my young days that a half-sister of mine by my father's first marriage with Mademoiselle de Beauvilliers had—when in advanced middle life he married a second time—conceived a dislike for her mother-in-law, and, being of age, with an independent fortune of her own, had quitted the house, taken up her residence with an elderly female relative, and there had contracted a marriage with a man who gave her lessons in drawing. After that marriage, which my father in vain tried to prevent, my sister was renounced by her family. That was all I knew till, after I came into my inheritance by the death of both my parents, I learned from my father's confidential lawyer that the drawing-master, M. Duval, had soon dissipated his wife's fortune,

become a widower with one child—a girl—and fallen into
great distress. He came to my father, begging for pecuniary aid. My father, though by no means rich, consented
to allow him a yearly pension, on condition that he never
revealed to his child her connection with our family. The
man agreed to the condition, and called at my father's lawyer quarterly for his annuity. But the lawyer informed
me that this deduction from my income had ceased, that
M. Duval had not for a year called or sent for the sum due
to him, and that he must therefore be dead. One day my
valet informed me that a young lady wished to see me—in
those days young ladies very often called on me. I desired
her to be shown in. There entered a young creature, almost of my own age, who, to my amazement, saluted me
as uncle. This was the child of my half-sister. Her father
had been dead several months, fulfilling very faithfully the
condition on which he had held his pension, and the girl
never dreaming of the claims that, if wise, poor child, she
ought not to have cared for, viz.,—to that obsolete useless
pauper birthright, a branch on the family tree of a French
noble. But in pinch of circumstance, and from female
curiosity, hunting among the papers her father had left for
some clue to the reasons for the pension he had received,
she found letters from her mother, letters from my father,
which indisputably proved that she was grandchild to the
feu Vicomte de Mauléon, and niece to myself. Her story
as told to me was very pitiable. Conceiving herself to be
nothing higher in birth than daughter to this drawing-master, at his death, poor, penniless orphan that she was, she
had accepted the hand of an English student of medicine
whom she did not care for. Miserable with this man, on
finding by the documents I refer to that she was my niece,
she came to me for comfort and counsel. What counsel
could I or any man give to her but to make the best of
what had happened, and live with her husband? But then
she started another question. It seems that she had been
talking with some one, I think her landlady, or some other

woman with whom she had made acquaintance—was she
legally married to this man? Had he not entrapped her
ignorance into a false marriage? This became a grave
question, and I sent at once to my lawyer. On hearing
the circumstances, he at once declared that the marriage
was not legal according to the laws of France. But, doubtless, her English *soi-disant* husband was not cognisant of
the French law, and a legal marriage could, with his assent, be at once solemnised. Monsieur Vane, I cannot
find words to convey to you the joy that poor girl showed
in her face and in her words when she learned that she was
not bound to pass her life with that man as his wife. It
was in vain to talk and reason with her. Then arose the
other question, scarcely less important. True, the marriage was not legal, but would it not be better on all accounts to take steps to have it formally annulled, thus free-
ing her from the harassment of any claim the Englishman
might advance, and enabling her to establish the facts in
a right position, not injurious to her honour in the eyes of
any future suitor to her hand? She would not hear of such
a proposal. She declared that she could not bring to the
family she pined to re-enter the scandal of disgrace. To
allow that she had made such a *mésalliance* would be bad
enough in itself; but to proclaim to the world that, though
nominally the wife, she had in fact been only the mistress
of this medical student—she would rather throw herself
into the Seine. All she desired was to find some refuge,
some hiding-place for a time, whence she could write to the
man informing him that he had no lawful hold on her.
Doubtless he would not seek then to molest her. He would
return to his own country, and be effaced from her life.
And then, her story unknown, she might form a more suitable alliance. Fiery young creature though she was—true
De Mauléon in being so fiery—she interested me strongly. I
should say that she was wonderfully handsome; and though
imperfectly educated, and brought up in circumstances so
lowly, there was nothing common about her—a certain *je*

ne sais quoi of stateliness and race.   At all events she did
with me what she wished.   I agreed to aid her desire of a
refuge and hiding-place.   Of course I could not lodge her in
my own apartment, but I induced a female relation of her
mother's, an old lady living at Versailles, to receive her, stating her birth, but of course concealing her illegal marriage.

"From time to time I went to see her.   But one day I
found this restless bright-plumaged bird flown.   Among
the ladies who visited at her relative's house was a certain
Madame Marigny, a very pretty young widow.   Madame
Marigny and Louise formed a sudden and intimate friendship.   The widow was moving from Versailles into an
apartment at Paris, and invited Louise to share it.   She
had consented.   I was not pleased at this; for the widow
was too young, and too much of a coquette, to be a safe
companion to Louise.   But though professing much gratitude and great regard for me, I had no power of controlling
the poor girl's actions.   Her nominal husband, meanwhile,
had left France, and nothing more was heard or known of
him.   I saw that the best thing that could possibly befall
Louise was marriage with some one rich enough to gratify
her taste for luxury and pomp; and that if such a marriage
offered itself, she might be induced to free it from all possible embarrassment by procuring the annulment of the
former, from which she had hitherto shrunk in such revolt.
This opportunity presented itself.   A man already rich,
and in a career that promised to make him infinitely richer,
an associate of mine in those days when I was rapidly
squandering the remnant of my inheritance—this man saw
her at the opera in company with Madame Marigny, fell
violently in love with her, and ascertaining her relationship
to me, besought an introduction.   I was delighted to give
it; and, to say the truth, I was then so reduced to the
bottom of my casket, I felt that it was becoming impossible
for me to continue the aid I had hitherto given to Louise,
and what then would become of her?   I thought it fair to
tell Louvier——"

" Louvier—the financier?"

" Ah, that was a slip of the tongue, but no matter; there is no reason for concealing his name.   I thought it right, I say, to tell Louvier confidentially the history of the unfortunate illegal marriage.   It did not damp his ardour.   He wooed her to the best of his power, but she evidently took him into great dislike.   One day she sent for me in much excitement, showed me some advertisements in the French journals which, though not naming her, evidently pointed at her, and must have been dictated by her *soi-disant* husband.   The advertisements might certainly lead to her discovery if she remained in Paris.   She entreated my consent to remove elsewhere.   Madame Marigny had her own reason for leaving Paris, and would accompany her.   I supplied her with the necessary means, and a day or two afterwards she and her friend departed, as I understood, for Brussels.   I received no letter from her; and my own affairs so seriously pre-occupied me, that poor Louise might have passed altogether out of my thoughts, had it not been for the suitor she had left in despair behind.   Louvier besought me to ascertain her address; but I could give him no other clue to it than that she said she was going to Brussels, but should soon remove to some quiet village.   It was not for a long time—I can't remember how long—it might be several weeks, perhaps two or three months,— that I received a short note from her stating that she waited for a small remittance, the last she would accept from me, as she was resolved, so soon as her health would permit, to find means to maintain herself—and telling me to direct to her, *Poste restante*, Aix-la-Chapelle.   I sent her the sum she asked, perhaps a little more, but with a confession reluctantly wrung from me that I was a ruined man; and I urged her to think very seriously before she refused the competence and position which a union with M. Louvier would insure.

"This last consideration so pressed on me that, when Louvier called on me, I think that day or the next, I gave

him Louise's note, and told him that, if he were still as
much in love with her as ever, *les absens ont toujours tort,*
and he had better go to Aix-la-Chapelle and find her out;
that he had my hearty approval of his wooing, and consent
to his marriage, though I still urged the wisdom and fair-
ness, if she would take the preliminary step—which, after
all, the French law frees as much as possible from pain and
scandal—of annulling the irregular marriage into which
her childlike youth had been decoyed.

"Louvier left me for Aix-la-Chapelle. The very next
day came that cruel affliction which made me a prey to the
most intolerable calumny, which robbed me of every friend,
which sent me forth from my native country penniless, and
resolved to be nameless—until—until—well, until my hour
could come again—every dog, if not hanged, has its day;
—when that affliction befell me, I quitted France, heard
no more of Louvier nor of Louise; indeed, no letter addressed to me at Paris would have reached——"

The man paused here, evidently with painful emotion.
He resumed in the quiet matter-of-fact way in which he
had commenced his narrative.

"Louise had altogether faded out of my remembrance
until your question revived it. As it happened, the question came at the moment when I meditated resuming my
real name and social position. In so doing, I should of
course come in contact with my old acquaintance Louvier;
and the name of Louise was necessarily associated with us.
I called on him, and made myself known. The slight information I gave you as to my niece was gleaned from him.
I may now say more. It appears that when he arrived at
Aix-la-Chapelle he found that Louise Duval had left it a
day or two previously, and according to scandal had been
for some time courted by a wealthy and noble lover, whom
she had gone to Munich to meet. Louvier believed this
tale: quitted Aix indignantly, and never heard more of
her. The probability is, M. Vane, that she must have
been long dead. But if living still, I feel quite sure that

she will communicate with me some day or other. Now
that I have reappeared in Paris in my own name—entered
into a career that, for good or for evil, must ere long bring
my name very noisily before the public—Louise cannot fail
to hear of my existence and my whereabouts; and unless I
am utterly mistaken as to her character, she will assuredly
inform me of her own. Oblige me with your address, and
in that case I will let you know. Of course I take for
granted the assurance you gave me last year, that you only
desire to discover her in order to render her some benefit,
not to injure or molest her?"

"Certainly. To that assurance I pledge my honour.
Any letter with which you may favour me had better be
directed to my London address; here is my card. But, M.
le Vicomte, there is one point on which pray pardon me if
I question you still. Had you no suspicion that there was
one reason why this lady might have quitted Paris so hastily, and have so shrunk from the thought of a marriage so
advantageous, in a worldly point of view, as that with M.
Louvier,—namely, that she anticipated the probability of
becoming the mother of a child by the man whom she refused to acknowledge as a husband?"

" That idea did not strike me until you asked me if she had
a child. Should your conjecture be correct, it would obvi-
ously increase her repugnance to apply for the annulment
of her illegal marriage. But if Louise is still living and
comes across me, I do not doubt that, the motives for concealment no longer operating, she will confide to me the
truth. Since we have been talking together thus frankly,
I suppose I may fairly ask whether I do not guess correctly
in supposing that this *soi-disant* husband, whose name I
forget,—Mac——something, perhaps, Scotch—I think she
said he was *Ecossais*,—is dead and has left by will some
legacy to Louise and any child she may have borne to
him?"

"Not exactly so. The man, as you say, is dead; but he
bequeathed no legacy to the lady who did not hold herself

married to him.   But there are those connected with him
who, knowing the history, think that some compensation
is due for the wrong so unconsciously done to her, and yet
more to any issue of a marriage not meant to be irregular
or illegal.   Permit me now to explain why I sought you in
another guise and name than my own.   I could scarcely
place in M. Lebeau the confidence which I now unreservedly
place in the Vicomte de Mauléon."

"*Cela va sans dire*.   You believed, then, that calumny
about the jewels; you do not believe it now?"

"Now! my amazement is, that any one who had known
you could believe it."

"Oh, how often, and with tears of rage in my exile—my
wanderings—have I asked that question of myself!   That
rage has ceased; and I have but one feeling left for that
credulous, fickle Paris, of which one day I was the idol,
the next the byword.   Well, a man sometimes plays chess
more skilfully for having been long a mere bystander.   He
understands better how to move, and when to sacrifice the
pieces.   Politics, M. Vane, is the only exciting game left
to me at my years.   At yours, there is still that of love.
How time flies! we are nearing the station at which I descend.   I have kinsfolk of my mother's in these districts.
They are not Imperialists; they are said to be powerful in
the department.   But before I apply to them in my own
name, I think it prudent that M. Lebeau should quietly
ascertain what is their real strength, and what would be
the prospects of success if Victor de Mauléon offered himself as *député* at the next election.   Wish him joy, M.
Vane!   If he succeed, you will hear of him some day
crowned in the Capitol, or hurled from the Tarpeian rock."

Here the train stopped.   The false Lebeau gathered up
his papers, readjusted his spectacles and his bag, descended lightly, and, pressing Graham's hand as he paused
at the door, said, "Be sure I will not forget your address
if I have anything to say.   *Bon voyage!*"

CHAPTER VII.

GRAHAM continued his journey to Strasbourg. On arriving there he felt very unwell. Strong though his frame was, the anguish and self-struggle through which he had passed since the day he had received in London Mrs. Morley's letter, till that on which he had finally resolved on his course of conduct at Paris, and the shock which had annihilated his hopes in Isaura's rejection, had combined to exhaust its endurance, and fever had already commenced when he took his place in the *coupé*. If there be a thing which a man should not do when his system is undermined, and his pulse between 90 and 100, it is to travel all night by a railway express. Nevertheless, as the Englishman's will was yet stronger than his frame, he would not give himself more than an hour's rest, and again started for Berlin. Long before he got to Berlin, the will failed him as well as the frame. He was lifted out of the carriage, taken to a hotel in a small German town, and six hours afterwards he was delirious. It was fortunate for him that under such circumstances plenty of money and Scott's circular-notes for some hundreds were found in his pocket-book, so that he did not fail to receive attentive nursing and skilful medical treatment. There, for the present, I must leave him—leave him for how long? But any village apothecary could say that fever such as his must run its course. He was still in bed, and very dimly—and that but at times—conscious, when the German armies were gathering round the penfold of Sedan.

CHAPTER VIII.

WHEN the news of the disastrous day at Sedan reached Paris, the first effect was that of timid consternation. There were a few cries of *Déchéance!* fewer still of *Vive la*

République among the motley crowds; but they were faint, and chiefly by ragged *gamins*. A small body repaired to Trochu and offered him the sceptre, which he politely declined. A more important and respectable body—for it comprised the majority of the *Corps Législatif*—urged Palikao to accept the temporary dictatorship, which the War Minister declined with equal politeness. In both these overtures it was clear that the impulse of the proposers was towards any form of government rather than republican. The *sergens de ville* were sufficient that day to put down riot. They did make a charge on a mob, which immediately ran away.

The morning of that day the Council of Ten were summoned by Lebeau—*minus* only Rameau, who was still too unwell to attend, and the Belgian, not then at Paris; but their place was supplied by the two travelling members, who had been absent from the meeting before recorded. These were conspirators better known in history than those I have before described; professional conspirators—personages who from their youth upwards had done little else but conspire. Following the discreet plan pursued elsewhere throughout this humble work, I give their names other than they bore. One, a very swarthy and ill-favoured man, between forty and fifty, I call Paul Grimm—by origin a German, but by rearing and character French; from the hair on his head, staring up rough and ragged as a bramble-bush, to the soles of small narrow feet, shod with dainty care, he was a personal coxcomb, and spent all he could spare on his dress. A clever man, not ill-educated—a vehement and effective speaker at a club. Vanity and an amorous temperament had made him a conspirator, since he fancied he interested the ladies more in that capacity than any other. His companion, Edgar Ferrier, would have been a journalist, only hitherto his opinions had found no readers; the opinions were those of Marat. He rejoiced in thinking that his hour for glory, so long deferred, had now arrived. He was thoroughly sincere: his father and grandfather had died in a madhouse. Both these men, insignificant in ordinary times, were likely to become of terrible importance in the crisis of a revolution. They both had great power with the elements that form a Parisian mob. The instructions given to these members of the Council by Lebeau were brief: they were summed up in the one word, *Déchéance*. The formidable nature of a council apparently so meanly constituted became strikingly evident at that moment, because it was so small in number, while each one of these could put in movement a large section of the populace; secondly, because, unlike a revolutionary club or a numerous association, no time was wasted in idle speeches, and all were under the orders of one man of clear head and resolute purpose; and thirdly, and above all, because one man supplied the treasury, and money for an object desired was liberally given and promptly at hand. The meeting did not last ten minutes, and about two hours afterwards its effects were visible. From Montmartre and Belleville and Montretout poured streams of *ouvriers*, with whom Armand Monnier was a chief, and the *Médecin des Pauvres* an oracle. Grimm and Ferrier headed other detachments that startled the well-dressed idlers on the Boulevards. The stalwart figure of the Pole was seen on the Place de la Concorde, towering amidst other refugees, amid which glided the Italian champion of humanity. The cry of *Déchéance* became louder. But as yet there were only few cries of *Vive la République!*—such a cry was not on the orders issued by Lebeau. At midnight the crowd round the hall of the *Corps Législatif* is large: cries of *La Déchéance* loud—a few cries, very feeble, of *Vive la République!*

What followed on the 4th—the marvellous audacity with which half-a-dozen lawyers belonging to a pitiful minority in a Chamber elected by universal suffrage walked into the Hotel de Ville and said, "The Republic is established, and we are its Government," history has told too recently for me to narrate. On the evening of the 5th the Council of

Ten met again: the Pole; the Italian radiant; Grimm and
Ferrier much excited and rather drunk; the *Médecin des
Pauvres* thoughtful; and Armand Monnier gloomy. A
rumour has spread that General Trochu, in accepting the
charge imposed on him, has exacted from the Government
the solemn assurance of respect for God, and for the rights
of Family and Property. The Atheist is very indignant at
the assent of the Government to the first proposition; Monnier equal indignant at the assent to the second and third.
What has that honest *ouvrier* conspired for?—what has he
suffered for?—of late nearly starved for?—but to marry
another man's wife, getting rid of his own, and to legalise
a participation in the property of his employer,—and now
he is no better off than before. "There must be another
revolution," he whispers to the Atheist.

"Certainly," whispers back the Atheist; "he who desires
to better this world must destroy all belief in another."

The conclave was assembled when Lebeau entered by the
private door. He took his place at the head of the table;
and, fixing on the group eyes that emitted a cold gleam
through the spectacles, thus spoke:

"Messieurs, or Citoyens, which ye will—I no longer call
ye *confrères*—you have disobeyed or blundered my instructions. On such an occasion disobedience and blunder are
crimes equally heinous."

Angry murmurs.

"Silence! Do not add mutiny to your other offences.
My instructions were simple and short. Aid in the abolition of the Empire. Do not aid in any senseless cry for a
Republic or any other form of government. Leave that to
the Legislature. What have you done? You swelled the
crowd that invaded the *Corps Législatif.* You, Dombinsky,
not even a Frenchman, dare to mount the President's ros-
trum, and brawl forth your senseless jargon. You, Edgar
Ferrier, from whom I expected better, ascend the tribune,
and invite the ruffians in the crowd to march to the prisons
and release the convicts; and all of you swell the mob at

the Hotel de Ville, and inaugurate the reign of folly by creating an oligarchy of lawyers to resist the march of triumphal armies. Messieurs, I have done with you. You are summoned for the last time: the Council is dissolved."

With these words Lebeau put on his hat, and turned to depart. But the Pole, who was seated near him, sprang to his feet, exclaiming, 'Traitor, thou shalt not escape! Comrades, he wants to sell us!"

"I have a right to sell *you* at least, for I bought you, and a very bad bargain I made," said Lebeau, in a tone of withering sarcasm.

"Liar!" cried the Pole, and seized Lebeau by the left hand, while with the right he drew forth a revolver. Ferrier and Grimm, shouting, "*A bas le renégat!*" would have rushed forward in support of the Pole, but Monnier thrust himself between them and their intended victim, crying with a voice that dominated their yell, "Back!—we are not assassins." Before he had finished the sentence the Pole was on his knees. With a vigour which no one could have expected from the seeming sexagenarian, Lebeau had caught the right arm of his assailant, twisted it back so mercilessly as almost to dislocate elbow and shoulder joint. One barrel of the revolver discharged itself harmlessly against the opposite wall, and the pistol itself then fell from the unnerved hand of the would-be assassin; and what with the pain and the sudden shock, the stalwart Dombinsky fell in the attitude of a suppliant at the feet of his unlooked-for vanquisher.

Lebeau released his hold, possessed himself of the pistol, pointing the barrels towards Edgar Ferrier, who stood with mouth agape and lifted arm arrested, and said quietly: "Monsieur, have the goodness to open that window." Ferrier mechanically obeyed. "Now, hireling," continued Lebeau, addressing the vanquished Pole, "choose between the door and the window." "Go, my friend," whispered the Italian. The Pole did not utter a word; but rising nimbly, and rubbing his arm, stalked to the door. There he paused a moment and said, "I retire overpowered by numbers," and vanished.

"Messieurs," resumed Lebeau, calmly, "I repeat that the Council is dissolved. In fact its object is fulfilled more abruptly than any of us foresaw, and by means which I at least had been too long out of Paris to divine as possible. I now see that every aberration of reason is possible to the Parisians. The object that united us was the fall of the Empire. As I have always frankly told you, with that object achieved, separation commences. Each of us has his own crotchet, which differs from the other man's. Pursue yours as you will—I pursue mine—you will find Jean Lebeau no more in Paris: *il s'efface. Au plaisir, mais pas au revoir.*"

He retreated to the masked door and disappeared.

Marc le Roux, the porter or custos of that ruinous council-hall, alarmed at the explosion of the pistol, had hurried into the room, and now stood unheeded by the door with mouth agape, while Lebeau thus curtly dissolved the assembly. But when the president vanished through the secret doorway, Le Roux also retreated. Hastily descending the stairs, he made as quickly as his legs could carry him for the mouth of the alley in the rear of the house, through which he knew that Lebeau must pass. He arrived, panting and breathless, in time to catch hold of the ex-president's arm. "Pardon, citizen," stammered he, "but do I understand that you have sent the Council of Ten to the devil?"

"I? Certainly not, my good Paul; I dismiss them to go where they like. If they prefer the direction you name, it is their own choice. I declined to accompany them, and I advise you not to do so."

"But, citizen, have you considered what is to become of Madame? Is she to be turned out of the lodge? Are my wages to stop, and Madame to be left without a crust to put into her soup?"

"Not so bad as that; I have just paid the rent of the

baraque for three months in advance, and there is your quarter's pay, in advance also. My kind regards to Madame, and tell her to keep your skin safe from the schemes of these lunatics." Thrusting some pieces of gold into the hands of the porter, Lebeau nodded his adieu, and hastened along his way.

Absorbed in his own reflections, he did not turn to look behind. But if he had, he could not have detected the dark form of the porter, creeping in the deep shadow of the streets with distant but watchful footsteps.

CHAPTER IX.

THE conspirators, when left by their president, dispersed in deep, not noisy resentment. They were indeed too stunned for loud demonstration; and belonging to different grades of life, and entertaining different opinions, their confidence in each other seemed lost now that the chief who had brought and kept them together was withdrawn from their union. The Italian and the Atheist slank away, whispering to each other. Grimm reproached Ferrier for deserting Dombinsky and obeying Lebeau. Ferrier accused Grimm of his German origin, and hinted at denouncing him as a Prussian spy. Gaspard le Noy linked his arm in Monnier's, and when they had gained the dark street without, leading into a labyrinth of desolate lanes, the *Médicin des Pauvres* said to the mechanic: "You are a brave fellow, Monnier. Lebeau owes you a good turn. But for your cry, 'We are not assassins,' the Pole might not have been left without support. No atmosphere is so infectious as that in which we breathe the same air of revenge: when the violence of one man puts into action the anger or suspicion of others, they become like a pack of hounds, which follow the spring of the first hound, whether

on the wild boar or their own master. Even I, who am by
no means hot-headed, had my hand on my case-knife when
the word 'assassin' rebuked and disarmed me."

"Nevertheless," said Monnier, gloomily, "I half repent
the impulse which made me interfere to save that man.
Better he should die than live to betray the cause we
allowed him to lead."

"Nay, *mon ami*, speaking candidly, we must confess that
he never from the first pretended to advocate the cause for
which you conspired. On the contrary, he always said that
with the fall of the Empire our union would cease, and each
become free to choose his own way towards his own after-
objects."

"Yes," answered Armand, reluctantly; "he said that to
me privately, with still greater plainness than he said it to
the Council. But I answered as plainly."

"How?"

"I told him that the man who takes the first step in a
revolution, and persuades others to go along with him, cannot in safety stand still or retreat when the next step is to
be taken. It is '*en avant*' or '*à la lanterne.*' So it shall be
with him. Shall a fellow-being avail himself of the power
over my mind which he derives from superior education or
experience,—break into wild fragments my life, heretofore
tranquil, orderly, happy,—make use of my opinions, which
were then but harmless desires, to serve his own purpose,
which was hostile to the opinions he roused into action,—
say to me, 'Give yourself up to destroy the first obstacle in
the way of securing a form of society which your inclina-
tions prefer,' and then, that first obstacle destroyed, cry,
'Halt! I go with you no further; I will not help you to
piece together the life I have induced you to shatter; I will
not aid you to susbtitute for the society that pained you
the society that would please; I leave you, struggling, bewildered, maddened, in the midst of chaos within and without you'? Shall a fellow-being do this, and vanish with a
mocking cry: 'Tool! I have had enough of thee; I cast thee

aside as worthless lumber'? Ah! let him beware! The tool is of iron, and can be shaped to edge and point."

The passion with which this rough eloquence was uttered, and the fierce sinister expression that had come over a countenance habitually open and manly, even when grave and stern, alarmed and startled Le Noy. "Pooh, my friend!" he said, rather falteringly, "you are too excited now to think justly. Go home and kiss your children. Never do anything that may make them shrink from their father. And as to Lebeau, try and forget him. He says he shall disappear from Paris. I believe him. It is clear to me that the man is not what he seemed to us. No man of sixty could by so easy a sleight of hand have brought that giant Pole to his knee. If Lebeau reappear it will be in some other form. Did you notice that in the momentary struggle his flaxen wig got disturbed, and beneath it I saw a dark curl. I suspect that the man is not only younger than he seemed, but of higher rank—a conspirator against one throne, perhaps, in order to be minister under another. There are such men."

Before Monnier, who seemed struck by these conjectures, collected his thoughts to answer, a tall man in the dress of a *sous lieutenant* stopped under a dim gas-lamp, and, catching sight of the artisan's face, seized him by the hand, exclaiming, "Armand, *mon frère!* well met; strange times, eh? Come and discuss them at the *Café de Lyon* yonder over a bowl of punch. I'll stand treat."

"Agreed, dear Charles."

"And if this monsieur is a friend of yours, perhaps he will join us."

"You are too obliging, Monsieur," answered Le Noy, not ill-pleased to get rid of his excited companion; "but it has been a busy day with me, and I am only fit for bed. Be abstinent of the punch, Armand. You are feverish already. Good-night, Messieurs."

The *Café de Lyon*, in vogue among the National Guard of the *quartier*, was but a few yards off, and the brothers turned towards it arm in arm. "Who is the friend?" asked Charles; "I don't remember to have seen him with thee before."

"He belongs to the medical craft—a good patriot and a kind man—attends the poor gratuitously. Yes, Charles, these are strange times; what dost thou think will come of them?"

They had now entered the *café;* and Charles had ordered the punch, and seated himself at a vacant table before he replied. "What will come of these times? I will tell thee. National deliverance and regeneration through the ascendency of the National Guard."

"Eh? I don't take," said Armand, bewildered.

"Probably not," answered Charles, with an air of compassionate conceit; "thou art a dreamer, but I am a politician." He tapped his forehead significantly. "At this custom-house, ideas are examined before they are passed."

Armand gazed at his brother wistfully, and with a deference he rarely manifested towards any one who disputed his own claims to superior intelligence. Charles was a few years older than Monnier; he was of large build; he had shaggy lowering eyebrows, a long obstinate upper lip, the face of a man who was accustomed to lay down the law. Inordinate self-esteem often gives that character to a physiognomy otherwise commonplace. Charles passed for a deep thinker in his own set, which was a very different set from Armand's—not among workmen but small shopkeepers. He had risen in life to a grade beyond Armand's; he had always looked to the main chance, married the widow of a hosier and glover much older than himself, and in her right was a very respectable tradesman, comfortably well off; a Liberal, of course, but a Liberal *bourgeois*, equally against those above him and those below. Needless to add that he had no sympathy with his brother's socialistic opinions. Still he loved that brother as well as he could love any one except himself. And Armand, who was very affectionate, and with whom family ties were very strong, returned that

love with ample interest; and though so fiercely at war with
the class to which Charles belonged, was secretly proud of
having a brother who was of that class. So in England I
have known the most violent antagonist of the landed aristocracy—himself a cobbler—who interrupts a discourse on
the crimes of the aristocracy by saying, "Though I myself
descend from a county family."

In an evil day Charles Monnier, enrolled in the National
Guard, had received promotion in that patriotic corps.
From that date he began to neglect his shop, to criticise
military matters, and to think that if merit had fair play
he should be a Cincinnatus or a Washington, he had not
decided which.

"Yes," resumed Charles, ladling out the punch, "thou
hast wit enough to perceive that our generals are imbeciles
or traitors; that *gredin* Bonaparte has sold the army for
ten millions of francs to Bismarck, and I have no doubt that
Wimpffen has his share of the bargain. McMahon was
wounded conveniently, and has his own terms for it. The
regular army is nowhere. Thou wilt see—thou wilt see—
they will not stop the march of the Prussians. Trochu
will be obliged to come to the National Guard. Then we
shall say, 'General, give us our terms, and go to sleep.'
I shall be summoned to the council of war. I have my
plan. I explain it—'tis accepted—it succeeds. I am
placed in supreme command—the Prussians are chased
back to their sour-krout. And I—well—I don't like to
boast, but thou'lt see—thou'lt see—what will happen."

"And thy plan, Charles—thou hast formed it already?"

"Ay, ay,—the really military genius is prompt, *mon
petit* Armand—a flash of the brain. Hark ye! Let the
Vandals come to Paris and invest it. Whatever their numbers on paper, I don't care a button; they can only have a
few thousands at any given point in the vast circumference
of the capital. Any fool must grant that—thou must grant
it, eh?"

"It seems just."

"Of course. Well, then, we proceed by sorties of 200,000 men repeated every other day, and in twelve days the Prussians are in full flight.[1] The country rises on their flight— they are cut to pieces. I depose Trochu—the National Guard elects the Saviour of France. I have a place in my eye for thee. Thou art superb as a decorator—thou shalt be Minister *des Beaux Arts*. But keep clear of the *canaille*. No more strikes then—thou wilt be an employer—respect thy future order."

Armand smiled mournfully. Though of intellect which, had it been disciplined, was far superior to his brother's, it was so estranged from practical opinions, so warped, so heated, so flawed and cracked in parts, that he did not see the ridicule of Charles's braggadocio. Charles had succeeded in life, Armand had failed; and Armand believed in the worldly wisdom of the elder born. But he was far too sincere for any bribe to tempt him to forsake his creed and betray his opinions. And he knew that it must be a very different revolution from that which his brother contemplated, that could allow him to marry another man's wife, and his "order" to confiscate other people's property.

"Don't talk of strikes, Charles. What is done is done. I was led into heading a strike, not on my own account, for I was well paid and well off, but for the sake of my fellow-workmen. I may regret now what I did, for the sake of Marie and the little ones. But it is an affair of honour, and I cannot withdraw from the cause till my order, as thou namest my class, has its rights."

"Bah! thou wilt think better of it when thou art an em-

---

[1] Charles Monnier seems to have indiscreetly blabbed out his "idea," for it was plagiarised afterwards at a meeting of the National Guards in the Salle de la Bourse by Citizen Rochebrune (slain 19th January, 1871, in the affair of Montretout). The plan, which he developed nearly in the same words as Charles Monnier, was received with lively applause; and at the close of his speech it was proposed to name at once Citizen Rochebrune General of the National Guard, an honour which, unhappily for his country, the citizen had the modesty to decline.

ployer. Thou hast suffered enough already. Remember
that I warned thee against that old fellow in spectacles
whom I met once at thy house. I told thee he would lead
thee into mischief, and then leave thee to get out of it. I
saw through him. I have a head! *Va!*"

"Thou wert a true prophet—he has duped me. But in
moving me he has set others in movement; and I suspect
he will find he has duped himself. Time will show."

Here the brothers were joined by some loungers belonging to the National Guard. The talk became general, the
potations large. Towards daybreak Armand reeled home,
drunk for the first time in his life. He was one of those
whom drink makes violent. Marie had been sitting up for
him, alarmed at his lengthened absence. But when she
would have thrown herself on his breast, her pale face and
her passionate sobs enraged him. He flung her aside roughly. From that night the man's nature was changed. If,
as a physiognomist has said, each man has in him a portion
of the wild beast, which is suppressed by mild civilising
circumstances, and comes uppermost when self-control is
lost, the nature of many an honest workman, humane and
tender-hearted as the best of us, commenced a change into
the wild beast that raged through the civil war of the
Communists, on the day when half-a-dozen Incapables,
with no more claim to represent the people of Paris than
half-a-dozen monkeys would have, were allowed to elect
themselves to supreme power, and in the very fact of that
election released all the elements of passion, and destroyed
all the bulwarks of order.

————————

CHAPTER X.

No man perhaps had more earnestly sought and more
passionately striven for the fall of the Empire than Victor
de Mauléon; and perhaps no man was more dissatisfied and

II.—10

disappointed by the immediate consequences of that fall. In first conspiring against the Empire, he had naturally enough, in common with all the more intelligent enemies of the dynasty, presumed that its fate would be worked out by the normal effect of civil causes—the alienation of the educated classes, the discontent of the artisans, the eloquence of the press and of popular meetings, strengthened in proportion as the Emperor had been compelled to relax the former checks upon the license of either. And De Mauléon had no less naturally concluded that there would be time given for the preparation of a legitimate and rational form of government to succeed that which was destroyed. For, as has been hinted or implied, this remarkable man was not merely an instigator of revolution through the Secret Council, and the turbulent agencies set in movement through the lower strata of society;—he was also in confidential communication with men eminent for wealth, station, and political repute, from whom he obtained the funds necessary for the darker purposes of conspiracy, into the elaboration of which they did not inquire; and these men, though belonging like himself to the Liberal party, were no hot-blooded democrats. Most of them were in favour of constitutional monarchy; all of them for forms of government very different from any republic in which socialists or communists could find themselves uppermost. Among these politicians were persons ambitious and able, who, in scheming for the fall of the Empire, had been prepared to undertake the task of conducting to ends compatible with modern civilisation the revolution they were willing to allow a mob at Paris to commence. The opening of the war necessarily suspended their designs. How completely the events of the 4th September mocked the calculations of their ablest minds, and paralysed the action of their most energetic spirits, will appear in the conversation I am about to record. It takes place between Victor de Mauléon and the personage to whom he had addressed the letter written on the night before the interview with Louvier, in which Victor had announced his intention of reappearing in Paris in his proper name and rank. I shall designate this correspondent as vaguely as possible; let me call him the Incognito. He may yet play so considerable a part in the history of France as a potent representative of the political philosophy of De Tocqueville—that is, of Liberal principles incompatible with the absolute power either of a sovereign or a populace, and resolutely opposed to experiments on the foundations of civilised society—that it would be unfair to himself and his partisans if, in a work like this, a word were said that could lead malignant conjecture to his identity with any special chief of the opinions of which I here present him only as a type.

The Incognito, entering Victor's apartment:

"My dear friend, even if I had not received your telegram, I should have hastened hither on the news of this astounding revolution. It is only in Paris that such a tragedy could be followed by such a farce. You were on the spot—a spectator. Explain it if you can."

DE MAULÉON.—"I was more than a spectator; I was an actor. Hiss me—I deserve it. When the terrible news from Sedan reached Paris, in the midst of the general stun and bewilderment I noticed a hesitating timidity among all those who had wares in their shops and a good coat on their backs. They feared that to proclaim the Empire defunct would be to install the Red Republic with all its paroxysm of impulsive rage and all its theories of wholesale confiscation. But since it was impossible for the object we had in view to let slip the occasion of deposing the dynasty which stood in its way, it was necessary to lose no time in using the revolutionary part of the populace for that purpose. I assisted in doing so; my excuse is this—that in a time of crisis a man of action must go straight to his immediate object, and in so doing employ the instruments at his command. I made, however, one error in judgment which admits no excuse: I relied on all I had heard, and all I had observed, of the character of Trochu, and I was deceived, in common, I believe, with all his admirers, and three parts of the educated classes of Paris."

INCOGNITO.—"I should have been equally deceived! Trochu's conduct is a riddle that I doubt if he himself can ever solve. He was master of the position; he had the military force in his hands if he combined with Palikao, which, whatever the jealousies between the two, it was his absolute duty to do. He had a great prestige——"

DE MAULEON.—"And for the moment a still greater popularity. His *ipse dixit* could have determined the wavering and confused spirits of the population. I was prepared for his abandonment of the Emperor—even of the Empress and the Regency. But how could I imagine that he, the man of moderate politics, of Orleanistic leanings, the clever writer, the fine talker, the chivalrous soldier, the religious Breton, could abandon everything that was legal, everything that could save France against the enemy, and Paris against civil discord; that he would connive at the annihilation of the Senate, of the popular Assembly, of every form of Government that could be recognised as legitimate at home or abroad, accept service under men whose doctrines were opposed to all his antecedents, all his professed opinions, and inaugurate a chaos under the name of a Republic!"

INCOGNITO.—"How, indeed? How suppose that the National Assembly, just elected by a majority of seven millions and a half, could be hurried into a conjuring-box, and reappear as the travesty of a Venetian oligarchy, composed of half-a-dozen of its most unpopular members! The sole excuse for Trochu is, that he deemed all other considerations insignificant compared with the defence of Paris, and the united action of the nation against the invaders. But if that were his honest desire in siding with this monstrous usurpation of power, he did everything by which the desire could be frustrated. Had there been any provisional body composed of men known and esteemed, elected by the Chambers, supported by Trochu and the troops at his back,

there would have been a rallying-point for the patriotism of
the provinces; and in the wise suspense of any constitution
to succeed that Government until the enemy were chased
from the field, all partisans—Imperialists, Legitimists, Orleanists, Republicans—would have equally adjourned their
differences. But a democratic Republic, proclaimed by a
Parisian mob for a nation in which sincere democratic Republicans are a handful, in contempt of an Assembly chosen
by the country at large; headed by men in whom the provinces have no trust, and for whom their own representa-
tives are violently cashiered;—can you conceive such a combination of wet blankets supplied by the irony of Fate for
the extinction of every spark of ardour in the population
from which armies are to be gathered in haste, at the beck
of usupers they distrust and despise? Paris has excelled
itself in folly. Hungering for peace, it proclaims a Government which has no legal power to treat for it. Shriek-
ing out for allies among the monarchies, it annihilates the
hope of obtaining them; its sole chance of escape from
siege, famine, and bombardment, is in the immediate and
impassioned sympathy of the provinces; and it revives all
the grudges which the provinces have long sullenly felt
against the domineering pretensions of the capital, and in-
vokes the rural populations, which comprise the pith and
sinew of armies, in the name of men whom I verily believe
they detest still more than they do the Prussians. Victor,
it is enough to make one despair of his country! All beyond the hour seems anarchy and ruin."

"Not so!" exclaimed De Mauléon. "Everything comes
to him who knows how to wait. The Empire is destroyed;
the usurpation that follows it has no roots. It will but
serve to expedite the establishment of such a condition as
we have meditated and planned—a constitution adapted to
our age and our people, not based wholly on untried experiments, taking the best from nations that do not allow Freedom and Order to be the sport of any popular breeze. From
the American Republic we must borrow the only safeguards

against the fickleness of the universal suffrage which,
though it was madness to concede in any ancient community, once conceded cannot be safely abolished,—viz., the
salutary law that no article of the Constitution, once settled,
can be altered without the consent of two-thirds of the legislative body.   By this law we insure permanence, and that
concomitant love for institutions which is engendered by time
and custom.   Secondly, the formation of a senate on such
principles as may secure to it in all times of danger a confidence and respect which counteract in public opinion the
rashness and heat of the popular assembly.   On what principles that senate should be formed, with what functions
invested, what share of the executive—especially in foreign
affairs, declarations of war, or treaties of peace—should be
accorded to it, will no doubt need the most deliberate care
of the ablest minds.   But a senate I thus sketch has alone
rescued America from the rashness of counsel incident to a
democratic Chamber; and it is still more essential to France,
with still more favourable elements for its creation.   From
England we must borrow the great principle that has alone
saved her from revolution—that the head of the State can
do no wrong.   He leads no armies, he presides over no
Cabinet.   All responsibility rests with his advisers; and
where we upset a dynasty, England changes an administration.   Whether the head of the State should have the title
of sovereign or president, whether he be hereditary or
elected, is a question of minor importance impossible now
to determine, but on which I heartily concur with you that
hereditary monarchy is infinitely better adapted to the
habits of Frenchmen, to their love of show and of honours—and infinitely more preservative from all the dangers
which result from constant elections to such a dignity, with
parties so heated, and pretenders to the rank so numerous—
than any principle by which a popular demagogue or a successful general is enabled to destroy the institutions he is
elected to guard.   On these fundamental doctrines for the
regeneration of France I think we are agreed.   And I believe

when the moment arrives to promulgate them, through an expounder of weight like yourself, they will rapidly commend themselves to the intellect of France. For they belong to common sense; and in the ultimate prevalence of common-sense I have a faith which I refuse to medievalists who would restore the right divine; and still more to fanatical quacks, who imagine that the worship of the Deity, the ties of family, and the rights of property are errors at variance with the progress of society. *Qui vivra, verra.*"

INCOGNITO.—"In the outlines of the policy you so ably enunciate I heartily concur. But if France is, I will not say to be regenerated, but to have fair play among the nations of Europe, I add one or two items to the programme. France must be saved from Paris, not by subterranean barracks and trains, the impotence of which we see to-day with a general in command of the military force, but by conceding to France its proportionate share of the power now monopolised by Paris. All this system of centralisation, equally tyrannical and corrupt, must be eradicated. Talk of examples from America, of which I know little—from England, of which I know much,—what can we more advantageously borrow from England than that diffusion of all her moral and social power which forbids the congestion of blood in one vital part? Decentralise! decentralise! decentralise! will be my incessant cry, if ever the time comes when my cry will be heard. France can never be a genuine France until Paris has no more influence over the destinies of France than London has over those of England. But on this theme I could go on till midnight. Now to the immediate point: what do you advise me to do in this crisis, and what do you propose to do yourself?"

De Mauléon put his hand to his brow, and remained a few moments silent and thoughtful. At last he looked up with that decided expression of face which was not the least among his many attributes for influence over those with whom he came into contact.

"For you, on whom so much of the future depends, my

advice is brief—have nothing to do with the present. All
who join this present mockery of a Government will share
the fall that attends it—a fall from which one or two of
their body may possibly recover by casting blame on their
confrères,—you never could. But it is not for you to oppose that Government with an enemy on its march to Paris.
You are not a soldier; military command is not in your
rôle. The issue of events is uncertain; but whatever it be,
the men in power cannot conduct a prosperous war nor obtain an honourable peace. Hereafter you may be the *Deus
ex machinâ.* No personage of that rank and with that mission appears till the end of the play: we are only in the
first act. Leave Paris at once, and abstain from all action."

INCOGNITO (dejectedly).—"I cannot deny the soundness
of your advice, though in accepting it I feel unutterably
saddened. Still you, the calmest and shrewdest observer
among my friends, think there is cause for hope, not despair. Victor, I have more than most men to make life
pleasant, but I would lay down life at this moment with
you. You know me well enough to be sure that I utter no
melodramatic fiction when I say that I love my country as a
young man loves the ideal of his dreams—with my whole
mind and heart and soul! and the thought that I cannot
now aid her in the hour of her mortal trial is—is——"

The man's voice broke down, and he turned aside, veil-
ing his face with a hand that trembled.

DE MAULEON.—"Courage—patience! All Frenchmen
have the first; set them an example they much need in the
second. I, too, love my country, though I owe to it little
enough, heaven knows. I suppose love of country is inherent in all who are not Internationalists. They profess only
to love humanity, by which, if they mean anything practical, they mean a rise in wages."

INCOGNITO (rousing himself, and with a half smile).—
"Always cynical, Victor—always belying yourself. But
now that you have advised my course, what will be your
own? Accompany me, and wait for better times."

"No, noble friend; our positions are different. Yours is made—mine yet to make. But for this war I think I could have secured a seat in the Chamber. As I wrote you, I found that my kinsfolk were of much influence in their department, and that my restitution to my social grade, and the repute I had made as an Orleanist, inclined them to forget my youthful errors and to assist my career. But the Chamber ceases to exist. My journal I shall drop. I cannot support the Government; it is not a moment to oppose it. My prudent course is silence."

INCOGNITO.—"But is not your journal essential to your support?"

DE MAULEON.—"Fortunately not. Its profits enabled me to lay by for the rainy day that has come; and having reimbursed you and all friends the sums necessary to start it, I stand clear of all debt, and, for my slender wants, a rich man. If I continued the journal I should be beggared; for there would be no readers to *Common Sense* in this interval of lunacy. Nevertheless, during this interval, I trust to other ways for winning a name that will open my rightful path of ambition whenever we again have a legislature in which *Common Sense* can be heard."

INCOGNITO.—"But how win that name, silenced as a writer?"

DE MAULEON.—"You forget that I have fought in Algeria. In a few days Paris will be in a state of siege; and then—and then," he added, and very quietly dilated on the renown of a patriot or the grave of a soldier.

"I envy you the chance of either," said the Incognito; and after a few more brief words he departed, his hat drawn over his brows, and entering a hired carriage which he had left at the corner of the quiet street, was consigned to the station du ——, just in time for the next train.

CHAPTER XI.

VICTOR dressed and went out. The streets were crowded. Workmen were everywhere employed in the childish operation of removing all insignia, and obliterating all names that showed where an Empire had existed. One greasy citizen, mounted on a ladder, was effacing the words "Boulevard Haussman," and substituting for Haussman, "Victor Hugo."

Suddenly De Mauléon came on a group of blouses, interspersed with women holding babies and ragged boys holding stones, collected round a well-dressed slender man, at whom they were hooting and gesticulating, with menaces of doing something much worse. By an easy effort of his strong frame the Vicomte pushed his way through the tormentors, and gave his arm to their intended victim.

"Monsieur, allow me to walk home with you."

Therewith the shrieks and shouts and gesticulations increased. "Another impertinent! Another traitor! Drown him! Drown them both! To the Seine! To the Seine!" A burly fellow rushed forward, and the rest made a plunging push. The outstretched arm of De Mauléon kept the ringleader at bay. "*Mes enfans*," cried Victor with a calm clear voice, "I am not an Imperialist. Many of you have read the articles signed Pierre Firmin, written against the tyrant Bonaparte when he was at the height of his power. I am Pierre Firmin—make way for me." Probably not one in the crowd had ever read a word written by Pierre Firmin, nor even heard of the name. But they did not like to own ignorance; and that burly fellow did not like to encounter that arm of iron which touched his throat. So he cried out, "Oh! if you are the great Pierre Firmin, that alters the case. Make way for the patriot Pierre!" "But," shrieked a virago, thrusting her baby into De Mauléon's face, "the other is the Imperialist, the

capitalist, the vile Duplessis. At least we will have him."
De Mauléon suddenly snatched the baby from her, and said,
with imperturbable good temper, "Exchange of prisoners.
I resign the man, and I keep the baby."

No one who does not know the humours of a Parisian
mob can comprehend the suddenness of popular change, or
the magical mastery over crowds which is effected by quiet
courage and a ready joke. The group was appeased at once.
Even the virago laughed; and when De Mauléon restored
the infant to her arms, with a gold piece thrust into its tiny
clasp, she eyed the gold, and cried, "God bless you, citizen!"
The two gentlemen made their way safely now.

"M. de Mauléon," said Duplessis, "I know not how to
thank you. Without your seasonable aid I should have
been in great danger of life; and—would you believe it?—
the woman who denounced and set the mob on me was one of
the objects of a charity which I weekly dispense to the poor."

"Of course I believe that. At the Red clubs no crime is
more denounced than that of charity. It is the 'fraud
against *Egalité*'—a vile trick of the capitalist to save to
himself the millions he ought to share with all by giving
a *sou* to one. Meanwhile, take my advice, M. Duplessis,
and quit Paris with your young daughter. This is no place
for rich Imperialists at present."

"I perceived that before to-day's adventure. I distrust
the looks of my very servants, and shall depart with Valérie
this evening for Bretagne."

"Ah! I heard from Louvier that you propose to pay off
his mortgage on Rochebriant, and make yourself sole proprietor of my young kinsman's property."

"I trust you only believe half what you hear. I mean
to save Rochebriant from Louvier, and consign it, free of
charge, to your kinsman, as the *dot* of his bride, my
daughter."

"I rejoice to learn such good news for the head of my
house. But Alain himself—is he not with the prisoners of
war?"

"No, thank heaven. He went forth an officer of a regiment of Parisian Mobiles—went full of sanguine confidence; he came back with his regiment in mournful despondency. The undiscipline of his regiment, of the Parisian Mobiles generally, appears incredible. Their insolent disobedience to their officers, their ribald scoffs at their general—oh, it is sickening to speak of it! Alain distinguished himself by repressing a mutiny and is honoured by a signal compliment from the commander in a letter of recommendation to Palikao. But Palikao is nobody now. Alain has already been sent into Bretagne, commissioned to assist in organising a corps of Mobiles in his neighbourhood. Trochu, as you know, is a Breton. Alain is confident of the good conduct of the Bretons. What will Louvier do? He is an arch Republican; is he pleased now he has got what he wanted?"

"I suppose he is pleased, for he is terribly frightened. Fright is one of the great enjoyments of a Parisian. Good day. Your path to your hotel is clear now. Remember me kindly to Alain."

De Mauléon continued his way through streets sometimes deserted, sometimes thronged. At the commencement of the Rue de Florentin he encountered the brothers Vandemar walking arm in arm.

"Ha, De Mauléon!" cried Enguerrand; "what is the last minute's news?"

"I can't guess. Nobody knows at Paris how soon one folly swallows up another. Saturn here is always devouring one or other of his children."

"They say that Vinoy, after a most masterly retreat, is almost at our gates with 80,000 men."

"And this day twelvemonth we may know what he does with them."

Here Raoul, who seemed absorbed in gloomy reflections, halted before the hotel in which the Contessa di Rimini lodged, and with a nod to his brother, and a polite, if not cordial salutation to Victor, entered the *porte cochère*.

"Your brother seems out of spirits,—a pleasing contrast to the uproarious mirth with which Parisians welcome the advance of calamity."

"Raoul, as you know, is deeply religious. He regards the defeat we have sustained, and the peril that threatens us, as the beginning of a divine chastisement, justly incurred by our sins—I mean, the sins of Paris. In vain my father reminds him of Voltaire's story, in which the ship goes down with a *fripon* on board. In order to punish the *fripon*, the honest folks are drowned."

"Is your father going to remain on board the ship, and share the fate of the other honest folks?"

"*Pas si bête.* He is off to Dieppe for sea-bathing. He says that Paris has grown so dirty since the 4th September, that it is only fit for the feet of the Unwashed. He wished my mother to accompany him; but she replies, 'No; there are already too many wounded not to need plenty of nurses.' She is assisting to inaugurate a society of ladies in aid of the *Sœurs de Charité*. Like Raoul, she is devout, but she has not his superstitions. Still his superstitions are the natural reaction of a singularly earnest and pure nature from the frivolity and corruption which, when kneaded well up together with a slice of sarcasm, Paris calls philosophy."

"And what, my dear Enguerrand, do you propose to do?"

"That depends on whether we are really besieged. If so, of course I become a soldier."

"I hope not a National Guard?"

"I care not in what name I fight, so that I fight for France."

As Enguerrand said these simple words, his whole countenance seemed changed. The crest rose; his eyes sparkled; the fair and delicate beauty which had made him the darling of women—the joyous sweetness of expression and dainty grace of high breeding which made him the most popular companion to men,—were exalted in a masculine nobleness of aspect, from which a painter might have taken hints for a study of the young Achilles separated for ever from effeminate companionship at the sight of the weapons of war. De Mauléon gazed on him admiringly. We have seen that he shared the sentiments uttered—had resolved on the same course of action. But it was with the tempered warmth of a man who seeks to divest his thoughts and his purpose of the ardour of romance, and who, in serving his country, calculates on the gains to his own ambition. Nevertheless he admired in Enguerrand the image of his own impulsive and fiery youth.

"And you, I presume," resumed Enguerrand, "will fight too, but rather with pen than with sword."

"Pens will now only be dipped in red ink, and common-sense never writes in that colour; as for the sword, I have passed the age of forty-five, at which military service halts. But if some experience in active service, some knowledge of the art by which soldiers are disciplined and led, will be deemed sufficient title to a post of command, however modest the grade be, I shall not be wanting among the defenders of Paris."

"My brave dear Vicomte, if you are past the age to serve, you are in the ripest age to command; and with the testimonials and the cross you won in Algeria, your application for employment will be received with gratitude by any general so able as Trochu."

"I don't know whether I shall apply to Trochu. I would rather be elected to command even by the Mobiles or the National Guard, of whom I have just spoken disparagingly; and no doubt both corps will soon claim and win the right to choose their officers. But if elected, no matter by whom, I shall make a preliminary condition; the men under me shall train, and drill, and obey,—soldiers of a very different kind from the youthful Pekins nourished on absinthe and self-conceit, and applauding that Bombastes Furioso, M. Hugo, when he assures the enemy that Paris will draw an idea from its scabbard. But here comes Savarin. *Bon jour*, my dear poet."

"Don't say good day. An evil day for journalists and

writers who do not out-Herod Blanqui and Pyat. I know not how I shall get bread and cheese. My poor suburban villa is to be pulled down by way of securing Paris; my journal will be suppressed by way of establishing the liberty of the press. It ventured to suggest that the people of France should have some choice in the form of their government."

"That was very indiscreet, my poor Savarin," said Victor; "I wonder your printing-office has not been pulled down. We are now at the moment when wise men hold their tongues."

"Perhaps so, M. de Mauléon. It might have been wiser for all of us, you as well as myself, if we had not allowed our tongues to be so free before this moment arrived. We live to learn; and if we ever have what may be called a passable government again, in which we may say pretty much what we like, there is one thing I will not do, I will not undermine that government without seeing a very clear way to the government that is to follow it. What say you, Pierre Firmin?"

"Frankly, I say that I deserve your rebuke," answered De Mauléon thoughtfully. "But, of course, you are going to take or send Madame Savarin out of Paris."

"Certainly. We have made a very pleasant party for our hegira this evening—among others the Morleys. Morley is terribly disgusted. A Red Republican slapped him on the shoulder and said, 'American, we have a republic as well as you.' 'Pretty much you know about republics,' growled Morley; 'a French republic is as much like ours as a baboon is like a man.' On which the Red roused the mob, who dragged the American off to the nearest station of the National Guard, where he was accused of being a Prussian spy. With some difficulty, and lots of brag about the sanctity of the stars and stripes, he escaped with a reprimand, and caution how to behave himself in future. So he quits a city in which there no longer exists freedom of speech. My wife hoped to induce Mademoiselle Cicogna to accompany us; I grieve to say she refuses. You know she is engaged in marriage to Gustave Rameau; and his mother dreads the effect that these Red Clubs and his own vanity may have upon his excitable temperament if the influence of Mademoiselle Cicogna be withdrawn."

"How could a creature so exquisite as Isaura Cicogna ever find fascination in Gustave Rameau!" exclaimed Enguerrand.

"A woman like her," answered De Mauléon, "always finds a fascination in self-sacrifice."

"I think you divine the truth," said Savarin, rather mournfully. "But I must bid you good-bye. May we live to shake hands *réunis sous des meilleurs auspices.*"

Here Savarin hurried off, and the other two men strolled into the Champs Elysées, which were crowded with loungers, gay and careless, as if there had been no disaster at Sedan, no overthrow of an Empire, no enemy on its road to Paris.

In fact the Parisians, at once the most incredulous and the most credulous of all populations, believed that the Prussians would never be so impertinent as to come in sight of the gates. Something would occur to stop them! The king had declared he did not war on Frenchmen, but on the Emperor: the Emperor gone, the war was over. A democratic republic was instituted. A horrible thing in its way, it is true; but how could the Pandour tyrant brave the infection of democratic doctrines among his own barbarian armies? Were not placards, addressed to our "German brethren," posted upon the walls of Paris, exhorting the Pandours to fraternise with their fellow-creatures? Was not Victor Hugo going to publish "a letter to the German people"? Had not Jules Favre graciously offered peace, with the assurance that "France would not cede a stone of her fortresses—an inch of her territory? She would pardon the invaders and not march upon Berlin!" To all these, and many more such incontestable proofs, that the idea of a siege was moonshine, did Enguerrand and Victor listen as they joined group after group of their fellow-countrymen : nor did Paris cease to harbour such pleasing illusions, amusing itself with piously laying crowns at the foot of the statue of Stras- bourg, swearing "they would be worthy of their Alsatian brethren," till on the 19th of September the last telegram was received, and Paris was cut off from the rest of the world by the iron line of the Prussian invaders. "Tran- quil and terrible," says Victor Hugo, "she awaits the in- vasion! A volcano needs no assistance."

CHAPTER XII.

WE left Graham Vane slowly recovering from the attack of fever which had arrested his journey to Berlin in quest of the Count von Rudesheim. He was, however, saved the prosecution of that journey, and his direction turned back to France by a German newspaper which informed him that the King of Prussia was at Rheims, and that the Count von Rudesheim was among the eminent personages gathered there around their sovereign. In conversing the same day with the kindly doctor who attended him, Gra- ham ascertained that this German noble held a high com- mand in the German armies, and bore a no less distin- guished reputation as a wise political counsellor than he had earned as a military chief. As soon as he was able to travel, and indeed before the good doctor sanctioned his departure, Graham took his way to Rheims, uncertain, however, whether the Count would still be found there. I spare the details of his journey, interesting as they were. On reaching the famous and, in the eyes of Legitimists, the sacred city, the Englishman had no difficulty in ascertaining the house, not far from the cathedral, in which the Count von Rudesheim had taken his temporary abode. Walking towards it from the small hotel in which he had been lucky enough to find a room disengaged—slowly, for he was still feeble—he was struck by the quiet conduct of the German soldiery, and, save in their appearance, the peaceful aspect of the streets. Indeed, there was an air of festive gaiety about the place, as in an English town in which some popular regiment is quartered. The German soldiers thronged the shops, buying largely; lounged into the *cafés;* here and there attempted flirtations with the *grisettes,* who laughed at their French and blushed at their compliments; and in their good-humoured, somewhat bashful cheeriness, there was no trace of the insolence of conquest.

But as Graham neared the precincts of the cathedral his ear caught a grave and solemn music, which he at first supposed to come from within the building. But as he paused and looked round, he saw a group of the German military, on whose stalwart forms and fair manly earnest faces the setting sun cast its calm lingering rays. They were chanting, in voices not loud but deep, Luther's majestic hymn *" Nun danket alle Gott."* The chant awed even the ragged beggar boys who had followed the Englishman, as they followed any stranger, would have followed King William himself, whining for alms. "What a type of the difference between the two nations!" thought Graham; "the Marseillaise, and Luther's Hymn!" While thus meditating and listening, a man in a general's uniform came slowly out of the cathedral, with his hands clasped behind his back, and his head bent slightly downwards. He, too, paused on hearing the hymn; then unclasped his hand and beckoned to one of the officers, to whom approaching he whispered a word or two, and passed on towards the Episcopal palace. The hymn hushed, and the singers quietly dispersed. Graham divined rightly that the general had thought a hymn thanking the God of battles might wound the feelings of the inhabitants of the vanquished city—not, however, that any of them were likely to understand the language in which the thanks were uttered. Graham followed the measured steps of the general, whose hands were again clasped behind his back—the musing habit of Von Moltke, as it had been of Napoleon the First.

Continuing his way, the Englishman soon reached the house in which the Count von Rudesheim was lodged, and, sending in his card, was admitted at once through an anteroom in which sate two young men, subaltern officers apparently employed in draughting maps, into the presence of the Count.

"Pardon me," said Graham, after the first conventional salutation, "if I interrupt you for a moment or so in the midst of events so grave, on a matter that must seem to you very trivial."

"Nay," answered the Count, "there is nothing so trivial in this world but what there will be some one to whom it is important. Say how I can serve you."

"I think, M. le Comte, that you once received in your household, as teacher or governess, a French lady, Madame Marigny."

"Yes, I remember her well—a very handsome woman. My wife and daughter took great interest in her. She was married out of my house."

"Exactly—and to whom?"

"An Italian of good birth, who was then employed by the Austrian Government in some minor post, and subsequently promoted to a better one in the Italian dominion, which then belonged to the house of Hapsburg, after which we lost sight of him and his wife."

"An Italian—what was his name?"

"Ludovico Cicogna."

"Cicogna!" exclaimed Graham, turning very pale. "Are you sure that was the name?"

"Certainly. He was a cadet of a very noble house, and disowned by relations too patriotic to forgive him for accepting employment under the Austrian Government."

"Can you not give me the address of the place in Italy to which he was transferred on leaving Austria?"

"No; but if the information be necessary to you, it can

be obtained easily at Milan, where the head of the family resides, or indeed in Vienna, through any ministerial bureau."

"Pardon me one or two questions more. Had Madame Marigny any children by a former husband?"

"Not that I know of: I never heard so. Signor Cicogna was a widower, and had, if I remember right, children by his first wife, who was also a Frenchwoman. Before he obtained office in Austria, he resided, I believe, in France. I do not remember how many children he had by his first wife. I never saw them. Our acquaintance began at the baths of Töplitz, where he saw and fell violently in love with Madame Marigny. After their marriage, they went to his post, which was somewhere, I think, in the Tyrol. We saw no more of them; but my wife and daughter kept up a correspondence with the Signora Cicogna for a short time. It ceased altogether when she removed into Italy."

"You do not even know if the Signora is still living?"

"No."

"Her husband, I am told, is dead."

"Indeed! I am concerned to hear it. A good-looking, lively, clever man. I fear he must have lost all income when the Austrian dominions passed to the house of Savoy."

"Many thanks for your information. I can detain you no longer," said Graham, rising.

"Nay, I am not very busy at this moment; but I fear we Germans have plenty of work on our hands."

"I had hoped that, now the French Emperor, against whom your king made war, was set aside, his Prussian majesty would make peace with the French people."

"Most willingly would he do so if the French people would let him. But it must be through a French Government legally chosen by the people. And they have chosen none! A mob at Paris sets up a provisional administration, that commences by declaring that it will not give up 'an inch of its territory nor a stone of its fortresses.' No terms of peace can be made with such men holding such talk." After a few words more over the state of public affairs,—in which Graham expressed the English side of affairs, which was all for generosity to the vanquished; and the Count argued much more ably on the German, which was all for security against the aggressions of a people that would not admit itself to be vanquished,—the short interview closed.

As Graham at night pursued his journey to Vienna, there came into his mind Isaura's song of the Neapolitan fisherman. Had he, too, been blind to the image on the rock? Was it possible that all the while he had been resisting the impulse of his heart, until the discharge of the mission intrusted to him freed his choice and decided his fortunes, the very person of whom he was in search had been before him, then to be for ever won, lost to him now for ever? Could Isaura Cicogna be the child of Louise Duval by Richard King? She could not have been her child by Cicogna: the dates forbade that hypothesis. Isaura must have been five years old when Louise married the Italian.

Arrived at Milan, Graham quickly ascertained that the post to which Ludovico Cicogna had been removed was in Verona, and that he had there died eight years ago. Nothing was to be learned as to his family or his circumstances at the time of his death. The people of whose history we know the least are the relations we refuse to acknowledge. Graham continued his journey to Verona. There he found on inquiry that the Cicognas had occupied an apartment in a house which stood at the outskirts of the town and had been since pulled down to make way for some public improvements. But his closest inquiries could gain him no satisfactory answers to the all-important questions as to Ludovico Cicogna's family. His political alienation from the Italian cause, which was nowhere more ardently espoused than at Verona, had rendered him very unpopular. He visited at no Italian houses. Such society as he had was confined to the Austrian military within the Quadrilateral or at Venice, to which city he made frequent ex-

cursions: was said to lead there a free and gay life, very
displeasing to the Signora, whom he left in Verona.   She
was but little seen, and faintly remembered as very handsome and proud-looking.   Yes, there were children—a girl,
and a boy several years younger than the girl; but whether
she was the child of the Signora by a former marriage, or
whether the Signora was only the child's stepmother, no
one could say.   The usual clue, in such doubtful matters
obtainable through servants, was here missing.   The Cicognas had only kept two servants, and both were Austrian
subjects, who had long left the country,—their very names
forgotten.

Graham now called to mind the Englishman Selby, for
whom Isaura had such grateful affection, as supplying to
her the place of her father.   This must have been the Englishman whom Louise Duval had married after Cicogna's
death.   It would be no difficult task, surely, to ascertain
where he had resided.   Easy enough to ascertain all that
Graham wanted to know from Isaura herself, if a letter
could reach her.   But, as he knew by the journals, Paris
was now invested—cut off from all communication with the
world beyond.   Too irritable, anxious, and impatient to
wait for the close of the siege, though he never suspected
it could last so long as it did, he hastened to Venice, and
there learned through the British consul that the late Mr.
Selby was a learned antiquarian, an accomplished general
scholar, a *fanatico* in music, a man of gentle temper though
reserved manners; had at one time lived much at Venice:
after his marriage with the Signora Cicogna he had taken
up his abode near Florence.   To Florence Graham now
went.   He found the villa on the skirts of Fiesole at which
Mr. Selby had resided.   The peasant who had officiated as
gardener and shareholder in the profits of vines and figs,
was still, with his wife, living on the place.   Both man
and wife remembered the *Inglese* well; spoke of him with
great affection, of his wife with great dislike.   They said
her manners were very haughty, her temper very violent;

that she led the *Inglese* a very unhappy life; that there
were a girl and a boy, both hers by a former marriage; but
when closely questioned whether they were sure that the
girl was the Signora's child by the former husband, or
whether she was not the child of that husband by a former
wife, they could not tell; they could only say that both
were called by the same name—Cicogna; that the boy was
the Signora's favourite—that indeed she seemed wrapt up
in him; that he died of a rapid decline a few months after
Mr. Selby had hired the place, and that shortly after his
death the Signora left the place and never returned to it;
that it was little more than a year that she had lived with
her husband before this final separation took place. The
girl remained with Mr. Selby, who cherished and loved her
as his own child. Her Christian name was Isaura, the
boy's Luigi. A few years later, Mr. Selby left the villa
and went to Naples, where they heard he had died. They
could give no information as to what had become of his
wife. Since the death of her boy that lady had become
very much changed—her spirits quite broken, no longer
violent. She would sit alone and weep bitterly. The only
person out of her family she would receive was the priest;
till the boy's death she had never seen the priest, nor been
known to attend divine service.

"Was the priest living?"

"Oh, no; he had been dead two years. A most excellent man—a saint," said the peasant's wife.

"Good priests are like good women," said the peasant,
drily; "there are plenty of them, but they are all under-
ground."

On which remark the wife tried to box his ears. The
contadino had become a freethinker since the accession of
the house of Savoy. His wife remained a good Catholic.

Said the peasant as, escaping from his wife, he walked
into the high-road with Graham, "My belief, *Eccellenza*,
is, that the priest did all the mischief."

"What mischief?"

"Persuaded the Signora to leave her husband. The *Inglese* was not a Catholic. I heard the priest call him a heretic. And the *padre*, who, though not so bad as some of his cloth, was a meddling bigot, thought it perhaps best for her soul that it should part company with a heretic's person. I can't say for sure, but I think that was it. The *padre* seemed to triumph when the Signora was gone."

Graham mused. The peasant's supposition was not improbable. A woman such as Louise Duval appeared to be— of vehement passions and ill-regulated mind—was just one of those who, in a moment of great sorrow, and estranged from the ordinary household affections, feel, though but imperfectly, the necessity of a religion, and, ever in extremes, pass at once from indifferentism into superstition.

Arrived at Naples, Graham heard little of Selby except as a literary recluse, whose only distraction from books was the operatic stage. But he heard much of Isaura; of the kindness which Madame de Grantmesnil had shown to her, when left by Selby's death alone in the world; of the interest which the friendship and the warm eulogies of one so eminent as the great French writer had created for Isaura in the artistic circles; of the intense sensation her appearance, her voice, her universal genius, had made in that society, and the brilliant hopes of her subsequent career on the stage the *cognoscenti* had formed. No one knew anything of her mother; no one entertained a doubt that Isaura was by birth a Cicogna. Graham could not learn the present whereabouts of Madame de Grantmesnil. She had long left Naples, and had been last heard of at Genoa; was supposed to have returned to France a little before the war. In France she had no fixed residence.

The simplest mode of obtaining authentic information whether Isaura was the daughter of Ludovico Cicogna by his first wife—namely, by registration of her birth—failed him; because, as von Rudesheim had said, his first wife was a Frenchwoman. The children had been born some-

where in France, no one could even guess where. No one
had ever seen the first wife, who had never appeared in
Italy, nor had even heard what was her maiden name.

Graham, meanwhile, was not aware that Isaura was still
in the besieged city, whether or not already married to
Gustave Rameau; so large a number of the women had
quitted Paris before the siege began, that he had reason to
hope she was among them. He heard through an American that the Morleys had gone to England before the Prussian investment; perhaps Isaura had gone with them. He
wrote to Mrs. Morley, inclosing his letter to the Minister
of the United States at the Court of St. James's, and while
still at Naples received her answer. It was short, and
malignantly bitter. "Both myself and Madame Savarin,
backed by Signora Venosta, earnestly entreated Mademoiselle Cicogna to quit Paris, to accompany us to England.
Her devotion to her affianced husband would not permit her
to listen to us. It is only an Englishman who could suppose
Isaura Cicogna to be one of those women who do not insist
on sharing the perils of those they love. You ask whether
she was the daughter of Ludovico Cicogna by his former
marriage, or of his second wife by him. I cannot answer.
I don't even know whether Signor Cicogna ever had a former wife. Isaura Cicogna never spoke to me of her parents. Permit me to ask what business is it of yours now?
Is it the English pride that makes you wish to learn whether
on both sides she is of noble family? How can that discovery alter your relations towards the affianced bride of
another?"

On receipt of this letter, Graham quitted Naples, and
shortly afterwards found himself at Versailles. He obtained permission to establish himself there, though the
English were by no means popular. Thus near to Isaura,
thus sternly separated from her, Graham awaited the close
of the siege. Few among those at Versailles believed that
the Parisians would endure it much longer. Surely they
would capitulate before the bombardment, which the Ger-

mans themselves disliked to contemplate as a last resource, could commence.

In his own mind Graham was convinced that Isaura was the child of Richard King. It seemed to him probable that Louise Duval, unable to assign any real name to the daughter of the marriage she disowned,—neither the name borne by the repudiated husband, nor her own maiden name,—would, on taking her daughter to her new home, have induced Cicogna to give the child his name, or that after Cicogna's death she herself had so designated the girl. A dispassionate confidant, could Graham have admitted any confidant whatever, might have suggested the more than equal probability that Isaura was Cicogna's daughter by his former espousal. But then what could have become of Richard King's child? To part with the fortune in his hands, to relinquish all the ambitious dreams which belonged to it, cost Graham Vane no pang: but he writhed with indignant grief when he thought that the wealth of Richard King's heiress was to pass to the hands of Gustave Rameau,—that this was to be the end of his researches— this the result of the sacrifice his sense of honour imposed on him. And now that there was the probability that he must convey to Isaura this large inheritance, the practical difficulty of inventing some reason for such a donation, which he had, while at a distance made light of, became seriously apparent. How could he say to Isaura that he had 200,000l. in trust for her, without naming any one so devising it? Still more, how constitute himself her guardian, so as to secure it to herself, independently of her husband? Perhaps Isaura was too infatuated with Rameau, or too romantically unselfish, to permit the fortune so mysteriously conveyed being exclusively appropriated to herself. And if she were already married to Rameau, and if he were armed with the right to inquire into the source of this fortune, how exposed to the risks of disclosure would become the secret Graham sought to conceal. Such a secret affecting the memory of the sacred dead, affixing a shame on the scutcheon of the living, in the irreverent hands of a Gustave Rameau,—it was too dreadful to contemplate such a hazard. And yet, if Isaura were the missing heiress, could Graham Vane admit any excuse for basely withholding from her, for coolly retaining to himself the wealth for which he was responsible? Yet, torturing as were these communings with himself, they were mild in their torture compared to the ever-growing anguish of the thought that in any case the only woman he had ever loved—ever could love,—who might but for his own scruples and prejudices have been the partner of his life, was perhaps now actually the wife of another, and, as such, in what terrible danger! Famine within the walls of the doomed city: without, the engines of death waiting for a signal. So near to her, and yet so far! So willing to die for her, if for her he could not live: and with all his devotion, all his intellect, all his wealth, so powerless!

CHAPTER XIII.

It is now the middle of November—a Sunday. The day has been mild, and is drawing towards its close. The Parisians have been enjoying the sunshine. Under the leafless trees in the public gardens and the Champs Elysées children have been at play. On the Boulevards the old elegance of gaiety is succeeded by a livelier animation. Itinerant musicians gather round them ragged groups. Fortune-tellers are in great request, especially among the once brilliant Laises and Thaises, now looking more shabby, to whom they predict the speedy restoration of Nabobs and Russians, and golden joys. Yonder Punch is achieving a victory over the Evil One, who wears the Prussian spiked helmet, and whose face has been recently beautified into a resemblance to Bismarck. Punch draws to his show a laughing audience of *Moblots* and recruits to the new companies of the National Guard. Members of the once for-

midable police, now threadbare and hunger-pinched, stand
side by side with unfortunate beggars and sinister-looking
patriots who have served their time in the jails or galleys.

Uniforms of all variety are conspicuous—the only evidence visible of an enemy at the walls. But the aspects of
the wearers of warlike accoutrements are *débonnaire* and
smiling, as of revellers on a holiday of peace. Among
these defenders of their country, at the door of a crowded
café, stands Frederic Lemercier, superb in the costume,
bran-new, of a National Guard,—his dog Fox tranquilly
reposing on its haunches, with eyes fixed upon its fellow-
dog philosophically musing on the edge of Punch's show,
whose master is engaged in the conquest of the Bismarck
fiend.

"Lemercier," cried the Vicomte de Brézé, approaching
the *café*, "I scarcely recognise you in that martial guise.
You look *magnifique*—the *galons* become you. *Peste!* an
officer already?"

"The National Guards and Mobiles are permitted to
choose their own officers, as you are aware. I have been
elected, but to subaltern grade, by the warlike patriots of
my department. Enguerrand de Vandemar is elected a
captain of the Mobiles in his, and Victor de Mauléon is
appointed to the command of a battalion of the National
Guards. But I soar above jealousy at such a moment,—

"'Rome a choisi mon bras ; je n'examine rien.'"

"You have no right to be jealous. De Mauléon has had
experience and won distinction in actual service, and from
all I hear is doing wonders with his men—has got them
not only to keep but to love drill. I heard no less an authority than General V—— say that if all the officers of
the National Guard were like De Mauléon, that body would
give an example of discipline to the line."

"I say nothing as to the promotion of a real soldier like
the Vicomte—but a Parisian dandy like Enguerrand de Vandemar!"

"You forget that Enguerrand received a military education—an advantage denied to you."

"What does that matter? Who cares for education nowadays? Besides, have I not been training ever since the 4th of September, to say nothing of the hard work on the ramparts?"

"*Parlez moi de cela :* it is indeed hard work on the ramparts. *Infandum dolorem quorum pars magna fui.* Take the day duty. What with rising at seven o'clock, and being drilled between a middle-aged and corpulent grocer on one side and a meagre beardless barber's apprentice on the other; what with going to the bastions at eleven, and seeing half one's companions drunk before twelve; what with trying to keep their fists off one's face when one politely asks them not to call one's general a traitor or a poltroon,—the work of the ramparts would be insupportable, if I did not take a pack of cards with me, and enjoy a quiet rubber with three other heroes in some sequestered corner. As for night work, nothing short of the indomitable fortitude of a Parisian could sustain it; the tents made expressly not to be waterproof, like the groves of the Muses,—

"'per
Quos et aquæ subeant et auræ.'

A fellow-companion of mine tucks himself up on my rug, and pillows his head on my knapsack. I remonstrate—he swears—the other heroes wake up and threaten to thrash us both; and just when peace is made, and one hopes for a wink of sleep, a detachment of spectators, chiefly *gamins*, coming to see that all is safe in the camp, strike up the Marseillaise. Ah, the world will ring to the end of time with the sublime attitude of Paris in the face of the Vandal invaders, especially when it learns that the very shoes we stand in are made of cardboard. In vain we complain. The contractor for shoes is a staunch Republican, and jobs by right divine. May I ask if you have dined yet?"

"Heavens! no, it is too early. But I am excessively

hungry. I had only a quarter of jugged cat for breakfast, and the brute was tough. In reply to your question, may I put another: Did you lay in plenty of stores?"

"Stores? no; I am a bachelor, and rely on the stores of my married friends."

"Poor De Brézé! I sympathise with you, for I am in the same boat, and dinner invitations have become monstrous rare."

"Oh, but you are so confoundedly rich! What to you are forty francs for a rabbit, or eighty francs for a turkey?"

"Well, I suppose I am rich, but I have no money, and the ungrateful *restaurants* will not give me credit. They don't believe in better days."

"How can *you* want money?"

"Very naturally. I had invested my capital famously— the best speculations—partly in house rents, partly in company shares; and houses pay no rents, and nobody will buy company shares. I had 1,000 napoleons on hand, it is true, when Duplessis left Paris—much more, I thought, than I could possibly need, for I never believed in the siege. But during the first few weeks I played at whist with bad luck, and since then so many old friends have borrowed of me that I doubt if I have 200 francs left. I have despatched four letters to Duplessis by pigeon and balloon, entreating him to send me 25,000 francs by some trusty fellow who will pierce the Prussian lines. I have had two answers: 1st, that he will find a man; 2nd, that the man is found and on his way. Trust to that man, my dear friend, and meanwhile lend me 200 francs."

"*Mon cher, désolé* to refuse; but I was about to ask you to share your 200 francs with me who live chiefly by my pen; and that resource is cut off. Still, *il faut vivre*—one must dine."

"That is a fact, and we will dine together to-day at my expense; limited liability, though—eight francs a head."

"Generous Monsieur, I accept. Meanwhile let us take a turn towards the Madeleine."

The two Parisians quit the *café*, and proceed up the Boulevard. On their way they encounter Savarin. "Why," said De Brézé, "I thought you had left Paris with Madame."

"So I did, and deposited her safely with the Morleys at Boulogne. These kind Americans were going to England, and they took her with them. But *I* quit Paris! I! No: I am old; I am growing obese. I have always been short-sighted. I can neither wield a sword nor handle a musket. But Paris needs defenders; and every moment I was away from her I sighed to myself, '*Il faut être là!*' I returned before the Vandals had possessed themselves of our railways, the *convoi* overcrowded with men like myself, who had removed wives and families; and when we asked each other why we went back, every answer was the same, '*Il faut être là.*' No, poor child, no—I have nothing to give you."

These last words were addressed to a woman young and handsome, with a dress that a few weeks ago might have been admired for taste and elegance by the lady leaders of the *ton*, but was now darned, and dirty, and draggled.

"Monsieur, I did not stop you to ask for alms. You do not seem to remember me, M. Savarin."

"But I do," said Lemercier, "surely I address Mademoiselle Julie Caumartin."

"Ah, excuse me, *le petit* Frederic," said Julie with a sickly attempt at coquettish sprightliness; "I had no eyes except for M. Savarin."

"And why only for me, my poor child?" asked the kind-hearted author.

"Hush!" She drew him aside. "Because you can give me news of that monster Gustave. It is not true, it cannot be true, that he is going to be married?"

"Nay, surely, Mademoiselle, all connection between you and young Rameau has ceased for months—ceased from the date of that illness in July which nearly carried him off."

"I resigned him to the care of his mother," said the girl; "but when he no longer needs a mother, he belongs to me. Oh, consider, M. Savarin, for his sake I refused the most splendid offers! When he sought me, I had my *coupé*, my opera-box, my *cachemires*, my jewels. The Russians—the English—vied for my smiles. But I loved the man. I never loved before: I shall never love again; and after the sacrifices I have made for him, nothing shall induce me to give him up. Tell me, I entreat, my dear M. Savarin, where he is hiding. He has left the parental roof, and they refused there to give me his address."

"My poor girl, don't be *méchante*. It is quite true that Gustave Rameau is engaged to be married; and any attempt of yours to create scandal——"

"Monsieur," interrupted Julie, vehemently, "don't talk to me about scandal! The man is mine, and no one else shall have him. His address?"

"Mademoiselle," cried Savarin, angrily, "find it out for yourself." Then—repentant of rudeness to one so young and so desolate—he added, in mild expostulatory accents: "Come, come, *ma belle enfant*, be reasonable: Gustave is no loss. He is reduced to poverty."

"So much the better. When he was well off I never cost him more than a supper at the Maison Dorée; and if he is poor he shall marry me, and I will support him!"

"You!—and how?"

"By my profession when peace comes; and meanwhile I have offers from a *café* to recite warlike songs. Ah! you shake your head incredulously. The ballet-dancer recite verses? Yes! *he* taught me to recite his own *Soyez bon pour moi*. M. Savarin! do say where I can find *mon homme*."

"No."

"That is your last word?

"It is."

The girl drew her thin shawl round her and hurried off. Savarin rejoined his friends. "Is that the way you console yourself for the absence of Madame?" asked De Brézé, drily.

"Fie!" cried Savarin, indignantly; "such bad jokes are ill-timed. What strange mixtures of good and bad, of noble and base, every stratum of Paris life contains! There is that poor girl, in one way contemptible, no doubt, and yet in another way she has an element of grandeur. On the whole, at Paris, the women, with all their faults, are of finer mould than the men."

"French gallantry has always admitted that truth," said Lemercier. "Fox, Fox, Fox." Uttering this cry, he darted forward after the dog, who had strayed a few yards to salute another dog led by a string, and caught the animal in his arms. "Pardon me," he exclaimed, returning to his friends, "but there are so many snares for dogs at present. They are just coming into fashion for roasts, and Fox is so plump."

"I thought," said Savarin, "that it was resolved at all the sporting clubs that, be the pinch of famine ever so keen, the friend of man should not be eaten."

"That was while the beef lasted; but since we have come to cats, who shall predict immunity to dogs? *Quid intactum ne-faste liquimus?* Nothing is sacred from the hand of rapine."

The church of the Madeleine now stood before them. *Moblots* were playing pitch-and-toss on its steps.

"I don't wish you to accompany me, Messieurs," said Lemercier, apologetically, "but I am going to enter the church."

"To pray?" asked De Brézé, in profound astonishment.

"Not exactly; but I want to speak to my friend Rochebriant, and I know I shall find him there."

"Praying?" again asked De Brézé.

"Yes."

"That is curious—a young Parisian exquisite at prayer— that is worth seeing. Let us enter, too, Savarin."

They enter the church. It is filled, and even the scepti-
ii—12

cal De Brézé is impressed and awed by the sight. An intense fervour pervades the congregation. The majority, it is true, are women, many of them in deep mourning, and many of their faces mourning deeper than the dress. Everywhere may be seen gushing tears, and everywhere faintly heard the sound of stifled sighs. Besides the women are men of all ages—young, middle-aged, old, with heads bowed and hands clasped, pale, grave, and earnest. Most of them were evidently of the superior grade of life— nobles, and the higher *bourgeoisie:* few of the *ouvrier* class, very few, and these were of an earlier generation. I except soldiers, of whom there were many, from the provincial Mobiles, chiefly Bretons; you know the Breton soldiers by the little cross worn on their *képis*.

Among them Lemercier at once distinguished the noble countenance of Alain de Rochebriant. De Brézé and Savarin looked at each other with solemn eyes. I know not when either had last been within a church; perhaps both were startled to find that religion still existed in Paris— and largely exist it does, though little seen on the surface of society, little to be estimated by the articles of journals and the reports of foreigners. Unhappily, those among whom it exists are not the ruling class—are of the classes that are dominated over and obscured in every country the moment the populace becomes master. And at that moment the journals chiefly read were warring more against the Deity than the Prussians—were denouncing soldiers who attended mass. "The Gospel certainly makes a bad soldier," writes the patriot Pyat.

Lemercier knelt down quietly. The other two men crept noiselessly out, and stood waiting for him on the steps, watching the *Moblots* (Parisian *Moblots*) at play.

"I should not wait for the *roturier* if he had not promised me a *rôti*," said the Vicomte de Brézé, with a pitiful attempt at the patrician wit of the *ancien régime*.

Savarin shrugged his shoulders. "I am not included in the invitation," said he, "and therefore free to depart. I

must go and look up a former *confrère* who was an enthusiastic Red Republican, and I fear does not get so much to
eat since he has no longer an Emperor to abuse."

So Savarin went away. A few minutes afterwards
Lemercier emerged from the church with Alain.

CHAPTER XIV.

"I KNEW I should find you in the Madeleine," said Lemercier, "and I wished much to know when you had news
from Duplessis. He and your fair *fiancée* are with your
aunt still staying at Rochebriant?"

"Certainly. A pigeon arrived this morning with a few
lines. All well there."

"And Duplessis thinks, despite the war, that he shall be
able, when the time comes, to pay Louvier the mortgage-
sum?"

"He never doubts that. His credit in London is so
good. But of course all works of improvement are
stopped."

"Pray did he mention me?—anything about the mes-
senger who was to pierce the Prussian lines?"

"What! has the man not arrived? It is two weeks since
he left."

"The Uhlans have no doubt shot him—the assassins,—
and drunk up my 25,000 francs—the thieves."

"I hope not. But in case of delay, Duplessis tells me I
am to remit to you 2,000 francs for your present wants. I
will send them to you this evening."

"How the deuce do you possess such a sum?"

"I came from Brittany with a purse well filled. Of
course I could have no scruples in accepting money from
my destined father-in-law."

"And you can spare this sum?"

"Certainly—the State now provides for me; I am in
command of a Breton company."

"True. Come and dine with me and De Brézé."

"Alas! I cannot. I have to see both the Vandemars before I return to the camp for the night. And now—hush—come this way (drawing Frederic further from De Brézé), I have famous news for you. A sortie on a grand scale is imminent; in a few days we may hope for it."

"I have heard that so often that I am incredulous."

"Take it as a fact now."

"What! Trochu has at last matured his plan?"

"He has changed its original design, which was to cut through the Prussian lines to Rouen, occupying there the richest country for supplies, guarding the left bank of the Seine and a watercourse to convoy them to Paris. The incidents of war prevented that: he has a better plan now. The victory of the army of the Loire at Orleans opens a new enterprise. We shall cut our way through the Prussians, join that army, and with united forces fall on the enemy at the rear. Keep this a secret as yet, but rejoice with me that we shall prove to the invaders what men who fight for their native soil can do under the protection of Heaven."

"Fox, Fox, *mon chéri*," said Lemercier, as he walked towards the *Café Riche* with De Brézé; "thou shalt have a *festin de Balthazar* under the protection of Heaven."

CHAPTER XV.

On leaving Lemercier and De Brézé, Savarin regained the Boulevard, and pausing every now and then to exchange a few words with acquaintances—the acquaintances of the genial author were numerous—turned into the *quartier* Chaussée d'Antin, and gaining a small neat house, with a richly-ornamented *façade*, mounted very clean, well-kept stairs to a third story. On one of the doors on the lanling-place was nailed a card, inscribed, "Gustave Rameau, *homme de lettres.*" Certainly it is not usual in Paris thus to *afficher* one's self as a "man of letters"? But Genius scorns what is usual. Had not Victor Hugo left in the hotel-books on the Rhine his designation "*homme de lettres*"? Did not the heir to one of the loftiest houses in the peerage of England, and who was also a first-rate amateur in painting, inscribe on his studio when in Italy, "——, *artiste*"? Such examples, no doubt, were familiar to Gustave Rameau, and "*homme de lettres*" was on the scrap of pasteboard nailed to his door.

Savarin rang; the door opened, and Gustave appeared. The poet was, of course, picturesquely attired. In his day of fashion he had worn within doors a very pretty fanciful costume, designed after portraits of the young Raffaele; that costume he had preserved—he wore it now. It looked very threadbare, and the *pourpoint* very soiled. But the beauty of the poet's face had survived the lustre of the garments. True, thanks to absinthe, the cheeks had become somewhat puffy and bloated. Grey was distinctly visible in the long ebon tresses. But still the beauty of the face was of that rare type which a Thorwaldsen or a Gibson seeking a model for a Narcissus would have longed to fix into marble.

Gustave received his former chief with a certain air of reserved dignity; led him into his chamber, only divided by a curtain from his accommodation for washing and slumber, and placed him in an arm-chair beside a drowsy fire—fuel had already become very dear.

"Gustavo," said Savarin, "are you in a mood favourable to a little serious talk?"

"Serious talk from M. Savarin is a novelty too great not to command my profoundest interest."

"Thank you,—and to begin: I who know the world and mankind advise you, who do not, never to meet a man who wishes to do you a kindness with an ungracious sarcasm. Irony is a weapon I ought to be skilled in, but weapons are used against enemies, and it is only a tyro who flourishes his rapier in the face of his friends."

"I was not aware that M. Savarin still permitted me to regard him as a friend."

"Because I discharged the duties of friend—remonstrated, advised, and warned. However, let bygones be bygones. I entreated you not to quit the safe shelter of the paternal roof. You insisted on doing so. I entreated you not to send to one of the most ferocious of the Red, or rather, the Communistic, journals, articles, very eloquent, no doubt, but which would most seriously injure you in the eyes of quiet, orderly people, and compromise your future literary career for the sake of a temporary flash in the pan during a very evanescent period of revolutionary excitement. You scorned my adjurations, but at all events you had the grace not to append your true name to those truculent effusions. In literature, if literature revive in France, we two are henceforth separated. But I do not forego the friendly interest I took in you in the days when you were so continually in my house. My wife, who liked you so cordially, implored me to look after you during her absence from Paris, and, *enfin, mon pauvre garçon*, it would grieve me very much if, when she comes back, I had to say to her, 'Gustave Rameau has thrown away the chance of redemption and of happiness which you deemed was secure to him.' *A l'œil malade, la lumière nuit.*"

So saying, he held out his hand kindly.

Gustave, who was far from deficient in affectionate or tender impulses, took the hand respectfully, and pressed it warmly.

"Forgive me if I have been ungracious, M. Savarin, and vouchsafe to hear my explanation."

"Willingly, *mon garçon.*"

"When I became convalescent, well enough to leave my father's house, there were circumstances which compelled me to do so. A young man accustomed to the life of a *garçon* can't be always tied to his mother's apron-strings."

"Especially if the apron-pocket does not contain a bottle of absinthe," said Savarin, drily. "You may well colour and try to look angry; but I know that the doctor strictly forbade the use of that deadly *liqueur*, and enjoined your mother to keep strict watch on your liability to its temptations. And hence one cause of your *ennui* under the paternal roof. But if there you could not imbibe absinthe, you were privileged to enjoy a much diviner intoxication. There you could have the foretaste of domestic bliss,—the society of the girl you loved, and who was pledged to become your wife. Speak frankly. Did not that society itself begin to be wearisome?"

"No," cried Gustave, eagerly, "it was not wearisome——"

"Yes, but——"

"But it could not be all-sufficing to a soul of fire like mine."

"Hem," murmured Savarin—"a soul of fire! This is very interesting; pray go on."

"The calm, cold, sister-like affection of a childish undeveloped nature, which knew no passion except for art, and was really so little emancipated from the nursery as to take for serious truth all the old myths of religion—such companionship may be very soothing and pleasant when one is lying on one's sofa, and must live by rule, but when one regains the vigour of youth and health——"

"Do not pause," said Savarin, gazing with more compassion than envy on that melancholy impersonation of youth and health. "When one regains that vigour of which I myself have no recollection, what happens?"

"The thirst for excitement, the goads of ambition, the irresistible claims which the world urges upon genius, return."

"And that genius, finding itself at the North Pole amid Cimmerian darkness in the atmosphere of a childish intellect—in other words, the society of a pure-minded virgin, who, though a good romance-writer, writes nothing but what a virgin may read, and, though a *bel esprit*, says her prayers and goes to church—then genius—well, pardon my ignorance, what does genius do?"

"Oh, M. Savarin, M. Savarin! don't let us talk any more. There is no sympathy between us. I cannot bear that bloodless, mocking, cynical mode of dealing with grand emotions, which belongs to the generation of the *Doctrinaires*. I am not a Thiers or a Guizot."

"Good heavens! who ever accused you of being either? I did not mean to be cynical. Mademoiselle Cicogna has often said I am, but I did not think you would. Pardon me. I quite agree with the philosopher who asserted that the wisdom of the past was an imposture, that the meanest intellect now living is wiser than the greatest intellect which is buried in Père la Chaise; because the dwarf who follows the giant, when perched on the shoulders of the giant, sees farther than the giant ever could. *Allez.* I go in for your generation. I abandon Guizot and Thiers. Do condescend and explain to my dull understanding, as the inferior mortal of a former age, what are the grand emotions which impel a soul of fire in your wiser generation. The thirst of excitement—what excitement? The goads of ambition—what ambition?"

"A new social system is struggling from the dissolving elements of the old one, as, in the fables of priestcraft, the soul frees itself from the body which has become ripe for the grave. Of that new system I aspire to be a champion— a leader. Behold the excitement that allures me, the ambition that goads."

"Thank you," said Savarin, meekly; "I am answered. I recognise the dwarf perched on the back of the giant. Quitting these lofty themes, I venture to address to you now one simple matter-of-fact question: How about Mademoiselle Cicogna? Do you think you can induce her to transplant herself to the new social system, which I presume will abolish, among other obsolete myths, the institution of marriage?"

"M. Savarin, your question offends me. Theoretically I am opposed to the existing superstitions that encumber the very simple principle by which may be united two persons so long as they desire the union, and separated so soon as the union becomes distasteful to either. But I am perfectly aware that such theories would revolt a young lady like Mademoiselle Cicogna. I have never even named them to her, and our engagement holds good."

"Engagement of marriage? No period for the ceremony fixed?"

"That is not my fault. I urged it on Isaura with all earnestness before I left my father's house."

"That was long after the siege had begun. Listen to me, Gustave. No persuasion of mine or my wife's, nor Mrs. Morley's, could induce Isaura to quit Paris while it was yet time. She said very simply that, having pledged her truth and hand to you, it would be treason to honour and duty if she should allow any considerations for herself to be even discussed so long as you needed her presence. You were then still suffering, and, though convalescent, not without danger of a relapse. And your mother said to her— I heard the words: ''Tis not for his bodily health I could dare to ask you to stay, when every man who can afford it is sending away his wife, sisters, daughters. As for that, I should suffice to tend him; but if you go, I resign all hope for the health of his mind and his soul.' I think at Paris there may be female poets and artists whom that sort of argument would not have much influenced. But it so happens that Isaura is not a *Parisienne*. She believes in those old myths which you think fatal to sympathies with yourself; and those old myths also lead her to believe that where a woman has promised she will devote her life to a man, she cannot forsake him when told by his mother that she is necessary to the health of his mind and his soul. Stay. Before you interrupt me, let me finish what I have to say. It appears that, so soon as your bodily health was improved, you felt that your mind and your soul could

take care of themselves; and certainly it seems to me that
Isaura Cicogna is no longer of the smallest use to either."

Rameau was evidently much disconcerted by this speech.
He saw what Savarin was driving at—the renunciation of
all bond between Isaura and himself. He was not prepared for such renunciation. He still felt for the Italian
as much of love as he could feel for any woman who did
not kneel at his feet, as at those of Apollo condescending
to the homage of Arcadian maids. But on the one hand,
he felt that many circumstances had occurred since the disaster at Sedan to render Isaura a very much less desirable
partie than she had been when he had first wrung from her
the pledge of betrothal. In the palmy times of a Government in which literature and art commanded station and
insured fortune, Isaura, whether as authoress or singer,
was a brilliant marriage for Gustave Rameau. She had
also then an assured and competent, if modest, income.
But when times change, people change with them. As the
income for the moment (and Heaven only can say how long
that moment might last), Isaura's income had disappeared.
It will be recollected that Louvier had invested her whole
fortune in the houses to be built in the street called after
his name. No houses, even when built, paid any rent
now. Louvier had quitted Paris; and Isaura could only
be subsisting upon such small sum as she might have had
in hand before the siege commenced. All career in such
literature and art as Isaura adorned was at a dead stop.
Now, to do Rameau justice, he was by no means an avari-
cious or mercenary man. But he yearned for modes of life
to which money was essential. He liked his "comforts;"
and his comforts included the luxuries of elegance and
show—comforts not to be attained by marriage with Isaura
under existing circumstances.

Nevertheless it is quite true that he had urged her to
marry him at once, before he had quitted his father's
house; and her modest shrinking from such proposal, however excellent the reasons for delay in the national calami-

ties of the time, as well as the poverty which the calamity threatened, had greatly wounded his *amour propre*. He had always felt that her affection for him was not love; and though he could reconcile himself to that conviction when many solid advantages were attached to the prize of her love, and when he was ill, and penitent, and maudlin, and the calm affection of a saint seemed to him infinitely preferable to the vehement passion of a sinner,—yet when Isaura was only Isaura by herself—Isaura *minus* all the *et cetera* which had previously been taken into account—the want of adoration for himself very much lessened her value.

Still, though he acquiesced in the delayed fulfilment of the engagement with Isaura, he had no thought of withdrawing from the engagement itself, and after a slight pause he replied: " You do me great injustice if you suppose that the occupations to which I devote myself render me less sensible to the merits of Mademoiselle Cicogna, or less eager for our union. On the contrary, I will confide to you—as a man of the world—one main reason why I quitted my father's house, and why I desire to keep my present address a secret. Mademoiselle Caumartin conceived for me a passion—a caprice—which was very flattering for a time, but which latterly became very troublesome. Figure to yourself—she daily came to our house while I was lying ill, and with the greatest difficulty my mother got her out of it. That was not all. She pestered me with letters containing all sorts of threats—nay, actually kept watch at the house; and one day when I entered the carriage with my mother and Signora Venosta for a drive in the Bois (meaning to call for Isaura by the way), she darted to the carriage-door, caught my hand, and would have made a scene if the coachman had given her leave to do so. Luckily he had the tact to whip on his horses, and we escaped. I had some little difficulty in convincing the Signora Venosta that the girl was crazed. But I felt the danger I incurred of her coming upon me some moment when in company with Isaura, and so I left my father's house; and naturally wishing to steer clear of this vehement little demon till I am safely married, I keep my address a secret from all who are likely to tell her of it."

"You do wisely if you are really afraid of her, and cannot trust your nerves to say to her plainly, 'I am engaged to be married; all is at an end between us. Do not force me to employ the police to protect myself from unwelcome importunities.'"

"Honestly speaking, I doubt if I have the nerve to do that, and I doubt still more if it would be of any avail. It is very *ennuyant* to be so passionately loved; but, *que voulez vous?* It is my fate."

"Poor martyr! I condole with you: and, to say truth, it was chiefly to warn you of Mademoiselle Caumartin's pertinacity that I call this evening."

Here Savarin related the particulars of his *rencontre* with Julie, and concluded by saying: "I suppose I may take your word of honour that you will firmly resist all temptation to renew a connection which would be so incompatible with the respect due to your *fiancée?* Fatherless and protectorless as Isaura is, I feel bound to act as a virtual guardian to one in whom my wife takes so deep an interest, and to whom, as she thinks, she had some hand in bringing about your engagement: she is committed to no small responsibilities. Do not allow poor Julie, whom I sincerely pity, to force on me the unpleasant duty of warning your *fiancée* of the dangers to which she might be subjected by marriage with an Adonis whose fate it is to be so profoundly beloved by the sex in general, and ballet nymphs in particular."

"There is no chance of so disagreeable a duty being incumbent on you, M. Savarin. Of course, what I myself have told you in confidence is sacred."

"Certainly. There are things in the life of a *garçon* before marriage which would be an affront to the modesty of his *fiancée* to communicate and discuss. But then those things must belong exclusively to the past and cast no shadow over the future. I will not interrupt you further. No doubt you have work for the night before you. Do the Red journalists for whom you write pay enough to support you in these terribly dear times?"

"Scarcely. But I look forward to wealth and fame in the future. And you?"

"I just escape starvation. If the siege last much longer, it is not of the gout I shall die. Good-night to you."

CHAPTER XVI.

ISAURA had, as we have seen, been hitherto saved by the siege and its consequences from the fulfilment of her engagement to Gustave Rameau; and since he had quitted his father's house she had not only seen less of him, but a certain chill crept into his converse in the visits he paid to her. The compassionate feeling his illness had excited, confirmed by the unwonted gentleness of his mood, and the short-lived remorse with which he spoke of his past faults and follies, necessarily faded away in proportion as he regained that kind of febrile strength which was his normal state of health, and with it the arrogant self-assertion which was ingrained in his character. But it was now more than ever that she became aware of the antagonism between all that constituted his inner life and her own. It was not that he volunteered in her presence the express utterance of those opinions, social or religious, which he addressed to the public in the truculent journal to which, under a *nom de plume,* he was the most inflammatory contributor. Whether it was that he shrank from insulting the ears of the pure virgin whom he had wooed as wife with avowals of his disdain of marriage bonds, or perhaps from shocking yet more her womanly humanity and her religious faith by cries for the blood of anti-republican traitors and the down-

fall of Christian altars; or whether he yet clung, though
with relapsing affection, to the hold which her promise had
imposed on him, and felt that that hold would be for ever
gone, and that she would recoil from his side in terror and
dismay, if she once learned that the man who had implored
her to be his saving angel from the comparatively mild
errors of youth, had so belied his assurance, so mocked her
credulity, as deliberately to enter into active warfare against
all that he knew her sentiments regarded as noble and her
conscience received as divine: despite the suppression of
avowed doctrine on his part, the total want of sympathy between these antagonistic natures made itself felt by
both—more promptly felt by Isaura.   If Gustave did not
frankly announce to her in that terrible time (when all that
a little later broke out on the side of the Communists was
more or less forcing ominous way to the lips of those who
talked with confidence to each other, whether to approve or
to condemn) the associates with whom he was leagued, the
path to which he had committed his career—still for her
instincts for genuine Art—which for its development needs
the serenity of peace, which for its ideal needs dreams that
soar into the Infinite—Gustave had only the scornful sneer
of the man who identifies with his ambition the violent
upset of all that civilisation has established in this
world, and the blank negation of all that patient hope
and heroic aspiration which humanity carries on into the
next.

On his side, Gustave Rameau, who was not without certain fine and delicate attributes in a complicated nature
over which the personal vanity and the mobile temperament of the Parisian reigned supreme, chafed at the re-
straints imposed on him.   No matter what a man's doctrines may be—however abominable you and I may deem
them—man desires to find, in the dearest fellowship he can
establish, that sympathy in the woman his choice singles
out from her sex—deference to his opinions, sympathy with
his objects, as man.   So, too, Gustave's sense of honour—

and according to his own Parisian code that sense was keen—
became exquisitely stung by the thought that he was
compelled to play the part of a mean dissimulator to the
girl for whose opinions he had the profoundest contempt.
How could these two, betrothed to each other, not feel,
though without coming to open dissension, that between
them had flowed the inlet of water by which they had been
riven asunder? What man, if he can imagine himself a
Gustave Rameau, can blame the revolutionist absorbed in
ambitious projects for turning the pyramid of society
topsy-turvy, if he shrank more and more from the companionship of a betrothed with whom he could not
venture to exchange three words without caution and
reserve? And what woman can blame an Isaura if
she felt a sensation of relief at the very neglect of
the affianced whom she had compassionated and could
never love?

Possibly the reader may best judge of the state of Isaura's
mind at this time by a few brief extracts from an imperfect
fragmentary journal, in which, amid saddened and lonely
hours, she held converse with herself.

"One day at Enghien I listened silently to a conversation between M. Savarin and the Englishman, who sought
to explain the conception of duty in which the German
poet has given such noble utterance to the thoughts of the
German philosopher—viz., that moral aspiration has the
same goal as the artistic,—the attainment to the calm delight wherein the pain of effort disappears in the content of
achievement. Thus in life, as in art, it is through discipline that we arrive at freedom, and duty only completes
itself when all motives, all actions, are attuned into one
harmonious whole, and it is not striven for as duty, but enjoyed as happiness. M. Savarin treated this theory with
the mockery with which the French wit is ever apt to treat
what it terms German mysticism. According to him, duty
must always be a hard and difficult struggle; and he said

laughingly, 'Whenever a man says, "I have done my duty," it is with a long face and a mournful sigh.'

"Ah, how devoutly I listened to the Englishman! how harshly the Frenchman's irony jarred upon my ears! And yet now, in the duty that life imposes on me, to fulfil which I strain every power vouchsafed to my nature, and seek to crush down every impulse that rebels, where is the promised calm, where any approach to the content of achievement? Contemplating the way before me, the Beautiful even of Art has vanished. I see but cloud and desert. Can this which I assume to be duty really be so? Ah, is it not sin even to ask my heart that question?

*   *   *   *

"Madame Rameau is very angry with her son for his neglect both of his parents and of me. I have had to take his part against her. I would not have him lose their love. Poor Gustave! But when Madame Rameau suddenly said to-day: 'I erred in seeking the union between thee and Gustave. Retract thy promise; in doing so thou wilt be justified,'—oh, the strange joy that flashed upon me as she spoke. Am I justified? Am I? Oh, if that Englishman had never crossed my path! Oh, if I had never loved! or if in the last time we met he had not asked for my love, and confessed his own! Then, I think, I could honestly reconcile my conscience with my longings, and say to Gustave, 'We do not suit each other; be we both released!' But now—is it that Gustave is really changed from what he was, when in despondence at my own lot, and in pitying belief that I might brighten and exalt his, I plighted my troth to him? or is it not rather that the choice I thus voluntarily made became so intolerable a thought the moment I knew I was beloved and sought by another; and from that moment I lost the strength I had before,—strength to silence the voice at my own heart? What! is it the image of that other one which is persuading me to be false?—to exaggerate the failings, to be blind to the merits of him who has a right to say, 'I

am what I was when thou didst pledge thyself to take me
for better or for worse'?

*   *   *   *   *

" Gustave has been here after an absence of several days.
He was not alone. The good Abbé Vertpré and Madame
de Vandemar, with her son, M. Raoul, were present. They
had come on matters connected with our ambulance. They
do not know of my engagement to Gustave; and seeing him
in the uniform of a National Guard, the Abbé courteously
addressed to him some questions as to the possibility of
checking the terrible increase of the vice of intoxication, so
alien till of late to the habits of the Parisians, and becoming fatal to discipline and bodily endurance,—could the
number of the *cantines* on the ramparts be more limited?
Gustave answered with rudeness and bitter sarcasm, 'Before priests could be critics in military matters they must
undertake military service themselves.'

" The Abbé replied with unalterable good-humour, 'But,
in order to criticise the effects of drunkenness, must one
get drunk one's self?' Gustave was put out, and retired
into a corner of the room, keeping sullen silence till my
other visitors left.

" Then before I could myself express the pain his words
and manner had given me, he said abruptly, 'I wonder how
you can tolerate the *tartuferie* which may amuse on the
comic stage, but in the tragedy of these times is revolting.'
This speech roused my anger, and the conversation that
ensued was the gravest that had ever passed between us.

" If Gustave were of stronger nature and more concen-
trated will, I believe that the only feelings I should have
for him would be antipathy and dread. But it is his very
weaknesses and inconsistencies that secure to him a certain
tenderness of interest. I think he could never be judged
without great indulgence by women; there is in him so
much of the child,—wayward, irritating one moment, and
the next penitent, affectionate. One feels as if persistence
in evil were impossible to one so delicate both in mind and

form. That peculiar order of genius to which he belongs
seems as if it ought to be so estranged from all directions,
violent or coarse. When in poetry he seeks to utter some
audacious and defying sentiment, the substance melts away
in daintiness of expression, in soft, lute-like strains of
slender music. And when he has stung, angered, revolted
my heart the most, suddenly he subsides into such pathetic
gentleness, such tearful remorse, that I feel as if resentment to one so helpless, desertion of one who must fall
without the support of a friendly hand, were a selfish
cruelty. It seems to me as if I were dragged towards a
precipice by a sickly child clinging to my robe.

"But in this last conversation with him, his language in
regard to subjects I hold most sacred drew forth from me
words which startled him, and which *may* avail to save
him from that worst insanity of human minds,—the mimi-
cry of the Titans who would have dethroned a God to restore a Chaos. I told him frankly that I had only promised to share his fate on my faith in his assurance of my
power to guide it heavenward; and that if the opinions he
announced were seriously entertained, and put forth in defiance of heaven itself, we were separated for ever. I told
him how earnestly, in the calamities of the time, my own
soul had sought to take refuge in thoughts and hopes beyond the earth; and how deeply many a sentiment that in
former days passed by me with a smile in the light talk of
the *salons*, now shocked me as an outrage on the reverence
which the mortal child owes to the Divine Father. I owned
to him how much of comfort, of sustainment, of thought
and aspiration, elevated beyond the sphere of Art in which
I had hitherto sought the purest air, the loftiest goal, I
owed to intercourse with minds like those of the Abbé de
Vertpré; and how painfully I felt as if I were guilty of
ingratitude when he compelled me to listen to insults on
those whom I recognised as *benefactors*.

"I wished to speak sternly; but it is my great misfortune, my prevalent weakness, that I cannot be stern when

I ought to be. It is with me in life as in art. I never
could on the stage have taken the part of a Norma or a
Medea. If I attempt in fiction a character which deserves
condemnation, I am untrue to poetic justice. I cannot condemn and execute; I can but compassionate and pardon
the creature I myself have created. I was never in the
real world stern but to one; and then, alas! it was because
I loved where I could no longer love with honour; and I,
knowing my weakness, had terror lest I should yield.

"So Gustave did not comprehend from my voice, my
manner, how gravely I was in earnest. But, himself softened, affected to tears, he confessed his own faults—ceased
to argue in order to praise; and—and—uttering protesta-
tions seemingly the most sincere, he left me bound to him
still—bound to him still—woe is me!"

It is true that Isaura had come more directly under the
influence of religion than she had been in the earlier dates
of this narrative. There is a time in the lives of most of
us, and especially in the lives of women, when, despondent
of all joy in an earthly future, and tortured by conflicts
between inclination and duty, we transfer all the passion
and fervour of our troubled souls to enthusiastic yearnings
for the Divine Love; seeking to rebaptise ourselves in the
fountain of its mercy, taking thence the only hopes that
can cheer, the only strength that can sustain us. Such a
time had come to Isaura. Formerly she had escaped from
the griefs of the work-a-day world into the garden-land of
Art. Now, Art had grown unwelcome to her, almost hate-
ful. Gone was the spell from the garden-land; its flowers
were faded, its paths were stony, its sunshine had vanished in mist and rain. There are two voices of Nature in
the soul of the genuine artist,—that is, of him who, because he can create, comprehends the necessity of the great
Creator. Those voices are never both silent. When one is
hushed, the other becomes distinctly audible. The one
speaks to him of Art, the other of Religion.

At that period several societies for the relief and tend-
ance of the wounded had been formed by the women of
Paris,—the earliest, if I mistake not, by ladies of the highest rank—amongst whom were the Comtesse de Vandemar
and the Contessa di Rimini—though it necessarily included
others of stations less elevated.   To this society, at the request of Alain de Rochebriant and of Enguerrand, Isaura
had eagerly attached herself.   It occupied much of her
time; and in connection with it she was brought much into
sympathetic acquaintance with Raoul de Vandemar—the
most zealous and active member of that Society of St.
François de Sales, to which belonged other young nobles of
the Legitimist creed.   The passion of Raoul's life was the
relief of human suffering.   In him was personified the
ideal of Christian charity.   I think all, or most of us, have
known what it is to pass under the influence of a nature
that is so far akin to ours that it desires to become something better and higher than it is—that desire being paramount in ourselves—but seeks to be that something in ways
not akin to, but remote from, the ways in which we seek it.
When this contact happens, either one nature, by the mere
force of will, subjugates and absorbs the other, or both,
while preserving their own individuality, apart and independent, enrich themselves by mutual interchange, and the
asperities which differences of taste and sentiment in detail
might otherwise provoke melt in the sympathy which unites
spirits striving with equal earnestness to rise nearer to the
unseen and unattainable Source, which they equally recognise as Divine.

Perhaps, had these two persons met a year ago in the
ordinary intercourse of the world, neither would have detected the sympathy of which I speak.   Raoul was not
without the prejudice against artists and writers of romance, that is shared by many who cherish the persuasion
that all is vanity which does not concentrate imagination
and intellect in the destinies of the soul hereafter; and
Isaura might have excited his compassion, certainly not his

reverence. While to her, his views on all that seeks to render the actual life attractive and embellished, through the accomplishments of Muse and Grace, would have seemed the narrow-minded asceticism of a bigot. But now, amid the direful calamities of the time, the beauty of both natures became visible to each. To the eyes of Isaura tenderness became predominant in the monastic self-denial of Raoul. To the eyes of Raoul, devotion became predominant in the gentle thoughtfulness of Isaura. Their intercourse was in ambulance and hospital—in care for the wounded, in prayer for the dying. Ah! it is easy to declaim against the frivolities and vices of Parisian society as they appear on the surface; and, in revolutionary times, it is the very worst of Paris that ascends in scum to the top. But descend below the surface, even in that demoralising suspense of order, and nowhere on earth might the angel have beheld the image of humanity more amply vindicating its claim to the heritage of heaven.

CHAPTER XVII.

THE warning announcement of some great effort on the part of the besieged, which Alain had given to Lemercier, was soon to be fulfilled.

For some days the principal thoroughfares were ominously lined with military *convois*. The loungers on the Boulevards stopped to gaze on the long defiles of troops and cannons, commissariat conveyances, and, saddening accompaniments! the vehicles of various ambulances for the removal of the wounded. With what glee the loungers said to each other "*Enfin!*" Among all the troops that Paris sent forth, none were so popular as those which Paris had not nurtured—the sailors. From the moment they arrived, the sailors had been the pets of the capital. They soon proved themselves the most notable contrast to that

force which Paris herself had produced—the National
Guard. Their frames were hardy, their habits active, their
discipline perfect, their manners mild and polite. "Oh, if
all our troops were like these!" was the common exclamation of the Parisians.

At last burst forth upon Paris the proclamations of General Trochu and General Ducrot; the first brief, calm, and
Breton-like, ending with "Putting our trust in God. March
on for our country:" the second more detailed, more candidly stating obstacles and difficulties, but fiery with eloquent enthusiasm, not unsupported by military statistics,
in the 400 cannon, two-thirds of which were of the largest
calibre, that no material object could resist; more than
150,000 soldiers, all well armed, well equipped, abundantly
provided with munitions, and all (*J'en ai l'espoir*) animated
by an irresistible ardour. "For me," concludes the General, "I am resolved. I swear before you, before the whole
nation, that I will not re-enter Paris except as dead or vic-
torious."

At these proclamations, who then at Paris does not recall
the burst of enthusiasm that stirred the surface? Trochu
became once more popular; even the Communistic or athe-
istic journals refrained from complaining that he attended
mass, and invited his countrymen to trust in God. Ducrot
was more than popular—he was adored.

The several companies in which De Mauléon and Enguerrand served departed towards their post early on the same
morning, that of the 28th. All the previous night, while
Enguerrand was buried in profound slumber, Raoul remained in his brother's room; sometimes on his knees before the ivory crucifix which had been their mother's last
birthday gift to her youngest son—sometimes seated beside
the bed in profound and devout meditation. At daybreak,
Madame de Vandemar stole into the chamber. Unconscious of his brother's watch, he had asked her to wake
him in good time, for the young man was a sound sleeper.
Shading the candle she bore with one hand, with the other

she drew aside the curtain, and looked at Enguerrand's calm fair face, its lips parted in the happy smile which seemed to carry joy with it wherever its sunshine played. Her tears fell noiselessly on her darling's cheek; she then knelt down and prayed for strength. As she rose she felt Raoul's arm around her; they looked at each other in silence; then she bowed her head and wakened Enguerrand with her lips. "*Pas de querelle, mes amis,*" he murmured, opening his sweet blue eyes drowsily. "Ah, it was a dream! I thought Jules and Emile [two young friends of his] were worrying each other; and you know, dear Raoul, that I am the most officious of peacemakers. Time to rise, is it? No peacemaking to-day. Kiss me again, mother, and say 'Bless thee.'"

"Bless thee, bless thee, my child," cried the mother, wrapping her arms passionately round him, and in tones choked with sobs.

"Now leave me, *maman,*" said Enguerrand, resorting to the infantine ordinary name, which he had not used for years. "Raoul, stay and help me to dress. I must be *très beau* to-day. I shall join thee at breakfast, *maman.* Early for such repast, but *l'appétit vient en mangeant.* Mind the coffee is hot."

Enguerrand, always careful of each detail of dress, was especially so that morning, and especially gay, humming the old air, "Partant pour la Syrie." But his gaiety was checked when Raoul, taking from his breast a holy talisman, which he habitually wore there, suspended it with loving hands round his brother's neck. It was a small crystal set in Byzantine filigree; imbedded in it was a small splinter of wood, said by pious tradition to be a relic of the Divine Cross. It had been for centuries in the family of the Contessa di Rimini, and was given by her to Raoul, the only gift she had ever made him, as an emblem of the sinless purity of the affection that united those two souls in the bonds of the beautiful belief.

"She bade me transfer it to thee to-day, my brother,"

said Raoul, simply; "and now without a pang I can gird on thee thy soldier's sword."

Enguerrand clasped his brother in his arms, and kissed him with passionate fervour. "Oh, Raoul, how I love thee! how good thou hast ever been to me! how many sins thou hast saved me from! how indulgent thou hast been to those from which thou couldst not save! Think on that, my brother, in case we do not meet again on earth."

"Hush, hush, Enguerrand! No gloomy forebodings now! Come, come hither, my half of life, my sunny half of life!" and uttering these words, he led Enguerrand towards the crucifix, and there, in deeper and more solemn voice, said, "Let us pray." So the brothers knelt side by side, and Raoul prayed aloud as only such souls can pray.

When they descended into the *salon* where breakfast was set out, they found assembled several of their relations, and some of Enguerrand's young friends not engaged in the sortie. One or two of the latter, indeed, were disabled from fighting by wounds in former fields; they left their sick-beds to bid him good-bye. Unspeakable was the affection this genial nature inspired in all who came into the circle of its winning magic; and when, tearing himself from them, he descended the stair, and passed with light step through the *porte cochère*, there was a crowd around the house—so widely had his popularity spread among even the lower classes, from which the Mobiles in his regiment were chiefly composed. He departed to the place of rendezvous amid a chorus of exhilarating cheers.

Not thus lovingly tended on, not thus cordially greeted, was that equal idol of a former generation, Victor de Mauléon. No pious friend prayed beside his couch, no loving kiss waked him from his slumbers. At the grey of the November dawn he rose from a sleep which had no smiling dreams, with that mysterious instinct of punctual will which cannot even go to sleep without fixing beforehand the exact moment in which sleep shall end. He, too, like Enguerrand, dressed himself with care—unlike Enguerrand, with care strictly soldier-like. Then, seeing he had some little time yet before him, he rapidly revisited the pigeonholes and drawers in which might be found by prying eyes anything he would deny to their curiosity. All that he found of this sort were some letters in female handwriting, tied together with faded ribbon, relics of earlier days, and treasured throughout later vicissitudes; letters from the English girl to whom he had briefly referred in his confession to Louvier,—the only girl he had ever wooed as his wife. She was the only daughter of highborn Roman Catholics, residing at the time of his youth in Paris. Reluctantly they had assented to his proposals; joyfully they had retracted their assent when his affairs had become so involved; yet possibly the motive that led him to his most ruinous excesses—the gambling of the turf—had been caused by the wild hope of a nature, then fatally sanguine, to retrieve the fortune that might suffice to satisfy the parents. But during his permitted courtship the lovers had corresponded. Her letters were full of warm, if innocent, tenderness—till came the last cold farewell. The family had long ago returned to England; he concluded, of course, that she had married another.

Near to these letters lay the papers which had served to vindicate his honour in that old affair, in which the unsought love of another had brought on him shame and affliction. As his eye fell on the last, he muttered to himself, "I kept *these*, to clear my repute. Can I keep *those*, when, if found, they might compromise the repute of her who might have been my wife had I been worthy of her? She is doubtless now another's; or, if dead,—honour never dies." He pressed his lips to the letters with a passionate, lingering, mournful kiss; then, raking up the ashes of yesterday's fire, and rekindling them, he placed thereon those leaves of a melancholy romance in his past, and watched them slowly, reluctantly smoulder away into tinder. Then he opened a drawer in which lay the only paper of a polit-

ical character which he had preserved. All that related
to plots or conspiracies in which his agency had committed
others, it was his habit to destroy as soon as received. For
the sole document thus treasured he alone was responsible;
it was an outline of his ideal for the future constitution of
France, accompanied with elaborate arguments, the heads
of which his conversation with the Incognito made known
to the reader. Of the soundness of this political programme, whatever its merits or faults (a question on which
I presume no judgment), he had an intense conviction.
He glanced rapidly over its contents, did not alter a word,
sealed it up in an envelope, inscribed, " My Legacy to my
Countrymen." The papers refuting a calumny relating
solely to himself he carried into the battle-field, placed
next to his heart,—significant of a Frenchman's love of
honour in this world—as the relic placed round the neck
of Enguerrand by his pious brother was emblematic of the
Christian hope of mercy in the next.

CHAPTER XVIII.

THE streets swarmed with the populace gazing on the
troops as they passed to their destination. Among those
of the Mobiles who especially caught the eye were two
companies in which Enguerrand de Vandemar and Victor
de Mauléon commanded. In the first were many young
men of good family, or in the higher ranks of the
bourgeoisie, known to numerous lookers-on; there was something inspiriting in their gay aspects, and in the easy carelessness of their march. Mixed with this company, however, and forming of course the bulk of it, were those who
belonged to the lower classes of the population; and though
they too might seem gay to an ordinary observer, the gaiety
was forced. Many of them were evidently not quite sober;
and there was a disorderly want of soldiership in their mien
and armament which inspired distrust among such *vieux*

moustaches as, too old for other service than that of the
ramparts, mixed here and there among the crowd.

But when De Mauléon's company passed, the *vieux
moustaches* impulsively touched each other. They recognised the march of well-drilled men; the countenances grave
and severe, the eyes not looking on this side and that for
admiration, the step regularly timed; and conspicuous
among these men the tall stature and calm front of the
leader.

"These fellows will fight well," growled a *vieux moustache*, "where did they fish out their leader?"

"Don't you know?" said a *bourgeoisie*. "Victor de Mauléon. He won the cross in Algeria for bravery. I recollect him when I was very young; the very devil for women
and fighting."

"I wish there were more such devils for fighting and
fewer for women," growled again *le vieux moustache*.

One incessant roar of cannon all the night of the 29th.
The populace had learned the names of the French cannons, and fancied they could distinguish the several sounds
of their thunder. "There spits 'Josephine'!" shouts an
invalid sailor. "There howls our own 'Populace'!" [1] cries
a Red Republican from Belleville. "There sings 'Le
Châtiment'!" laughed Gustave Rameau, who was now become an enthusiastic admirer of the Victor Hugo he had
before affected to despise. And all the while, mingled
with the roar of the cannon, came, far and near from the
streets, from the ramparts, the gusts of song—song sometimes heroic, sometimes obscene, more often carelessly joyous. The news of General Vinoy's success during the early
part of the day had been damped by the evening report of
Ducrot's delay in crossing the swollen Marne. But the
spirits of the Parisians rallied from a momentary depres-
sion on the excitement at night of that concert of martial
music.

[1] The "Populace" had been contributed to the artillery, *sou à sou*,
by the working class.

During that night, close under the guns of the double redoubt of Gravelle and La Faisanderie, eight pontoon-bridges were thrown over the Marne; and at daybreak the first column of the third army under Blanchard and Renoult crossed with all their artillery, and, covered by the fire of the double redoubts, of the forts of Vincennes, Nogent, Rossney, and the batteries of Mont Avron, had an hour before noon carried the village of Champigny, and the first *échelon* of the important plateau of Villiers, and were already commencing the work of intrenchment, when, rally·ing from the amaze of a defeat, the German forces burst upon them, sustained by fresh batteries. The Prussian pieces of artillery established at Chennevières and at Neuilly opened fire with deadly execution; while a numerous infantry, descending from the intrenchments of Villiers, charged upon the troops under Renoult. Among the French in that strife were Enguerrand and the Mobiles of which he was in command. Dismayed by the unexpected fire, these Mobiles gave way, as indeed did many of the line. Enguerrand rushed forward to the front: "On, *mes enfans*, on! What will our mothers and wives say of us if we fly? *Vive la France !*—On!" Among those of the bet·ter class in that company there rose a shout of applause, but it found no sympathy among the rest. They wavered, they turned. "Will you suffer me to go on alone, country-men?" cried Enguerrand; and alone he rushed on towards the Prussian line—rushed, and fell, mortally wounded, by a musket-ball. "Revenge, revenge!" shouted some of the foremost; "Revenge!" shouted those in the rear; and, so shouting, turned on their heels and fled. But ere they could disperse they encountered the march, steadfast though rapid, of the troop led by Victor de Mauléon. "Poltroons!" he thundered, with the sonorous depth of his strong voice, "halt and turn, or my men shall fire on you as deserters." " *Va, citoyen*," said one fugitive, an officer—popularly elected, because he was the loudest brawler in the club of the Salle Favre,—we have seen him before—Charles, the brother of Armand Monnier;—"men can't fight when they despise their generals. It is our generals who are poltroons and fools both."

"Carry my answer to the ghosts of cowards," cried De Mauléon, and shot the man dead.

His followers, startled and cowed by the deed, and the voice and the look of the death-giver, halted. The officers, who had at first yielded to the panic of their men, took fresh courage, and finally led the bulk of the troop back to their post "*enlevés à la baïonette*," to use the phrase of a candid historian of that day.

Day, on the whole, not inglorious to France. It was the first, if it was the last, really important success of the besieged. They remained masters of the ground, the Prussians leaving to them the wounded and the dead.

That night what crowds thronged from Paris to the top of the Montmartre heights, from the observatory on which the celebrated inventor Bazin had lighted up, with some magical electric machine, all the plain of Gennevilliers from Mont Valérien to the Fort de la Briche! The splendour of the blaze wrapped the great city;—distinctly above the roofs of the houses soared the Dôme des Invalides, the spires of Nôtre Dame, the giant turrets of the Tuileries; —and died away on resting on the *infames scapulos Acroceraunia*, the "thunder crags" of the heights occupied by the invading army.

Lemercier, De Brézé, and the elder Rameau—who, despite his peaceful habits and grey hairs, insisted on joining in the aid of *la patrie*—were among the National Guards attached to the Fort de la Briche and the neighbouring eminence, and they met in conversation.

"What a victory we have had!" said the old Rameau.

"Rather mortifying to your son, M. Rameau," said Lemercier.

"Mortifying to my son, sir!—the victory of his countrymen. What do you mean?"

"I had the honour to hear M. Gustave the other night at the club *de la Vengeance.*"

"*Bon Dieu!* do you frequent those tragic reunions?" asked De Brézé.

"They are not at all tragic: they are the only comedies left us, as one must amuse one's self somewhere, and the club *de la Vengeance* is the prettiest thing of the sort going. I quite understand why it should fascinate a poet like your son, M. Rameau. It is held in a *salle de café chantant*— style *Louis Quinze*—decorated with a pastoral scene from Watteau. I and my dog Fox drop in. We hear your son haranguing. In what poetical sentences he despaired of the Republic! The Government (he called them *les charlatans de l'Hôtel de Ville*) were imbeciles. They pretended to inaugurate a revolution, and did not employ the most obvious of revolutionary means. There Fox and I pricked up our ears: what were those means? Your son proceeded to explain: 'All mankind were to be appealed to against individual interests. The commerce of luxury was to be abolished: clearly luxury was not at the command of all mankind. *Cafés* and theatres were to be closed for ever— all mankind could not go to *cafés* and theatres. It was idle to expect the masses to combine for anything in which the masses had not an interest in common. The masses had no interest in any property that did not belong to the masses. Programmes of the society to be founded, called the *Ligue Cosmopolite Démocratique*, should be sent at once into all the States of the civilised world—how? by balloons. Money corrupts the world as now composed: but the money at the command of the masses could buy all the monarchs and courtiers and priests of the universe.' At that sentiment, vehemently delivered, the applauses were frantic, and Fox in his excitement began to bark. At the sound of his bark one man cried out, 'That's a Prussian!' another, 'Down with the spy!' another, 'There's an *aristo* present—he keeps alive a dog which would be a week's meal for a family!' I snatch up Fox at the last cry, and clasp him to a bosom protected by the uniform of the National Guard.

"When the hubbub had subsided, your son, M. Rameau, proceeded, quitting mankind in general, and arriving at the question in particular most interesting to his audience—the mobilisation of the National Guard; that is, the call upon men who like talking and hate fighting to talk less and fight more. 'It was the sheerest tyranny to select a certain number of free citizens to be butchered. If the fight was for the mass, there ought to be *la levée en masse*. If one did not compel everybody to fight, why should anybody fight?' Here the applause again became vehement, and Fox again became indiscreet. I subdued Fox's bark into a squeak by pulling his ears. 'What!' cries your poet-son, '*la levée en masse* gives us fifteen millions of soldiers, with which we could crush, not Prussia alone, but the whole of Europe. (Immense sensation.) Let us, then, resolve that the charlatans of the Hôtel de Ville are incapable of delivering us from the Prussians; that they are deposed; that the *Ligue* of the *Démocratie Cosmopolite* is installed; that meanwhile the Commune shall be voted the Provisional Government, and shall order the Prussians to retire within three days from the soil of Paris.'

"Pardon me this long description, my dear M. Rameau, but I trust I have satisfactorily explained why victory obtained in the teeth of his eloquent opinions, if gratifying to him as a Frenchman, must be mortifying to him as a politician."

The old Rameau sighed, hung his head, and crept away.

While, amid this holiday illumination, the Parisians enjoyed the panorama before them, the *Frères Chrétiens* and the attendants of the various ambulances were moving along the battle-plains; the first in their large-brimmed hats and sable garbs, the last in strange motley costume, many of them in glittering uniform—all alike in their serene indifference to danger; often pausing to pick up among the dead their own brethren who had been slaughtered in

the midst of their task.   Now and then they came on sinister forms apparently engaged in the same duty of tending
the wounded and dead, but in truth murderous plunderers,
to whom the dead and the dying were equal harvests.   Did
the wounded man attempt to resist the foul hands searching for their spoil, they added another wound more immediately mortal, grinning as they completed on the dead the
robbery they had commenced on the dying.

Raoul de Vandemar had been all the earlier part of the
day with the assistants of the ambulance over which he
presided, attached to the battalions of the National Guard
in a quarter remote from that in which his brother had
fought and fallen.   When those troops, later in the day,
were driven from the Montmedy plateau, which they had
at first carried, Raoul repassed towards the plateau at
Villiers, on which the dead lay thickest.   On the way he
heard a vague report of the panic which had dispersed
the Mobiles of whom Enguerrand was in command, and of
Enguerrand's vain attempt to inspirit them.   But his
fate was not known.   There, at midnight, Raoul is still
searching among the ghastly heaps and pools of blood,
lighted from afar by the blaze from the observatory of
Montmartre, and more near at hand by the bivouac fires
extended along the banks to the left of the Marne, while
everywhere about the field flitted the lanterns of the *Frères
Chrétiens*.   Suddenly, in the dimness of a spot cast into
shadow by an incompleted earthwork, he observed a small
sinister figure perched on the breast of some wounded soldier, evidently not to succour.   He sprang forward and
seized a hideous-looking urchin, scarcely twelve years old,
who held in one hand a small crystal locket, set in filigree
gold, torn from the soldier's breast, and lifted high in the
other a long case-knife.   At a glance Raoul recognised the
holy relic he had given to Enguerrand, and, flinging the
precocious murderer to be seized by his assistants, he cast
himself beside his brother.   Enguerrand still breathed, and
his languid eyes brightened as he knew the dear familiar

face. He tried to speak, but his voice failed, and he shook his head sadly, but still with a faint smile on his lips. They lifted him tenderly, and placed him on a litter. The movement, gentle as it was, brought back pain, and with the pain strength to mutter, "My mother—I would see her once more."

As at daybreak the loungers on Montmartre and the ramparts descended into the streets—most windows in which were open, as they had been all night, with anxious female faces peering palely down—they saw the conveyances of the ambulances coming dismally along, and many an eye turned wistfully towards the litter on which lay the idol of the pleasure-loving Paris, with the dark, bareheaded figure walking beside it,—onwards, onwards, till it reached the Hôtel de Vandemar, and a woman's cry was heard at the entrance—the mother's cry, "My son! my son!"

II.—14

BOOK XII.

CHAPTER I.

THE last book closed with the success of the Parisian sortie on the 30th of November, to be followed by the terrible engagements no less honourable to French valour, on the 2nd of December. There was the sanguine belief that deliverance was at hand; that Trochu would break through the circle of iron, and effect that junction with the army of Aurelles de Paladine which would compel the Germans to raise the investment;—belief rudely shaken by Ducrot's proclamation of the 4th, to explain the recrossing of the Marne, and the abandonment of the positions conquered, but not altogether dispelled till von Moltke's letter to Trochu on the 5th announcing the defeat of the army of the Loire and the recapture of Orleans. Even then the Parisians did not lose hope of succour; and even after the desperate and fruitless sortie against Le Bourget on the 21st, it was not without witticisms on defeat and predictions of triumph, that Winter and Famine settled sullenly on the city.

Our narrative reopens with the last period of the siege.

It was during these dreadful days, that if the vilest and the most hideous aspects of the Parisian population showed themselves at the worst, so all its loveliest, its noblest, its holiest characteristics—unnoticed by ordinary observers in the prosperous days of the capital—became conspicuously prominent. The higher classes, including the remnant of the old *noblesse*, had, during the whole siege, exhibited qualities in notable contrast to those assigned them by the enemies of aristocracy. Their sons had been foremost among those soldiers who never calumniated a leader, never fled before a foe; their women had been among the most zealous and the most tender nurses of the ambulances they had founded and served; their houses had been freely opened, whether to the families exiled from the suburbs, or in supplement to the hospitals. The amount of relief they afforded unostentatiously, out of means that shared the general failure of accustomed resource, when the famine commenced, would be scarcely credible if stated. Admirable, too, were the fortitude and resignation of the genuine Parisian *bourgeoisie*,—the thrifty tradesfolk and small *rentiers*,—that class in which, to judge of its timidity when opposed to a mob, courage is not the most conspicuous virtue. Courage became so now—courage to bear hourly increasing privation, and to suppress every murmur of suffering that would discredit their patriotism, and invoke "peace at any price." It was on this class that the calamities of the siege now pressed the most heavily. The stagnation of trade, and the stoppage of the rents, in which they had invested their savings, reduced many of them to actual want. Those only of their number who obtained the pay of one-and-a-half franc a day as National Guards, could be sure to escape from starvation. But this pay had already begun to demoralise the receivers. Scanty for supply of food, it was ample for supply of drink. And drunkenness, hitherto rare in that rank of the Parisians, became a prevalent vice, aggravated in the case of a National Guard, when it wholly unfitted him for the duties he undertook, especially such National Guards as were raised from the most turbulent democracy of the working class.

But of all that population, there were two sections in which the most beautiful elements of our human nature were most touchingly manifest—the women and the priesthood, including in the latter denomination all the various brotherhoods and societies which religion formed and inspired.

It was on the 27th of December that Frederic Lemercier
stood gazing wistfully on a military report affixed to a blank
wall, which stated that "the enemy, worn out by a resistance of over one hundred days," had commenced the bombardment. Poor Frederic was sadly altered; he had escaped the Prussian's guns, but not the Parisian winter—
the severest known for twenty years. He was one of the
many frozen at their posts—brought back to the ambulance
with Fox in his bosom trying to keep him warm. He had
only lately been sent forth as convalescent,—ambulances
were too crowded to retain a patient longer than absolutely
needful,—and had been hunger-pinched and frost-pinched
ever since. The luxurious Frederic had still, somewhere or
other, a capital yielding above three thousand a year, and
of which he could not now realise a franc, the title-deeds
to various investments being in the hands of Duplessis,—
the most trustworthy of friends, the most upright of men,—
but who was in Bretagne, and could not be got at. And
the time had come at Paris when you could not get trust for
a pound of horse-flesh, or a daily supply of fuel. And
Frederic Lemercier, who had long since spent the 2000
francs borrowed from Alain (not ignobly, but somewhat
ostentatiously, in feasting any acquaintance who wanted a
feast), and who had sold to any one who could afford to
speculate on such dainty luxuries,—clocks, bronzes, amber-
mounted pipes,—all that had made the envied garniture of
his bachelor's apartment—Frederic Lemercier was, so far
as the task of keeping body and soul together, worse off
than any English pauper who can apply to the Union. Of
course he might have claimed his half-pay of thirty sous as
a National Guard. But he little knows the true Parisian
who imagines a seigneur of the Chaussée d'Antin, the oracle
of those with whom he lived, and one who knew life so well
that he had preached prudence to a seigneur of the Faubourg like Alain de Rochebriant, stooping to apply for the
wages of thirty sous. Rations were only obtained by the
wonderful patience of women, who had children to whom

they were both saints and martyrs. The hours, the weary hours, one had to wait before one could get one's place on the line for the distribution of that atrocious black bread, defeated men,—defeated most wives if only for husbands,— were defied only by mothers and daughters. Literally speaking, Lemercier was starving. Alain had been badly wounded in the sortie of the 21st, and was laid up in an ambulance. Even if he could have been got at, he had probably nothing left to bestow upon Lemercier.

Lemercier gazed on the announcement of the bombardment, and the Parisian gaiety, which some French historian of the siege calls *douce philosophie*, lingering on him still, he said, audibly, turning round to any stranger who heard: "Happiest of mortals that we are! Under the present Government we are never warned of anything disagreeable that can happen; we are only told of it when it has happened, and then as rather pleasant than otherwise. I get up. I meet a civil *gendarme*. 'What is that firing? which of our provincial armies is taking Prussia in the rear?' 'Monsieur,' says the *gendarme*, 'it is the Prussian Krupp guns.' I look at the proclamation, and my fears vanish,— my heart is relieved. I read that the bombardment is a sure sign that the enemy is worn out."

Some of the men grouped round Frederic ducked their heads in terror; others, who knew that the thunderbolt launched from the plateau of Avron would not fall on the pavements of Paris, laughed and joked. But in front, with no sign of terror, no sound of laughter, stretched, moving inch by inch, the female procession towards the bakery in which the morsel of bread for their infants was doled out.

"Hist, *mon ami*," said a deep voice beside Lemercier. "Look at those women, and do not wound their ears by a jest."

Lemercier, offended by that rebuke, though too susceptible to good emotions not to recognise its justice, tried with feeble fingers to turn up his moustache, and to turn a defiant crest upon the rebuker. He was rather startled to see

the tall martial form at his side, and to recognise Victor de
Mauléon. "Don't you think, M. Lemercier," resumed the
Vicomte, half sadly, "that these women are worthy of better
husbands and sons than are commonly found among the soldiers whose uniform we wear?"

"The National Guard! You ought not to sneer at them,
Vicomte,—you whose troop covered itself with glory on the
great days of Villiers and Champigny,—you in whose
praise even the grumblers of Paris became eloquent, and
in whom a future Marshal of France is foretold."

"But, alas! more than half of my poor troop was left on
the battle-field, or is now wrestling for mangled remains
of life in the ambulances. And the new recruits with which
I took the field on the 21st are not likely to cover themselves
with glory, or to insure their commander the *bâton* of a
marshal."

"Ay, I heard when I was in the hospital that you had
publicly shamed some of these recruits, and declared that
you would rather resign than lead them again to battle."

"True; and at this moment, for so doing, I am the man
most hated by the rabble who supplied those recruits."

The men, while thus conversing, had moved slowly on,
and were now in front of a large *café*, from the interior of
which came the sound of loud bravos and clappings of
hands. Lemercier's curiosity was excited. "For what
can be that applause?" he said; "let us look in and see."

The room was thronged. In the distance, on a small
raised platform, stood a girl dressed in faded theatrical
finery, making her obeisance to the crowd.

"Heavens!" exclaimed Frederic—"can I trust my eyes?
Surely that is the once superb Julie: has she been dancing
here?"

One of the loungers, evidently belonging to the same
world as Lemercier, overheard the question and answered
politely: "No, Monsieur: she has been reciting verses,
and really declaims very well, considering it is not her
vocation. She has given us extracts from Victor Hugo and

De Musset: and crowned all with a patriotic hymn by Gustave Rameau,—her old lover, if gossip be true."

Meanwhile De Mauléon, who at first had glanced over the scene with his usual air of calm and cold indifference, became suddenly struck by the girl's beautiful face, and gazed on it with a look of startled surprise.

"Who and what did you say that poor fair creature is, M. Lemercier?"

"She is a Mademoiselle Julie Caumartin, and was a very popular *coryphée*. She has hereditary right to be a good dancer, as the daughter of a once more famous ornament of the ballet, *la belle* Léonie—whom you must have seen in your young days."

"Of course. Léonie—she married a M. Surville, a silly *bourgeois gentilhomme*, who earned the hatred of Paris by taking her off the stage. So that is her daughter I see no likeness to her mother—much handsomer. Why does she call herself Caumartin?"

"Oh," said Frederic, "a melancholy but trite story. Léonie was left a widow, and died in want. What could the poor young daughter do? She found a rich protector, who had influence to get her an appointment in the ballet: and there she did as most girls so circumstanced do—appeared under an assumed name, which she has since kept."

"I understand," said Victor, compassionately. "Poor thing! she has quitted the platform, and is coming this way, evidently to speak to you. I saw her eyes brighten as she caught sight of your face."

Lemercier attempted a languid air of modest self-complacency as the girl now approached him. "*Bon jour*, M. Frederic! *Ah, mon Dieu!* how thin you have grown! You have been ill?"

"The hardships of a military life, Mademoiselle. Ah, for the *beaux jours* and the peace we insisted on destroying under the Empire which we destroyed for listening to us! But you thrive well, I trust. I have seen you better dressed, but never in greater beauty."

The girl blushed as she replied, "Do you really think as you speak?"

"I could not speak more sincerely if I lived in the legendary House of Glass."

The girl clutched his arm, and said in suppressed tones, "Where is Gustave?"

"Gustave Rameau? I have no idea. Do you never see him now?"

"Never,—perhaps I never shall see him again; but when you do meet him, say that Julie owes to him her livelihood. An honest livelihood, Monsieur. He taught her to love verses—told her how to recite them. I am engaged at this *café*---you will find me here the same hour every day, in case—in case—— You are good and kind, and will come and tell me that Gustave is well and happy even if he forgets me. *Au revoir!* Stop, you do look, my poor Frederic, as if—as if——pardon me, Monsieur Lemercier, is there anything I can do? Will you condescend to borrow from me? I am in funds."

Lemercier at that offer was nearly moved to tears. Famished though he was, he could not, however, have touched that girl's earnings.

"You are an angel of goodness, Mademoiselle! Ah, how I envy Gustave Rameau! No, I don't want aid. I am always a—*rentier*."

"*Bien!* and if you see Gustave, you will not forget."

"Rely on me. Come away," he said to De Mauléon; "I don't want to hear that girl repeat the sort of bombast the poets indite nowadays. It is fustian; and that girl may have a brain of feather, but she has a heart of gold."

"True," said Victor, as they regained the street. "I overheard what she said to you. What an incomprehensible thing is a woman! how more incomprehensible still is a woman's love! Ah, pardon me; I must leave you. I see in the procession a poor woman known to me in better days."

De Mauléon walked towards the woman he spoke of—one

of the long procession to the bakery—a child clinging to her robe. A pale grief-worn woman, still young, but with the weariness of age on her face, and the shadow of death on her child's.

"I think I see Madame Monnier," said De Mauléon, softly.

She turned and looked at him drearily. A year ago, she would have blushed if addressed by a stranger in a name not lawfully hers.

"Well," she said, in hollow accents broken by cough; "I don't know you, Monsieur."

"Poor woman!" he resumed, walking beside her as she moved slowly on, while the eyes of other women in the procession stared at him hungrily. "And your child looks ill too. It is your youngest?"

"My only one! The others are in *Père la Chaise.* There are but few children alive in my street now. God has been very merciful, and taken them to Himself."

De Mauléon recalled the scene of a neat comfortable apartment, and the healthful happy children at play on the floor. The mortality among the little ones, especially in the *quartier* occupied by the working classes, had of late been terrible. The want of food, of fuel, the intense severity of the weather, had swept them off as by a pestilence.

"And Monnier—what of him? No doubt he is a National Guard, and has his pay?"

The woman made no answer, but hung down her head. She was stifling a sob. Till then her eyes seemed to have exhausted the last source of tears.

"He lives still?" continued Victor, pityingly: "he is not wounded?"

"No: he is well—in health; thank you kindly, Monsieur."

"But his pay is not enough to help you, and of course he can get no work. Excuse me if I stopped you. It is because I owed Armand Monnier a little debt for work, and I am ashamed to say that it quite escaped my memory in these terrible events. Allow me, Madame, to pay it to you," and he thrust his purse into her hand. "I think this contains about the sum I owed; if more or less, we will settle the difference later. Take care of yourself."

He was turning away when the woman caught hold of him.

"Stay, Monsieur. May Heaven bless you!—but—but—tell me what name I am to give to Armand. I can't think of any one who owed him money. It must have been before that dreadful strike, the beginning of all our woes. Ah, if it were allowed to curse any one, I fear my last breath would not be a prayer."

"You would curse the strike, or the master who did not forgive Armand's share in it?"

"No, no,—the cruel man who talked him into it—into all that has changed the best workman, the kindest heart—the—the——" again her voice died in sobs.

"And who was that man?" asked De Mauléon, falteringly.

"His name was Lebeau. If you were a poor man, I should say 'Shun him.'"

"I have heard of the name you mention; but if we mean the same person, Monnier cannot have met him lately. He has not been in Paris since the siege."

"I suppose not, the coward! He ruined us—us who were so happy before; and then, as Armand says, cast us away as instruments he had done with. But—but if you do know him, and do see him again, tell him—tell him not to complete his wrong—not to bring murder on Armand's soul. For Armand isn't what he was—and has become, oh, so violent! I dare not take this money without saying who gave it. He would not take money as alms from an aristocrat. Hush! he beat me for taking money from the good Monsieur Raoul de Vandemar—my poor Armand beat me!"

De Mauléon shuddered. "Say that it is from a customer whose rooms he decorated in his spare hours on his own account before the strike,—Monsieur ——;" here he uttered indistinctly some unpronounceable name and hurried off, soon lost as the streets grew darker. Amid groups of a higher order of men—military men, nobles, *ci-devant* deputies—among such ones his name stood very high. Not only his bravery in the recent sorties had been signal, but a strong belief in his military talents had become prevalent; and conjoined with the name he had before established as a political writer, and the remembrance of the vigour and sagacity with which he had opposed the war, he seemed certain, when peace and order became established, of a brilliant position and career in a future administration: not less because he had steadfastly kept aloof from the existing Government, which it was rumoured, rightly or erroneously, that he had been solicited to join; and from every combination of the various democratic or discontented factions.

Quitting these more distinguished associates, he took his way alone towards the ramparts. The day was closing; the thunders of the cannon were dying down.

He passed by a wine-shop round which were gathered many of the worse specimens of the *Moblots* and National Guards, mostly drunk, and loudly talking in vehement abuse of generals and officers and commissariat. By one of the men, as he came under the glare of a petroleum lamp (there was gas no longer in the dismal city), he was recognised as the commander who had dared to insist on discipline, and disgrace honest patriots who claimed to themselves the sole option between fight and flight. The man was one of those patriots—one of the new recruits whom Victor had shamed and dismissed for mutiny and cowardice. He made a drunken plunge at his former chief, shouting, "*A bas l'aristo!* Comrades, this is the *coquin* De Mauléon who is paid by the Prussians for getting us killed: *à la lanterne!*" "*A la lanterne!*" stammered and hiccupped others of the group; but they did not stir to execute their threat. Dimly seen as the stern face and sinewy form of the threatened man was by their drowsied eyes, the name of De Mauléon, the man without fear of a foe, and without ruth for a mutineer, sufficed to protect him from outrage; and with a slight movement of his arm that sent his denouncer reeling against the lamp-post, De Mauléon passed on:—when another man, in the uniform of a National Guard, bounded from the door of the tavern, crying with a loud voice, "Who said De Mauléon?—let me look on him:" and Victor, who had strode on with slow lion-like steps, cleaving the crowd, turned, and saw before him in the gleaming light a face, in which the bold frank, intelligent aspect of former days was lost in a wild, reckless, savage expression—the face of Armand Monnier.

"Ha! are you really Victor de Mauléon?" asked Monnier, not fiercely, but under his breath,—in that sort of stage whisper which is the natural utterance of excited men under the mingled influence of potent drink and hoarded rage.

"Certainly; I am Victor de Mauléon."

"And you were in command of the —— company of the National Guard on the 30th of November at Champigny and Villiers?"

"I was."

"And you shot with your own hand an officer belonging to another company who refused to join yours?"

"I shot a cowardly soldier who ran away from the enemy, and seemed a ringleader of other runaways; and in so doing, I saved from dishonour the best part of his comrades."

"The man was no coward. He was an enlightened Frenchman, and worth fifty of such *aristos* as you; and he knew better than his officers that he was to be led to an idle slaughter. Idle—I say idle. What was France the better, how was Paris the safer, for the senseless butchery of that day? You mutinied against a wiser general than Saint Trochu when you murdered that mutineer."

"Armand Monnier, you are not quite sober to-night, or I would argue with you that question. But you no doubt are brave: how and why do you take the part of a runaway?"

"How and why? He was my brother, and you own

you murdered him: my brother—the sagest head in Paris.
If I had listened to him, I should not be,—*bah!*—no matter
now what I am."

"I could not know he was your brother; but if he had
been mine I would have done the same."

Here Victor's lip quivered, for Monnier griped him by
the arm, and looked him in the face with wild stony eyes.

"I recollect that voice! Yet—yet—you say you are a
noble, a Vicomte—Victor de Mauléon, and you shot my
brother!"

Here he passed his left hand rapidly over his forehead.
The fumes of wine still clouded his mind, but rays of intelligence broke through the cloud. Suddenly he said in a
loud, and calm, and natural voice:

"Mons. le Vicomte, you accost me as Armand Monnier—
pray how do you know my name?"

"How should I not know it? I have looked into the
meetings of the 'Clubs *rouges*.' I have heard you speak, and
naturally asked your name. *Bon soir*, M. Monnier! When
you reflect in cooler moments, you will see that if patriots
excuse Brutus for first dishonouring and then executing his
own son, an officer charged to defend his country may be
surely pardoned for slaying a runaway to whom he was no
relation, when in slaying he saved the man's name and
kindred from dishonour—unless, indeed, you insist on telling the world why he was slain."

"I know your voice—I know it. Every sound becomes
clearer to my ear. And if——"

But while Monnier thus spoke, De Mauléon had hastened
on. Monnier looked round, saw him gone, but did not pursue. He was just intoxicated enough to know that his footsteps were not steady, and he turned back to the wine-shop
and asked surlily for more wine. Could you have seen him
then as he leant swinging himself to and fro against the
wall,—had you known the man two years ago, you would
have been a brute if you felt disgust. You could only have
felt that profound compassion with which we gaze on a

great royalty fallen. For the grandest of all royalties is that which takes its crown from Nature, needing no accident of birth. And Nature made the mind of Armand Monnier king-like; endowed it with lofty scorn of meanness and falsehood and dishonour, with warmth and tenderness of heart which had glow enough to spare from ties of kindred and hearth and home, to extend to those distant circles of humanity over which royal natures would fain extend the shadow of their sceptre.

How had the royalty of the man's nature fallen thus? Royalty rarely falls from its own constitutional faults. It falls when, ceasing to be royal, it becomes subservient to bad advisers. And what bad advisers, always appealing to his better qualities and so enlisting his worser, had discrowned this mechanic?

"A little knowledge is a dangerous thing, "

says the old-fashioned poet. "Not so," says the modern philosopher; "a little knowledge is safer than no knowledge." Possibly, as all individuals and all communities must go through the stage of a little knowledge before they can arrive at that of much knowledge, the philosopher's assertion may be right in the long-run, and applied to humankind in general. But there is a period, as there is a class, in which a little knowledge tends to terrible demoralisation. And Armand Monnier lived in that period and was one of that class. The little knowledge that his mind, impulsive and ardent, had picked up out of books that warred with the great foundations of existing society, had originated in ill advices. A man stored with much knowledge would never have let Madame de Grantmesnil's denunciations of marriage rites, or Louis Blanc's vindication of Robespierre as the representative of the working against the middle class, influence his practical life. He would have assessed such opinions at their real worth; and whatever that worth might seem to him, would not to such opinions have committed the conduct of his life. Opinion is not fateful: conduct is. A little knowledge crazes an earnest, warm-blooded, powerful creature like Armand Monnier into a fanatic. He takes an opinion which pleases him as a revelation from the gods; that opinion shapes his conduct; that conduct is his fate. Woe to the philosopher who serenely flings before the little knowledge of the artisan dogmas as harmless as the Atlantis of Plato if only to be discussed by philosophers, and deadly as the torches of Até if seized as articles of a creed by fanatics! But thrice woe to the artisan who makes himself the zealot of the Dogma!

Poor Armand acts on the opinions he adopts; proves his contempt for the marriage state by living with the wife of another; resents, as natures so inherently manly must do, the Society that visits on her his defiance of its laws; throws himself, head foremost, against that society altogether; necessarily joins all who have other reasons for hostility to Society; he himself having every inducement not to join indiscriminate strikes—high wages, a liberal employer, ample savings, the certainty of soon becoming employer himself. No; that is not enough to the fanatic: he persists on being dupe and victim. He, this great king of labour, crowned by Nature, and cursed with that degree of little knowledge which does not comprehend how much more is required before a schoolboy would admit it to be knowledge at all,—he rushes into the maddest of all speculations—that of the artisan with little knowledge and enormous faith—that which intrusts the safety and repose and dignity of life to some ambitious adventurer, who uses his warm heart for the adventurer's frigid purpose, much as the lawyer-government of September used the Communists,—much as, in every revolution of France, a Bertrand has used a Raton—much as, till the sound of the last trumpet, men very much worse than Victor de Mauléon will use men very much better than Armand Monnier, if the Armand Monniers disdain the modesty of an Isaac Newton on hearing that a theorem to which he had given all the strength of his patient intellect was disputed: "It may be so;" meaning, I suppose, that it requires a large amount of experience ascertained before a man of much knowledge becomes that which a man of little knowledge is at a jump—the fanatic of an experiment untried.

CHAPTER II.

SCARCELY had De Mauléon quitted Lemercier before the latter was joined by two loungers scarcely less famished than himself—Savarin and De Brézé. Like himself, too, both had been sufferers from illness, though not of a nature to be consigned to an hospital. All manner of diseases then had combined to form the pestilence which filled the streets with unregarded hearses—bronchitis, pneumonia, smallpox, a strange sort of spurious dysentery much more speedily fatal than the genuine. The three men, a year before so sleek, looked like ghosts under the withering sky; yet all three retained embers of the native Parisian humour, which their very breath on meeting sufficed to kindle up into jubilant sparks or rapid flashes.

"There are two consolations," said Savarin, as the friends strolled or rather crawled towards the Boulevards—"two consolations for the *gourmet* and for the proprietor in these days of trial for the gourmand, because the price of truffles is come down."

"Truffles!" gasped De Brézé, with watering mouth; "impossible! They are gone with the age of gold."

"Not so. I speak on the best authority—my laundress; for she attends the *succursale* in the Rue de Chateaudun; and if the poor woman, being, luckily for me, a childless widow, gets a morsel she can spare, she sells it to me."

"Sells it!" feebly exclaimed Lemercier. "Crœsus! you have money then, and can buy?"

"Sells it—on credit! I am to pension her for life if I live to have money again. Don't interrupt me. This honest woman goes this morning to the *succursale*. I promise myself a delicious *bifteck* of horse. She gains the *succursale*, and the *employé* informs her that there is nothing left in his store except—truffles. A glut of those in the market allows him to offer her a bargain—seven francs *la boîte*. Send me seven francs, De Brézé, and you shall share the banquet."

De Brézé shook his head expressively.

"But," resumed Savarin, "though credit exists no more except with my laundress, upon terms of which the usury is necessarily proportioned to the risk, yet, as I had the honour before to observe, there is comfort for the proprietor. The instinct of property is imperishable."

"Not in the house where I lodge," said Lemercier. "Two soldiers were billeted there; and during my stay in the ambulance they enter my rooms, and cart away all of the little furniture left there, except a bed and a table. Brought before a court-martial, they defend themselves by saying, 'The rooms were abandoned.' The excuse was held valid. They were let off with a reprimand and a promise to restore what was not already disposed of. They have restored me another table and four chairs."

"Nevertheless, they had the instinct of property, though erroneously developed, otherwise they would not have deemed any excuse for their act necessary. Now for my instance of the inherent tenacity of that instinct. A worthy citizen in want of fuel sees a door in a garden wall, and naturally carries off the door. He is apprehended by a *gendarme* who sees the act. '*Voleur*,' he cries to the *gendarme*, 'do you want to rob me of my property?' 'That door your property? I saw you take it away.' 'You confess,' cries the citizen, triumphantly—'you confess that it is my property; for you saw me appropriate it.' Thus you see how imperishable is the instinct of property. No sooner does it disappear as yours than it reappears as mine."

"I would laugh if I could," said Lemercier, "but such a convulsion would be fatal. *Dieu des dieux,* how empty I

II.—15

am!" He reeled as he spoke, and clung to De Brézé for
support. De Brézé had the reputation of being the most
selfish of men. But at that moment, when a generous man
might be excused for being selfish enough to desire to keep
the little that he had for his own reprieve from starvation,
this egotist became superb. "Friends," he cried, with enthusiasm, "I have something yet in my pocket; we will
dine, all three of us."

"Dine!" faltered Lemercier. "Dine! I have not dined
since I left the hospital. I breakfasted yesterday—on two
mice upon toast. Dainty, but not nutritious. And I
shared them with Fox."

"Fox! Fox lives still, then?" cried De Brézé, startled.

"In a sort of way he does. But one mouse since yesterday morning is not much; and he can't expect that every
day."

"Why don't you take him out?" asked Savarin. "Give
him a chance of picking up a bone somewhere."

"I dare not; he would be picked up himself. Dogs are
getting very valuable: they sell for 50 francs apiece.
Come, De Brézé, where are we to dine?"

"I and Savarin can dine at the London Tavern upon rat
pâté or jugged cat. But it would be impertinence to invite a satrap like yourself who has a whole dog in his larder—a dish of 50 francs—a dish for a king. Adieu, my
dear Frederic. *Allons*, Savarin."

"I feasted you on better meats than dog when I could
afford it," said Frederic, plaintively; "and the first time
you invite me you retract the invitation. Be it so. *Bon
appetit.*"

"*Bah!*" said De Brézé, catching Frederic's arm as he
turned to depart. "Of course I was but jesting. Only
another day, when my pockets will be empty, do think
what an excellent thing a roasted dog is, and make up your
mind while Fox has still some little flesh on his bones."

"Flesh!" said Savarin, detaining them. Look! See
how right Voltaire was in saying, 'Amusement is the first

necessity of civilised man.' Paris can do without bread: Paris still retains Polichinello."

He pointed to the puppet-show, round which a crowd, not of children alone, but of men—middle-aged and old—were collected; while sous were dropped into the tin handed round by a squalid boy.

"And, *mon ami*," whispered De Brézé to Lemercier, with the voice of a tempting fiend, "observe how Punch is without his dog."

It was true. The dog was gone,—its place supplied by a melancholy emaciated cat.

Frederic crawled towards the squalid boy. "What has become of Punch's dog?"

"We ate him last Sunday. Next Sunday we shall have the cat in a pie," said the urchin, with a sensual smack of the lips.

"O Fox! Fox!" murmured Frederic, as the three men went slowly down through the darkening streets—the roar of the Prussian guns heard afar, while distinct and near rang the laugh of the idlers round the Punch without a dog.

CHAPTER III.

WHILE De Brézé and his friends were feasting at the *Café Anglais*, and faring better than the host had promised—for the bill of fare comprised such luxuries as ass, mule, peas, fried potatoes, and champagne (champagne in some mysterious way was inexhaustible during the time of famine)—a very different group had assembled in the rooms of Isaura Cicogna. She and the Venosta had hitherto escaped the extreme destitution to which many richer persons had been reduced. It is true that Isaura's fortune placed in the hands of the absent Louvier, and invested in the new street that was to have been, brought no return. It was true that in that street the Venosta, dreaming of cent. per

cent., had invested all her savings. But the Venosta, at
the first announcement of war, had insisted on retaining in
hand a small sum from the amount Isaura had received from
her "*roman*," that might suffice for current expenses, and
with yet more acute foresight had laid in stores of provisions
and fuel immediately after the probability of a siege became
apparent. But even the provident mind of the Venosta had
never foreseen that the siege would endure so long, or that
the prices of all articles of necessity would rise so high.
And meanwhile all resources—money, fuel, provisions—
had been largely drawn upon by the charity and benevolence of Isaura, without much remonstrance on the part of
the Venosta, whose nature was very accessible to pity. Un-
fortunately, too, of late money and provisions had failed to
Monsieur and Madame Rameau, their income consisting
partly of rents no longer paid, and the profits of a sleeping
partnership in the old shop, from which custom had departed; so that they came to share the fireside and meals at
the rooms of their son's *fiancée* with little scruple, because
utterly unaware that the money retained and the provisions
stored by the Venosta were now nearly exhausted.

The patriotic ardour which had first induced the elder
Rameau to volunteer his services as a National Guard had
been ere this cooled if not suppressed, first by the hardships
of the duty, and then by the disorderly conduct of his associates, and their ribald talk and obscene songs. He was
much beyond the age at which he could be registered. His
son was, however, compelled to become his substitute,
though from his sickly health and delicate frame attached
to that portion of the National Guard which took no part
in actual engagements, and was supposed to do work on the
ramparts and maintain order in the city.

In that duty, so opposed to his tastes and habits, Gustave
signalised himself as one of the loudest declaimers against
the imbecility of the Government, and in the demand for
immediate and energetic action, no matter at what loss of
life, on the part of all—except the heroic force to which he

himself was attached. Still, despite his military labours, Gustave found leisure to contribute to Red journals, and his contributions paid him tolerably well. To do him justice, his parents concealed from him the extent of their destitution; they, on their part, not aware that he was so able to assist them, rather fearing that he himself had nothing else for support but his scanty pay as a National Guard. In fact, of late the parents and son had seen little of each other. M. Rameau, though a Liberal politician, was Liberal as a tradesman, not as a Red Republican or a Socialist. And, though little heeding his son's theories while the Empire secured him from the practical effect of them, he was now as sincerely frightened at the chance of the Communists becoming rampant as most of the Parisian tradesmen were. Madame Rameau, on her side, though she had the dislike to aristocrats which was prevalent with her class, was a stanch Roman Catholic; and seeing in the disasters that had befallen her country the punishment justly incurred by its sins, could not but be shocked by the opinions of Gustave, though she little knew that he was the author of certain articles in certain journals, in which these opinions were proclaimed with a vehemence far exceeding that which they assumed in his conversation. She had spoken to him with warm anger, mixed with passionate tears, on his irreligious principles; and from that moment Gustave shunned to give her another opportunity of insulting his pride and depreciating his wisdom.

Partly to avoid meeting his parents, partly because he recoiled almost as much from the *ennui* of meeting the other visitors at her apartments—the Paris ladies associated with her in the ambulance, Raoul de Vandemar, whom he especially hated, and the Abbé Vertpré, who had recently come into intimate friendship with both the Italian ladies—his visits to Isaura had become exceedingly rare. He made his incessant military duties the pretext for absenting himself; and now, on this evening, there were gathered round Isaura's hearth—on which burned almost the last of the hoarded fuel—the Venosta, the two Rameaus, the Abbé Vertpré, who was attached as confessor to the society of which Isaura was so zealous a member. The old priest and the young poetess had become dear friends. There is in the nature of a woman (and especially of a woman at once so gifted and so childlike as Isaura, combining an innate tendency towards faith with a restless inquisitiveness of intellect, which is always suggesting query or doubt) a craving for something afar from the sphere of her sorrow, which can only be obtained through that "bridal of the earth and sky" which we call religion. And hence, to natures like Isaura's, that link between the woman and the priest, which the philosophy of France has never been able to dissever.

"It is growing late," said Madame Rameau; "I am beginning to feel uneasy. Our dear Isaura is not yet returned."

"You need be under no apprehension," said the Abbé. "The ladies attached to the ambulance of which she is so tender and zealous a sister incur no risk. There are always brave men related to the sick and wounded who see to the safe return of the women. My poor Raoul visits that ambulance daily. His kinsman, M. de Rochebriant, is there among the wounded."

"Not seriously hurt, I hope," said the Venosta; "not disfigured? He was so handsome; it is only the ugly warrior whom a scar on the face improves."

"Don't be alarmed, Signora; the Prussian guns spared his face. His wounds in themselves were not dangerous, but he lost a good deal of blood. Raoul and the Christian brothers found him insensible among a heap of the slain."

"M. de Vandemar seems to have very soon recovered the shock of his poor brother's death," said Madame Rameau. "There is very little heart in an aristocrat."

The Abbé's mild brow contracted. "Have more charity, my daughter. It is because Raoul's sorrow for his lost brother is so deep and so holy that he devotes himself more than ever to the service of the Father which is in heaven. He said, a day or two after the burial, when plans for a monument to Enguerrand were submitted to him: 'May my prayer be vouchsafed, and my life be a memorial of him more acceptable to his gentle spirit than monuments of bronze or marble. May I be divinely guided and sustained in my desire to do such good acts as he would have done had he been spared longer to earth. And whenever tempted to weary, may my conscience whisper, Betray not the trust left to thee by thy brother, lest thou be not reunited to him at last.'"

"Pardon me, pardon!" murmured Madame Rameau humbly, while the Venosta burst into tears.

The Abbé, though a most sincere and earnest ecclesiastic, was a cheery and genial man of the world; and, in order to relieve Madame Rameau from the painful self-reproach he had before excited, he turned the conversation. "I must beware, however," he said, with his pleasant laugh, "as to the company in which I interfere in family questions; and especially in which I defend my poor Raoul from any charge brought against him. For some good friend this day sent me a terrible organ of communistic philosophy, in which we humble priests are very roughly handled, and I myself am especially singled out by name as a pestilent intermeddler in the affairs of private households. I am said to set the women against the brave men who are friends of the people, and am cautioned by very truculent threats to cease from such villainous practices." And here, with a dry humour that turned into ridicule what would otherwise have excited disgust and indignation among his listeners, he read aloud passages replete with the sort of false eloquence which was then the vogue among the Red journals. In these passages, not only the Abbé was pointed out for popular execration, but Raoul de Vandemar, though not expressly named, was clearly indicated as a pupil of the Abbé's, the type of a lay Jesuit.

The Venosta alone did not share in the contemptuous

laughter with which the inflated style of these diatribes inspired the Rameaus. Her simple Italian mind was horror-stricken by language which the Abbe treated with ridicule.

"Ah!" said M. Rameau, "I guess the author—that firebrand Felix Pyat."

"No," answered the Abbé; "the writer signs himself by the name of a more learned atheist—Diderot *le jeune*."

Here the door opened, and Raoul entered, accompanying Isaura. A change had come over the face of the young Vandemar since his brother's death. The lines about the mouth had deepened, the cheeks had lost their rounded contour and grown somewhat hollow. But the expression was as serene as ever, perhaps even less pensively melancholy. His whole aspect was that of a man who has sorrowed, but been supported in sorrow; perhaps it was more sweet—certainly it was more lofty.

And, as if there were in the atmosphere of his presence something that communicated the likeness of his own soul to others, since Isaura had been brought into his companionship, her own lovely face had caught the expression that prevailed in his—that, too, had become more sweet—that, too, had become more lofty.

The friendship that had grown up between these two young mourners was of a very rare nature. It had in it no sentiment that could ever warm into the passion of human love. Indeed, had Isaura's heart been free to give away, love for Raoul de Vandemar would have seemed to her a profanation. He was never more priestly than when he was most tender. And the tenderness of Raoul towards her was that of some saint-like nature towards the acolyte whom it attracted upwards. He had once, just before Enguerrand's death, spoken to Isaura with a touching candour as to his own predilection for a monastic life. "The worldly avocations that open useful and honourable careers for others have no charm for me. I care not for riches nor power, nor honours nor fame. The austerities of the conventual life have no terror for me; on the contrary, they have a charm, for with them are abstraction from earth and meditation on heaven. In earlier years I might, like other men, have cherished dreams of human love, and felicity in married life, but for the sort of veneration with which I regarded one to whom I owe—humanly speaking—whatever of good there may be in me. Just when first taking my place among the society of young men who banish from their life all thought of another, I came under the influence of a woman who taught me to see that holiness was beauty. She gradually associated me with her acts of benevolence, and from her I learned to love God too well not to be indulgent to his creatures. I know not whether the attachment I felt to her could have been inspired in one who had not from childhood conceived a romance, not perhaps justified by history, for the ideal images of chivalry. My feeling for her at first was that of the pure and poetic homage which a young knight was permitted, *sans reproche*, to render to some fair queen or *châtelaine*, whose colours he wore in the lists, whose spotless repute he would have perilled his life to defend. But soon even that sentiment, pure as it was, became chastened from all breath of earthly love, in proportion as the admiration refined itself into reverence. She has often urged me to marry, but I have no bride on this earth. I do but want to see Enguerrand happily married, and then I quit the world for the cloister."

But after Enguerrand's death, Raoul resigned all idea of the convent. That evening, as he attended to their homes Isaura and the other ladies attached to the ambulance, he said, in answer to inquiries about his mother, "She is resigned and calm. I have promised her I will not, while she lives, bury her other son: I renounce my dreams of the monastery."

Raoul did not remain many minutes at Isaura's. The Abbé accompanied him on his way home. "I have a request to make to you," said the former; "you know, of course, your distant cousin the Vicomte de Mauléon?"

"Yes. Not so well as I ought, for Enguerrand liked him."

"Well enough, at all events, to call on him with a request which I am commissioned to make, but it might come better from you as a kinsman. I am a stranger to him, and I know not whether a man of that sort would not regard as an officious intermeddling any communication made to him by a priest. The matter, however, is a very simple one. At the convent of —— there is a poor nun who is, I fear, dying. She has an intense desire to see M. de Mauléon, whom she declares to be her uncle, and her only surviving relative. The laws of the convent are not too austere to prevent the interview she seeks in such a case. I should add that I am not acquainted with her previous history. I am not the confessor of the sisterhood; he, poor man, was badly wounded by a chance ball a few days ago when attached to an ambulance on the ramparts. As soon as the surgeon would allow him to see any one, he sent for me, and bade me go to the nun I speak of—Sister Ursula. It seems that he had informed her that M. de Mauléon was at Paris, and had promised to ascertain his address. His wound had prevented his doing so, but he trusted to me to procure the information. I am well acquainted with the Supérieure of the convent, and I flatter myself that she holds me in esteem. I had therefore no difficulty to obtain her permission to see this poor nun, which I did this evening. She implored me for the peace of her soul to lose no time in finding out M. de Mauléon's address, and entreating him to visit her. Lest he should demur, I was to give him the name by which he had known her in the world—Louise Duval. Of course I obeyed. The address of a man who has so distinguished himself in this unhappy siege I very easily obtained, and repaired at once to M. de Mauléon's apartment. I there learned that he was from home, and it was uncertain whether he would not spend the night on the ramparts."

"I will not fail to see him early in the morning," said Raoul, "and execute your commission."

CHAPTER IV.

DE MAULEON was somewhat surprised by Raoul's visit the next morning. He had no great liking for a kinsman whose politely distant reserve towards him, in contrast to poor Enguerrand's genial heartiness, had much wounded his sensitive self-respect; nor could he comprehend the religious scruples which forbade Raoul to take a soldier's share in the battle-field, though in seeking there to save the lives of others so fearlessly hazarding his own life.

"Pardon," said Raoul, with his sweet mournful smile, "the unseasonable hour at which I disturb you. But your duties on the ramparts and mine in the hospital begin early, and I have promised the Abbé Vertpré to communicate a message of a nature which perhaps you may deem pressing." He proceeded at once to repeat what the Abbé had communicated to him the night before relative to the illness and the request of the nun.

"Louise Duval!" exclaimed the Vicomte, "discovered at last, and a *religieuse!* Ah! I now understand why she never sought me out when I reappeared at Paris. Tidings of that sort do not penetrate the walls of a convent. I am greatly obliged to you, M. de Vandemar, for the trouble you have so kindly taken. This poor nun is related to me, and I will at once obey the summons. But this convent *des* —— I am ashamed to say I know not where it is. A long way off, I suppose?"

"Allow me to be your guide," said Raoul; "I should take it as a favour to be allowed to see a little more of a man whom my lost brother held in such esteem."

Victor was touched by this conciliatory speech, and in a few minutes more the two men were on their way to the convent on the other side of the Seine.

Victor commenced the conversation by a warm and heart-felt tribute to Enguerrand's character and memory. "I never," he said, "knew a nature more rich in the most endearing qualities of youth; so gentle, so high-spirited, rendering every virtue more attractive, and redeeming such few faults or foibles as youth so situated and so tempted cannot wholly escape, with an urbanity not conventional, not artificial, but reflected from the frankness of a genial temper and the tenderness of a generous heart. Be comforted for his loss, my kinsman. A brave death was the proper crown of that beautiful life."

Raoul made no answer, but pressed gratefully the arm now linked within his own. The companions walked on in silence; Victor's mind settling on the visit he was about to make to the niece so long mysteriously lost, and now so unexpectedly found. Louise had inspired him with a certain interest from her beauty and force of character, but never with any warm affection. He felt relieved to find that her life had found its close in the sanctuary of the convent. He had never divested himself of a certain fear, inspired by Louvier's statement that she might live to bring scandal and disgrace on the name he had with so much difficulty, and after so lengthened an anguish, partially cleared in his own person.

Raoul left De Mauléon at the gate of the convent, and took his way towards the hospitals where he visited, and the poor whom he relieved.

Victor was conducted silently into the convent *parloir;* and, after waiting there several minutes, the door opened, and the Supérieure entered. As she advanced towards him, with stately step and solemn visage, De Mauléon recoiled, and uttered a half-suppressed exclamation that partook both of amaze and awe. Could it be possible? Was this majestic woman, with the grave impassible aspect, once the ardent girl whose tender letters he had cherished through stormy years, and only burned on the night before the most perilous of his battle-fields? This the one, the sole one, whom in his younger dreams he had seen as his destined wife? It was so—it was. Doubt vanished when he heard her voice; and yet how different every tone, every accent, from those of the low, soft, thrilling music that had breathed in the voice of old!

"M. de Mauléon," said the Supérieure, calmly, "I grieve to sadden you by very mournful intelligence. Yesterday evening, when the Abbé undertook to convey to you the request of our Sister Ursula, although she was beyond mortal hope of recovery—as otherwise you will conceive that I could not have relaxed the rules of this house so as to sanction your visit—there was no apprehension of immediate danger. It was believed that her sufferings would be prolonged for some days. I saw her late last night before retiring to my cell, and she seemed even stronger than she had been for the last week. A sister remained at watch in her cell. Towards morning she fell into apparently quiet sleep, and in that sleep she passed away." The Supérieure here crossed herself, and murmured pious words in Latin.

"Dead! my poor niece!" said Victor, feelingly, roused from his stun at the first sight of the Supérieure by her measured tones, and the melancholy information she so composedly conveyed to him. "I cannot, then, even learn why she so wished to see me once more,—or what she might have requested at my hands!"

"Pardon, M. le Vicomte. Such sorrowful consolation I have resolved to afford you, not without scruples of conscience, but not without sanction of the excellent Abbé Vertpré, whom I summoned early this morning to decide my duties in the sacred office I hold. As soon as Sister Ursula heard of your return to Paris, she obtained my permission to address to you a letter, subjected, when finished, to my perusal and sanction. She felt that she had much on her mind which her feeble state might forbid her to make known to you in conversation with sufficient fulness; and as she could only have seen you in presence of one of the sisters she imagined that there would also be less restraint in a written communication. In fine, her request was that, when you called, I might first place this letter in your hands, and allow you time to read it, before being admitted to her presence; when a few words conveying your promise to attend to the wishes with which you would then be acquainted, would suffice for an interview in her exhausted condition.   Do I make myself understood?"

"Certainly, Madame,—and the letter?"

"She had concluded last evening; and when I took leave of her later in the night, she placed it in my hands for approval.   M. le Vicomte, it pains me to say that there is much in the tone of that letter which I grieve for and condemn.   And it was my intention to point this out to our sister at morning, and tell her that passages must be altered before I could give to you the letter.   Her sudden decease deprived me of this opportunity.   I could not, of course, alter or erase a line—a word.   My only option was to suppress the letter altogether, or give it you intact.   The Abbé thinks that, on the whole, my duty does not forbid the dictate of my own impulse—my own feelings; and I now place this letter in your hands."

De Mauléon took a packet, unsealed, from the thin white fingers of the Supérieure; and as he bent to receive it, lifted towards her eyes eloquent with sorrowful, humble pathos, in which it was impossible for the heart of a woman who had loved not to see a reference to the past which the lips did not dare to utter.

A faint, scarce-perceptible blush stole over the marble cheek of the nun.   But, with an exquisite delicacy, in which survived the woman while reigned the nun, she replied to the appeal.

"M. Victor de Mauléon, before, having thus met, we part for ever, permit a poor *religieuse* to say with what joy— a joy rendered happier because it was tearful—I have learned through the Abbé Vertpré that the honour which, as between man and man, no one who had once known you could ever doubt, you have lived to vindicate from calumny."

"Ah; you have heard that—at last, at last!"

"I repeat—of the honour thus deferred, I never doubted."
The Supérieure hurried on. "Greater joy it has been to
me to hear from the same venerable source that, while
found bravest among the defenders of your country, you
are clear from all alliance with the assailants of your God.
Continue so, continue so, Victor de Mauléon,"

She retreated to the door, and then turned towards him
with a look in which all the marble had melted away; adding, with words more formally nunlike, yet unmistakably
womanlike, than those which had gone before, "That to
the last you may be true to God, is a prayer never by me
omitted."

She spoke, and vanished.

In a kind of dim and dreamlike bewilderment, Victor de
Mauléon found himself without the walls of the convent.
Mechanically, as a man does when the routine of his life
is presented to him, from the first Minister of State to the
poor clown at a suburban theatre, doomed to appear at their
posts, to prose on a Beer Bill, or grin through a horse-col-
lar, though their hearts are bleeding at every pore with
some household or secret affliction,—mechanically De Mauléon went his way towards the ramparts, at a section of
which he daily drilled his raw recruits. Proverbial for his
severity towards those who offended, for the cordiality of
his praise of those who pleased his soldierly judgment, no
change of his demeanour was visible that morning, save
that he might be somewhat milder to the one, somewhat
less hearty to the other. This routine duty done, he passed
slowly towards a more deserted because a more exposed
part of the defences, and seated himself on the frozen
sward alone. The cannon thundered around him. He
heard unconsciously: from time to time an *obus* hissed and
splintered close at his feet;—he saw with abstracted eye.
His soul was with the past; and, brooding over all that in
the past lay buried there, came over him a conviction of
the vanity of the human earth-bounded objects for which
we burn or freeze, far more absolute than had grown out of

the worldly cynicism connected with his worldly ambition. The sight of that face, associated with the one pure romance of his reckless youth, the face of one so estranged, so serenely aloft from all memories of youth, of romance, of passion, smote him in the midst of the new hopes of the new career, as the look on the skull of the woman he had so loved and so mourned, when disburied from her grave, smote the brilliant noble who became the stern reformer of La Trappe. And while thus gloomily meditating, the letter of the poor Louise Duval was forgotten. She whose existence had so troubled, and crossed, and partly marred the lives of others,—she, scarcely dead, and already forgotten by her nearest kin. Well—had she not forgotten, put wholly out of her mind, all that was due to those much nearer to her than is an uncle to a niece?

The short, bitter, sunless day was advancing towards its decline before Victor roused himself with a quick impatient start from his reverie, and took forth the letter from the dead nun.

It began with expressions of gratitude, of joy at the thought that she should see him again before she died, thank him for his past kindness, and receive, she trusted, his assurance that he would attend to her last remorseful injunctions. I pass over much that followed in the explanation of events in her life sufficiently known to the reader. She stated, as the strongest reason why she had refused the hand of Louvier, her knowledge that she should in due time become a mother—a fact concealed from Victor, secure that he would then urge her not to annul her informal marriage, but rather insist on the ceremonies that would render it valid. She touched briefly on her confidential intimacy with Madame Marigny, the exchange of name and papers, her confinement in the neighbourhood of Aix, the child left to the care of the nurse, the journey to Munich to find the false Louise Duval was no more. The documents obtained through the agency of her easy-tempered kinsman, the late Marquis de Rochebriant, and her subsequent do-

mestication in the house of the von Rudesheims,—all this
it is needless to do more here than briefly recapitulate.
The letter then went on: " While thus kindly treated by the
family with whom nominally a governess, I was on the
terms of a friend with Signor Ludovico Cicogna, an Italian
of noble birth.   He was the only man I ever cared for.   I
loved him with frail human passion.   I could not tell him
my true history.   I could not tell him that I had a child;
such intelligence would have made him renounce me at
once.   He had a daughter, still but an infant, by a former
marriage, then brought up in France.   He wished to take
her to his house, and his second wife to supply the place
of her mother.   What was I to do with the child I had
left near Aix?   While doubtful and distracted, I read an
advertisement in the journals to the effect that a French
lady, then staying in Coblentz, wished to adopt a female
child not exceeding the age of six: the child to be wholly
resigned to her by the parents, she undertaking to rear and
provide for it as her own.   I resolved to go to Coblentz at
once.   I did so.   I saw this lady.   She seemed in affluent
circumstances, yet young, but a confirmed invalid, confined
the greater part of the day to her sofa by some malady of
the spine.   She told me very frankly her story.   She had
been a professional dancer on the stage, had married re-
spectably, quitted the stage, become a widow, and shortly
afterwards been seized with the complaint that would probably for life keep her a secluded prisoner in her room.
Thus afflicted, and without tie, interest, or object in the
world, she conceived the idea of adopting a child that she
might bring up to tend and cherish her as a daughter.   In
this, the imperative condition was that the child should
never be sought by the parents.   She was pleased by my
manner and appearance: she did not wish her adopted
daughter to be the child of peasants.   She asked me for no
references,—made no inquiries.   She said cordially that
she wished for no knowledge that, through any indiscretion
of her own, communicated to the child might lead her to

II.—16

seek the discovery of her real parents. In fine, I left Coblentz on the understanding that I was to bring the infant,
and if it pleased Madame Surville, the agreement was concluded.

"I then repaired to Aix. I saw the child. Alas! unnatural mother that I was, the sight only more vividly
brought before me the sense of my own perilous position.
Yet the child was lovely! a likeness of myself, but lovelier
far, for it was a pure, innocent, gentle loveliness. And
they told her to call me '*Maman.*' Oh, did I not relent
when I heard that name? No; it jarred on my ear as a
word of reproach and shame. In walking with the infant
towards the railway station, imagine my dismay when suddenly I met the man who had been taught to believe me
dead. I soon discovered that his dismay was equal to my
own,—that I had nothing to fear from his desire to claim
me. It did occur to me for a moment to resign his child
to him. But when he shrank reluctantly from a half suggestion to that effect, my pride was wounded, my conscience
absolved. And, after all, it might be unsafe to my future
to leave with him any motive for tracing me. I left him
hastily. I have never seen nor heard of him more. I
took the child to Coblentz. Madame Surville was charmed
with its prettiness and prattle,—charmed still more when
I rebuked the poor infant for calling me '*Maman,*' and
said, 'Thy real mother is here.' Freed from my trouble,
I returned to the kind German roof I had quitted, and
shortly after became the wife of Ludovico Cicogna.

"My punishment soon began. His was a light, fickle,
pleasure-hunting nature. He soon grew weary of me. My
very love made me unamiable to him. I became irritable,
jealous, exacting. His daughter, who now came to live
with us, was another subject of discord. I knew that he
loved her better than me. I became a harsh step-mother;
and Ludovico's reproaches, vehemently made, nursed all
my angriest passions. But a son of this new marriage was
born to myself. My pretty Luigi! how my heart became

wrapt up in him! Nursing him, I forgot resentment
against his father. Well, poor Cicogna fell ill and died.
I mourned him sincerely; but my boy was left. Poverty
then fell on me,—poverty extreme. Cicogna's sole income
was derived from a post in the Austrian dominion in Italy,
and ceased with it. He received a small pension in compensation; that died with him.

"At this time, an Englishman, with whom Ludovico had
made acquaintance in Venice, and who visited often at our
house in Verona, offered me his hand. He had taken an
extraordinary liking to Isaura, Cicogna's daughter by his
first marriage. But I think his proposal was dictated
partly by compassion for me, and more by affection for her.
For the sake of my boy Luigi I married him. He was a
good man, of retired learned habits with which I had no
sympathy. His companionship overwhelmed me with
ennui. But I bore it patiently for Luigi's sake. God
saw that my heart was as much as ever estranged from
Him, and He took away my all on earth—my boy. Then
in my desolation I turned to our Holy Church for comfort.
I found a friend in the priest, my confessor. I was startled
to learn from him how guilty I had been—was still. Pushing to an extreme the doctrines of the Church, he would
not allow that my first marriage, though null by law, was
void in the eyes of Heaven. Was not the death of the
child I so cherished a penalty due to my sin towards the
child I had abandoned?

"These thoughts pressed on me night and day. With
the consent and approval of the good priest, I determined
to quit the roof of M. Selby, and to devote myself to the
discovery of my forsaken Julie.

"I had a painful interview with M. Selby. I announced
my intention to separate from him. I alleged as a reason
my conscientious repugnance to live with a professed heretic—an enemy to our Holy Church. When M. Selby
found that he could not shake my resolution, he lent himself to it with the forbearance and generosity which he had

always exhibited. On our marriage he had settled on me five thousand pounds, to be absolutely mine in the event of his death. He now proposed to concede to me the interest on that capital during his life, and he undertook the charge of my step-daughter Isaura, and secured to her all the rest he had to leave; such landed property as he possessed in England passing to a distant relative.

"So we parted, not with hostility—tears were shed on both sides. I set out for Coblentz. Madame Surville had long since quitted that town, devoting some years to the round of various mineral spas in vain hope of cure. Not without some difficulty I traced her to her last residence in the neighbourhood of Paris, but she was then no more—her death accelerated by the shock occasioned by the loss of her whole fortune, which she had been induced to place in one of the numerous fraudulent companies by which so many have been ruined. Julie, who was with her at the time of her death, had disappeared shortly after it—none could tell me whither; but from such hints as I could gather, the poor child, thus left destitute, had been betrayed into sinful courses.

"Probably I might yet by searching inquiry have found her out; you will say it was my duty at least to institute such inquiry. No doubt; I now remorsefully feel that it was. I did not think so at the time. The Italian priest had given me a few letters of introduction to French ladies with whom, when they had sojourned at Florence, he had made acquaintance. These ladies were very strict devotees, formal observers of those decorums by which devotion proclaims itself to the world. They had received me not only with kindness but with marked respect. They chose to exalt into the noblest self-sacrifice the act of my leaving M. Selby's house. Exaggerating the simple cause assigned to it in the priest's letter, they represented me as quitting a luxurious home and an idolising husband rather than continue intimate intercourse with the enemy of my religion. This new sort of flattery intoxicated me with its fumes. I recoiled from the thought of shattering the pedestal to which 1 had found myself elevated. What if I should discover my daughter in one from the touch of whose robe these holy women would recoil as from the rags of a leper! No; it would be impossible for me to own her—impossible for me to give her the shelter of my roof. Nay, if discovered to hold any commune with such an outcast, no explanation, no excuse short of the actual truth, would avail with these austere judges of human error. And the actual truth would be yet deeper disgrace. I reasoned away my conscience. If I looked for example in the circles in which I had obtained reverential place, I could find no instance in which a girl who had fallen from virtue was not repudiated by her nearest relatives. Nay, when I thought of my own mother, had not her father refused to see her, to acknowledge her child, from no other offence than that of a *mésalliance* which wounded the family pride? That pride, alas! was in my blood—my sole inheritance from the family I sprang from.

"Thus it went on, till I had grave symptoms of a disease which rendered the duration of my life uncertain. My conscience awoke and tortured me. I resolved to take the veil. Vanity and pride again! My resolution was applauded by those whose opinion had so swayed my mind and my conduct. Before I retired into the convent from which I write, I made legal provision as to the bulk of the fortune which, by the death of M. Selby, has become absolutely at my disposal. One thousand pounds amply sufficed for donation to the convent: the other four thousand pounds are given in trust to the eminent notary, M. Nadaud, Rue ——. On applying to him, you will find that the sum, with the accumulated interest, is bequeathed to you,—a tribute of gratitude for the assistance you afforded me in the time of your own need, and the kindness with which you acknowledged our relationship and commiserated my misfortunes.

"But oh, my uncle, find out—a man can do so with a

facility not accorded to a woman—what has become of this poor Julie, and devote what you may deem right and just of the sum thus bequeathed to place her above want and temptation. In doing so, I know you will respect my name: I would not have it dishonour you, indeed.

"I have been employed in writing this long letter since the day I heard you were in Paris. It has exhausted the feeble remnants of my strength. It will be given to you before the interview I at once dread and long for, and in that interview you will not rebuke me. Will you, my kind uncle? No, you will only soothe and pity!

"Would that I were worthy to pray for others, that I might add, 'May the Saints have you in their keeping and lead you to faith in the Holy Church, which has power to absolve from sins those who repent as I do.'"

The letter dropped from Victor's hand. He took it up, smoothed it mechanically, and with a dim, abstracted, bewildered, pitiful wonder. Well might the Supérieure have hesitated to allow confessions, betraying a mind so little regulated by genuine religious faith, to pass into other hands. Evidently it was the paramount duty of rescuing from want or from sin the writer's forsaken child, that had overborne all other considerations in the mind of the Woman and the Priest she consulted.

Throughout that letter, what a strange perversion of understanding! what a half-unconscious confusion of wrong and right!—the duty marked out so obvious and so neglected; even the religious sentiment awakened by the conscience so dividing itself from the moral instinct! the dread of being thought less religious by obscure comparative strangers stronger than the moral obligation to discover and reclaim the child for whose errors, if she had erred, the mother who so selfishly forsook her was alone responsible! even at the last, at the approach of death, the love for a name she had never made a self-sacrifice to preserve unstained; and that concluding exhortation,—that reliance on a repentance in which there was so qualified a reparation!

More would Victor de Mauléon have wondered had he known those points of similarity in character, and in the nature of their final bequests, between Louise Duval and the husband she had deserted. By one of those singular coincidences which, if this work be judged by the ordinary rules presented to the ordinary novel-reader, a critic would not unjustly impute to defective invention in the author, the provision for this child, deprived of its natural parents during their lives, is left to the discretion and honour of trustees, accompanied on the part of the consecrated Louise and "the blameless King," with the injunction of respect to their worldly reputations—two parents so opposite in condition, in creed, in disposition, yet assimilating in that point of individual character in which it touches the wide vague circle of human opinion. For this, indeed, the excuses of Richard King are strong, inasmuch as the secrecy he sought was for the sake, not of his own memory, but that of her whom the world knew only as his honoured wife. The conduct of Louise admits no such excuse; she dies as she had lived; an Egotist. But, whatever the motives of the parents, what is the fate of the deserted child? What revenge does the worldly opinion, which the parents would escape for themselves, inflict on the innocent infant to whom the bulk of their worldly possessions is to be clandestinely conveyed? Would all the gold of Ophir be compensation enough for her?

Slowly De Mauléon roused himself, and turned from the solitary place where he had been seated to a more crowded part of the ramparts. He passed a group of young *Moblots*, with flowers wreathed round their gun-barrels. "If," said one of them gaily, "Paris wants bread, it never wants flowers." His companions laughed merrily, and burst out into a scurrile song in ridicule of St. Trochu. Just then an *obus* fell a few yards before the group. The sound only for a moment drowned the song, but the splinters struck a man in a coarse, ragged dress, who had stopped to listen to the singers. At his sharp cry, two men hastened to his side: one was Victor de Mauléon; the other was a surgeon, who quitted another group of idlers—National Guards—attracted by the shriek that summoned his professional aid. The poor man was terribly wounded. The surgeon, glancing at De Mauléon, shrugged his shoulders, and muttered, "Past help!" The sufferer turned his haggard eyes on the Vicomte, and gasped out, "M. de Mauléon?"

"That is my name," answered Victor, surprised, and not immediately recognising the sufferer.

"Hist, Jean Lebeau!—look at me: you recollect me now, —Marc le Roux, *concierge* to the Secret Council. Ay, I found out who you were long ago—followed you home from the last meeting you broke up. But I did not betray you, or you would have been murdered long since. Beware of the old set—beware of—of——" Here his voice broke off into shrill exclamations of pain. Curbing his last agonies with a powerful effort, he faltered forth, "You owe me a service—see to the little one at home—she is starving." The death-*râle* came on; in a few moments he was no more.

Victor gave orders for the removal of the corpse, and hurried away. The surgeon, who had changed countenance when he overheard the name in which the dying man had addressed De Mauléon, gazed silently after De Mauléon's retreating form, and then, also quitting the dead, rejoined the group he had quitted. Some of those who composed it acquired evil renown later in the war of the Communists, and came to disastrous ends: among that number the Pole Loubinsky and other members of the Secret Council. The Italian Raselli was there too, but, subtler than his French *confrères*, he divined the fate of the Communists, and glided from it—safe now in his native land, destined there, no doubt, to the funereal honours and lasting renown which Italy bestows on the dust of her sons who have advocated assassination out of love for the human race.

Amid this group, too, was a National Guard, strayed from his proper post, and stretched on the frozen ground;

and, early though the hour, in the profound sleep of intoxication.

"So," said Loubinsky, "you have found your errand in
vain, Citizen le Noy; another victim to the imbecility of
our generals."

"And partly one of us," replied the *Médecin des Pauvres*.
"You remember poor le Roux, who kept the old *baraque*
where the Council of Ten used to meet? Yonder he lies."

"Don't talk of the Council of Ten. What fools and
dupes we were made by that *vieux gredin*, Jean Lebeau!
How I wish I could meet him again!"

Gaspard le Noy smiled sarcastically. "So much the
worse for you, if you did. A muscular and a ruthless fellow is that Jean Lebeau!" Therewith he turned to the
drunken sleeper and woke him up with a shake and a kick.

"Armand—Armand Monnier, I say, rise, rub your eyes.
What if you are called to your post? What if you are
shamed as a deserter and a coward?"

Armand turned, rose with an effort from the recumbent
to the sitting posture, and stared dizzily in the face of the
Médecin des Pauvres.

"I was dreaming that I had caught by the throat," said
Armand, wildly, "the *aristo* who shot my brother; and lo,
there were two men, Victor de Mauléon and Jean Lebeau."

"Ah! there is something in dreams," said the surgeon.
"Once in a thousand times a dream comes true."

CHAPTER V.

THE time now came when all provision of food or of fuel
failed the modest household of Isaura; and there was not
only herself and the Venosta to feed and warm—there were
the servants whom they had brought from Italy, and had
not the heart now to dismiss to the certainty of famine.
True, one of the three, the man, had returned to his native

land before the commencement of the siege; but the two
women had remained. They supported themselves now as
they could on the meagre rations accorded by the Government. Still Isaura attended the ambulance to which she
was attached. From the ladies associated with her she
could readily have obtained ample supplies: but they had
no conception of her real state of destitution; and there
was a false pride generally prevalent among the respectable
classes, which Isaura shared, that concealed distress lest
alms should be proffered.

The destitution of the household had been carefully concealed from the parents of Gustave Rameau, until, one day,
Madame Rameau, entering at the hour at which she generally, and her husband sometimes, came for a place by the
fireside and a seat at the board, found on the one only
ashes, on the other a ration of the black nauseous com-
pound which had become the substitute for bread.

Isaura was absent on her duties at the ambulance hospital,—purposely absent, for she shrank from the bitter task
of making clear to the friends of her betrothed the impos-
sibility of continuing the aid to their support which their
son had neglected to contribute; and still more from the
comment which she knew they would make on his conduct,
in absenting himself so wholly of late, and in the time of
such trial and pressure, both from them and from herself.
Truly, she rejoiced at that absence so far as it affected
herself. Every hour of the day she silently asked her conscience whether she were not now absolved from a promise
won from her only by an assurance that she had power to
influence for good the life that now voluntarily separated
itself from her own. As she had never loved Gustave, so
she felt no resentment at the indifference his conduct manifested. On the contrary, she hailed it as a sign that the
annulment of their betrothal would be as welcome to him
as to herself. And if so, she could restore to him the sort
of compassionate friendship she had learned to cherish in
the hour of his illness and repentance. She had resolved

to seize the first opportunity he afforded to her of speaking to him with frank and truthful plainness. But, meanwhile, her gentle nature recoiled from the confession of her resolve to appeal to Gustave himself for the rupture of their engagement.

Thus the Venosta alone received Madame Rameau; and while that lady was still gazing round her with an emotion too deep for immediate utterance, her husband entered with an expression of face new to him—the look of a man who has been stung to anger, and who has braced his mind to some stern determination. This altered countenance of the good-tempered *bourgeois* was not, however, noticed by the two women. The Venosta did not even raise her eyes to it, as with humbled accents she said, "Pardon, dear Monsieur, pardon, Madame, our want of hospitality; it is not our hearts that fail. We kept our state from you as long as we could. Now it speaks for itself: '*la fame è una bretta festin.*'"

"Oh, Madame! and oh, my poor Isaura!" cried Madame Rameau, bursting into tears. "So we have been all this time a burden on you,—aided to bring such want on you! How can we ever be forgiven? And my son—to leave us thus,—not even to tell us where to find him!"

"Do not degrade us, my wife," said M. Rameau, with unexpected dignity, "by a word to imply that we would stoop to sue for support to our ungrateful child. No, we will not starve! I am strong enough still to find food for you. I will apply for restoration to the National Guard. They have augmented the pay to married men; it is now nearly two francs and a half a-day to a *père de famille*, and on that pay we all can at least live. Courage, my wife! I will go at once for employment. Many men older than I am are at watch on the ramparts, and will march to the battle on the next sortie."

"It shall not be so," exclaimed Madame Rameau, vehemently, and winding her arm round her husband's neck. "I loved my son better than thee once—more shame to me.

Now, I would rather lose twenty such sons than peril thy life, my Jacques! Madame," she continued, turning to the Venosta, "thou wert wiser than I. Thou wert ever opposed to the union between thy young friend and my son. I felt sore with thee for it—a mother is so selfish when she puts herself in the place of her child. I thought that only through marriage with one so pure, so noble, so holy, Gustave could be saved from sin and evil. I am deceived. A man so heartless to his parents, so neglectful of his affianced, is not to be redeemed. I brought about this betrothal: tell Isaura that I release her from it. I have watched her closely since she was entrapped into it. I know how miserable the thought of it has made her, though, in her sublime devotion to her plighted word, she sought to conceal from me the real state of her heart. If the betrothal bring such sorrow, what would the union do! Tell her this from me. Come, Jacques, come away!"

"Stay, Madame!" exclaimed the Venosta, her excitable nature much affected by this honest outburst of feeling. "It is true that I did oppose, so far as I could, my poor *Piccola's* engagement with M. Gustave. But I dare not do your bidding. Isaura would not listen to me. And let us be just! M. Gustave may be able satisfactorily to explain his seeming indifference and neglect. His health is always very delicate; perhaps he may be again dangerously ill. He serves in the National Guard; perhaps—" she paused, but the mother conjectured the word left unsaid, and, clasping her hands, cried out in anguish, "Perhaps dead!—and we have wronged him! Oh, Jacques, Jacques! how shall we find out—how discover our boy? Who can tell us where to search? at the hospital—or in the cemeteries?" At the last word she dropped into a seat, and her whole frame shook with her sobs.

Jacques approached her tenderly, and kneeling by her side, said:

"No, *m'amie*, comfort thyself, if it be indeed comfort to learn that thy son is alive and well. For my part, I know not if I would not rather he had died in his innocent childhood. I have seen him—spoken to him. I know where he is to be found."

"You do, and concealed it from me? Oh, Jacques!"

"Listen to me, wife, and you, too, Madame; for what I have to say should be made known to Mademoiselle Cicogna. Some time since, on the night of the famous sortie, when at my post on the ramparts, I was told that Gustave had joined himself to the most violent of the Red Republicans, and had uttered at the *Club de la Vengeance* sentiments, of which I will only say that I, his father and a Frenchman, hung my head with shame when they were repeated to me. I resolved to go to the club myself. I did. I heard him speak—heard him denounce Christianity as the instrument of tyrants."

"Ah!" cried the two women, with a simultaneous shudder.

"When the assembly broke up, I waylaid him at the door. I spoke to him seriously. I told him what anguish such announcement of blasphemous opinions would inflict on his pious mother. I told him I should deem it my duty to inform Mademoiselle Cicogna, and warn her against the union on which he had told us his heart was bent. He appeared sincerely moved by what I said; implored me to keep silence towards his mother and his betrothed; and promised, on that condition, to relinquish at once what he called 'his career as an orator,' and appear no more at such execrable clubs. On this understanding I held my tongue. Why, with such other causes of grief and suffering, should I tell thee, poor wife, of a sin that I hoped thy son had repented and would not repeat? And Gustave kept his word. He has never, so far as I know, attended, at least spoken, at the Red clubs since that evening."

"Thank heaven so far," murmured Madame Rameau.

"So far, yes; but hear more. A little time after I thus met him he changed his lodging, and did not confide to us his new address, giving as a reason to us that he wished to avoid all clue to his discovery by that pertinacious Mademoiselle Julie."

Rameau had here sunk his voice into a whisper, intended only for his wife, but the ear of the Venosta was fine enough to catch the sound, and she repeated, "Mademoiselle Julie! Santa Maria! who is she?"

"Oh!" said M. Rameau, with a shrug of his shoulders, and with true Parisian *sang froid* as to such matters of morality, "a trifle not worth considering. Of course, a good-looking *garçon* like Gustave must have his little affairs of the heart before he settles for life. Unluckily, amongst those of Gustave was one with a violent-tempered girl who persecuted him when he left her, and he naturally wished to avoid all chance of a silly scandal, if only out of respect to the dignity of his *fiancée*. But I found that was not the true motive, or at least the only one, for concealment. Prepare yourself, my poor wife. Thou hast heard of these terrible journals which the *déchéance* has let loose upon us. Our unhappy boy is the principal writer of one of the worst of them, under the name of 'Diderot le Jeune.'"

"What!" cried the Venosta. "That monster! The good Abbé Vertpré was telling us of the writings with that name attached to them. The Abbé himself is denounced by name as one of those meddling priests who are to be constrained to serve as soldiers or pointed out to the vengeance of the *canaille*. Isaura's *fiancée* a blasphemer!"

"Hush, hush!" said Madame Rameau, rising, very pale but self-collected. "How do you know this, Jacques?"

"From the lips of Gustave himself. I heard first of it yesterday from one of the young reprobates with whom he used to be familiar, and who even complimented me on the rising fame of my son, and praised the eloquence of his article that day. But I would not believe him. I bought the journal—here it is; saw the name and address of the printer—went this morning to the office—was there told that 'Diderot le Jeune' was within revising the press—stationed myself by the street door, and when Gustave came out I seized his arm, and asked him to say Yes or No if he was the author of this infamous article,—this, which I now hold in my hand. He owned the authorship with pride; talked wildly of the great man he was—of the great things he was to do; said that, in hitherto concealing his true name, he had done all he could to defer to the bigoted prejudices of his parents and his *fiancée;* and that if genius, like fire, would find its way out, he could not help it; that a time was rapidly coming when his opinions would be uppermost; that since October the Communists were gaining ascendancy, and only waited the end of the siege to put down the present Government, and with it all hypocrisies and shams, religious or social. My wife, he was rude to me, insulting! but he had been drinking—that made him incautious: and he continued to walk by my side towards his own lodging, on reaching which he ironically invited me to enter, saying, 'I should meet there men who would soon argue me out of my obsolete notions.' You may go to him, wife, now, if you please. I will not, nor will I take from him a crust of bread. I came hither, determined to tell the young lady all this, if I found her at home. I should be a dishonoured man if I suffered her to be cheated into misery. There, Madame Venosta, there! Take that journal, show it to Mademoiselle; and report to her all I have said."

M. Rameau, habitually the mildest of men, had, in talking, worked himself up into positive fury.

His wife, calmer but more deeply affected, made a piteous sign to the Venosta not to say more; and without other salutation or adieu took her husband's arm, and led him from the house.

CHAPTER VI.

OBTAINING from her husband Gustave's address, Madame Rameau hastened to her son's apartment alone through the darkling streets. The house in which he lodged was in a

different quarter from that in which Isaura had visited
him.   Then, the street selected was still in the centre of
the *beau monde*—now, it was within the precincts of that
section of the many-faced capital in which the *beau monde*
was held in detestation or scorn; still the house had certain pretensions, boasting a courtyard and a porter's lodge.
Madame Rameau, instructed to mount *au second*, found the
door ajar, and, entering, perceived on the table of the little
salon the remains of a feast which, however untempting it
might have been in happier times, contrasted strongly with
the meagre fare of which Gustave's parents had deemed
themselves fortunate to partake at the board of his betrothed; remnants of those viands which offered to the inquisitive epicure an experiment in food much too costly for
the popular stomach—dainty morsels of elephant, hippo-
potamus, and wolf, interspersed with half-emptied bottles
of varied and high-priced wines.   Passing these evidences
of unseasonable extravagance with a mute sentiment of
anger and disgust, Madame Rameau penetrated into a
small cabinet, the door of which was also ajar, and saw her
son stretched on his bed half dressed, breathing heavily in
the sleep which follows intoxication.   She did not attempt
to disturb him.   She placed herself quietly by his side,
gazing mournfully on the face which she had once so
proudly contemplated, now haggard and   faded,—still
strangely beautiful, though it was the beauty of ruin.

From time to time he stirred uneasily, and muttered
broken words, in which fragments of his own delicately-
worded verse were incoherently mixed up with ribald slang,
addressed to imaginary companions.   In his dreams he was
evidently living over again his late revel, with episodical
diversions into the poet-world, of which he was rather a
vagrant nomad than a settled cultivator.   Then she would
silently bathe his feverish temples with the perfumed water
she found on his dressing-table.   And so she watched till,
in the middle of the night, he woke up, and recovered the
possession of his reason with a quickness that surprised

Madame Rameau. He was, indeed, one of those men in whom excess of drink, when slept off, is succeeded by extreme mildness, the effect of nervous exhaustion, and by a dejected repentance, which, to his mother, seemed a propitious lucidity of the moral sense.

Certainly on seeing her he threw himself on her breast, and began to shed tears. Madame Rameau had not the heart to reproach him sternly. But by gentle degrees she made him comprehend the pain he had given to his father, and the destitution in which he had deserted his parents and his affianced. In his present mood Gustave was deeply affected by these representations. He excused himself feebly by dwelling on the excitement of the times, the preoccupation of his mind, the example of his companions; but with his excuses he mingled passionate expressions of remorse, and before daybreak mother and son were completely reconciled. Then he fell into a tranquil sleep; and Madame Rameau, quite worn out, slept also in the chair beside him, her arm around his neck. He awoke before she did at a late hour in the morning; and stealing from her arm, went to his *escritoire*, and took forth what money he found there, half of which he poured into her lap, kissing her till she awoke.

"Mother," he said, "henceforth I will work for thee and my father. Take this trifle now; the rest I reserve for Isaura."

"Joy! I have found my boy again. But Isaura, I fear that she will not take thy money, and all thought of her must also be abandoned."

Gustave had already turned to his looking-glass, and was arranging with care his dark ringlets: his personal vanity—his remorse appeased by this pecuniary oblation—had revived.

"No," he said gaily, "I don't think I shall abandon her; and it is not likely, when she sees and hears me, that she can wish to abandon me! Now let us breakfast, and then I will go at once to her."

II.—17

In the mean while, Isaura, on her return to her apartment at the wintry nightfall, found a cart stationed at the door, and the Venosta on the threshold, superintending the removal of various articles of furniture—indeed, all such articles as were not absolutely required.

"Oh, *Piccola!*" she said, with an attempt at cheerfulness, "I did not expect thee back so soon. Hush! I have made a famous bargain. I have found a broker to buy these things which we don't want just at present, and can replace by new and prettier things when the siege is over and we get our money. The broker pays down on the nail and thou wilt not go to bed without supper. There are no ills which are not more supportable after food."

Isaura smiled faintly, kissed the Venosta's cheek, and ascended with weary steps to the sitting-room. There she seated herself quietly, looking with abstracted eyes round the bare dismantled space by the light of the single candle.

When the Venosta re-entered, she was followed by the servants, bringing in a daintier meal than they had known for days—a genuine rabbit, potatoes, *marrons glacés*, a bottle of wine, and a pannier of wood. The fire was soon lighted, the Venosta plying the bellows. It was not till this banquet, of which Isaura, faint as she was, scarcely partook, had been remitted to the two Italian women-servants, and another log been thrown on the hearth, that the Venosta opened the subject which was pressing on her heart. She did this with a joyous smile, taking both Isaura's hands in her own, and stroking them fondly.

"My child, I have such good news for thee! Thou hast escaped—thou art free!" and then she related all that M. Rameau had said, and finished by producing the copy of Gustave's unhallowed journal.

When she had read the latter, which she did with compressed lips and varying colour, the girl fell on her knees—not to thank Heaven that she would now escape a union from which her soul so recoiled—not that she was indeed free, but to pray, with tears rolling down her cheeks, that

God would yet save to Himself, and to good ends, the soul that she had failed to bring to Him. All previous irritation against Gustave was gone: all had melted into an ineffable compassion.

--------●--------

CHAPTER VII.

WHEN, a little before noon, Gustave was admitted by the servant into Isaura's *salon*, its desolate condition, stripped of all its pretty feminine elegancies, struck him with a sense of discomfort to himself which superseded any more remorseful sentiment. The day was intensely cold: the single log on the hearth did not burn; there were only two or three chairs in the room; even the carpet, which had been of gaily coloured Aubusson, was gone. His teeth chattered; and he only replied by a dreary nod to the servant who informed him that Madame Venosta was gone out, and Mademoiselle had not yet quitted her own room.

If there be a thing which a true Parisian of Rameau's stamp associates with love of woman, it is a certain sort of elegant surroundings, a pretty *boudoir*, a cheery hearth, an easy *fauteuil*. In the absence of such attributes, "*fugit retro Venus.*" If the Englishman invented the word comfort, it is the Parisian who most thoroughly comprehends the thing. And he resents the loss of it in any house where he has been accustomed to look for it, as a personal wrong to his feelings.

Left for some minutes alone, Gustave occupied himself with kindling the log, and muttering, "*Par tous les diables, quel chien de rhume je vais attraper!*" He turned as he heard the rustle of a robe and a light slow step. Isaura stood before him. Her aspect startled him. He had come prepared to expect grave displeasure and a frigid reception. But the expression of Isaura's face was more kindly, more gentle, more tender, than he had seen it since the day she had accepted his suit.

Knowing from his mother what his father had said to his prejudice, he thought within himself, "After all, the poor girl loves me better than I thought. She is sensible and enlightened; she cannot pretend to dictate an opinion to a man like me."

He approached with a complacent self-assured mien, and took her hand, which she yielded to him quietly, leading her to one of the few remaining chairs, and seating himself beside her.

"Dear Isaura," he said, talking rapidly all the while he performed this ceremony, "I need not assure you of my utter ignorance of the state to which the imbecility of our Government, and the cowardice, or rather the treachery, of our generals, has reduced you. I only heard of it late last night from my mother. I hasten to claim my right to share with you the humble resources which I have saved by the intellectual labours that have absorbed all such moments as my military drudgeries left to the talents which, even at such a moment, paralysing minds less energetic, have sustained me:"—and therewith he poured several pieces of gold and silver on the table beside her chair.

"Gustave," then said Isaura, "I am well pleased that you thus prove that I was not mistaken when I thought and said that, despite all appearances, all errors, your heart was good. Oh, do but follow its true impulses, and——"

"Its impulses lead me ever to thy feet," interrupted Gustave, with a fervour which sounded somewhat theatrical and hollow.

The girl smiled, not bitterly, not mockingly; but Gustave did not like the smile.

"Poor Gustave," she said, with a melancholy pathos in her soft voice, "do you not understand that the time has come when such commonplace compliments ill suit our altered positions to each other? Nay, listen to me patiently; and let not my words in this last interview pain you to recall. If either of us be to blame in the engagement hastily contracted, it is I. Gustave, when you, exaggerating in your imagination the nature of your sentiments for me, said with such earnestness that on my consent to our union depended your health, your life, your career; that if I withheld that consent you were lost, and in despair would seek distraction from thought in all from which your friends, your mother, the duties imposed upon Genius for the good of Man to the ends of God, should withhold and save you—when you said all this, and I believed it, I felt as if Heaven commanded me not to desert the soul which appealed to me in the crisis of its struggle and peril. Gustave, I repent; I was to blame."

"How to blame?"

"I overrated my power over your heart: I overrated still more, perhaps, power over my own."

"Ah, your own! I understand now. You did not love me?"

"I never said that I loved you in the sense in which you use the word. I told you that the love which you have described in your verse, and which," she added, falteringly, with heightened colour and with hands tightly clasped, "I have conceived possible in my dreams, it was not mine to give. You declared you were satisfied with such affection as I could bestow. Hush! let me go on. You said that affection would increase, would become love, in proportion as I knew you more. It has not done so. Nay, it passed away; even before this time of trial and of grief, I became aware how different from the love you professed was the neglect which needs no excuse, for it did not pain me."

"You are cruel indeed, Mademoiselle."

"No, indeed, I am kind. I wish you to feel no pang at our parting. Truly I had resolved, when the siege terminated, and the time to speak frankly of our engagement came, to tell you that I shrank from the thought of a union between us; and that it was for the happiness of both that our promises should be mutually cancelled. The moment has come sooner than I thought. Even had I loved you, Gustave, as deeply as—as well as the beings of Romance love, I would not dare to wed one who calls upon mortals to deny God, demolish His altars, treat His worship as a crime. No; I would sooner die of a broken heart, that I might the sooner be one of those souls privileged to pray the Divine Intercessor for merciful light on those beloved and left dark on earth."

"Isaura!" exclaimed Gustave, his mobile temperament impressed, not by the words of Isaura, but by the passionate earnestness with which they were uttered, and by the exquisite spiritual beauty which her face took from the combined sweetness and fervour of its devout expression, —"Isaura, I merit your censure, your sentence of condemnation; but do not ask me to give back your plighted troth. I have not the strength to do so. More than ever, more than when first pledged to me, I need the aid, the companionship, of my guardian angel. You were that to me once; abandon me not now. In these terrible times of revolution, excitable natures catch madness from each other. A writer in the heat of his passion says much that he does not mean to be literally taken, which in cooler moments he repents and retracts. Consider, too, the pressure of want, of hunger. It is the opinions that you so condemn which alone at this moment supply bread to the writer. But say you will yet pardon me,—yet give me trial if I offend no more—if I withdraw my aid to any attacks on your views, your religion—if I say, 'Thy God shall be my God, and thy people shall be my people.'"

"Alas!" said Isaura, softly, "ask thyself if those be words which I can believe again. Hush!" she continued, checking his answer with a more kindling countenance and more impassioned voice. "Are they, after all, the words that man should address to woman? Is it on the strength of Woman that Man should rely? Is it to her that he should say, 'Dictate my opinions on all that belongs to the Mind of man; change the doctrines that I have thoughtfully formed and honestly advocate; teach me how to act on earth, clear all my doubts as to my hopes of heaven'?

No, Gustave; in this task man never should repose on woman. Thou are honest at this moment, my poor friend; but could I believe thee to-day, thou wouldst laugh to-morrow at what woman can be made to believe."

Stung to the quick by the truth of Isaura's accusation, Gustave exclaimed with vehemence: "All that thou sayest is false, and thou knowest it. The influence of woman on man for good or for evil defies reasoning. It does mould his deeds on earth; it does either make or mar all that future which lies between his life and his gravestone, and of whatsoever may lie beyond the grave. Give me up now, and thou art responsible for me, for all I do, it may be against all that thou deemest holy. Keep thy troth yet awhile, and test me. If I come to thee showing how I could have injured, and how for thy dear sake I have spared, nay, aided, all that thou dost believe and reverence, then wilt thou dare to say, 'Go thy ways alone—I forsake thee!'"

Isaura turned aside her face, but she held out her hand—it was as cold as death. He knew that she had so far yielded, and his vanity exulted: he smiled in secret triumph as he pressed his kiss on that icy hand and was gone.

"This is duty—it must be duty," said Isaura to herself. "But where is the buoyant delight that belongs to a duty achieved?—where? oh where?" And then she stole with drooping head and heavy step into her own room, fell on her knees, and prayed.

CHAPTER VIII.

In vain persons, be they male or female, there is a complacent self-satisfaction in any momentary personal success, however little that success may conduce to—nay, however much it may militate against—the objects to which their vanity itself devotes its more permanent desires. A vain woman may be very anxious to win A——, the magnificent, as a partner for life, and yet feel a certain triumph when a glance of her eye has made an evening's conquest of the pitiful B——, although by that achievement she incurs the imminent hazard of losing A—— altogether. So, when Gustave Rameau quitted Isaura, his first feeling was that of triumph. His eloquence had subdued her will; she had not finally discarded him. But as he wandered abstractedly in the biting air, his self-complacency was succeeded by mortification and discontent. He felt that he had committed himself to promises which he was by no means prepared to keep. True, the promises were vague in words; but in substance they were perfectly clear—"to spare, nay, to aid all that Isaura esteemed and reverenced." How was this possible to him? How could he suddenly change the whole character of his writings?—how become the defender of marriage and property, of church and religion?—how proclaim himself so utter an apostate? If he did, how become a leader of the fresh revolution? how escape being its victim? Cease to write altogether? But then how live? His pen was his sole subsistence, save 30 sous a-day as a National Guard—30 sous a day to him, who, in order to be Sybarite in tastes, was Spartan in doctrine. Nothing better just at that moment than Spartan doctrine, "Live on black broth and fight the enemy." And the journalists in vogue so thrived upon that patriotic sentiment, that they were the last persons compelled to drink the black broth or to fight the enemy.

"Those women are such idiots when they meddle in politics," grumbled between his teeth the enthusiastic advocate of Woman's Rights on all matters of love. "And," he continued, soliloquising, "it is not as if the girl had any large or decent *dot;* it is not as if she said, 'In return for the sacrifice of your popularity, your prospects, your opinions, I give you not only a devoted heart, but an excellent table and a capital fire and plenty of pocket-money.' *Sacrebleu!* when I think of that frozen *salon,* and possibly the

leg of a mouse for dinner, and a virtuous homily by way
of grace, the prospect is not alluring; and the girl herself
is not so pretty as she was—grown very thin. *Sur mon
âme,* I think she asks too much—far more than she is
worth. No, no; I had better have accepted her dismissal.
Elle n'est pas digne de moi."

Just as he arrived at that conclusion, Gustave Rameau
felt the touch of a light, a soft, a warm, yet a firm hand,
on his arm. He turned, and beheld the face of the woman
whom, through so many dreary weeks, he had sought to
shun—the face of Julie Caumartin. Julie was not, as Savarin had seen her, looking pinched and wan, with faded
robes, nor, as when met in the *café* by Lemercier, in the
faded robes of a theatre. Julie never looked more beautiful, more radiant, than she did now; and there was a wonderful heartfelt fondness in her voice when she cried, "*Mon
homme! mon homme! seul homme au monde à mon cœur,
Gustave, chéri adoré!* I have found thee—at last—at
last!" Gustave gazed upon her, stupefied. Involuntarily
his eye glanced from the freshness of bloom in her face
which the intense cold of the atmosphere only seemed to
heighten into purer health, to her dress, which was new
and handsome—black—he did not know that it was mourning—the cloak trimmed with costly sables. Certainly it
was no mendicant for alms who thus reminded the shivering Adonis of the claims of a pristine Venus. He stammered out her name, "Julie!"—and then he stopped.

"*Oui, ta Julie! Petit ingrat!* how I have sought for
thee! how I have hungered for the sight of thee! That
monster Savarin! he would not give me any news of thee.
That is ages ago. But at least Frederic Lemercier, whom I
saw since, promised to remind thee that I lived still. He
did not do so, or I should have seen thee—*n'est ce pas?*"

"Certainly, certainly—only—*chère amie*—you know that
—that—as I before announced to thee, I—I—was engaged
in marriage—and—and——"

"But are you married?"

"No, no.   Hark!   Take care—is not that the hiss of an *obus?*"

"What then?   Let it come!   Would it might slay us both while my hand is in thine!"

"Ah!" muttered Gustave, inwardly, "what a difference! This is love!   No preaching here!   *Elle est plus digne de moi que l'autre.*"

"No," he said, aloud, "I am not married.   Marriage is at best a pitiful ceremony.   But if you wished for news of me, surely you must have heard of my effect as an orator not despised in the Salle Favre.   Since, I have withdrawn from that arena.   But as a journalist I flatter myself that I have had a *beau succès.*"

"Doubtless, doubtless, my Gustave, my Poet!   Wherever thou art, thou must be first among men.   But, alas! it is my fault—my misfortune.   I have not been in the midst of a world that perhaps rings of thy name."

"Not my name.   Prudence compelled me to conceal that.   Still, Genius pierces under any name.   You might have discovered me under my *nom de plume.*"

"Pardon me—I was always *bête.*   But, oh! for so many weeks I was so poor—so destitute.   I could go nowhere, except—don't be ashamed of me—except——"

"Yes?   Go on."

"Except where I could get some money.   At first to dance—you remember my *bolero.*   Then I got a better engagement.   Do you not remember that you taught me to recite verses?   Had it been for myself alone, I might have been contented to starve.   Without thee, what was life? But thou wilt recollect Madeleine, the old *bonne* who lived with me.   Well, she had attended and cherished me since I was so high—lived with my mother.   Mother! no; it seems that Madame Surville was not my mother after all. But, of course, I could not let my old Madeleine starve; and therefore, with a heart as heavy as lead, I danced and declaimed.   My heart was not so heavy when I recited thy songs."

"My songs! *Pauvre ange!*" exclaimed the Poet.

"And then, too, I thought, 'Ah, this dreadful siege! He, too, may be poor—he may know want and hunger;' and so all I could save from Madeleine I put into a box for thee, in case thou shouldst come back to me some day. *Mon homme,* how could I go to the Salle Favre? How could I read journals, Gustave? But thou art not married, Gustave? *Parole d'honneur?*"

"*Parole d'honneur!* What does that matter?"

"Everything! Ah! I am not so *méchante,* so *mauvaise tête* as I was some months ago. If thou wert married, I should say, 'Blessed and sacred be thy wife! Forget me.' But as it is, one word more. Dost thou love the young lady, whoever she be? or does she love thee so well that it would be sin in thee to talk trifles to Julie? Speak as honestly as if thou wert not a poet."

"Honestly, she never said she loved me. I never thought she did. But, you see, I was very ill, and my parents and friends and my physician said that it was right for me to arrange my life, and marry, and so forth. And the girl had money, and was a good match. In short, the thing was settled. But oh, Julie, she never learned my songs by heart! She did not love as thou didst, and still dost. And—ah! well—now that we meet again—now that I look in thy face—now that I hear thy voice—— No, I do not love her as I loved, and might yet love thee. But—but——"

"Well, but? oh, I guess. Thou seest me well dressed, no longer dancing and declaiming at *cafés:* and thou thinkest that Julie has disgraced herself? she is unfaithful?"

Gustave had not anticipated that frankness, nor was the idea which it expressed uppermost in his mind when he said, "but, but——" There were many *buts* all very confused, struggling through his mind as he spoke. However, he answered as a Parisian sceptic, not ill-bred, naturally would answer:

"My dear friend, my dear child" (the Parisian is very

fond of the word child or *enfant* in addressing a woman),
"I have never seen thee so beautiful as thou art now; and
when thou tellest me that thou are no longer poor, and the
proof of what thou sayest is visible in the furs, which,
alas! I cannot give thee, what am I to think?"

"Oh, *mon homme, mon homme!* thou art very *spirituel*,
and that is why I loved thee. I am very *bête*, and that is
excuse enough for thee if thou couldst not love me. But
canst thou look me in the face and not know that my eyes
could not meet thine as they do, if I had been faithless to
thee even in a thought, when I so boldly touched thine
arm? *Viens chez moi*, come and let me explain all. Only—
only let me repeat, if another has rights over thee which
forbid thee to come, say so kindly, and I will never trouble
thee again."

Gustave had been hitherto walking slowly by the side of
Julie, amidst the distant boom of the besiegers' cannon,
while the short day began to close; and along the dreary
boulevards sauntered idlers turning to look at the young,
beautiful, well-dressed woman who seemed in such contrast
to the capital whose former luxuries the "Ondine" of imperial Paris represented. He now offered his arm to Julie;
and, quickening his pace, said, "There is no reason why I
should refuse to attend thee home, and listen to the explanations thou dost generously condescend to volunteer."

CHAPTER IX.

"Ah, indeed! what a difference! what a difference!"
said Gustave to himself when he entered Julie's apartment. In her palmier days, when he had first made her
acquaintance, the apartment no doubt had been infinitely
more splendid, more abundant in silks and fringes and
flowers and nicknacks; but never had it seemed so cheery
and comfortable and home-like as now. What a contrast

to Isaura's dismantled chilly *salon!* She drew him towards the hearth, on which, blazing though it was, she piled
fresh billets, seated him in the easiest of easy-chairs, knelt
beside him, and chafed his numbed hands in hers; and as
her bright eyes fixed tenderly on his, she looked so young
and so innocent! You would not then have called her the
"Ondine of Paris."

But when, a little while after, revived by the genial
warmth and moved by the charm of her beauty, Gustave
passed his arm round her neck and sought to draw her on
his lap, she slid from his embrace, shaking her head gently,
and seated herself, with a pretty air of ceremonious de-
corum, at a little distance.

Gustave looked at her amazed.

" *Causons,*" said she, gravely: "thou wouldst know why
I am so well dressed, so comfortably lodged, and I am long-
ing to explain to thee all. Some days ago I had just finished my performance at the Café ——, and was putting
on my shawl, when a tall Monsieur, *fort bel homme*, with
the air of a *grand seigneur*, entered the *café*, and approaching me politely, said, 'I think I have the honour to address Mademoiselle Julie Caumartin?' 'That is my name,'
I said, surprised; and, looking at him more intently, I recognised his face. He had come into the *café* a few days
before with thine old acquaintance Frederic Lemercier, and
stood by when I asked Frederic to give me news of thee.
'Mademoiselle,' he continued, with a serious melancholy
smile, 'I shall startle you when I say that I am appointed
to act as your guardian by the last request of your mother.'
'Of Madame Surville?' 'Madame Surville adopted you, but
was not your mother. We cannot talk at ease here. Allow me to request that you will accompany me to Monsieur
N——, the *avoué*. It is not very far from this: and by
the way I will tell you some news that may sadden, and
some news that may rejoice.'

"There was an earnestness in the voice and look of this
Monsieur that impressed me. He did not offer me his

arm; but I walked by his side in the direction he chose.
As we walked he told me in very few words that my mother had been separated from her husband, and for certain
family reasons had found it so difficult to rear and provide
for me herself, that she had accepted the offer of Madame
Surville to adopt me as her own child. While he spoke,
there came dimly back to me the remembrance of a lady
who had taken me from my first home, when I had been,
as I understood, at nurse, and left me with poor dear Madame Surville, saying, 'This is henceforth your mamma.'
I never again saw that lady. It seems that many years
afterwards my true mother desired to regain me. Madame
Surville was then dead. She failed to trace me out, owing,
alas! to my own faults and change of name. She then entered a nunnery, but, before doing so, assigned a sum of
100,000 francs to this gentleman, who was distantly connected with her, with full power to him to take it to himself, or give it to my use should he discover me, at his discretion. 'I ask you,' continued the Monsieur, 'to go with
me to Mons. N——'s, because the sum is still in his hands.
He will confirm my statement. All that I have now to say
is this: If you accept my guardianship, if you obey implicitly my advice, I shall consider the interest of this sum
which has accumulated since deposited with M. N—— due
to you; and the capital will be your *dot* on marriage, if the
marriage be with my consent.'"

Gustave had listened very attentively, and without interruption, until now; when he looked up, and said with his
customary sneer, "Did your Monsieur, *fort bel homme*, you
say, inform you of the value of the advice, rather of the
commands, you were implicitly to obey?"

"Yes," answered Julie, "not then, but later. Let me
go on. We arrived at M. N——'s, an elderly grave man.
He said that all he knew was that he held the money in
trust for the Monsieur with me, to be given to him, with
the accumulations of interest, on the death of the lady who
had deposited it. If that Monsieur had instructions how

to dispose of the money, they were not known to him. All he had to do was to transfer it absolutely to him on the proper certificate of the lady's death. So you see, Gustave, that the Monsieur could have kept all from me if he had liked."

"Your Monsieur is very generous. Perhaps you will now tell me his name."

"No; he forbids me to do it yet."

"And he took this apartment for you, and gave you money to buy that smart dress and these furs. Bah! *mon enfant*, why try to deceive me? Do I not know my Paris? A *fort bel homme* does not make himself guardian to a *fort belle fille* so young and fair as Mademoiselle Julie Caumartin without certain considerations which shall be nameless, like himself."

Julie's eyes flashed. "Ah, Gustave! ah, Monsieur!" she said, half angrily, half plaintively, "I see that my guardian knew you better than I did. Never mind; I will not reproach. Thou hast the right to despise me."

"Pardon! I did not mean to offend thee," said Gustave, somewhat disconcerted. "But own that thy story is strange; and this guardian, who knows me better than thou—does he know me at all? Didst thou speak to him of me?"

"How could I help it? He says that this terrible war, in which he takes an active part, makes his life uncertain from day to day. He wished to complete the trust bequeathed to him by seeing me safe in the love of some worthy man who"—she paused for a moment with an expression of compressed anguish, and then hurried on—" who would recognise what was good in me,—would never reproach me for—for—the past. I then said that my heart was thine: I could never marry any one but thee."

"Marry me," faltered Gustave—"marry!"

"And," continued the girl, not heeding his interruption, "he said thou wert not the husband he would choose for me: that thou wert not—no, I cannot wound thee by re-

peating what he said unkindly, unjustly. He bade me
think of thee no more. I said again, that is impossible."

"But," resumed Rameau, with an affected laugh, "why
think of anything so formidable as marriage? Thou lovest
me, and——" He approached again, seeking to embrace
her. She recoiled. "No, Gustave, no. I have sworn—
sworn solemnly by the memory of my lost mother—that I
will never sin again. I will never be to thee other than thy
friend—or thy wife."

Before Gustave could reply to these words, which took
him wholly by surprise, there was a ring at the outer door,
and the old *bonne* ushered in Victor de Mauléon. He halted
at the threshold, and his brow contracted.

"So you have already broken faith with me, Mademoiselle?"

"No, Monsieur, I have not broken faith," cried Julie,
passionately. "I told you that I would not seek to find
out Monsieur Rameau. I did not seek, but I met him unexpectedly. I owed to him an explanation. I invited him
here to give that explanation. Without it, what would he
have thought of me? Now he may go, and I will never
admit him again without your sanction."

The Vicomte turned his stern look upon Gustave, who
though, as we know, not wanting in personal courage, felt
cowed by his false position; and his eye fell, quailed before
De Mauléon's gaze.

"Leave us for a few minutes alone, Mademoiselle," said
the Vicomte. "Nay, Julie," he added, in softened tones,
"fear nothing. I, too, owe explanation—friendly explanation—to M. Rameau."

With his habitual courtesy towards women, he extended
his hand to Julie, and led her from the room. Then, closing the door, he seated himself, and made a sign to Gustave to do the same.

"Monsieur," said De Mauléon, "excuse me if I detain
you. A very few words will suffice for our present interview. I take it for granted that Mademoiselle has told you

that she is no child of Madame Surville's: that her own
mother bequeathed her to my protection and guardianship
with a modest fortune which is at my disposal to give or
withhold. The little I have seen already of Mademoiselle
impresses me with sincere interest in her fate. I look with
compassion on what she may have been in the past; I anticipate with hope what she may be in the future. I do
not ask you to see her in either with my eyes. I say
frankly that it is my intention, and I may add, my resolve,
that the ward thus left to my charge shall be henceforth
safe from the temptations that have seduced her poverty,
her inexperience, her vanity, if you will, but have not yet
corrupted her heart. *Bref,* I must request you to give me
your word of honour that you will hold no further communication with her. I can allow no sinister influence to
stand between her fate and honour."

"You speak well and nobly, M. le Vicomte," said Rameau, "and I give the promise you exact." He added,
feelingly: "It is true her heart has never been corrupted:
that is good, affectionate, unselfish as a child's. *J'ai l'honneur de vous saluer,* M. le Vicomte."

He bowed with a dignity unusual to him, and tears were
in his eyes as he passed by De Mauléon and gained the ante-
room. There a side-door suddenly opened, and Julie's
face, anxious, eager, looked forth.

Gustave paused: "Adieu, Mademoiselle! Adieu, though
we may never meet again,—though our fates divide us,—believe me that I shall ever cherish your memory—and——"

The girl interrupted him, impulsively seizing his arm,
and looking him in the face with a wild fixed stare.

"Hush! dost thou mean to say that we are parted,—
parted for ever?"

"Alas!" said Gustave, "what option is before us? Your
guardian rightly forbids my visits; and even were I free to
offer you my hand, you yourself say that I am not a suitor
he would approve."

Julie turned her eyes towards De Mauléon, who, following Gustave into the ante-room, stood silent and impassive, leaning against the wall.

He now understood and replied to the pathetic appeal in the girl's eyes.

"My young ward," he said, "M. Rameau expresses himself with propriety and truth. Suffer him to depart. He belongs to the former life; reconcile yourself to the new."

He advanced to take her hand, making a sign to Gustave to depart. But as he approached Julie, she uttered a weak piteous wail, and fell at his feet senseless. De Mauléon raised and carried her into her room, where he left her to the care of the old *bonne*. On re-entering the ante-room, he found Gustave still lingering by the outer door.

"You will pardon me, Monsieur," he said to the Vicomte, "but in fact I feel so uneasy, so unhappy. Has she——? You see, you see that there is danger to her health, perhaps to her reason, in so abrupt a separation, so cruel a rupture between us. Let me call again, or I may not have strength to keep my promise."

De Mauléon remained a few minutes musing. Then he said in a whisper, "Come back into the *salon*. Let us talk frankly."

CHAPTER X.

"M. RAMEAU," said De Mauléon, when the two men had reseated themselves in the *salon*, "I will honestly say that my desire is to rid myself as soon as I can of the trust of guardian to this young lady. Playing as I do with fortune, my only stake against her favours is my life. I feel as if it were my duty to see that Mademoiselle is not left alone and friendless in the world at my decease. I have in my mind for her a husband that I think in every way suitable: a handsome and brave young fellow in my battalion, of respectable birth, without any living relations to consult as to his choice. I have reason to believe that if Julie married him, she need never fear a reproach to her antecedents. Her *dot* would suffice to enable him to realise his own wish of a country town in Normandy. And in that station, Paris and its temptations would soon pass from the poor child's thoughts, as an evil dream. But I cannot dispose of her hand without her own consent; and if she is to be reasoned out of her fancy for you, I have no time to devote to the task. I come to the point. You are not the man I would choose for her husband. But, evidently, you are the man she would choose. Are you disposed to marry her? You hesitate, very naturally; I have no right to demand an immediate answer to a question so serious. Perhaps you will think over it, and let me know in a day or two? I take it for granted that if you were, as I heard, engaged before the siege to marry the Signora Cicogna, that engagement is annulled?"

"Why take it for granted?" asked Gustave, perplexed.

"Simply because I find you here. Nay, spare explanations and excuses. I quite understand that you were invited to come. But a man solemnly betrothed to a *demoiselle* like the Signora Cicogna, in a time of such dire calamity and peril, could scarcely allow himself to be tempted to accept the invitation of one so beautiful, and so warmly attached to him, as is Mademoiselle Julie; and on witnessing the passionate strength of that attachment, say that he cannot keep a promise not to repeat his visits. But if I mistake, and you are still betrothed to the Signorina, of course all discussion is at an end."

Gustave hung his head in some shame, and in much bewildered doubt.

The practised observer of men's characters, and of shifting phases of mind, glanced at the poor poet's perturbed countenance with a half-smile of disdain.

"It is for you to judge how far the very love to you so ingenuously evinced by my ward—how far the reasons against marriage with one whose antecedents expose her to reproach—should influence one of your advanced opinions upon social ties. Such reasons do not appear to have with artists the same weight they have with the *bourgeoisie*. I have but to add that the husband of Julie will receive with her hand a *dot* of nearly 120,000 francs; and I have reason to believe that that fortune will be increased—how much, I cannot guess—when the cessation of the siege will allow communication with England. One word more. I should wish to rank the husband of my ward in the number of my friends. If he did not oppose the political opinions with which I identify my own career, I should be pleased to make any rise in the world achieved by me assist to the raising of himself. But my opinions, as during the time we were brought together you were made aware, are those of a practical man of the world, and have nothing in common with Communists, Socialists, Internationalists, or whatever sect would place the aged societies of Europe in Medea's caldron of youth. At a moment like the present, fanatics and dreamers so abound that the number of such sinners will necessitate a general amnesty when order is restored. What a poet so young as you may have written or said at such a time will be readily forgotten and forgiven a year or two hence, provided he does not put his notions into violent action. But if you choose to persevere in the views you now advocate, so be it. They will not make poor Julie less a believer in your wisdom and genius. Only they will separate you from me, and a day may come when I should have the painful duty of ordering you to be shot—*Dii meliora*. Think over all I have thus frankly said. Give me your answer within forty-eight hours; and meanwhile hold no communication with my ward. I have the honour to wish you good-day."

CHAPTER XI.

THE short grim day was closing when Gustave, quitting
Julie's apartment, again found himself in the streets. His
thoughts were troubled and confused. He was the more
affected by Julie's impassioned love for him, by the contrast with Isaura's words and manner in their recent interview. His own ancient fancy for the "Ondine of Paris"
became revived by the difficulties between their ancient intercourse which her unexpected scruples and De Mauléon's
guardianship interposed. A witty writer thus defines *une
passion*, "*une caprice inflammé par des obstacles.*" In the
ordinary times of peace, Gustave, handsome, aspiring to
reputable position in the *beau monde*, would not have admitted any considerations to compromise his station by
marriage with a *figurante*. But now the wild political doctrines he had embraced separated his ambition from that
beau monde, and combined it with ascendancy over the revolutionists of the populace—a direction which he must abandon if he continued his suit to Isaura. Then, too, the immediate possession of Julie's *dot* was not without temptation
to a man who was so fond of his personal comforts, and
who did not see where to turn for a dinner, if, obedient to
Isaura's "prejudices," he abandoned his profits as a writer
in the revolutionary press. The inducements for with-
drawal from the cause he had espoused, held out to him
with so haughty a coldness by De Mauléon, were not wholly
without force, though they irritated his self-esteem. He
was dimly aware of the Vicomte's masculine talents for
public life; and the high reputation he had already acquired among military authorities, and even among experienced and thoughtful civilians, had weight upon Gustave's
impressionable temperament. But though De Mauléon's
implied advice here coincided in much with the tacit com-
pact he had made with Isaura, it alienated him more from

Isaura herself, for Isaura did not bring to him the fortune which would enable him to suspend his lucubrations, watch the turn of events, and live at ease in the meanwhile; and the *dot* to be received with De Mauléon's ward had those advantages.

While thus meditating Gustave turned into one of the *cantines* still open, to brighten his intellect with a *petit verre*, and there he found the two colleagues in the extinct Council of Ten, Paul Grimm and Edgar Ferrier. With the last of these revolutionists Gustave had become intimately *lié*. They wrote in the same journal, and he willingly accepted a distraction from his self-conflict which Edgar offered him in a dinner at the Café Riche, which still offered its hospitalities at no exorbitant price. At this repast, as the drink circulated, Gustave waxed confidential. He longed, poor youth, for an adviser. Could he marry a girl who had been a ballet-dancer, and who had come into an unexpected heritage? " *Est tu fou d'en douter?*" cried Edgar. " What a sublime occasion to manifest thy scorn of the miserable *banalités* of the *bourgeoisie!* It will but increase thy moral power over the people. And then think of the money. What an aid to the cause! What a capital for the launch!—journal all thine own! Besides, when our principles triumph—as triumph they must—what would be marriage but a brief and futile ceremony, to be broken the moment thou hast cause to complain of thy wife or chafe at the bond? Only get the *dot* into thine own hands. *L'amour passe—reste la cassette.*"

Though there was enough of good in the son of Madame Rameau to revolt at the precise words in which the counsel was given, still, as the fumes of the punch yet more addled his brains, the counsel itself was acceptable; and in that sort of maddened fury which intoxication produces in some excitable temperaments, as Gustave reeled home that night leaning on the arm of stouter Edgar Ferrier, he insisted on going out of his way to pass the house in which Isaura lived, and, pausing under her window, gasped out some

verses of a wild song, then much in vogue among the vo-
taries of Felix Pyat, in which everything that existent society deems sacred was reviled in the grossest ribaldry.
Happily Isaura's ear heard it not. The girl was kneeling
by her bedside absorbed in prayer.

CHAPTER XII.

THREE days after the evening thus spent by Gustave
Rameau, Isaura was startled by a visit from M. de Mauléon. She had not seen him since the commencement of
the siege, and she did not recognise him at first glance in
his military uniform.

"I trust you will pardon my intrusion, Mademoiselle,"
he said, in the low sweet voice habitual to him in his gen-
tler moods, "but I thought it became me to announce to
you the decease of one who, I fear, did not discharge with
much kindness the duties her connection with you imposed.
Your father's second wife, afterwards Madame Selby, is
no more. She died some days since in a convent to which
she had retired."

Isaura had no cause to mourn the dead, but she felt a
shock in the suddenness of this information; and in that
sweet spirit of womanly compassion which entered so
largely into her character, and made a part of her genius
itself, she murmured tearfully, "The poor Signora! Why
could I not have been with her in illness? She might then
have learned to love me. And she died in a convent, you
say? Ah, her religion was then sincere! Her end was
peaceful?"

"Let us not doubt that, Mademoiselle. Certainly she
lived to regret any former errors, and her last thought was
directed towards such atonement as might be in her power.
And it is that desire of atonement which now strangely
mixes me up, Mademoiselle, in your destinies. In that de-

sire for atonement, she left to my charge, as a kinsman distant indeed, but still, perhaps, the nearest with whom she was personally acquainted—a young ward. In accepting that trust, I find myself strangely compelled to hazard the risk of offending you."

"Offending me? How? Pray speak openly."

"In so doing, I must utter the name of Gustave Rameau."

Isaura turned pale and recoiled, but she did not speak.

"Did he inform me rightly that, in the last interview with him three days ago, you expressed a strong desire that the engagement between him and yourself should cease; and that you only, and with reluctance, suspended your rejection of the suit he had pressed on you, in consequence of his entreaties, and of certain assurances as to the changed direction of the talents of which we will assume that he is possessed?"

"Well, well, Monsieur," exclaimed Isaura, her whole face brightening; "and you come on the part of Gustave Rameau to say that on reflection he does not hold me to our engagement—that in honour and in conscience I am free?"

"I see," answered De Mauléon, smiling, "that I am pardoned already. It would not pain you if such were my instructions in the embassy I undertake?"

"Pain me? No. But——"

"But what?"

"Must he persist in a course which will break his mother's heart, and make his father deplore the hour that he was born? Have you influence over him, M. de Mauléon? If so, will you not exert it for his good?"

"You interest yourself still in his fate, Mademoiselle?"

"How can I do otherwise? Did I not consent to share it when my heart shrank from the thought of our union? And now when, if I understand you rightly, I am free, I cannot but think of what was best in him."

"Alas! Mademoiselle, he is but one of many—a spoilt child of that Circe, imperial Paris. Everywhere I look

around, I see but corruption.   It was hidden by the halo
which corruption itself engenders.   The halo is gone, the
corruption is visible.   Where is the old French manhood?
Banished from the heart, it comes out only at the tongue.
Were our deeds like our words, Prussia would beg on her knee
to be a province of France.   Gustave is the fit poet for this
generation.   Vanity—desire to be known for something,
no matter what, no matter by whom—that is the Parisian's
leading motive power;—orator, soldier, poet, all alike.
Utterers of fine phrases; despising knowledge, and toil,
and discipline; railing against the Germans as barbarians,
against their generals as traitors; against God for not taking
their part.   What can be done to weld this mass of hollow
bubbles into the solid form of a nation—the nation it affects
to be?   What generation can be born out of the unmanly
race, inebriate with brag and absinthe?   Forgive me this
tirade; I have been reviewing the battalion I command.
As for Gustave Rameau,—if we survive the siege, and see
once more a Government that can enforce order, and a public that will refuse renown for balderdash,—I should not be
surprised if Gustave Rameau were among the prettiest imi-
tators of Lamartine's early *Meditations*.   Had he been born
under Louis XIV. how loyal he would have been!   What
sacred tragedies in the style of *Athalie* he would have
written, in the hope of an audience at Versailles!   But I
detain you from the letter I was charged to deliver you.   I
have done so purposely, that I might convince myself that
you welcome that release which your too delicate sense of
honour shrank too long from demanding."

Here he took forth and placed a letter in Isaura's hand;
and, as if to allow her to read it unobserved, retired to the
window recess.

Isaura glanced over the letter.   It ran thus:

"I feel that it was only to your compassion that I owed
your consent to my suit.   Could I have doubted that before,
your words when we last met sufficed to convince me.   In

my selfish pain at the moment, I committed a great wrong.
I would have held you bound to a promise from which you
desired to be free. Grant me pardon for that; and for all
the faults by which I have offended you. In cancelling our
engagement, let me hope that I may rejoice in your friendship, your remembrance of me, some gentle and kindly
thought. My life may henceforth pass out of contact with
yours; but you will ever dwell in my heart, an image pure
and holy as the saints in whom you may well believe—they
are of your own kindred."

"May I convey to Gustave Rameau any verbal reply to
his letter?" asked De Mauléon, turning as she replaced the
letter on the table.

"Only my wishes for his welfare. It might wound him
if I added, my gratitude for the generous manner in which
he has interpreted my heart, and acceded to its desires."

"Mademoiselle, accept my congratulations. My condo-
lences are for the poor girl left to my guardianship. Unhappily she loves this man; and there are reasons why I
cannot withhold my consent to her union with him, should
he demand it, now that, in the letter remitted to you, he
has accepted your dismissal. If I can keep him out of all
the follies and all the evils into which he suffers his vanity
to mislead his reason, I will do so;—would I might say,
only in compliance with your compassionate injunctions.
But henceforth the infatuation of my ward compels me to
take some interest in his career. Adieu, Mademoiselle! I
have no fear for your happiness now."

Left alone, Isaura stood as one transfigured. All the
bloom of her youth seemed suddenly restored. Round her
red lips the dimples opened, countless mirrors of one happy
smile. "I am free, I am free," she murmured—"joy,
joy!" and she passed from the room to seek the Venosta,
singing clear, singing loud, as a bird that escapes from the
cage and warbles to the heaven it regains the blissful tale
of its release.

CHAPTER XIII.

IN proportion to the nearer roar of the besiegers' cannon, and the sharper gripe of famine within the walls, the Parisians seemed to increase their scorn for the skill of the enemy, and their faith in the sanctity of the capital. All false news was believed as truth; all truthful news abhorred as falsehood. Listen to the groups round the *cafés*. "The Prussian funds have fallen three per cent. at Berlin," says a threadbare ghost of the Bourse (he had been a clerk of Louvier's). "Ay," cries a National Guard, "read extracts from *La Liberté*. The barbarians are in despair. Nancy is threatened, Belfort is freed. Bourbaki is invading Baden. Our fleets are pointing their cannon upon Hamburg. Their country endangered, their retreat cut off, the sole hope of Bismarck and his trembling legions is to find a refuge in Paris. The increasing fury of the bombardment is a proof of their despair."

"In that case," whispered Savarin to De Brézé, "suppose we send a flag of truce to Versailles with a message from Trochu that, on disgorging their conquests, ceding the left bank of the Rhine, and paying the expenses of the war, Paris, ever magnanimous to the vanquished, will allow the Prussians to retire."

"The Prussians! Retire!" cried Edgar Ferrier, catching the last word and glancing fiercely at Savarin. "What Prussian spy have we among us? Not one of the barbarians shall escape. We have but to dismiss the traitors who have usurped the government, proclaim the Commune and the rights of labour, and we give birth to a Hercules that even in its cradle can strangle the vipers."

Edgar Ferrier was the sole member of his political party among the group which he thus addressed; but such was the terror which the Communists already began to inspire among the *bourgeoisie* that no one volunteered a reply.

Savarin linked his arm in De Brézé's, and prudently drew him off.

"I suspect," said the former, "that we shall soon have worse calamities to endure than the Prussian *obus* and the black loaf. The Communists will have their day."

"I shall be in my grave before then," said De Brézé, in hollow accents. "It is twenty-four hours since I spent my last fifty sous on the purchase of a rat, and I burnt the legs of my bedstead for the fuel by which that quadruped was roasted."

"*Entre nous*, my poor friend, I am much in the same condition," said Savarin, with a ghastly attempt at his old pleasant laugh. "See how I am shrunken! My wife would be unfaithful to the Savarin of her dreams if she accepted a kiss from the slender gallant you behold in me. But I thought you were in the National Guard, and therefore had not to vanish into air."

"I was a National Guard, but I could not stand the hardships, and being above the age, I obtained my exemption. As to pay, I was then too proud to claim my wage of 1 franc 25 centimes. I should not be too proud now. Ah, blessed be Heaven! here comes Lemercier; he owes me a dinner—he shall pay it. *Bon jour*, my dear Frederic! How handsome you look in your *képi!* Your uniform is brilliantly fresh from the soil of powder. What a contrast to the tatterdemalions of the Line!"

"I fear," said Lemercier, ruefully, "that my costume will not look so well a day or two hence. I have just had news that will no doubt seem very glorious—in the news-papers. But then newspapers are not subjected to cannon-balls."

"What do you mean?" answered De Brézé.

"I met, as I emerged from my apartment a few minutes ago, that fire-eater, Victor de Mauléon, who always contrives to know what passes at headquarters. He told me that preparations are being made for a great sortie. Most prob-ably the announcement will appear in a proclamation to-

morrow, and our troops march forth to-morrow night. The
National Guard (fools and asses who have been yelling out
for decisive action) are to have their wish, and to be placed
in the van of battle,—amongst the foremost, the battalion
in which I am enrolled. Should this be our last meeting
on earth, say that Frederic Lemercier has finished his part
in life with *éclat*."

"Gallant friend," said De Brézé, feebly seizing him by
the arm, "if it be true that thy mortal career is menaced,
die as thou hast lived. An honest man leaves no debt un-
paid. Thou owest me a dinner."

"Alas! ask of me what is possible. I will give thee
three, however, if I survive and regain my *rentes*. But to-
day I have not even a mouse to share with Fox."

"Fox lives then?" cried De Brézé, with sparkling hungry
eyes.

"Yes. At present he is making the experiment how long
an animal can live without food."

"Have mercy upon him, poor beast! Terminate his
pangs by a noble death. Let him save thy friends and
thyself from starving. For myself alone I do not plead;
I am but an amateur in polite literature. But Savarin, the
illustrious Savarin,—in criticism the French Longinus—in
poetry the Parisian Horace—in social life the genius of
gaiety in pantaloons,—contemplate his attenuated frame!
Shall he perish for want of food while thou hast such super-
fluity in thy larder? I appeal to thy heart, thy conscience,
thy patriotism. What, in the eyes of France, are a thousand
Foxes compared to a single Savarin?"

"At this moment," sighed Savarin, "I could swallow
anything, however nauseous, even thy flattery, De Brézé.
But, my friend Frederic, thou goest into battle—what will
become of Fox if thou fall? Will he not be devoured by
strangers? Surely it were a sweeter thought to his faithful
heart to furnish a repast to thy friends?—his virtues
acknowledged, his memory blest!"

"Thou dost look very lean, my poor Savarin! And how

hospitable thou wert when yet plump!" said Frederic,
pathetically. "And certainly, if I live, Fox will starve;
if I am slain, Fox will be eaten. Yet, poor Fox, dear Fox,
who lay on my breast when I was frostbitten. No; I have
not the heart to order him to the spit for you. Urge it
not."

"I will save thee that pang," cried De Brézé. "We are
close by thy rooms. Excuse me for a moment: I will run
in and instruct thy *bonne.*"

So saying, he sprang forward with an elasticity of step
which no one could have anticipated from his previous lan-
guor. Frederic would have followed, but Savarin clung to
him, whimpering: "Stay; I shall fall like an empty sack,
without the support of thine arm, young hero. Pooh! of
course De Brézé is only joking—a pleasant joke. Hist!—
a secret: he has moneys, and means to give us once more a
dinner at his own cost, pretending that we dine on thy dog.
He was planning this when thou camest up. Let him have
his joke, and we shall have a *festin de Balthazar.*"

"*Hein!*" said Frederic, doubtfully; "thou art sure he
has no designs upon Fox?"

"Certainly not, except in regaling us. Donkey is not
bad, but it is 14 francs a pound. A pullet is excellent, but
it is 30 francs. Trust to De Brézé; we shall have donkey
and pullet, and Fox shall feast upon the remains."

Before Frederic could reply, the two men were jostled
and swept on by a sudden rush of a noisy crowd in their
rear. They could but distinguish the words—Glorious
news—victory—Faidherbe—Chanzy. But these words
were sufficient to induce them to join willingly in the rush.
They forgot their hunger; they forget Fox. As they were
hurried on, they learned that there was a report of a complete defeat of the Prussians by Faidherbe near Amiens, —
of a still more decided one on the Loire by Chanzy. These
generals, with armies flushed with triumph, were pressing
on towards Paris to accelerate the destruction of the hated
Germans. How the report arose no one exactly knew.

All believed it, and were making their way to the Hotel de Ville to hear it formally confirmed.

Alas! before they got there they were met by another crowd returning, dejected but angry. No such news had reached the Government. Chanzy and Faidherbe were no doubt fighting bravely, with every probability of success; but——

The Parisian imagination required no more. "We should always be defeating the enemy," said Savarin, "if there were not always a *but;*" and his audience, who, had he so expressed himself ten minutes before, would have torn him to pieces, now applauded the epigram; and with execrations on Trochu, mingled with many a peal of painful sarcastic laughter, vociferated and dispersed.

As the two friends sauntered back towards the part of the Boulevards on which De Brézé had parted company with them, Savarin quitted Lemercier suddenly, and crossed the street to accost a small party of two ladies and two men who were on their way to the Madeleine. While he was exchanging a few words with them, a young couple, arm in arm, passed by Lemercier,—the man in the uniform of the National Guard—uniform as unsullied as Frederic's, but with as little of a military air as can well be conceived. His gait was slouching; his head bent downwards. He did not seem to listen to his companion, who was talking with quickness and vivacity, her fair face radiant with smiles. Lemercier looked at them as they passed by. "*Sur mon âme,*" muttered Frederic to himself, "surely that is *la belle* Julie; and she has got back her truant poet at last."

While Lemercier thus soliloquised, Gustave, still looking down, was led across the street by his fair companion, and into the midst of the little group with whom Savarin had paused to speak. Accidentally brushing against Savarin himself, he raised his eyes with a start, about to mutter some conventional apology, when Julie felt the arm on which she leant tremble nervously. Before him stood

Isaura, the Countess de Vandemar by her side; her two other companions, Raoul and the Abbé Vertpré, a step or two behind.

Gustave uncovered, bowed low, and stood mute and still for a moment, paralysed by surprise and the chill of a painful shame.

Julie's watchful eyes, following his, fixed themselves on the same face. On the instant she divined the truth. She beheld her to whom she had owed months of jealous agony, and over whom, poor child, she thought she had achieved a triumph. But the girl's heart was so instinctively good that the sense of triumph was merged in a sense of compassion. Her rival had lost Gustave. To Julie the loss of Gustave was the loss of all that makes life worth having. On her part, Isaura was moved not only by the beauty of Julie's countenance, but still more by the childlike ingenuousness of its expression.

So, for the first time in their lives, met the child and the stepchild of Louise Duval. Each so deserted, each so left alone and inexperienced amid the perils of the world, with fates so different, typifying orders of Womanhood so opposed. Isaura was naturally the first to break the silence that weighed like a sensible load on all present.

She advanced towards Rameau, with sincere kindness in her look and tone.

"Accept my congratulations," she said, with a grave smile. "Your mother informed me last evening of your nuptials. Without doubt I see Madame Gustave Rameau;"—and she extended her hand towards Julie. The poor Ondine shrank back for a moment, blushing up to her temples. It was the first hand which a woman of spotless character had extended to her since she had lost the protection of Madame Surville. She touched it timidly, humbly, then drew her bridegroom on; and with head more downcast than Gustave, passed through the group without a word.

She did not speak to Gustave till they were out of sight

and hearing of those they had left. Then, pressing his arm passionately, she said: "And that is the *demoiselle* thou hast resigned for me! Do not deny it. I am so glad to have seen her; it has done me so much good. How it has deepened, purified, my love for thee! I have but one return to make; but that is my whole life. Thou shalt never have cause to blame me—never—never!"

Savarin looked very grave and thoughtful when he rejoined Lemercier.

"Can I believe my eyes?" said Frederic. "Surely that was Julie Caumartin leaning on Gustave Rameau's arm! And had he the assurance, so accompanied, to salute Madame de Vandemar, and Mademoiselle Cicogna, to whom I understood he was affianced? Nay, did I not see Mademoiselle shake hands with the Ondine? or am I under one of the illusions which famine is said to engender in the brain?"

"I have not strength now to answer all these interrogatives. I have a story to tell; but I keep it for dinner. Let us hasten to thy apartment. De Brézé is doubtless there waiting us."

CHAPTER XIV.

UNPRESCIENT of the perils that awaited him, absorbed in the sense of existing discomfort, cold, and hunger, Fox lifted his mournful visage from his master's dressing-gown, in which he had encoiled his shivering frame, on the entrance of De Brézé and the *concierge* of the house in which Lemercier had his apartment. Recognising the Vicomte as one of his master's acquaintances, he checked the first impulse that prompted him to essay a feeble bark, and permitted himself, with a petulant whine, to be extracted from his covering, and held in the arms of the murderous visitor.

"*Dieu des dieux!*" ejaculated De Brézé, "how light the poor beast has become!" Here he pinched the sides and

II.—19

thighs of the victim. "Still," he said, "there is some flesh yet on these bones. You may grill the paws, *fricasser* the shoulders, and roast the rest. The *rognons* and the head accept for yourself as a perquisite." Here he transferred Fox to the arms of the *concierge*, adding, "*Vite au besogne, mon ami.*"

"Yes, Monsieur. I must be quick about it while my wife is absent. She has a *faiblesse* for the brute. He must be on the spit before she returns."

"Be it so; and on the table in an hour—five o'clock precisely—I am famished."

The *concierge* disappeared with Fox. De Brézé then amused himself by searching into Frederic's cupboards and *buffets*, from which he produced a cloth and utensils necessary for the repast. These he arranged with great neatness, and awaited in patience the moment of participation in the feast.

The hour of five had struck before Savarin and Frederic entered the *salon;* and at their sight De Brézé dashed to the staircase and called out to the *concierge* to serve the dinner.

Frederic, though unconscious of the Thyestean nature of the banquet, still looked round for the dog; and, not perceiving him, began to call out, "Fox! Fox! where hast thou hidden thyself?"

"Tranquillise yourself," said De Breze. "Do not suppose that I have not . . . ."

NOTE BY THE AUTHOR'S SON.[1]—The hand that wrote thus far has left unwritten the last scene of the tragedy of poor Fox. In the deep where Prospero has dropped his wand are now irrevocably buried the humour and the pathos of this cynophagous banquet. One detail of it, however, which the author imparted to his son, may here be faintly indicated. Let the sympathising reader recognise all that is dramatic in the conflict between hunger and affection; let him recall to mind the lachrymose loving kindness of his own post-prandial emotions after blissfully breaking some fast, less mercilessly prolonged, we will hope, than that of these besieged banqueters,

[1] See also Prefatory Note.

and then, though unaided by the fancy which conceived so quaint a situation, he may perhaps imagine what tearful tenderness would fill the eyes of the kind-hearted Frederic, as they contemplate the well-picked bones of his sacrificed favourite on the plate before him; which he pushes away, sighing, "Ah, poor Fox! how he would have enjoyed those bones!"

The chapter immediately following this one also remains unfinished. It was not intended to close the narrative thus left uncompleted; but of those many and so various works which have not unworthily associated with almost every department of literature the name of a single English writer, it is CHAPTER THE LAST. Had the author lived to finish it, he would doubtless have added to his Iliad of the Siege of Paris its most epic episode, by here describing the mighty combat between those two princes of the Parisian Bourse, the magnanimous Duplessis and the redoubtable Louvier. Amongst the few other pages of the book which have been left unwritten, we must also reckon with regret some pages descriptive of the reconciliation between Graham Vane and Isaura Cicogna, but, fortunately for the satisfaction of every reader who may have followed thus far the fortunes of *The Parisians*, all that our curiosity is chiefly interested to learn has been recorded in the *Envoi*, which was written before the completion of the novel.

We know not, indeed, what has become of these two Parisian types of a Beauty not of Holiness, the poor vain Poet of the *Pavé*, and the good-hearted Ondine of the Gutter. It is obvious, from the absence of all allusion to them in Lemercier's letter to Vane, that they had passed out of the narrative before that letter was written. We must suppose the catastrophe of their fates to have been described, in some preceding chapter, by the author himself, who would assuredly not have left M. Gustave Rameau in permanent possession of his ill-merited and ill-ministered fortune. That French representative of the appropriately popular poetry of modern ideas, which prefers "the roses and raptures of vice" to "the lilies and languors of virtue," cannot have been irredeemably reconciled by the sweet savours of the domestic *pot-au-feu*, even when spiced with pungent whiffs of repudiated disreputability, to any selfish betrayal of the cause of universal social emancipation from the personal proprieties. If poor Julie Caumartin has perished in the siege of Paris, with all the grace of a self-wrought redemption still upon her, we shall doubtless deem her fate a happier one than any she could have found in prolonged existence as Madame Rameau; and a certain modicum of this world's good things will, in that case, have been rescued for worthier employment by Graham Vane. To that assurance nothing but Lemercier's description of the fate of Victor de Mauléon (which will be found in the *Envoi*) need be added for the satisfaction of our sense of poetic justice . and if on the mimic stage, from which they now disappear, all these puppets have rightly played their parts in the drama of an empire's fall, each will have helped to " point a moral" as well as to "adorn a tale. " *Valete et plaudite!*

CHAPTER THE LAST.

AMONG the refugees which the *convoi* from Versailles disgorged on the Paris station were two men, who, in pushing through the crowd, came suddenly face to face with each other.

"Aha! *Bon jour*, M. Duplessis," said a burly voice.

"*Bon jour*, M. Louvier," replied Duplessis.

"How long have you left Bretagne?"

"On the day that the news of the armistice reached it, in order to be able to enter Paris the first day its gates were open. And you—where have you been?"

"In London."

"Ah! in London!" said Duplessis, paling. "I knew I had an enemy there."

"Enemy! I? Bah! my dear Monsieur. What makes you think me your enemy?"

"I remember your threats."

"*A propos* of Rochebriant. By the way, when would it be convenient to you and the dear Marquis to let me into prompt possession of that property? You can no longer pretend to buy it as a *dot* for Mademoiselle Valérie."

"I know not that yet. It is true that all the financial operations attempted by my agent in London have failed. But I may recover myself yet, now that I re-enter Paris. In the mean time, we have still six months before us; for, as you will find—if you know it not already—the interest due to you has been lodged with Messrs. —— of ——, and you cannot foreclose, even if the law did not take into consideration the national calamities as between debtor and creditor."

"Quite true. But if you cannot buy the property it must pass into my hands in a very short time. And you and the Marquis had better come to an amicable arrangement with me. *A propos,* I read in the *Times* newspaper that Alain was among the wounded in the sortie of December."

"Yes; we learnt that through a pigeon-post. We were afraid . . . ."

L'ENVOI.

THE intelligent reader will perceive that the story I relate is virtually closed with the preceding chapter; though I rejoice to think that what may be called its plot does not find its *dénoûment* amidst the crimes and the frenzy of the *Guerre des Communeaux.* Fit subjects these, indeed, for the social annalist in times to come. When crimes that outrage humanity have their motive or their excuse in principles that demand the demolition of all upon which the civilisation of Europe has its basis—worship, property, and marriage—in order to reconstruct a new civilisation adapted to a new humanity, it is scarcely possible for the serenest contemporary to keep his mind in that state of abstract reasoning with which Philosophy deduces from some past evil some existent good. For my part, I believe that throughout the whole known history of mankind, even in epochs when reason is most misled and conscience most perverted, there runs visible, though fine and threadlike, the chain of destiny, which has its roots in the throne of an All-wise and an All-good; that in the wildest illusions by which multitudes are frenzied, there may be detected gleams of prophetic truths; that in the fiercest crimes which, like the disease of an epidemic, characterise a peculiar epoch under abnormal circumstances, there might be found instincts or aspirations towards some social virtues to be realised ages afterwards by happier generations, all tending to save man from despair of the future, were the whole society to unite for the joyless hour of his race in the abjuration of soul and the denial of God, because all irre-

sistibly establishing that yearning towards an unseen future
which is the leading attribute of soul, evincing the government of a divine Thought which evolves out of the discords
of one age the harmonies of another, and, in the world
within us as in the world without, enforces upon every un-
clouded reason the distinction between Providence and
chance.

The account subjoined may suffice to say all that rests to
be said of those individuals in whose fate, apart from the
events or personages that belong to graver history, the
reader of this work may have conceived an interest.   It is
translated from the letter of Frederic Lemercier to Graham
Vane, dated June ——, a month after the defeat of the
Communists.

"Dear and distinguished Englishman, whose name I
honour but fail to pronounce, accept my cordial thanks for
your interests in such remains of Frederic Lemercier as yet
survive the ravages of Famine, Equality, Brotherhood,
Petroleum, and the Rights of Labour.   I did not desert my
Paris when M. Thiers, '*parmula non bene relictâ*,' led his
sagacious friends and his valiant troops to the groves of
Versailles, and confided to us unarmed citizens the preser-
vation of order and property from the insurgents whom he
left in possession of our forts and cannon.   I felt spell-
bound by the interest of the *sinistre mélodrame*, with its
quick succession of scenic effects and the metropolis of the
world for its stage.   Taught by experience, I did not aspire
to be an actor; and even as a spectator, I took care neither
to hiss nor applaud.   Imitating your happy England, I observed a strict neutrality; and, safe myself from danger,
left my best friends to the care of the gods.

"As to political questions, I dare not commit myself to
a conjecture.   At this *rouge et noir* table, all I can say is,
that whichever card turns up, it is either a red or a black
one.   One gamester gains for the moment by the loss of the
other; the table eventually ruins both.

"No one believes that the present form of government can last; every one differs as to that which can. Raoul de Vandemar is immovably convinced of the restoration of the Bourbons. Savarin is meditating a new journal devoted to the cause of the Count of Paris. De Brézé and the old Count de Passy, having in turn espoused and opposed every previous form of government, naturally go in for a perfectly novel experiment, and are for constitutional dictatorship under the Duc d'Aumale, which he is to hold at his own pleasure, and ultimately resign to his nephew the Count, under the mild title of a constitutional king;—that is, if it ever suits the pleasure of a dictator to depose himself. To me this seems the wildest of notions. If the Duc's administration were successful, the French would insist on keeping it; and if the uncle were unsuccessful, the nephew would not have a chance. Duplessis retains his faith in the Imperial dynasty; and that Imperialist party is much stronger than it appears on the surface. So many of the *bourgeoisie* recall with a sigh eighteen years of prosperous trade; so many of the military officers, so many of the civil officials, identify their career with the Napoleonic favour; and so many of the Priesthood, abhorring the Republic, always liable to pass into the hands of those who assail religion,—unwilling to admit the claim of the Orleanists, are at heart for the Empire.

"But I will tell you one secret. I and all the quiet folks like me (we are more numerous than any one violent faction) are willing to accept any form of government by which we have the best chance of keeping our coats on our backs. *Liberté, Egalité, Fraternité*, are gone quite out of fashion; and Mademoiselle —— has abandoned her great chant of the Marseillaise, and is drawing tears from enlightened audiences by her pathetic delivery of '*O Richard! O mon roi!*'"

"Now about the other friends of whom you ask for news.

"Wonders will never cease. Louvier and Duplessis are

no longer deadly rivals. They have become sworn friends, and are meditating a great speculation in common, to commence as soon as the Prussian debt is paid off. Victor de Mauléon brought about this reconciliation in a single interview during the brief interregnum between the Peace and the *Guerre des Communeaux*. You know how sternly Louvier was bent upon seizing Alain de Rochebriant's estates. Can you conceive the true cause? Can you imagine it possible that a hardened money-maker like Louvier should ever allow himself to be actuated, one way or the other, by the romance of a sentimental wrong? Yet so it was. It seems that many years ago he was desperately in love with a girl who disappeared from his life, and whom he believed to have been seduced by the late Marquis de Rochebriant. It was in revenge for this supposed crime that he had made himself the principal mortgagee of the late Marquis; and, visiting the sins of the father on the son, had, under the infernal disguise of friendly interest, made himself sole mortgagee to Alain, upon terms apparently the most generous. The demon soon showed his *griffe*, and was about to foreclose, when Duplessis came to Alain's relief; and Rochebriant was to be Valérie's *dot* on her marriage with Alain. The Prussian war, of course, suspended all such plans, pecuniary and matrimonial. Duplessis, whose resources were terribly crippled by the war, attempted operations in London with a view of raising the sum necessary to pay off the mortgage;—found himself strangely frustrated and baffled. Louvier was in London, and defeated his rival's agent in every speculation. It became impossible for Duplessis to redeem the mortgage. The two men came to Paris with the peace. Louvier determined both to seize the Breton lands and to complete the ruin of Duplessis, when he learned from De Mauléon that he had spent half his life in a baseless illusion; that Alain's father was innocent of the crime for which his son was to suffer;—and Victor, with that strange power over men's minds which was so peculiar to him, talked Louvier into mercy if not into

repentance. In short, the mortgage is to be paid off by in-
stalments at the convenience of Duplessis. Alain's marriage with Valérie is to take place in a few weeks. The
fournisseurs are already gone to fit up the old château for
the bride, and Louvier is invited to the wedding.

"I have all this story from Alain, and from Duplessis
himself. I tell the tale as 'twas told to me, with all the
gloss of sentiment upon its woof. But between ourselves,
I am too Parisian not to be sceptical as to the unalloyed
amiability of sudden conversions. And I suspect that Louvier was no longer in a condition to indulge in the unprofi-
table whim of turning rural seigneur. He had sunk large
sums and incurred great liabilities in the new street to be
called after his name; and that street has been twice ravaged, first by the Prussian siege, and next by the *Guerre
des Communeaux;* and I can detect many reasons why Louvier should deem it prudent not only to withdraw from the
Rochebriant seizure, and make sure of peacefully recovering
the capital lent on it, but establishing joint interest and
quasi partnership with a financier so brilliant and successful
as Armand Duplessis has hitherto been.

"Alain himself is not quite recovered from his wound,
and is now at Rochebriant, nursed by his aunt and Valérie.
I have promised to visit him next week. Raoul de Vandemar is still at Paris with his mother, saying, there is no
place where one Christian man can be of such service. The
old Count declines to come back, saying there is no place
where a philosopher can be in such danger.

"I reserve as my last communication, in reply to your
questions, that which is the gravest. You say that you
saw in the public journals brief notice of the assassination
of Victor de Mauléon; and you ask for such authentic particulars as I can give of that event, and of the motives of
the assassin.

"I need not, of course, tell you how bravely the poor
Vicomte behaved throughout the siege; but he made many
enemies among the worst members of the National Guard

by the severity of his discipline; and had he been caught
by the mob the same day as Clement Thomas, who committed the same offence, would have certainly shared the
fate of that general.   Though elected a *député*, he remained
at Paris a few days after Thiers & Co. left it, in the hope
of persuading the party of Order, including then no small
portion of the National Guards, to take prompt and vigorous
measures to defend the city against the Communists.   Indignant at their pusillanimity, he then escaped to Versailles.   There he more than confirmed the high reputation
he had acquired during the siege, and impressed the ablest
public men with the belief that he was destined to take a
very leading part in the strife of party.   When the Versailles troops entered Paris, he was, of course, among them
in command of a battalion.

"He escaped safe through that horrible war of barricades,
though no man more courted danger.   He inspired his men
with his own courage.   It was not till the revolt was
quenched on the evening of the 28th May that he met his
death.   The Versailles soldiers, naturally exasperated,
were very prompt in seizing and shooting at once every
passenger who looked like a foe.   Some men under De
Mauléon had seized upon one of these victims, and were
hurrying him into the next street for execution, when,
catching sight of the Vicomte, he screamed out, 'Lebeau,
save me!'

"At that cry De Mauléon rushed forward, arrested his
soldiers, cried, 'This man is innocent—a harmless physician.   I answer for him.'   As he thus spoke, a wounded
Communist, lying in the gutter amidst a heap of the slain,
dragged himself up, reeled towards De Mauléon, plunged a
knife between his shoulders, and dropped down dead.

"The Vicomte was carried into a neighbouring house,
from all the windows of which the tricolour was suspended;
and the *Médecin* whom he had just saved from summary
execution examined and dressed his wound.   The Vicomte
lingered for more than an hour, but expired in the effort to

utter some words, the sense of which those about him en-deavoured in vain to seize.

"It was from the *Médecin* that the name of the assassin and the motive for the crime were ascertained. The mis-creant was a Red Republican and Socialist named Armand Monnier. He had been a very skilful workman, and earn-ing, as such, high wages. But he thought fit to become an active revolutionary politician, first led into schemes for up-setting the world by the existing laws of marriage, which had inflicted on him one woman who ran away from him, but being still legally his wife, forbade him to marry another woman with whom he lived, and to whom he seems to have been passionately attached.

"These schemes, however, he did not put into any posi-tive practice till he fell in with a certain Jean Lebeau, who exercised great influence over him, and by whom he was admitted into one of the secret revolutionary societies which had for their object the overthrow of the Empire. After that time his head became turned. The fall of the Empire put an end to the society he had joined: Lebeau dissolved it. During the siege Monnier was a sort of leader among the *ouvriers;* but as it advanced and famine commenced, he contracted the habit of intoxication. His children died of cold and hunger. The woman he lived with followed them to the grave. Then he seems to have become a ferocious madman, and to have been implicated in the worst crimes of the Communists. He cherished a wild desire of revenge against this Jean Lebeau, to whom he attributed all his calamities, and by whom, he said, his brother had been shot in the sortie of December.

"Here comes the strange part of the story. This Jean Lebeau is alleged to have been one and the same person with Victor de Mauléon. The *Médecin* I have named, and who is well known in Belleville and Montmartre as the *Médecin des Pauvres*, confesses that he belonged to the secret society organised by Lebeau; that the disguise the Vicomte assumed was so complete, that he should not have recognised his identity with the conspirator but for an accident. During the latter time of the bombardment, he, the *Médecin des Pauvres,* was on the eastern ramparts, and his attention was suddenly called to a man mortally wounded by the splinter of a shell. While examining the nature of the wound, De Mauléon, who was also on the ramparts, came to the spot. The dying man said, 'M. le Vicomte, you owe me a service. My name is Marc le Roux. I was on the police before the war. When M. de. Mauléon reassumed his station, and was making himself obnoxious to the Emperor, I might have denounced him as Jean Lebeau the conspirator. I did not. The siege has reduced me to want. I have a child at home—a pet. Don't let her starve.' 'I will see to her,' said the Vicomte. Before we could get the man into the ambulance cart he expired.

"The *Médecin* who told this story I had the curiosity to see myself, and cross-question. I own I believe his statement. Whether De Mauléon did or did not conspire against a fallen dynasty, to which he owed no allegiance, can little, if at all, injure the reputation he has left behind of a very remarkable man—of great courage and great ability—who might have had a splendid career if he had survived. But, as Savarin says truly, the first bodies which the car of revolution crushes down are those which first harness themselves to it.

"Among De Mauléon's papers is the programme of a constitution fitted for France. How it got into Savarin's hands I know not. De Mauléon left no will, and no relations came forward to claim his papers. I asked Savarin to give me the heads of the plan, which he did. They are as follows: .

"'The American republic is the sole one worth studying, for it has lasted. The causes of its duration are in the checks to democratic fickleness and disorder. 1st. No law affecting the Constitution can be altered without the consent of two-thirds of Congress. 2nd. To counteract the impulses natural to a popular Assembly chosen by universal suffrage, the greater legislative powers, especially in foreign affairs, are vested in the Senate, which has even executive as well as legislative functions. 3rd. The Chief of the State, having elected his government, can maintain it independent of hostile majorities in either Assembly.

"' These three principles of safety to form the basis of any new constitution for France.

"' For France it is essential that the chief magistrate, under whatever title he assume, should be as irresponsible as an English sovereign. Therefore he should not preside at his councils; he should not lead his armies. The day for personal government is gone, even in Prussia. The safety for order in a State is that, when things go wrong, the Ministry changes, the State remains the same. In Europe, Republican institutions are safer where the chief magistrate is hereditary than where elective.'

" Savarin says these axioms are carried out at length, and argued with great ability.

" I am very grateful for your proffered hospitalities in England. Some day I shall accept them—viz., whenever I decide on domestic life, and the calm of the conjugal *foyer*. I have a *penchant* for an English *Mees*, and am not exacting as to the *dot*. Thirty thousand livres sterling would satisfy me—a trifle, I believe, to you rich islanders.

" Meanwhile I am naturally compelled to make up for the miseries of that horrible siege. Certain moralising journals tell us that, sobered by misfortunes, the Parisians are going to turn over a new leaf, become studious and reflective, despise pleasure and luxury, and live like German professors. Don't believe a word of it. My conviction is that, whatever may be said as to our frivolity, extravagance, &c., under the Empire, we shall be just the same under any form of government—the bravest, the most timid, the most ferocious, the kindest-hearted, the most irrational, the most intelligent, the most contradictory, the most consistent people whom Jove, taking counsel of Venus and the Graces, Mars

and the Furies, ever created for the delight and terror of the world;—in a word, the Parisians.— *Votre tout dévoué,*
                    "FREDERIC LEMERCIER."

It is a lovely noon on the bay of Sorrento, towards the close of the autumn of 1871. Upon the part of the craggy shore, to the left of the town, on which her first perusal of the loveliest poem in which the romance of Christian heroism has ever combined elevation of thought with silvery delicacies of speech, had charmed her childhood, reclined the young bride of Graham Vane. They were in the first month of their marriage. Isaura had not yet recovered from the effects of all that had preyed upon her life, from the hour in which she had deemed that in her pursuit of fame she had lost the love that had coloured her genius and inspired her dreams, to that in which . . . .

The physicians consulted agreed in insisting on her passing the winter in a southern climate; and after their wedding, which took place in Florence, they thus came to Sorrento.

As Isaura is seated on the small smoothed rocklet, Graham reclines at her feet, his face upturned to hers with an inexpressible wistful anxiety in his impassioned tenderness. "You are sure you feel better and stronger since we have been here?"

THE END.